Debbie Macomber is a #1 *New York Times* bestselling author and a leading voice in women's fiction worldwide. Her work has appeared on every major bestseller list, with more than 170 million copies in print, and she is a multiple award winner. Hallmark Channel based a television series on Debbie's popular Cedar Cove books. For more information, visit her website, www.debbiemacomber.com.

New York Times and *USA TODAY* bestselling author **Lee Tobin McClain** read *Gone with the Wind* in the third grade and has been an incurable romantic ever since. When she's not writing angst-filled love stories with happy endings, she's probably Snapchatting with her college-student daughter, mediating battles between her goofy goldendoodle and her rescue cat or teaching aspiring writers in Seton Hill University's MFA program. She is probably not cleaning her house. For more about Lee, visit her website at www.leetobinmcclain.com.

#1 *New York Times* Bestselling Author

DEBBIE MACOMBER

READY FOR MARRIAGE

HARLEQUIN
BESTSELLING
AUTHOR
COLLECTION

HARLEQUIN®
BESTSELLING
AUTHOR
COLLECTION

Recycling programs
for this product may
not exist in your area.

ISBN-13: 978-1-335-49841-0

Ready for Marriage
First published in 1994. This edition published in 2023.
Copyright © 1994 by Debbie Macomber

A Family for Easter
First published in 2018. This edition published in 2023.
Copyright © 2018 by Lee Tobin McClain

For questions and comments about the quality of this book, please contact us at CustomerService@Harlequin.com.

Harlequin Enterprises ULC
22 Adelaide St. West, 41st Floor
Toronto, Ontario M5H 4E3, Canada
www.Harlequin.com

Printed in U.S.A.

CONTENTS

READY FOR MARRIAGE

Debbie Macomber

Dedicated to Carole Grande and her family
for their loving support through the years

Chapter 1

She could always grovel at Evan's feet. Knowing him as well as she did, Mary Jo Summerhill figured he'd probably like that. The very fact that she'd made this appointment—and then had the courage to show up—proved how desperate she was. But she'd had no choice; her parents' future rested in her hands and she knew of no better attorney to help with this mess than Evan Dryden.

If only he'd *agree* to help her...

Generally, getting in touch with an old boyfriend wouldn't create such anxiety, but Evan was more than just someone she'd dated a few times.

They'd been in love, deeply in love, and had planned to marry. In ways she hadn't yet fully grasped, Mary Jo still loved him. Terminating their relationship had nearly devastated her.

And him.

Mary Jo wasn't proud of the way she'd ended it. Mailing him back the beautiful pearl engagement ring had been cowardly, but she'd known she couldn't tell him face-to-face. She should've realized Evan would never leave it at that. She'd been a fool to think he'd take back the ring without confronting her.

He'd come to her angry and hurt, demanding an explanation. It quickly became apparent that he wouldn't accept the truth, and given no option, Mary Jo concocted a wild story about meeting another teacher and falling in love with him.

Telling such a bold-faced lie had magnified her guilt a hundredfold. But it was the only way she could make Evan believe her. The only way she could extricate herself from his life.

Her lie had worked beautifully, she noted with a twinge of pain. He'd recovered—just like his mother had said he would. He hadn't wasted any time getting on with his life, either.

Within a matter of months he was dating again. Pictures of Evan, with Jessica Kellerman at his side, had appeared regularly in the newspaper society pages. Unable to resist finding out more, Mary Jo had researched the Kellerman family. Her investigation had told her everything she needed to know. Jessica would make the perfect Dryden wife. The Kellermans were wealthy and established, unlike the Summerhills, who didn't rate so much as a mention in Boston's social register.

Later the same year, Mary Jo had heard about the extravagant Dryden family wedding. She been out of town that week at a teaching seminar, so she'd missed the newspaper coverage, and she'd avoided the society pages ever since. She didn't need any reminders of the wedding that had been the social event of the year.

That was nearly three years ago. Evan and Jessica were an old married couple by now. For all she knew, they might already have started a family. The twinge of regret became a knot in her stomach. Evan would make a wonderful father. They'd talked of a family, and she remembered how eager he was for children.

This wasn't exactly the best time for her to reenter his life, but she had no alternative. Her parents' future depended on Evan.

"Mr. Dryden will see you now," the receptionist said, breaking into Mary Jo's thoughts.

She nearly lost her nerve right then and there. Her heart pounded furiously. In a dead panic she tightened her hold on her purse strap, fighting the urge to dash straight out of her chair and out of the office.

"If you'll come this way."

"Of course," Mary Jo managed, although the words came out in gurglelike sounds, as if she were submerged in ten feet of water.

She followed the receptionist down a wide, plush-carpeted hallway to Evan's office. His name was on the door, engraved on a gold plate. The receptionist ushered her in, and left.

Mary Jo recognized Evan's personal assistant immediately, although they'd never met. Mrs. Sterling was exactly the way he'd described her. Late middle-age. Short and slim, with the energy of a Tasmanian devil. Formidably efficient. He'd claimed the woman could easily reorganize the world if she had to, and that she'd willingly take on any project he asked of her. She was loyal to a fault.

"Evan asked me to send you right in," Mrs. Sterling said, leading her to the closed inner door. She opened it, then asked, "Can I get you a cup of coffee?" Her tone was friendly but unmistakably curious.

"No, thank you." Mary Jo stepped over the threshold, her heart in her throat. She wondered how she'd feel seeing Evan again after all this time. She'd already decided that a facade was necessary. She planned to approach him as if they were long-lost friends. Casual friends. With a smile, she'd shake his hand, inquire about Jessica and catch up on events in his life.

Now that there were only a few feet between her and the man she loved, Mary Jo found she couldn't move, could barely even breathe.

Nothing could have prepared her for the force of these emotions. Within seconds she was drowning in feelings she didn't know how to handle. She felt swamped and panicky, as if she were going down for the third time.

She conjured up Gary's face, the man she'd dated off and on for the past few months, but that didn't help. Next she struggled to come up with some clever comment, some joke, anything. Instead, all she could remember was that the man she'd loved three years ago, loved now, was married to someone else.

Evan sat at his desk, writing; only now did he look up. Their eyes met and for the briefest moment, he seemed to experience the same sense of loss and regret she was feeling. He blinked and the emotion disappeared, wiped out with a mere movement of his eyes.

"Hello, Evan," she said, amazed at how offhand she sounded. "I imagine it's a surprise to see me after all this time."

He stood and extended his hand for a perfunctory shake, and when he spoke his voice was crisp and professional. "Mary Jo. It's great to see you."

Mary Jo nearly laughed out loud. Evan never did know how to tell a good lie. He was anything but pleased to see her again.

He motioned toward the chair on the other side of his desk. "Sit down."

She did, gratefully, uncertain how much longer her knees would support her. She set her purse on the carpet and waited for her heart rate to return to normal before she told him the purpose of her visit.

"Did Mary offer you a cup of coffee?"

"Yes. I'm fine, thank you," she said hurriedly. Her hands were trembling.

Evan sat down again and waited.

"I—guess you're wondering why I'm here...."

He leaned back in his chair, looking cool and composed. It'd been three long years since she'd seen him. He hadn't changed, at least not outwardly. He remained one of the handsomest men she'd ever seen. His hair was as dark as his eyes, the color of rich Swiss chocolate. His features were well defined, almost chiseled, but that was too harsh a word for the finely cut, yet pronounced lines of his face. Walter Dryden, Evan's father, was a Massachusetts senator, and it was commonly accepted that Evan would one day enter politics himself. He certainly had the smooth, clean-cut good looks for such a calling.

What had made him fall in love with Mary Jo? She'd always wondered, always been fascinated by that question. She suspected it had to do with being different from the other women he'd dated. She'd amused him, hadn't taken him too seriously, made him laugh.

"You have something you wanted to discuss with me?" he prompted, his tone revealing the slightest hint of irritation.

"Yes…sorry," she said, quickly returning her attention to the matter at hand. "My parents…actually, my father…he retired not long ago," she said, rushing the words together, "and he invested his savings with a financial company, Adison Investments. Have you ever heard of the firm?"

"No, I can't say I have."

This didn't surprise Mary Jo. Wealthy men like Evan had huge financial portfolios with varied and multiple investments. Her father had taken his life's savings and entrusted it to a man he'd met and trusted completely.

"Dad invested everything he had with the company," she continued. "According to the terms of the agreement, he was to receive monthly interest checks. He hasn't. At first there were a number of plausible excuses, which Dad readily accepted. He wanted to believe this Bill Adison so much that it was easier to accept the excuses than face the truth."

"Which is?" Evan asked.

"I… I don't know. That's why I'm here. My father worked for thirty-five years as a construction electrician. He's raised six children, scrimped and saved all that time to put something extra away for his retirement. He wanted to be able to travel with Mom. They've dreamed of touring the South Pacific, and now I'm afraid they're going to be cheated out of everything."

Evan scribbled down a few notes.

"I'm coming to you because I'm afraid my brothers

are about to take things into their own hands. Jack and Rich went to Adison's office last week and made such a fuss they were almost arrested. It'd destroy my parents if my brothers ended up in jail over this. As far as I can see, the only way to handle it is through an attorney."

Evan made another note. "Did you bring the papers your father signed?"

"No. I didn't tell anyone I was coming to see you. I thought if I could convince you to take this case for my family, I'd bring my parents in and you could discuss the details with them. You need to understand that it's more than the money. My dad's embarrassed that he could have trusted such a man. He feels like an old fool." Her father had become very depressed. Adison Investments had robbed him of far more than his retirement savings. They'd taken his self-confidence and left him feeling vulnerable and inept.

"There are strict laws governing investments in this state."

Anxious to hear what he had to say, Mary Jo leaned forward in her chair. This was the very reason she'd swallowed her pride and come to Evan. He had the knowledge and political clout to be effective in ways her family never could.

"Then you can help us?" she asked eagerly. Evan's hesitation sent her heart plummeting. "I'll be happy to pay you whatever your fee is," she added, as if that was his sole concern. "I wouldn't expect you to charge less than you'd receive from anyone else."

Evan stood and walked over to the window, his back to her. "Our firm specializes in corporate law."

"That doesn't mean you can't take this case, does it?"

Evan clenched his hands at his sides, then flexed his

fingers. "No, but these sorts of cases have a tendency to become involved. You may end up having to sue."

"My family's willing to do whatever to takes to settle this matter," she said with a stubborn tilt to her jaw.

"Lawsuits don't come cheap," he warned, turning around to face her.

"I don't care and neither do my brothers. True, they don't know I made an appointment to see you, but once I tell them, I'm sure they'll be willing to chip in whatever they can to cover your fee." They wouldn't be able to afford much. Mary Jo was the youngest of six and the only girl. Her brothers were all married and raising young families. There never seemed to be enough money to go around. The burden of the expense would fall on her shoulders, but Mary Jo accepted that.

"You're sure you want me to handle this?" Evan asked, frowning.

"Positive. There isn't anyone I trust more," she said simply. Her eyes met his and she refused to look away.

"I could recommend another attorney, someone far more qualified in the area of investment fraud—"

"No," she broke in. "I don't trust anyone but you." She hadn't meant to tell him that and, embarrassed, quickly lowered her gaze.

He didn't say anything for what seemed like a very long time. Mary Jo held her breath, waiting. If he expected her to plead, she'd do it willingly. It was fair compensation for the appalling way she'd treated him. "Please," she said, her voice low and trembling.

Evan's shoulders lifted in a drawn-out sigh. "Before I decide, fill me in on what you've been doing for the past three years."

Mary Jo hadn't anticipated this, wasn't prepared to discuss her life. "I'm still teaching."

"Kindergarten?"

"Yes," she said enthusiastically. She loved her job. "Five-year-olds are still my favorites."

"I notice you're not wearing a wedding band."

Her gaze automatically fell to her ring finger, and she pinched her lips tightly together.

"So you didn't marry lover boy, after all."

"No."

"What happened?" he asked. He almost seemed to enjoy questioning her. Mary Jo felt as though she were on the witness stand being cross-examined.

She shrugged, not wanting to become trapped in a growing web of untruths. She'd regretted that stupid lie every day for the past three years.

"It didn't work out?" he suggested.

This was agony for her. "You're right. It didn't work out."

He grinned then, for the first time, as if that delighted him.

"Are you seeing someone now?"

"I don't believe that information's necessary to the case. You're my attorney, not my confessor."

"I'm nothing to you," he said and his words were sharp. "At least not yet."

"Will you take the case or won't you?" she demanded.

"I haven't decided."

He did want her to grovel. And they said hell hath no fury like a *woman* scorned. Apparently women didn't hold the patent on that.

"Gary Copeland," she said stiffly, without emotion. "Gary and I've been seeing each other for several months."

"Another teacher?"

"He's a fireman."

Evan nodded thoughtfully.

"Will you or won't you help my parents?" she asked again, growing tired of this silly game.

He was silent for a moment, then said abruptly, "All right. I'll make some inquiries and learn what I can about Adison Investments."

Mary Jo was so relieved and grateful she sagged in her chair.

"Make an appointment with Mrs. Sterling for next week, and bring your father with you. Friday would be best. I'll be in court most of the week."

"Thank you, Evan," she whispered, blinking rapidly in an effort to fight back tears.

She stood, eager now to escape. Resisting the urge to hug him, she hurried out of his office, past Mrs. Sterling and into the hallway. She was in such a blind rush she nearly collided with a woman holding a toddler in her arms.

"Oh, I'm so sorry," Mary Jo said, catching herself. "I'm afraid I wasn't watching where I was going."

"No problem," the other woman said with a friendly smile. She held the child protectively against her hip. The little boy, dressed in a blue-and-white sailor suit, looked up at her with eyes that were dark and solemn. Dark as rich Swiss chocolate.

Evan's eyes.

Mary Jo stared at the tall lovely woman. This was Jessica, Evan's wife, and the baby in her arms was Evan's son. The flash of pain nearly paralyzed her.

"I shouldn't have been standing so close to the door," Jessica went on to say. "My husband said he was taking us to lunch, and asked me to meet him here."

"You must be Jessica Dryden," Mary Jo said, finding the strength to offer her a genuine smile. She couldn't take her eyes off Evan's son. He now wore a cheerful grin and waved small chubby arms. If circumstances had been different, this child might have been her own. The void inside her widened; she'd never felt so bleak, so empty.

"This is Andy." Jessica did a small curtsy with her son in her arms.

"Hello, Andy." Mary Jo gave him her hand, and like a proper gentleman, he took it and promptly tried to place it in his mouth.

Jessica laughed. "I'm afraid he's teething. Everything goes to his mouth first." She walked with Mary Jo toward the elevator, bouncing the impatient toddler against her hip. "You look familiar," she said casually. "Do I know you?"

"I don't think so. My name's Mary Jo Summerhill."

Jessica's face went blank, then recognition swept into her eyes as her smile slowly evaporated. Any censure, however, was quickly disguised.

"It was nice meeting you," Mary Jo said, speeding up as they neared the door.

"Evan's mentioned you," Jessica told her.

Mary Jo stopped suddenly. "He has?" She couldn't help it. Curiosity got the better of her.

"Yes. He…thought very highly of you."

That Jessica used the past tense didn't escape Mary Jo. "He's a top-notch attorney."

"He's wonderful," Jessica agreed. "By the way, I understand we have a mutual friend. Earl Kress."

Earl had been a volunteer at Mary Jo's school. He'd tutored slow readers, and she'd admired his patience and persistence, and especially his sense of humor. The children loved him.

Earl mentioned Evan's name at every opportunity. He seemed to idolize Evan for taking on his civil suit against the school district—and winning.

Earl had graduated from high school functionally illiterate. Because he was a talented athlete, he'd been passed from one grade to the next. Sports were important to the schools, and the teachers were coerced into giving him passing grades. Earl had been awarded a full-ride college scholarship but suffered a serious knee injury in football training camp two weeks after he arrived. Within a couple of months, he'd flunked out of college. In a landmark case, Earl had sued the school district for his education. Evan had been his attorney.

The case had been in the headlines for weeks. During the trial, Mary Jo had been glued to the television every night, eager for news. As a teacher, she was, of course, concerned with this crucial education issue. But in all honesty, her interest had less to do with Earl Kress than with Evan. Following the case gave her the opportunity to see him again, even if it was only on a television screen and for a minute or two at a time.

She'd cheered when she heard Earl had won his case.

In the kind of irony that life sometimes presents, Mary Jo met Earl about a year later. He was attending college classes and volunteering part-time as a tutor at the grade school. They'd become friends. She admired the young man and missed him now that he'd returned to the same university where he'd once failed. Again he'd gone on a scholarship, but this time it was an academic one.

"Yes, I know Earl," Mary Jo said.

"He told Evan he'd been working with you. We were surprised to learn you weren't married."

Evan knew! He'd made her squirm and forced her to tell him the truth when all along he'd been perfectly aware that she was still single. Mary Jo's hands knotted at her sides. He'd taken a little too much delight in squeezing the information out of her.

"Darling," a husky male voice said from behind Mary Jo. "I hope I didn't keep you waiting." He walked over to Jessica, lifted Andy out of her arms and kissed her on the cheek.

Mary Jo's jaw fell open as she stared at the couple.

"Have you met my husband?" Jessica asked. "Damian, this is Mary Jo Summerhill."

"How…hello." Mary Jo was so flustered she could barely think.

Evan wasn't married to Jessica. His *brother* was.

Chapter 2

"Can you help us?" Norman Summerhill asked Evan anxiously.

Mary Jo had brought both her parents. Evan was reading over the agreement her father had signed with Adison Investments. With a sick feeling in the pit of her stomach, she noticed he was frowning. The frown deepened the longer he read.

"What's wrong?" Mary Jo asked.

Her mother's hands were clenched so tightly that her fingers were white. Financial affairs confused and upset Marianna Summerhill. From the time Marianna had married Norman, she'd been a housewife and mother, leaving the financial details of their lives to her husband.

Mary Jo was fiercely proud of her family. Her father might not be a United States senator, but he was an honest and honorable man. He'd dedicated his life to his family, and worked hard through the years to provide for them. Mary Jo had been raised firmly rooted in her parents' love for each other and for their children.

Although close to sixty, her mother was still a beautiful woman, inside and out. Mary Jo had inherited her dark hair and brown eyes and her petite five-foot-four-inch frame. But the prominent high cheekbones and square jaw were undeniably from her father's side of the family. Her brothers towered above her and, like her parents, were delighted their youngest sibling was a girl.

That affection was returned. Mary Jo adored her older brothers, but she knew them and their quirks and foibles well. Living with five boys—all very different personalities—had given her plenty of practice in deciphering the male psyche. Evan might have come from a rich, upper-crust family, but he was a man, and she'd been able to read him like a book from the first. She believed that her ability to see through his playboy facade was what had originally attracted him. That attraction had grown and blossomed until...

"Come by for Sunday dinner. We eat about three, and we'd enjoy getting to know you better," her mother was saying. "It'd be an honor to have you at our table again."

The words cut into Mary Jo's thoughts like a scythe through wheat. "I'm sure Evan's too busy for that, Mother," she blurted out.

"I appreciate the invitation," Evan said, ignoring Mary Jo.

"You're welcome to stop by the house any time you like, young man," her father added, sending his daughter a frown of disapproval.

"Thank you. I'll keep it in mind," Evan said absently

as he returned his attention to the investment papers. "If you don't object, I'd like an attorney friend of mine to read this over. I should have an answer for you in the next week or so."

Her father nodded. "You do whatever you think is necessary. And don't you worry about your fee."

"Dad, I already told you! I've talked to Evan about that. This is my gift to you."

"Nonsense," her father argued, scowling. "I was the one who was fool enough to trust this shyster. If anyone pays Evan's fee, it'll be me."

"We don't need to worry about that right now," Evan interjected smoothly. "We'll work out the details of my bill later."

"That sounds fair to me." Norman Summerhill was quick to agree, obviously eager to put the subject behind him. Her father had carried his own weight all his life and wouldn't take kindly to Mary Jo's accepting responsibility for this debt. She hoped she could find a way to do so without damaging his formidable pride.

"Thank you for your time," she said to Evan, desperate to leave.

"It was good to see you again, young man," Norman said expansively, shaking hands with Evan. "No need to make yourself scarce. You're welcome for dinner any Sunday of the year."

"Daddy, please," Mary Jo groaned under her breath. The last thing she wanted was to have Evan show up for Sunday dinner with her five brothers and their assorted families. Her one dinner with his family had sufficiently pointed out the glaring differences between their backgrounds.

"Before you go," Evan said to Mary Jo, "my brother

asked me to give you this. I believe it's from Jessica." He handed her a sealed envelope.

"Thank you," Mary Jo mumbled. For the better part of their meeting, he'd avoiding speaking to her. He hadn't been rude or tactless, just businesslike and distant. At least toward her. With her parents, he'd been warm and gracious. She doubted they'd even recognized the subtle difference between how he'd treated them and how he'd treated her.

Mary Jo didn't open the envelope until she'd arrived back at her cozy duplex apartment. She stared at it for several minutes, wondering what Jessica Dryden could possibly have to say to her.

No need to guess, she decided, and tore open the envelope.

Dear Mary Jo,
I just wanted you to know how much I enjoyed meeting you. When I asked Evan why you were in to see him, he clammed right up. I should've known better—prying information out of Evan is even more difficult than it is with Damian.
From your reaction the other day, I could tell you assumed I was married to Evan. Damian and I got quite a chuckle out of that. You see, just about everyone tried to match me up with Evan, but I only had eyes for Damian. If you're free some afternoon, give me a call. Perhaps we could have lunch.
Warmest regards,
Jessica

Jessica had written her telephone number beneath her signature.

Mary Jo couldn't understand why Damian's wife would seek her out. They were virtual strangers. Perhaps Jessica knew something Mary Jo didn't—something about Evan. The only way to find out was to call.

Although Mary Jo wasn't entirely sure about doing this, she reached for the phone.

Jessica Dryden answered almost immediately.

"Mary Jo! I'm so glad to hear from you," she said. "I wondered what you'd think about my note. I don't usually do that sort of thing, but I was just so pleased you'd been to see Evan."

"You said he's mentioned me?"

"A number of times. Look, why don't you come over one afternoon soon and we can talk? You're not teaching right now, are you?"

"School let out a week ago."

"That's what I thought. Could you stop by next week? I'd really enjoy talking to you."

Mary Jo hesitated. Her first introduction to Evan's family had been a catastrophe, and she'd come away knowing their love didn't stand a chance. A second sortie might prove equally disastrous.

"I'd like that very much," Mary Jo found herself saying. If Evan had been talking about her, she wanted to know what he'd said.

"Great. How about next Tuesday afternoon? Come for lunch and we can sit on the patio and have a nice long chat."

"That sounds great," Mary Jo said.

It wasn't until later that evening, when she was filling a croissant with a curried shrimp mixture for dinner, that Mary Jo stopped to wonder exactly *why* Jessica was so eager to "chat" with her.

She liked Gary. She really did. Though why she felt it was necessary to remind herself of this, she didn't know. She didn't even want to know.

It had been like this from the moment she'd broken off her relationship with Evan. She'd found fault with every man she'd dated. Regardless of how attractive he was. Or how successful. How witty, how considerate...it didn't matter.

Gary was very *nice,* she repeated to herself.

Unfortunately he bored her to tears. He talked about his golf game, his bowling score and his prow-ess on the handball court. Never anything that was important to her. But his biggest fault, she'd realized early on in their relationship, was that he wasn't Evan.

They'd dated infrequently since the beginning of the year. To be honest, Mary Jo was beginning to think that, to Gary, her biggest attraction was her mother's cooking. Invariably, Gary stopped by early on Sunday afternoon, just as she was about to leave for her parents' home. It'd happened three out of the past five weeks. She suspected he'd been on duty at the fire hall the two weeks he'd missed.

"You look lovely this afternoon," he said when she opened her front door to him now. He held out a bouquet of pink carnations, which she took with a smile, pleased by his thoughtfulness.

"Hello, Gary."

He kissed her cheek, but it seemed perfunctory, as if he felt some display of affection was expected of him.

"How've you been?" he muttered, easing himself into the old rocking chair next to the fireplace.

Although Mary Jo's rooms were small, she'd carefully decorated each one. The living room had an Early American look. Her brother Lonny, who did beautiful woodwork, had carved her an eagle for Christmas, which she'd hung above the fireplace. In addition to her antique rocking chair, she had a small sofa and an old oak chest that she'd restored herself. Her mother had crocheted an afghan for the back of the sofa in a patriotic blend of red, white and blue.

Her kitchen was little more than a wide hallway that led to a compact dining space in a window alcove. Mary Jo loved to sit there in the morning sunshine with a cup of coffee and a book.

"You're lucky, you know," Gary said, gesturing around the room.

"How do you mean?"

"Well, first off, you don't have to work in the summer."

This was an old argument and Mary Jo was tired of hearing it. True, school wasn't in session for those two and a half months, but she didn't spend them lolling on a beach. This was the first summer in years that she wasn't attending courses to upgrade her skills.

"You've got the time you need to fix up this place the way you want it," he went on. "You have real decorating talent, you know. My place is a mess, but then I'm only there three or four days out of the week, if that."

If he was hinting that he'd like her to help him decorate his apartment, she refused to take the bait.

"Are you going over to your parents' this afternoon?" Gary asked cheerfully. "I don't mean to horn in, but your family doesn't seem to mind, and the two of us have an understanding, don't we?"

"An…understanding?" This was news to Mary Jo.

"Yeah. We're… I don't know, going together, I guess."

"I thought we were just friends." That was all Mary Jo intended the relationship to be.

"Just friends." Gary's face fell. His gaze wandered to the carnations he'd brought.

"When was the last time we went out on a date?" she asked, crossing her arms. "A real date."

"You mean to the movies or something?"

"Sure." Surveying her own memory, she could count on one hand the number of times he'd actually spent money taking her out. The carnations were an exception.

"We went to the Red Sox game, remember?"

"That was in April," she reminded him.

Gary frowned. "That long ago? Time certainly flies, doesn't it?"

"It sure does."

Gary rubbed his face. "You're right, Mary Jo. I've taken you for granted, haven't I?"

She was about to say they really didn't have much of an understanding, after all, did they. Yet a serious relationship with Gary didn't interest her and, difficult as it was to admit now, never had. She'd used him to block out the loneliness. She'd used him so her parents wouldn't worry about her. They firmly believed that a woman, especially a young woman, needed a man in her life, so she'd trotted out Gary in order to keep the peace. She wasn't exactly proud of her motives.

Gary reached for her hand. "How about a movie this

afternoon?" he suggested contritely. "We'll leave right after dinner at your parents'. We can invite anyone who wants to come along. You wouldn't mind, would you?"

Gary was honestly trying. He couldn't help it that he wasn't Evan Dryden. The thought slipped uncensored into her mind.

"A movie sounds like a great idea," she said firmly. She was going, and furthermore, she was determined to have a wonderful time. Just because Evan Dryden had briefly reentered her life was no reason to wallow in the impossible. He was way out of her league.

"Great." A smile lighted his boyish face. "Let's drive over to your mom and dad's place now."

"All right," Mary Jo said. She felt better already. Her relationship with Gary wasn't ideal—it wasn't even close to ideal—but he was her friend. Love and marriage had been built on a whole lot less.

Before they left the house, Gary grabbed the bouquet of carnations. Mary Jo blinked in surprise, and he hesitated, looking mildly chagrined. "I thought we'd give these to your mother. You don't mind, do you?"

"Of course not," she mumbled, but she did, just a little.

Gary must have realized it because he added, "Next time I'll bring some just for you."

"You owe me one, Mr. Copeland."

He laughed good-naturedly and with an elaborate display of courtesy, opened the car door for her.

Mary Jo slid into the seat and snapped her seat belt in place. During the brief drive to her parents' house, less than two miles away, she and Gary didn't speak; instead, they listened companionably to part of a Red Sox game.

Her nephews and nieces were out in the huge side yard, playing a rousing game of volleyball when they arrived. Gary parked his car behind her oldest brother's station wagon.

"I get a kick out of how much fun your family has together," he said a bit wistfully.

"We have our share of squabbles, too." But disagreements were unusual and quickly resolved. Three of her brothers, Jack, Rich and Lonny, were construction electricians like their father. Rob and Mark had both become mechanics and opened a shop together. They were still struggling to get on their feet financially, but both worked hard. With time, they'd make a go of it; Mary Jo was convinced of that.

"I wonder what your mother decided to cook today," Gary mused, and Mary Jo swore he all but licked his chops.

Briefly she wondered if Gary bothered to eat during the week, or if he stored up his appetite for Sunday dinners with her family.

"I've been introduced to all your brothers, haven't I?" he asked, frowning slightly as he helped her out of the car.

Mary Jo had to think about that. He must have been. Not every brother came every Sunday, but over the course of the past few months surely Gary had met each of her five brothers.

"I don't recognize the guy in the red sweatshirt," he said as they moved up the walk toward the house.

Mary Jo was distracted from answering by her mother, who came rushing down the porch steps, holding out her arms as if it'd been weeks since they'd last seen each other. She wore an apron and a smile that sparkled with delight. "Mary Jo! I'm so glad you're here." She hugged her daughter close for a long moment, then turned toward Gary.

"How sweet," she said, taking the bouquet of carnations and kissing his cheek.

Still smiling, Marianna turned back to her daughter. "You'll never guess who came by!"

It was then that Mary Jo noticed Evan walking toward them. Dressed in jeans and a red sweatshirt, he carried Lenny, her six-year-old nephew, tucked under one arm, and Robby, his older brother by a year, under the other. Both boys were kicking and laughing.

Evan stopped abruptly when he saw Mary Jo and Gary. The laughter drained out of his eyes.

"Hello," Gary said, stepping forward. "You must be one of Mary Jo's brothers. I don't believe we've met. I'm Gary Copeland."

Chapter 3

"What are you *doing* here?" Mary Jo demanded the minute she could get Evan alone. With a house full of people, it had taken her the better part of two hours to corner him. As it was, they were standing in the hallway and could be interrupted at any moment.

"If you'll recall, your mother invited me."

"The only reason you're here is to embarrass me." The entire meal had been an exercise in frustration for Mary Jo. Evan had been the center of attention and had answered a multitude of questions from her parents and brothers. As for the way he'd treated Gary— every time she thought about it, she seethed. Anyone watching them would think Evan and Gary were old pals. Evan had joked with Gary, even going so far as to mention that Mary Jo's ears grew red whenever she was uncomfortable with a subject.

The second he'd said it, she felt the blood rush to her ears. Soon they were so hot she was afraid Gary might mistake them for a fire engine.

What upset her most was the fact that Evan had her family eating out of his hand. Everyone acted as though he was some sort of celebrity! Her mother had offered him the first slice of chocolate cake, something Mary Jo could never remember happening. No matter who was seated at the dinner table, her father had always been served first.

"I didn't mean to make you uncomfortable," Evan said now, his eyes as innocent as a preschooler's.

Mary Jo wasn't fooled. She knew exactly why he'd come—to humiliate her in front of her family. Rarely had she been angrier. Rarely had she felt more frustrated. Tears filled her eyes and blurred her vision.

"You can think what you want of me, but don't *ever* laugh at my family," she said from between gritted teeth. She whirled away and had taken all of two steps when he caught hold of her shoulder and yanked her around.

Now he was just as angry. His dark eyes burned with it. They scowled at each other, faces tight, hands clenched.

"I would never laugh at your family," he said evenly.

Mary Jo straightened her shoulders defiantly. "But you look forward to make a laughingstock out of *me*. Let me give you an example. You knew I wasn't married, yet you manipulated me into admitting it. You *enjoy* making me uncomfortable!"

He grinned then, a sly off-center grin. "I figured you owed me that much."

"I don't owe you anything!" she snapped.

"Perhaps not," he agreed. He was laughing at her, had been from the moment she'd stepped into his high-priced office. Like an unsuspecting fly, she'd carelessly gotten caught in a spider's web.

"Stay out of my life," she warned, eyes narrowed.

Evan glared back at her. "Gladly."

Just then Sarah, one of Mary Jo's favorite nieces, came skipping down the hallway as only a five-year-old can, completely unaware of the tension between her and Evan. Sarah stopped when she saw Mary Jo with Evan.

"Hi," she said, looking up at them.

"Hello, sweetheart," Mary Jo said, forcing herself to smile. Her mouth felt as if it would crack.

Sarah stared at Evan, her eyes wide with curiosity. "Are you going to be my uncle someday?"

"No," Mary Jo answered immediately, mortified. It seemed that even her own family had turned against her.

"Why not?" Sarah wanted to know. "I like him better than Gary, and he likes you, too. I can tell. When we were eating dinner, he kept looking at you. Like Daddy looks at Mommy."

"I'm dating Gary," Mary Jo insisted, "and he's taking me to a movie. You can come if you want."

Sarah shook her head. "Gary likes *you,* but he doesn't like kids very much."

Mary Jo's heart sank. She'd noticed that about Gary herself. He wasn't accustomed to small children; he tolerated them, but kid noise irritated him. Evan, on the other hand, was an instant hit with both the adults and the kids. Nothing her nieces or nephews said or did seemed to bother him. If anything, he appeared to enjoy himself. He'd played volleyball and baseball with her brothers, chess with her father, and wrestled with the kids—ten against one.

"I hope you marry Evan," Sarah said, her expression serious. Having stated her opinion, she skipped on down to the end of the hallway.

"Mary Jo."

Before she could say anything else to Evan—although she didn't know what—Gary came looking for her. He stopped abruptly when he saw who she was with.

"I didn't mean to interrupt anything," he said, shoving his hands in his pockets, obviously uncomfortable.

"You didn't," Mary Jo answered decisively. "Now, what movie do you think we should see?" She turned her back on Evan and walked toward Gary, knowing in her heart that Sarah was right. Evan was the man for her. Not Gary.

"I'm absolutely thrilled that you came," Jessica Dryden said, opening the front door. Mary Jo stepped into the Dryden home, mildly surprised that a maid or other household help hadn't greeted her. From what she remembered of the older Drydens' home, Whispering Willows, the domestic staff had been with them for nearly thirty years.

"Thank you for inviting me," Mary Jo said, looking around. The house was a sprawling rambler decorated with comfortable modern furniture. An ocean scene graced the wall above the fireplace, but it wasn't by an artist Mary Jo recognized. Judging by the decor and relaxed atmosphere, Damian and Jessica seemed to be a fairly typical young couple.

"I fixed us a seafood salad," Jessica said, leading

Mary Jo into the large, spotless kitchen. She followed, her eyes taking in everything around her. Jessica and Damian's home was spacious and attractive, but it was nothing like Whispering Willows.

"You made the salad yourself?" Mary Jo asked. She didn't mean to sound rude, but she'd assumed Jessica had kitchen help.

"Yes," Jessica answered pleasantly. "I'm a fairly good cook. At least Damian hasn't complained. Much," she added with a dainty laugh. "I thought we'd eat on the patio. That is, if you don't mind. It's such a beautiful afternoon. I was working in the garden earlier and I cut us some roses. They're so lovely this time of year."

Sliding glass doors led to a brick-lined patio. A round glass table, shaded by a brightly striped umbrella, was set with two pink placemats and linen napkins. A bouquet of yellow roses rested in the middle.

"Would you like iced tea with lunch?" Jessica asked next.

"Please."

"Sit down and I'll bring everything out."

"Let me help." Mary Jo wasn't accustomed to being waited on and would've been uncomfortable letting Jessica do all the work. She followed her into the kitchen and carried out the pitcher of tea while Jessica brought the seafood salad.

"Where's Andy?" Mary Jo asked.

"Napping." She set the salad bowl and matching plates on the table and glanced at her watch. "We'll have a solid hour of peace. I hope."

They sat down together. Jessica gazed at her earnestly and began to speak. "You must think I'm terribly presumptuous to have written you that note, but I'm dying to talk to you."

"I'll admit curiosity is what brought me here," Mary Jo confessed. She'd expected to feel awkward and out of place, but Jessica was so easygoing and unpretentious Mary Jo felt perfectly at ease.

"I've known Evan from the time I was a kid. We grew up next door to each other," Jessica explained. "When I was a teenager I had the biggest crush on him. I made an absolute fool of myself." She shook her head wryly.

Mary Jo thought it was no wonder she found herself liking Jessica so much. They obviously had a great deal in common—especially when it came to Evan!

"As you may be aware, I worked with Evan when he represented Earl Kress. Naturally Evan and I spent a lot of time together. We became good friends and he told me about you."

Mary Jo nervously smoothed the linen napkin across her lap. She wasn't sure she wanted to hear what Jessica had to say.

"I hurt him badly, didn't I?" she asked, keeping her head lowered.

"Yes." Apparently Jessica didn't believe in mincing words. "I don't know what happened between you and the man you left Evan for, but clearly it didn't work out the way you expected."

"Few things in life work out the way we expect them to, do they?" Mary Jo answered cryptically.

"No." Jessica set down her fork. "For a while I was convinced there wasn't any hope for Damian and me. You see, I loved Damian, but everyone kept insisting Evan and I should be a couple. It gets confusing, so I won't go into the details, but Damian seemed to think he was doing the noble thing by stepping aside so I could marry Evan. It didn't seem to matter that I was in love with *him*. Everything was complicated even more by family expectations. Oh, my heavens," she said with a heartfelt sigh, "those were very bleak days."

"But you figured everything out."

"Yes," Jessica said with a relaxed smile. "It wasn't easy, but it was sure worth the effort." She paused, resting her hands in her lap. "This is the reason I asked you to have lunch with me. What happens between you and Evan is none of my business. And knowing Evan, he'd be furious with me if he knew I was even speaking to you, but…" She stopped and took in a deep breath. "You once had something very special with Evan. I'm hoping that with a little effort on both your parts you can reclaim it."

A cloak of sadness seemed to settle over Mary Jo's shoulders, and when she spoke her words were little more than a whisper. "It isn't possible anymore."

"Why isn't it? I don't know why you've come to Evan. That's not my affair. But I do realize how much courage it must have taken. You're already halfway there, Mary Jo. Don't give up now."

Mary Jo wished she could believe that, but it was too late for her and Evan now. Whatever chance they'd had as a couple had been destroyed long ago.

By her own hand.

Her reasons for breaking off the relationship hadn't changed. She'd done it because she had to, and she'd done it in such a way that Evan would never forgive her. That was part of her plan—for his sake.

"I almost think Evan hates me," she murmured. Speaking was painful; there was a catch in her voice.

"Nonsense," Jessica said briskly. "I don't believe that for a moment."

Mary Jo wished she could accept her friend's words, but Jessica hadn't been there when Evan suggested she hire another attorney. Jessica hadn't seen the look in Evan's eyes when she'd confronted him in the hallway of her family home. Nor had she been there when Mary Jo had introduced him to Gary.

He despised her, and the ironic thing was that she couldn't blame him.

"Just remember what I said," Jessica urged. "Be patient with Evan, and with yourself. But most of all, don't give up, not until you're absolutely convinced it'll never work. I speak from experience, Mary Jo—the rewards are well worth whatever it costs your pride. I can't imagine my life without Damian and Andy."

After a brief silence, Mary Jo resolutely changed the subject, and the two women settled down to their meal. Conversation was lighthearted—books and movies they'd both enjoyed, anecdotes about friends and family, opinions about various public figures.

They were continuing a good-natured disagreement over one of the Red Sox pitchers as they carried their plates inside. Just as they reached the kitchen, the doorbell chimed.

"I'll get that," Jessica said.

Smiling, Mary Jo rinsed off the plates and placed them in the dishwasher. She liked Jessica very much. Damian's wife was open and natural and had a wonderful sense of humor. She was also deeply in love with her husband.

"It's Evan," Jessica said, returning to the kitchen. Her voice was strained and tense. Evan stood stiffly behind his sister-in-law. "He dropped off some papers for Damian."

"Uh, hello, Evan," Mary Jo said awkwardly.

Jessica's gaze pleaded with her to believe she hadn't arranged this accidental meeting.

Andy let out a piercing cry, and Mary Jo thought the toddler had the worst sense of timing of any baby she'd ever known.

Jessica excused herself, and Mary Jo was left standing next to the dishwasher, wishing she was anywhere else in the world.

"What are you doing here?" he demanded the minute Jessica was out of earshot.

"You showed up at *my* family's home. Why is it so shocking that I'm at your brother's house?"

"I was invited," he reminded her fiercely.

"So was I."

He looked for a moment as if he doubted her. "Fine. I suppose you and Jessica have decided to become bosom buddies. That sounds like something you'd do."

Mary Jo didn't have a response to such a patently unfair remark.

"As it happens," Evan said in an obvious attempt to put his anger behind him, "I was meaning to call you this afternoon, anyway."

"About my parents' case?" she asked anxiously.

"I've talked with my colleague about Adison Investments, and it looks as if it'll involve some lengthy litigation."

Mary Jo leaned against the kitchen counter. "Lengthy is another word for expensive, right?"

"I was prepared to discuss my fee with you at the same time," he went on in a businesslike tone.

"All right," she said, tensing.

"I can't see this costing anything less than twenty or thirty thousand."

She couldn't help a sharp intake of breath. That amount of money was a fortune to her parents. To her, too.

"It could go even higher."

Which was another way of saying he wasn't willing to handle the case. Mary Jo felt the sudden need to sit down. She walked over to the table, pulled out a chair and sank into it.

"I'd be willing to do what I can, but—"

"Don't lie to me, Evan," she said, fighting back her hurt and frustration. She'd come to him because he had the clout and the influence to help her family. Because he was a damn good attorney. Because she'd trusted him to be honest and ethical.

"I'm not lying."

"That kind of money is far beyond what my parents or I can afford. It may not be a lot to you or your family, but there's no way we could hope to raise that much in a short amount of time."

"I'm willing to take payments."

How very generous of him, she mused sarcastically.

"There might be another way," he said.

"What?"

"If you agree, of course."

Mary Jo wasn't sure she liked the sound of this.

"A summer job. You're out of school, aren't you?" She nodded.

"My personal assistant, Mrs. Sterling, is taking an

extended European vacation this summer. I'd intended to hire a replacement, but as I recall your computer and dictation skills are excellent."

"My computer skills are very basic and I never took shorthand."

He grinned as if that didn't matter. Obviously, what did matter was making her miserable for the next two months.

"But you're a fast learner. Am I right or wrong?" he pressed.

"Well… I do pick up things fairly easily."

"That's what I thought." He spread out his hands. "Now, do you want the job or not?"

Chapter 4

"Mr. Dryden's a real pleasure to work for. I'm sure you won't have any problems," Mrs. Sterling said, looking relieved and happy that Mary Jo would be substituting for her. "Evan's not the least bit demanding, and I can't think of even one time he's been unreasonable."

Mary Jo suspected that might not be the case with her.

"I could have retired with my husband, but I enjoy my job so much I decided to stay on," Mrs. Sterling continued. "I couldn't bear leaving that young man. In some ways, I think of Evan as my own son."

"I'm sure he reciprocates your feelings," Mary Jo said politely. She didn't know how much longer she could endure listening to this list of Evan's finer qualities. Not that she doubted they were true. For Mrs. Sterling.

Thus far, Evan had embarrassed her in front of her family and blackmailed her into working for him. She had a problem picturing him as Prince Charming to her Cinderella. As for his being a "real pleasure" to work for, Mary Jo entertained some serious reservations.

"I'm glad you've got the opportunity to travel with your husband," Mary Jo said.

"That's another thing," Evan's personal assistant gushed. "What boss would be willing to let his personal assistant go for two whole months like this? It's a terrible inconvenience to him. Nevertheless, Mr. Dryden encouraged me to take this trip with Dennis. Why, he *insisted* I go. I promise you, they don't come any better than Mr. Dryden. You're going to thoroughly enjoy your summer."

Mary Jo's smile was weak at best.

Evan wanted her under his thumb, and much as she disliked giving in to the pressure, she had no choice. Twenty or thirty thousand dollars would financially cripple her parents. Evan knew that. He was also well aware that her brothers weren't in any position to contribute.

With the slump in the economy, new construction starts had been way down. Jack, Rich and Lonny had collected unemployment benefits most of the winter and were just scraping by now. Rob and Mark's automotive business was barely on its feet.

She was the one who'd gone to Evan for help, and she was the one who'd accepted the financial responsibility. When she'd told her parents she'd be working for Evan, they were both delighted. Her mother seemed to think it was the perfect solution. Whether Evan had planned it this way or not, his employing her had smoothed her father's ruffled feathers about Evan's fee. Apparently, letting her pick up any out-of-pocket expenses was unacceptable to Norman Summerhill, but an exchange of services, so to speak, was fine.

Evan, who could do no wrong as far as her parents were concerned, came out of this smelling like a rose— to use one of her dad's favorite expressions.

Mary Jo wondered if she was being unfair to assume that Evan was looking for vengeance, for a means of making her life miserable. Perhaps she'd misjudged him.

Perhaps. But she doubted it.

"I'm taking my lunch now," Mrs. Sterling said, pulling open the bottom drawer of her desk and taking out her handbag. She hesitated. "You will be all right here by yourself, won't you?"

"Of course." Mary Jo made an effort to sound infinitely confident, even if she wasn't. Evan's legal assistant, Peter McNichols, was on vacation for the next couple of weeks, so she'd be dealing with Evan entirely on her own.

Mary Jo wasn't emotionally prepared for that just yet. The shaky, unsure feeling in the pit of her stomach reminded her of the first time she'd stood in front of a classroom filled with five-year-olds.

No sooner had Mrs. Sterling left than Evan summoned Mary Jo. Grabbing a pen and pad, she hurried into his office, determined to be the best substitute personal assistant he could have hired.

"Sit down," he instructed in a curt, businesslike tone.

Mary Jo complied, sitting on the very edge of the chair, her back ramrod-straight, her shoulders stiff.

He reached for a small, well-worn black book and

flipped through the flimsy pages, scrutinizing the names. Mary Jo figured it had to be the typical bachelor's infamous "little black book." She knew he had a reputation, after all, as one of Boston's most eligible bachelors. Every six months or so, gossip columns speculated on Evan Dryden's current love interest. A little black book was exactly what she expected of him.

"Order a dozen red roses to be sent to Catherine Moore," he said, and rattled off the address. Mary Jo immediately recognized it as being in a prestigious neighborhood. "Suggest we meet for lunch on the twenty-fifth. Around twelve-thirty." He mentioned one of Boston's most elegant restaurants. "Have you got that?" he asked.

"I'll see to it right away," Mary Jo said crisply, revealing none of her feelings. Evan had done this on purpose. He was having her arrange a lunch date with one of his many conquests in order to humiliate her, to teach her a lesson. It was his way of telling her he'd completely recovered from their short-lived romance. There were any number of women who'd welcome his attentions.

Well, Mary Jo got the message, loud and clear. She got up, ready to return to her desk.

"There's more," Evan said.

Mary Jo sat back down and was barely able to keep up with him as he listed name after name, followed by phone number and address. Each woman was to receive a dozen red roses and an invitation to lunch, with time and place suggested.

When he'd finished, Mary Jo counted six names, each conjuring up a statuesque beauty. No doubt every one of them could run circles around her in looks, talent and, most important, social position.

Mary Jo didn't realize one man would know that many places to eat with so many different women, but she wisely kept her opinion to herself. If he was hoping she'd give him the satisfaction of a response, he was dead wrong.

She'd just finished ordering the flowers when Damian Dryden stepped into the office.

"Hello," he said. His eyes widened with surprise at finding her sitting at Mrs. Sterling's desk.

Mary Jo stood and extended her hand. "I'm Mary Jo Summerhill. We met briefly last week." She didn't mention the one other time she'd been introduced to Damian, certain he wouldn't remember.

It was well over three years ago. Evan and Mary Jo had been sailing, and they'd run into Damian at the marina. Her first impression of Evan's older brother was that of a shrewd businessman. Damian had seemed rather distant. He'd shown little interest in their cheerful commentary on sailing and the weather. From conversations she'd previously had with Evan regarding his brother, she'd learned he was a serious and hardworking lawyer, and that was certainly how he'd struck her—as someone with no time for fun or frivolity. Now he was a Superior Court judge, but he often dropped by the family law firm. Apparently the two brothers were close friends.

The man she'd met on the dock that day and the one who stood before her now might have been two entirely different men. Damian was still serious and hardworking, but he seemed more relaxed now, more apt to smile. Mary Jo was convinced that marriage and fatherhood had made the difference, and she was genuinely happy for him and for Jessica.

"You're working for the firm now?" Damian asked.

"Mrs. Sterling will be traveling in Europe this summer," Mary Jo said, "and Evan, uh, offered me the job." Which was a polite way of saying he'd coerced her into accepting the position.

"But I thought—" Damian stopped abruptly, then grinned. "Is Evan in?"

"Yes. I'll tell him you're here." She reached for the intercom switch and announced Damian, who walked directly into Evan's office.

Mary Jo was acquainting herself with the filing system when she heard Evan burst out laughing. It really wasn't fair to assume it had anything to do with her, but she couldn't help believing that was the case.

Damian left a couple of minutes later, smiling. He paused in front of Mary Jo's desk. "Don't let him give you a hard time," he said pleasantly. "My wife mentioned having you over for lunch last week, but she didn't say you'd accepted a position with the firm."

"I... I didn't know it myself at the time," Mary Jo mumbled. She hadn't actually agreed to the job until much later, after she'd spent a few days examining her limited options.

"I see. Well, it's good to have you on board, Mary Jo. If you have any questions or concerns, don't hesitate to talk to Evan. And if he does give you a hard time, just let me know and I'll straighten him out."

"Thank you," she said, and meant it. Although she couldn't very well see herself complaining to one brother about the other...

She decided to change her attitude about the whole

situation. She'd forget about Evan's probable motives and, instead, start looking at the positive side of this opportunity. She'd be able to help her parents now, without dipping into her own savings. Things could definitely be worse.

Mary Jo didn't learn just how *much* worse until Wednesday—the first day she was working on her own. Mrs. Sterling had spent the first two days of the week acquainting Mary Jo with office procedures and the filing system. She'd updated her on Evan's current cases, and Mary Jo felt reasonably confident she could handle whatever came up.

He called her into his office around eleven. "I need the William Jenkins file."

"I'll have it for you right away," she assured him. Mary Jo returned to the outer office and the filing cabinet, and sorted through the colored tabs. She located three clients named Jenkins, none of whom was William. Her heart pounded with dread as she hurried to another drawer, thinking it might have been misfiled.

Five minutes passed. Evan came out of his office, his movements as brusque and irritated as his voice. "Is there a problem?"

"I...can't seem to find the William Jenkins file," she said, hurriedly going through the files one more time. "Are you sure it isn't on your desk?"

"Would I have asked you to find it if I had it on my desk?" She could feel his cold stare directly between her shoulder blades.

"No, I guess not. But it isn't out here."

"It has to be. I distinctly remember giving it to Mrs. Sterling on Monday."

"She had me replace all the files on Monday," Mary Jo admitted reluctantly.

"Then you must have misfiled it."

"I don't recall any file with the name Jenkins," she said stubbornly. She didn't want to make an issue of this, but she'd been extremely careful with every file, even double-checking her work.

"Are you telling me I *didn't* return the file? Are you calling me a liar?"

This wasn't going well. "No," she said in a slow, deliberate voice. "All I'm saying is that I don't recall replacing any file with the name Jenkins on it." Their gazes met and locked in silent battle.

Evan's dark eyes narrowed briefly. "Are you doing this on purpose, Mary Jo?" he asked, crossing his arms over his chest.

"Absolutely not." Outraged, she brought her chin up and returned his glare. "You can think whatever you like, but I'd never do anything so underhanded as hide an important file."

She wasn't sure if he believed her or not, and his lack of trust hurt her more than any words he might have spoken. "If you honestly suspect I'd sabotage your office, then I suggest you fire me immediately."

Evan walked over to the cabinet and pulled open the top drawer. He was searching through the files, the same way she had earlier.

Silently Mary Jo prayed she hadn't inadvertently missed seeing the requested file. The humiliation of having him find it would be unbearable.

"It isn't here," he murmured, sounding almost surprised.

Mary Jo gave an inward sigh of relief.

"Where could it possibly be?" he asked impatiently. "I need it for an appointment this afteroon."

Mary Jo edged a couple of steps toward him. "Would you mind if I looked in your office?"

He gestured toward the open door. "Be my guest."

She sorted through the stack of files on the corner of his desk and leafed through his briefcase, all to no avail. Glancing at the clock, she groaned inwardly. "You have a lunch appointment," she reminded him.

"I need that file!" he snapped.

Mary Jo bristled. "I'm doing my best."

"Your best clearly isn't good enough. *Find that file.*"

"I'll do a much better job of it if you aren't here breathing down my neck. Go have lunch, and I'll find the Jenkins file." She'd dismantle the filing cabinets one by one until she'd located it, if that was what it took.

Evan hesitated, then checked his watch. "I won't be long," he muttered, reaching for his jacket and thrusting his arms into the sleeves. "I'll give you a call from the restaurant."

"All right."

"If worse comes to worst, we can reschedule the client," he said as he buttoned the jacket. Evan had always been a smart dresser, she reflected irrelevantly. No matter what the circumstances, he looked as if he'd just stepped off a page in *Esquire* or *GQ*.

"Listen," Evan said, pausing at the door. "Don't worry about it. The file has to surface sometime." He seemed to be apologizing, however indirectly, for his earlier bout of bad temper.

She nodded, feeling guilty although she had no reason. But the file was missing and she felt responsible, despite the fact that she'd never so much as seen it.

Since she'd brought her lunch to work, Mary Jo nibbled at it as she sorted through every single file drawer in every single cabinet. Mrs. Sterling was meticulously neat, and not a single file had been misplaced.

Mary Jo was sitting on the carpet, files spread around her, when Evan phoned.

"Did you find it?"

"No, I'm sorry, Evan... Mr. Dryden," she corrected quickly.

His lengthy pause added to her feelings of guilt and confusion. She'd been so determined to be a good replacement. She'd vowed she was going to give him his money's worth. Yet here it was—her first day of working alone—and already she'd failed him.

By the time Evan was back at the office, she'd reassembled everything. He made the call to reschedule the appointment with William Jenkins, saving her the task of inventing an excuse.

At three o'clock her phone rang. It was Gary, and the instant she recognized his voice, Mary Jo groaned.

"How'd you know where to reach me?" she asked, keeping her voice low. Evan was sure to frown on personal phone calls, especially from a male friend. After their confrontation that morning, she felt bad enough.

"Your mom told me you were working for Daddy Warbucks now."

"Don't call him that," she said heatedly, surprised at the flash of anger she experienced.

Gary didn't immediately respond—as if he, too, was taken aback by her outburst. "I apologize," he said, his voice contrite. "I didn't phone to start an argument. I wanted to tell you I've taken our talk last Sunday to heart. How about dinner and dancing this Saturday?

We could go to one of those all-you-can-eat places that serve barbecued ribs, and shuffle our feet a little afterward."

"Uh, maybe we could talk about this later."

"Yes or no?" Gary cajoled. "Just how difficult can it be? I thought you'd be pleased."

"It isn't a good idea to call me at the office, Gary."

"But I'll be at the fire station by the time you're off work," he explained. "I thought you wanted us to spend more time together. That's what you said, isn't it?"

Was that what she'd said? She didn't think so. Not exactly. "Uh, well…" Why, oh why, was life so complicated?

"I'm glad you spoke up," Gary continued when she didn't, "because I tend to get lazy in a relationship. I want you to know how much I appreciate your company."

"All right, I'll go," she said ungraciously, knowing it was the only way she'd get him off the phone quickly. "Saturday evening. What time?"

"Six okay? I'll pick you up."

"Six is fine."

"We're going to have a great time, Mary Jo. Just you wait and see."

She wasn't at all convinced of that, but she supposed she didn't have any right to complain. Eager to please, Gary was doing exactly what she'd asked of him. And frankly, dinner with Gary was a damn sight better than sitting home alone.

No sooner had she hung up the phone than Evan opened his door and stared at her, his look hard and disapproving. He didn't say a word about personal phone calls. He didn't have to. The heat radiated from her cheeks.

"Th-that was Gary," she said, then wanted to kick herself for volunteering the information. "I told him I can't take personal calls at the office. He won't be phoning again."

"Good," he said, and closed the door. It clicked sharply into place, as if to underline his disapproval. She returned to the letter she was typing into the computer.

Just before five, Mary Jo collected the letters that required Evan's signature and carried them to his office. He was reading over a brief, and momentarily looked up when she knocked softly and entered the room.

"Is there anything else you'd like me to do before I leave?" she asked, depositing the unsigned letters on the corner of his desk.

He shook his head. "Nothing, thank you. Good night, Ms. Summerhill."

He sounded so stiff and formal. As if he'd never held her, never kissed her. As if she'd never meant anything to him and never would.

"Good night, Mr. Dryden." She turned quickly and walked out of the office.

After their brief exchange regarding the missing file, they'd been coolly polite to each other during the rest of the day.

If his intention was to punish her, he couldn't have devised a more effective means.

Because she loved Evan. She'd never stopped loving him, no matter how she tried to convince herself otherwise. Being with him every day and maintaining this crisp, professional facade was the cruelest form of punishment.

Once she was home, Mary Jo kicked off her low heels, slumped into the rocking chair and closed her eyes in a desperate attempt to relax. She hadn't worked for Evan a full week yet, and already she wondered if she could last another day.

The rest of the summer didn't bear thinking about.

"What I don't understand," Marianna Summerhill said as she chopped up chicken for the salad, "is why you and Evan ever broke up."

"Mom, please, it was a long time ago."

"Not so long. Two, three years."

"Do you want me to set the table?" Mary Jo asked, hoping to distract her mother. That she hadn't seen through this unexpected dinner invitation only showed how weary she was, how low her defenses. Her mother had phoned the evening before, when Mary Jo was still recovering from working on her own with Evan; she'd insisted Mary Jo join them for dinner and "a nice visit."

"So, how's the job going?" her father asked, sitting down at the kitchen table. The huge dining room table was reserved for Sunday dinners.

"Oh, just great," Mary Jo said, working up enough energy to offer him a reassuring smile. She didn't want her parents to know what the job was costing her emotionally.

"I was just saying to Mary Jo what a fine young man Evan Dryden is." Her mother set the salad in the center of the table and pulled out a chair.

"He certainly is a decent sort. You were dating him a while back, weren't you?"

"Yes, Dad."

"Seems to me the two of you were real serious."

When she didn't answer, he added, "As I recall, he gave you an engagement ring, didn't he? You had him come to dinner that one time. Whatever happened, Mary Jo? Did our family scare him off?"

Mary Jo was forever bound to hide the truth. Evan had been an instant hit with her family. They'd thrown open their arms and welcomed him, delighted that Mary Jo had found a man to love. Not for the world would she let her parents be hurt. Not for the world would she tell them the truth.

How could she possibly explain that their only daughter, whom they adored, wasn't good enough for the high-and-mighty Drydens? The minute Mary Jo met Evan's mother, she'd sensed the older woman's disappointment in her. Lois Dryden was looking for more in a daughter-in-law than Mary Jo could ever be.

Their private chat after dinner had set the record straight. Evan was destined for politics and would need a certain kind of wife, Mrs. Dryden had gently explained. Mary Jo didn't hear much beyond that.

Mrs. Dryden had strongly implied that Mary Jo would hinder Evan's political aspirations. She might very well ruin his life. There'd been some talk about destiny and family expectations and the demands on a political wife—Mary Jo's memories of the conversation were vague. But her understanding of Mrs. Dryden's message had been anything but.

Evan needed a woman who would be an asset—socially and politically. As an electrician's daughter, Mary Jo couldn't possibly be that woman. End of discussion.

"Mary Jo?"

Her mother's worried voice cut into her thoughts.

She shook her head and smiled. "I'm sorry, Mom, what were you saying?"

"Your father asked you a question."

"About you and Evan," Norman elaborated. "I thought you two were pretty serious."

"We were at one time," she admitted, seeing no other way around it. "We were even engaged. But we…drifted apart. Those things happen, you know. Luckily we realized that before it was too late."

"But he's such a dear boy."

"He's a charmer, Mom," Mary Jo said, making light of his appeal. "But he's not the man for me. Besides, I'm dating Gary now."

Her parents exchanged meaningful glances.

"You don't like Gary?" Mary Jo prodded.

"Of course we like him," Marianna said cautiously. "It's just that…well, he's very sweet, but I just don't think Gary's right for you."

Frankly, Mary Jo didn't, either.

"It seems to me," her father said slowly as he buttered a slice of bread, "that your young man's more interested in your mother's cooking than he is in you."

So the family had noticed. Not that Gary'd made any secret of it. "Gary's just a friend, Dad. You don't need to worry—we aren't really serious."

"What about Evan?" Marianna studied Mary Jo carefully, wearing the concerned expression she always wore whenever she suspected one of her children was ill. An intense, narrowed expression—as if staring at Mary Jo long enough would reveal the problem.

"Oh, Evan's a friend, too," Mary Jo said airily, but she didn't really believe it. She doubted they could ever be friends again.

* * *

Late Friday afternoon, just before she began getting ready to leave for the weekend, Evan called Mary Jo into his office. He was busy writing, and she waited until he'd finished before she asked, "You wanted to see me?"

"Yes," he said absently, picking up a file folder. "I'm afraid I'm going to need you tomorrow."

"On Saturday?" She'd assumed the weekends were her own.

"I'm sure Mrs. Sterling mentioned I might occasionally need you to travel with me."

"No, she didn't," Mary Jo said, holding her shoulders rigid. She could guess what was coming. Somehow he was going to keep her from seeing Gary Saturday night. A man who lunched with a different woman every day of the week wanted to cheat her out of one dinner date with a friend.

"As it happens, I'll need you tomorrow afternoon and evening. I'm driving up to—"

"As it happens I already have plans for tomorrow evening," she interrupted defiantly.

"Then I suggest you cancel," he said impassively. "According to the terms of our agreement, you're to be at my disposal for the next two months. I need you this Saturday afternoon and evening."

"Yes, but—"

"May I remind you, that you're being well compensated for your time?"

It would take more than counting to ten to cool Mary Jo's rising temper. She wasn't fooled. Not for a second. Evan was doing this on purpose. He'd overheard her conversation with Gary.

"And if I refuse?" she asked, her outrage and defiance evident in every syllable.

Evan shrugged, as if it wasn't his concern one way or the other. "Then I'll have no choice but to fire you."

The temptation to throw the job back in his face was so strong she had to close her eyes to control it. "You're doing this intentionally, aren't you?" she said angrily. "I have a date with Gary Saturday night—you know I do—and you want to ruin it."

Evan leaned forward in his black leather chair; he seemed to weigh his words carefully. "Despite what you might think, I'm not a vindictive man. But, Ms. Summerhill, it doesn't really matter *what* you think."

She bit down so hard, her teeth hurt. "You're right, of course," she said quietly. "It doesn't matter what I think." She whirled around and stalked out of his office.

The force of her anger was too great to let her sit still. For ten minutes, she paced the floor, then sank into her chair. Resting her elbows on the desk, she buried her face in her hands, feeling very close to tears. It wasn't that this date with Gary was so important. It was that Evan would purposely ruin it for her.

"Mary Jo."

She dropped her hands to find Evan standing in front of her desk. They stared at each other for a long, still moment, then Mary Jo looked away. She wanted to wipe out the past and find the man she'd once loved. But she knew that what *he* wanted was to hurt her, to pay her back for the pain she'd caused him.

"What time do you need me?" she asked in an expressionless voice. She refused to meet his eyes.

"Three-thirty. I'll pick you up at your place."

"I'll be ready."

In the ensuing silence, Damian walked casually into the room. He stopped when he noticed them, glancing from Evan to Mary Jo and back again.

"I'm not interrupting anything, am I?"

"No." Evan recovered first and was quick to reassure his older brother. "What can I do for you, Damian?"

Damian gestured with the file he carried. "I read over the Jenkins case like you asked and jotted down some notes. I thought you might want to go over them with me."

The name leapt out at Mary Jo. "Did you say *Jenkins?*" she asked excitedly.

"Why, yes. Evan gave me the file the other day and asked me for my opinion."

"I did?" Evan sounded genuinely shocked.

Damian frowned. "Don't you remember?"

"No," Evan said. "Mary Jo and I've been searching for that file since yesterday."

"All you had to do, little brother," Damian chided, "was ask me."

The two men disappeared into Evan's office while Mary Jo finished tidying up for the day. Damian left as she was gathering her personal things.

"Evan would like to see you for a moment," he said on his way out the door.

Setting her purse aside, she walked into Evan's office. "You wanted to see me?" she asked coldly, standing just inside the doorway.

He stood at the window, staring down at the street far below, his hands clasped behind his back. His shoulders were slumped as if he'd grown weary. He turned to face her, his expression composed, even cool. "I apologize for the screw-up over the Jenkins file. I was entirely at fault. I did give it to Damian to read. I'm afraid it completely slipped my mind."

His apology came as a surprise. "It's no problem," she murmured.

"About tomorrow," he said next, lowering his voice slightly, "I won't be needing you, after all. Enjoy your evening with lover boy."

Chapter 5

"Is Evan coming?" Mary Jo's oldest brother, Jack, asked as he passed the bowl of mashed potatoes to his wife, Carrie.

"Yeah," Lonny piped in. "Where's Evan?"

"I heard you were working for him now," Carrie said, adding under her breath, "Lucky you."

Mary Jo's family was sitting around the big dining room table. Her parents, Jack, Carrie and their three children, Lonny and his wife, Sandra, and their two kids—they'd all focused their attention on Mary Jo.

"Mr. Dryden doesn't tell me his plans," she said, uncomfortable with their questions.

"You call him 'Mr. Dryden?'" her father asked, frowning.

"I'm his employee," Mary Jo replied.

"His father's a senator," Marianna reminded her husband, as if this was crucial information he didn't already know.

"I thought you said Evan's your friend." Her father wasn't going to give up, Mary Jo realized, until he had the answers he wanted.

"He *is* my friend," she returned evenly, "but while I'm an employee of the law firm it's important to maintain a certain decorum." That was a good response, she thought a bit smugly. One her father couldn't dispute.

"Did you invite him to Sunday dinner, dear?" her mother wanted to know.

"No."

"Then that explains it," Marianna said with a disappointed sigh. "Next week I'll see to it myself. We owe him a big debt of thanks."

Mary Jo resisted telling her mother that a man like Evan Dryden had more important things to do than plan his Sunday afternoons around her family's dinner. He'd come once as a gesture of friendliness, but they shouldn't expect him again. Her mother would learn that soon enough.

"How's the case with Adison Investments going, M.J.?" Jack asked, stabbing his fork into a marinated vegetable. "Have you heard anything?"

"Not yet," Mary Jo answered. "Evan had Mrs. Sterling type up a letter last week. I believe she mailed Mom and Dad a copy."

"She did," her father inserted.

"From my understanding, Evan, er, Mr. Dryden, gave Adison Investments two weeks to respond. If he hasn't heard from them by then, he'll prepare a lawsuit."

"Does he expect them to answer?" Rich burst out, his dark eyes flashing with anger.

"Now, son, don't get all riled up over this. Evan and Mary Jo are handling it now, and I have complete faith that justice will be served."

The family returned their attention to their food, and when the conversation moved on to other subjects, Mary Jo was grateful. Then, out of the blue, when she least expected it, her mother asked, "How was your dinner date with Gary?"

Taken aback, she stopped chewing, the fork poised in front of her mouth. Why was her life of such interest all of a sudden?

"Fine," she murmured when she'd swallowed. Once again the family's attention was on her. "Why is everyone looking at me?" she demanded.

Lonny chuckled. "It might be that we're wondering why you'd date someone like Gary Copeland when you could be going out with Evan Dryden."

"I doubt very much that Evan dates his employees," she said righteously. "It's bad business practice."

"I like Evan a whole lot," five-year-old Sarah piped up. "You do, too, don't you, Aunt Mary Jo?"

"Hmm...yes," she admitted, knowing she'd never get away with a lie, at least not with her own family. They knew her too well.

"Where's Gary now?" her oldest brother asked as though he'd only just noticed that he hadn't joined them for dinner. "It seems to me he's generally here. You'd think the guy had never tasted home cooking."

Now was as good a time as any to explain, Mary Jo decided. "Gary and I decided not to see each other anymore, Jack," she said, hoping to gloss over the details. "We're both doing different things now, and we've... drifted apart."

"Isn't that what you were telling me about you and Evan Dryden?" her father asked thoughtfully.

Mary Jo had forgotten that. Indeed, it was exactly what she'd said.

"Seems to me," her father added with a knowing parental look, "that you've been doing a lot of drifting apart from people lately."

Her mother, bless her heart, cast Mary Jo's father a frown. "If you ask me, it's the other way around." She nodded once as if to say the subject was now closed.

In some ways, Mary Jo was going to miss Gary. He was a friend and they'd parted on friendly terms. She hadn't intended to end their relationship, but over dinner Gary had suggested they think seriously about their future together.

To put it mildly, she'd been shocked. She'd felt comfortable in their rather loose relationship. Now Gary was looking for something more. She wasn't.

She knew he'd been disappointed, but he'd accepted her decision.

"I like Evan better, anyway," Sarah said solemnly. It seemed to be a recurring theme with her. She nodded once, the way her grandmother had just done, and the pink ribbons on her pigtails bobbed. "You'll bring him to dinner now, won't you?"

"I don't know, sweetheart."

"I do," her mother said, smiling confidently. "A mother knows these things, and it seems to me that Evan Dryden is the perfect man for our Mary Jo."

Evan was in the office when Mary Jo arrived early Monday morning. She quickly prepared a pot of coffee and brought him a mug as soon as it was ready.

He was on the phone but glanced up when she entered his office and smiled as he accepted the coffee. She returned to the outer office, amazed—and a little frightened—by how much one of his smiles could affect her.

Mary Jo's greatest fear was that the longer they worked together the more difficult it would be to maintain her guard. Without being aware of it, she might reveal her true feelings for Evan.

The phone rang and she automatically reached for it, enjoying her role as Evan's personal-assistant. She and Evan had had their share of differences, but seemed to have resolved them. In the office, anyway.

"Mary Jo." It was Jessica Dryden.

Mary Jo stiffened, fearing Evan might hear her taking a personal call. She didn't want anything to jeopardize their newly amicable relationship. The door to his office was open and he had a clear view of her from his desk.

"May I help you?" she asked in her best personal assistant voice.

Jessica hesitated at her cool, professional tone. "Hey, it's me. Jessica."

"I realize that."

Jessica laughed lightly. "I get it. Evan must be listening."

"That's correct." Mary Jo had trouble hiding a smile. One chance look in her direction, and he'd know this was no client she had on the line.

"Damian told me you're working for Evan now. What happened?" Jessica's voice lowered to a whisper as if she feared Evan would hear her, too.

Mary Jo carefully weighed her words. "I believe that case involved blackmail."

"Blackmail?" Jessica repeated, and laughed outright. "This I've got to hear. Is he being a real slave driver?"

"No. Not exactly."

"Can you escape one afternoon and meet me for lunch?"

"I might be able to arrange a lunch appointment. What day would you suggest?"

"How about tomorrow at noon? There's an Italian restaurant around the corner in the basement of the Wellman building. The food's great and the people who own it are like family."

"That sounds acceptable."

Evan appeared in the doorway between his office and hers. He studied her closely. Mary Jo swallowed uncomfortably at the obvious censure in his expression.

"Uh, perhaps I could confirm the details with you later."

Jessica laughed again. "Judging by your voice, Evan's standing right there—and he's figured out this isn't a business call."

"I believe you're right," she said stiffly.

Jessica seemed absolutely delighted. "I can't wait to hear all about this. I'll see you tomorrow, and Mary Jo…"

"Yes?" she urged, eager to get off the line.

"Have you thought any more about what I said? About working things out with Evan?"

"I… I'm thinking."

"Good. That's just great. I'll see you tomorrow, then."

Mary Jo replaced the receiver and darted a look in

Evan's direction. He averted his eyes and slammed the door. As if he was furious with her. Worse, as if she disgusted him.

Stunned, Mary Jo sat at her desk, fighting back a rush of outrage. He was being unfair. At the very least, he could've given her the opportunity to explain!

The morning, which had started out so well, with a smile and a sense of promise, had quickly disintegrated into outright hostility. Evan ignored her for the rest of the morning, not speaking except about office matters. And even then, his voice was cold and impatient. The brusque, hurried instructions, the lack of eye contact—everything seemed to suggest that he could barely tolerate the sight of her.

Without a word of farewell, he left at noon for his lunch engagement and came back promptly at one-thirty, a scant few minutes before his first afternoon appointment. Mary Jo had begun to wonder if he planned to return at all, worrying about how she'd explain his absence.

The temperature seemed to drop perceptibly the moment Evan walked in the door. She tensed, debating whether or not to confront him about his attitude.

Evan had changed, Mary Jo mused defeatedly. She couldn't remember him ever being this temperamental. She felt she was walking on the proverbial eggshells, afraid of saying or doing something that would irritate him even more.

Her afternoon was miserable. By five o'clock she knew she couldn't take much more of this silent treatment. She waited until the switchboard had been turned over to the answering service; that way there was no risk of being interrupted by a phone call.

The place was quiet—presumably staff in the nearby offices had gone home—when she approached his door. She knocked, then immediately walked inside. He was working and seemed unaware of her presence. She stood there until he glanced up.

"Could I speak to you for a moment?" she asked, standing in front of his desk. She heard the small quaver in her voice and groaned inwardly. She'd wanted to sound strong and confident.

"Is there a problem?" Evan asked, raising his eyebrows as if surprised—and not pleasantly—by her request.

"I'm afraid my position here isn't working out."

"Oh?" Up went the eyebrows again. "And why isn't it?"

It was much too difficult to explain how deeply his moods affected her. A mere smile and she was jubilant, a frown and she was cast into despair.

"It…it just isn't," was the best she could do.

"Am I too demanding?"

"No," she admitted reluctantly.

"Unreasonable?"

She lowered her gaze and shook her head.

"Then what is it?"

She gritted her teeth. "I want you to know that I've never made a personal phone call from this office during working hours."

"True, but you've received them."

"I assured you Gary wouldn't be phoning again."

"But he did," Evan inserted smoothly.

"He most certainly did not."

"Mary Jo," he said with exaggerated patience, as

though he were speaking to a child, "I heard you arranging a lunch date with him myself."

"That was Jessica. Damian mentioned running into me at the office and she called and suggested we meet for lunch."

"Jessica," Evan muttered. He grew strangely quiet.

"I think it might be best if I sought employment elsewhere," Mary Jo concluded. "Naturally I'll be happy to train my replacement." She turned abruptly and started to leave.

"Mary Jo." He sighed heavily. "Listen, you're right. I've behaved like a jerk all day. I apologize. Your personal life, your phone calls—it's none of my business. I promise you this won't happen again."

Mary Jo paused, unsure what to think. She certainly hadn't expected an apology.

"I want you to stay on," he added. "You're doing an excellent job, and I've been unfair. Will you?"

She should refuse, walk out while she had the excuse to do so. Leave without regrets. But she couldn't. She simply couldn't.

She offered him a shaky smile and nodded. "You know, you're not such a curmudgeon to work for, after all."

"I'm not?" He sounded downright cheerful. "This calls for a celebration, don't you think? Do you still enjoy sailing as much as you used to?"

She hadn't been on the water since the last time they'd taken out his sailboat. "I think so," she murmured, head spinning at his sudden reversal.

"Great. Run home and change clothes and meet me at the marina in an hour. We'll take out my boat and discover if you've still got your sea legs."

The prospect of spending time with Evan was too wonderful to turn down. For her sanity's sake, she should think twice before accepting the invitation, but she didn't. Whatever the price, she'd pay it—later.

"Remember when I taught you to sail?" Evan asked, his eyes smiling.

Mary Jo couldn't keep herself from smiling back. He'd been infinitely patient with her. She came from a long line of landlubbers and was convinced she'd never be a sailor.

"I still remember the first time we pulled out of the marina with me at the helm. I rammed another sailboat," she reminded him, and they both laughed.

"You'll meet me?" Evan asked, oddly intense after their moment of lightness.

Mary Jo doubted she could have refused him anything. "Just don't ask me to motor the boat out of the slip."

"You've got yourself a deal."

A little while earlier, she'd believed she couldn't last another hour with Evan. Now here she was, agreeing to meet him after work for a sailing lesson.

Rushing home, she threw off her clothes, not bothering to hang them up the way she usually did. She didn't stay longer than the few minutes it took to pull on a pair of jeans, a sweatshirt and her deck shoes. If she allowed any time for reflection, Mary Jo was afraid she'd talk herself out of going. She wanted these few hours with Evan so much it hurt.

Right now she refused to think about anything except the evening ahead of them. For this one night she wanted to put the painful past behind them—wipe out the memory of the last three lonely years.

She could see Evan waiting for her when she arrived at the marina. The wind had turned brisk, perfect for sailing, and the scent of salt and sea was carried on the breeze. Grabbing her purse, she trotted across the parking lot. Evan reached for her hand as if doing so was an everyday occurrence. Unthinkingly, Mary Jo gave it to him.

Both seemed to recognize in the same instant what they'd done. Evan turned to her, his eyes questioning; he seemed to expect Mary Jo to remove her hand from his. She met his gaze evenly and offered him a bright smile.

"I brought us something to eat," he said. "I don't know about you, but I'm starved."

Mary Jo was about to make some comment about his not eating an adequate lunch, when she recalled that he'd been out with Catherine Moore. Mary Jo wondered if the other woman was as elegant as her name suggested.

Evan leapt aboard, then helped her onto the small deck. He went below to retrieve the jib and the mainsail, and when he emerged Mary Jo asked, "Do you want me to rig the jib sail?"

He seemed surprised and pleased by the offer.

"That was the first thing you taught me, remember? I distinctly recall this long lecture about the importance of the captain and the responsibilities of the crew. Naturally, *you* were the distinguished captain and I was the lowly crew."

Evan laughed and the sound floated out to sea on the tail end of a breeze. "You remember all that, do you?"

"Like it was yesterday."

"Then have a go," he said, motioning toward the mast. But he didn't actually leave all the work to her.

They both moved forward and attached the stay for the jib to the mast, working together as if they'd been partners for years. When they were finished, Evan motored the sleek sailboat out of its slip and toward the open waters of Boston Harbor.

For all her earlier claims about not being a natural sailor, Mary Jo was still astonished by how much she'd enjoyed her times on the water. Her fondest memories of Evan had revolved around the hours spent aboard his boat. There was something wildly romantic about sailing together, gliding across the open water with the wind in their faces. She would always treasure those times with Evan.

Once they were safely out of the marina, they raised the mainsail and sliced through the emerald-green waters toward Massachusetts Bay.

"So you've been talking to Jessica?" he asked with a casualness that didn't deceive her.

"Mostly I've been working for you," she countered. "That doesn't leave me much time for socializing."

The wind whipped Evan's hair about his face, and he squinted into the sun. From the way he pinched his lips together, she guessed he was thinking about her date with Gary that weekend. She considered telling him it was over between her and Gary, but before she'd figured out how to bring up the subject, Evan spoke again.

"There's a bucket of fried chicken below," he said with a knowing smile, "if you're hungry, that is."

"Fried chicken," she repeated. She had no idea why sailing made her ravenous. And Evan was well aware of her weakness for southern-fried chicken. "Made with a secret recipe of nine special herbs and spices? Plus coleslaw and potato salad?"

Evan wiggled his eyebrows and smiled wickedly. "I seem to remember you had a fondness for a certain brand of chicken. There's a bottle of Chardonnay to go with it."

Mary Jo didn't need a second invitation to hurry below. She loaded up their plates, collected the bottle and two wineglasses and carried everything carefully up from the galley.

Sitting beside Evan, her plate balanced on her knees, she ate her dinner, savoring every bite. She must have been more enthusiastic than she realized, because she noticed him studying her. With a chicken leg poised near her mouth, she looked back at him.

"What's wrong?"

He grinned. "Nothing. I appreciate a woman who enjoys her food, that's all."

"I'll have you know I skipped lunch." But she wasn't going to tell him it was because every time she thought about him with Catherine Moore, she lost her appetite.

"I hope your employer values your dedication."

"I hope he does, too."

When they'd eaten, Mary Jo carried their plates below and packed everything away.

She returned and sat next to Evan. They finished their wine, then he let her take a turn at the helm. Almost before she was aware of it, his arms were around her. She stood there, hardly breathing, then allowed herself to lean back against his chest. It was as if those three painful years had been obliterated and they were both so much in love they couldn't see anything beyond the stars in their eyes.

Those had been innocent days for Mary Jo, that summer when she'd actually believed that an electrician's daughter could fit into the world of a man as rich and influential as Evan Dryden.

If she closed her eyes, she could almost forget everything that had happened since....

The wind blew more strongly and dusk began to darken the water. Mary Jo realized with intense regret that it was time for them to head back to the marina. Evan seemed to feel the same unwillingness to return to land—and reality.

They were both quiet as they docked. Together, they removed and stowed the sails.

Once everything was locked up, Evan walked her to the dimly lighted parking area. Mary Jo stood by the driver's side of her small car, reluctant to leave.

"I had a wonderful time," she whispered. "Thank you."

"I had a good time, too. Perhaps *too* good."

Mary Jo knew what he was saying; she felt it herself. It would be so easy to forget the past and pick up where they'd left off. Without much encouragement, she could easily find herself in his arms.

When he'd held her those few minutes on the boat, she'd experienced a feeling of warmth and completeness. Of happiness.

Sadness settled over her now, the weight of it almost unbearable. "Thank you again." She turned away and with a trembling hand inserted the car key into the lock. She wished Evan would leave before she did something ridiculous, like break into tears.

"Would you come sailing with me again some time?" he asked, and Mary Jo could have sworn his voice was tentative, uncertain. Which was ridiculous. Evan was one of the most supremely confident men she'd ever known.

Mary Jo waited for an objection to present itself. Several did. But not a single one of them seemed worth worrying about. Not tonight...

"I'd enjoy that very much." It was odd to be carrying on a conversation with her back to him, but she didn't dare turn around for fear she'd throw herself in his arms.

"Soon," he suggested, his voice low.

"How soon?"

"Next Saturday afternoon."

She swallowed and nodded. "What time?"

"Noon. Meet me here, and we'll have lunch first."

"All right."

From the light sound of his footsteps, she knew he'd moved away. "Evan," she called, whirling around, her heart racing.

He turned toward her and waited for her to speak.

"Are you sure?" Mary Jo felt as if her heart hung in the balance.

His face was half-hidden by shadows, but she could see the smile that slowly grew. "I'm very sure."

Mary Jo's hands shook as she climbed into her car. It was happening all over again and she was *letting* it happen. She was trembling so badly she could hardly fasten her seat belt.

What did she hope to prove? She already *knew* that nothing she could do would make her the right woman for Evan. Eventually she'd have to face the painful truth—again—and walk away from him. Eventually she'd have to look him in the eye and tell him she couldn't be part of his life.

Mary Jo didn't sleep more than fifteen minutes at a

stretch that night. When the alarm went off, her eyes burned, her head throbbed and she felt as lifeless as the dish of last week's pasta still sitting in her fridge.

She got out of bed, showered and put on the first outfit she pulled out of her closet. Then she downed a cup of coffee and two aspirin.

Evan was already at the office when she arrived. "Good morning," he said cheerfully as she walked in the door.

"Morning."

"Beautiful day, isn't it?"

Mary Jo hadn't noticed. She sat down at her desk and stared at the blank computer screen.

Evan brought her a cup of coffee and she blinked up at him. "I thought I was the one who was supposed to make coffee."

"I got here a few minutes early," he explained. "Drink up. You look like you could use it."

Despite her misery, she found the strength to grin. "I could."

"What's the matter? Bad night?"

She cupped the steaming mug with both hands. "Something like that." She couldn't very well confess *he* was the reason she hadn't slept. "Give me a few minutes and I'll be fine." A few minutes to dredge up the courage to tell him she had other plans for Saturday and couldn't meet him, after all. A few minutes to control the searing disappointment. A few minutes to remind herself she could survive without him. The past three years had proved that.

"Let me know if there's anything I can get you," he said.

She was about to suggest an appointment with a psychiatrist, then changed her mind. Evan would think she was joking; Mary Jo wasn't so sure it *was* a joke. What sensible woman would put herself through this kind of torture?

"I've already sorted through the mail," Evan announced. "There's something here from Adison Investments."

That bit of information perked Mary Jo up. "What did they say?"

"I haven't read it yet, but as soon as I do, I'll tell you. I'm hoping my letter persuaded Adison to agree to a refund."

"That's what you hope, not what you expect."

Evan's dark eyes were serious. "Yes."

He walked into his office but was back out almost immediately. Shaking his head, he handed Mary Jo the brief letter. She read the two curt paragraphs and felt a sense of discouragement. She had to hand it to Bill Adison. He came across as confident. Believable. He had to be, otherwise her father would never have trusted him. Adison reiterated that he had a signed contract and that the initial investment wouldn't be returned until the terms of their agreement had been fully met. Never mind that he hadn't upheld *his* side of the contract.

"Do you want to make an appointment with my parents?" she asked, knowing Evan would want to discuss the contents of the letter with her mother and father.

Evan took a moment to consider the question. "No. I think it'd be better for me to stop by their house myself and explain it to them. Less formal that way."

"Fine," she said, praying he wouldn't suggest Sunday. If he arrived on Sunday afternoon, one or more of her family members would be sure to tell him she'd broken up with Gary. No doubt her niece Sarah would blurt out that Evan could marry her now.

"I should probably talk to them today or tomorrow."

Mary Jo nodded, trying to conceal her profound relief.

"Why don't we plan on going there this evening after work?"

The "we" part didn't escape her.

"I'll call my folks and tell them," she said, figuring she'd set a time with them and then—later—make some plausible excuse for not joining Evan. Like a previous date. Or an emergency appointment with a manicurist. She'd break one of her nails and...

She was being ridiculous. She *should* be there. She *would* be there. She owed it to her parents. And it was business, after all, not a social excursion with Evan. Or a date. There was nothing to fear.

Mary Jo had just arrived at this conclusion when Evan called her into his office.

"Feeling better?" he asked, closing the door behind her.

"A little." She managed a tremulous smile.

He stared at her for an uncomfortable moment. She would've walked around him and seated herself, but he blocked the way.

"I know what might help," he said after a moment.

Thinking he was going to suggest aspirin, Mary Jo opened her mouth to tell him she'd already taken some. Before she could speak, he removed the pen and pad from her unresisting fingers and set them aside.

"What are you doing?" she asked, frowning in confusion.

He grinned almost boyishly. "I am, as they say in the movies, about to kiss you senseless."

Chapter 6

"You're going to kiss me?" Mary Jo's heart lurched as Evan drew her into his arms. His breath was warm against her face, and a wonderful, wicked feeling spread through her. She sighed and closed her eyes.

Evan eased his mouth over hers and it felt so natural, so familiar. So right.

He kissed her again, and tears gathered in Mary Jo's eyes. He wrapped her tightly in his arms and took several long breaths.

"I wanted to do this last night," he whispered.

She'd wanted him to kiss her then, too, yet—paradoxically—she'd been grateful he hadn't. It occurred to her now that delaying this moment could have been a mistake. They'd both thought about it, wondered how it would be, anticipated being in each other's arms again. And after all that intense speculation, their kiss might have disappointed them both.

It hadn't.

Nevertheless, Mary Jo was relieved when the phone rang. Evan cursed under his breath. "We need to talk about this," he muttered, still holding her.

The phone pealed a second time.

"We'll talk later," she promised quickly.

Evan released her, and she leapt for the telephone on his desk. Thankfully, the call was for him. Thankfully, it wasn't Jessica. Or her mother. Or Gary.

Mary Jo left his office and sank slowly into her chair, trying to make sense of what had happened.

All too soon Evan was back. He sat on the edge of her desk. "All right," he said, his eyes as bright and happy as a schoolboy's on the first day of summer vacation. "We're going to have this out once and for all."

"Have this out?"

"I don't know what happened between you and the man you fell in love with three years ago. But apparently it didn't last, which is fine with me."

"Evan, please!" She glanced desperately around. "Not here. Not now." She was shaking inside. Her stomach knotted and her chest hurt with the effort of holding back her emotions. Eventually she'd have to tell Evan there'd never been another man, but she wasn't looking forward to admitting that lie. Or her reasons for telling it.

"You're right." He sounded reluctant, as if he wanted to settle everything between them then and there. "This isn't the place. We need to be able to talk freely." He looked at his watch and his mouth tightened. "I've got to be in court this morning."

"Yes, I know." She was pathetically grateful that he'd be out of the office for a few hours. She needed time to think. She'd already made one decision, though: she refused to lie to him again. She was older now, more mature, and she recognized that, painful though it was, Evan's mother had been right. Mary Jo could do nothing to enhance Evan's career.

But she wasn't going to run away and hide, which was what she'd done three years ago. Nor could she bear the thought of pitting Evan against his parents. The Drydens were a close family, like her own. No, she'd have to find some other approach, some other way of convincing him this relationship couldn't possibly work. Just *how* she was going to do this, she had no idea.

Forcing her attention back to her morning tasks, she reached for the mail and quickly became absorbed in her work. In fact, she was five minutes late meeting Jessica.

Her friend was waiting in the Italian restaurant, sitting at a table in the back. A grandmotherly woman was holding Andy, using a bread stick to entertain the toddler.

"Lucia, this is my friend Mary Jo," Jessica said when she approached the table.

"Hello," Mary Jo murmured, pulling out a chair.

"Leave lunch to me," Lucia insisted, giving Andy back to his mother, who placed him in the high chair beside her. Jessica then handed her son another bread stick, which delighted him. Apparently Andy didn't understand he was supposed to *eat* the bread. He seemed to think it was a toy to wave gleefully overhead, and Mary Jo found herself cheered by his antics.

The older woman returned with large bowls of minestrone, plus a basket of bread so fresh it was still warm. "You eat now," she instructed, waiting for them to sample the delectable-smelling soup. "Enjoy your food first. You can talk later."

"It would be impossible *not* to enjoy our food," Jessica told Lucia, who beamed with pride.

"Lucia's right, of course," Jessica said, "but we've got less than an hour and I'm dying to hear what's happening with you and Evan."

"Not much." Which was the truth. For now, anyway. Mary Jo described how Evan had coerced her into working for him. She'd expected expressions of sympathy from her friend. Instead, Jessica seemed downright pleased.

"Damian said there'd been some misunderstanding about a file. He said Evan had suspected you of being careless—or worse—and when Damian showed up with it, Evan felt wretched."

"That's all behind us now." The uncertainty of their future loomed before them, and that was what concerned her most. Mary Jo weighed the decision to confide in Jessica about their kiss that morning. If Jessica had been someone other than Evan's sister-in-law, she might've done so. But it would be unfair to involve his family in this.

Jessica dipped her spoon into the thick soup. "I explained earlier that Evan and I became fairly close while I was working for the firm. What I didn't mention was how often he talked about you. He really loved you, Mary Jo."

Uncomfortable, Mary Jo lowered her gaze.

"I'm not saying this to make you feel guilty, but so you'll know that Evan's feelings for you were genuine. You weren't just a passing fancy to him. In some ways, I don't believe he's ever gotten over you."

Mary Jo nearly choked on her soup. "I wish that was true. I've arranged no less than six lunch appointments for him. All the names came directly out of his little black book. The invitations were accompanied by a dozen red roses." Until that moment, Mary Jo hadn't realized how jealous she was, and how much she'd been suffering while he'd wined and dined his girlfriends.

"Don't get me wrong," Jessica said. "Evan's dated other women. But there's never been anyone serious."

Mary Jo energetically ripped off a piece of bread. "He's gone out of his way to prove the opposite."

"What were these women's names?"

Lucia returned to the table with a large platter heaped with marinated vegetables, sliced meats and a variety of cheeses. Andy stretched out his hand, wanting a piece of cheese, which Jessica gave him.

"One was Catherine Moore."

A smile hovered at the edges of Jessica's mouth. "Catherine Moore is around seventy and she's his great-aunt."

Shocked, Mary Jo jerked up her head. "His great-aunt? What about..." and she rolled off the other names she remembered.

"All relatives," Jessica said, shaking her head. "The poor boy was desperate to make you jealous."

Mary Jo had no intention of admitting how well his scheme had worked. "Either that, or he was being thoughtful," she suggested offhandedly—just to be fair to Evan. She wanted to be angry with him, but found she was more amused.

"Trust me," Jessica said, smiling broadly. "Evan was desperate. He's dated, true, but he seldom goes out with the same woman more than three or four times. His mother's beginning to wonder if he'll ever settle down."

At the mention of Lois Dryden, Mary Jo paid close attention to her soup. "It was my understanding that Evan was planning to go into politics."

"I believe he will someday," Jessica answered enthusiastically. "In my opinion, he should. Evan has a generous, caring heart. He genuinely wants to help people. More importantly, he's the kind of man who's capable of finding solutions and making a difference.

"He's a wonderful diplomat, and people like him. It doesn't matter what walk of life they're from, either. The best way I can describe it is that Evan's got charisma."

Mary Jo nodded. It was the truth.

"Although he went into corporate law," Jessica continued, "I don't think his heart's ever really been in it. You should've seen him when he represented Earl Kress. He was practically a different person. No, I don't think he's at all happy as a corporate attorney."

"Then why hasn't he decided to run for office?"

"I'm not sure," Jessica said. "I assumed, for a while, that he was waiting until he was a bit older, but I doubt that's the reason. I know his family encourages him, especially his mother. Lois has always believed Evan's destined for great things."

"I...got that impression from her, as well."

"Evan and Damian have had long talks about his running for office. Damian's encouraged him, too, but Evan says the time's not right."

Mary Jo's heart felt heavy. Everything Jessica said seconded Lois Dryden's concerns about the role Evan's wife would play in his future.

"You're looking thoughtful."

Mary Jo managed a small smile. "I never understood what it was about me that attracted Evan."

"I know exactly what it was," Jessica said without a pause. "He told me himself, and more than once. He said it was as though you knew him inside and out. Apparently you could see right through him. I suspect it has something to do with the fact that you have five older brothers."

"Probably."

"Evan's been able to charm his way around just about everyone. Not you. You laughed at him and told him to save his breath on more than one occasion. Am I right?"

Mary Jo nodded, remembering the first day they'd met on the beach. He'd tried to sweet-talk her into a dinner date, and she'd refused. She'd realized immediately that Evan Dryden didn't know how to take no for an answer. In the end they'd compromised. They'd built a small fire, roasted hot dogs and marshmallows and sat on the beach talking until well past midnight.

They saw each other regularly after that. Mary Jo knew he was wealthy by the expensive sports car he drove, the kind of money he flashed around. In the beginning she'd assumed it was simply because he was a high-priced attorney. Fool that she'd been, Mary Jo hadn't even recognized the name.

It wasn't until much later, after she was already head over heels in love with him, that she learned the truth. Evan was more than wealthy. He came from a family whose history stretched back to the *Mayflower*.

"You were different from the other women he'd known," Jessica was saying. "He could be himself with you. One time he told me he felt an almost spiritual connection with you. It's something he's never expected to find with anyone else."

"Evan told you all that?" Mary Jo asked breathlessly.

"Yes, and much more," Jessica said, leaning forward. "You see, Mary Jo, I know how much Evan loved you—and still loves you."

Mary Jo felt as if she was about to break into deep, racking sobs. She loved Evan, too. Perhaps there *was* hope for them. Jessica made her feel they might have a future. She seemed to have such faith that, whatever their problems, love and understanding could work them out.

Mary Jo returned to the office, her heart full of hope. She'd been wrong not to believe in their love, wrong not to give them a chance. Her insecurities had wasted precious years.

When Evan walked in, it was almost five o'clock. Mary Jo resisted the urge to fly into his arms, but immediately sensed something was wrong. He was frowning and every line of his body was tense.

"What happened?" she asked, following him into his office.

"I lost," he said pacing. "You know something? I'm a damn poor loser."

She *had* noticed, but he hadn't experienced loss often enough to grow accustomed to accepting it. "Listen, it happens to the best of us," she assured him.

"But it shouldn't have in this case. We were in the right."

"You win some and you lose some. That's the nature of the legal game."

He glared at her and she laughed outright. He reminded her of one of her brothers after a highly contested high-school basketball game. Mark, the youngest, had always loved sports and was fiercely competitive. He'd had to be in order to compete against his four brothers. In his desire to win, Evan was similar to Mark.

"I can always count on you to soothe my battered ego, can't I?" he asked, his tone more than a little sarcastic.

"No. You can always count on me to tell you the truth." *Almost always,* she amended sadly, recalling her one lie.

"A kiss would make me feel better."

"Certainly not," she said briskly, but it was difficult to refuse him. "Not here, anyway."

"You're right," he admitted grudgingly, "but at least let me hold you." She wasn't given the opportunity to say no, not that she would've found the strength to do so.

He brought her into his arms and held her firmly against him, breathing deeply as if to absorb everything about her. "I can't believe I'm holding you like this," he whispered.

"Neither will anyone else who walks into this room." But she didn't care who saw them. She burrowed deeper into his embrace and rested her head against the solid strength of his chest.

He eased himself away from her and framed her face with his hands. His eyes were intense as he gazed down on her. "I don't care about the past, Mary Jo. It's water under the bridge. None of it matters. The only thing that matters is *right now.* Can we put everything else behind us and move forward?"

She bit her lower lip, her heart full of a new confidence. Nothing in this world would ever stand between them again. She would've said the words, but couldn't speak, so she nodded her head in abrupt little movements.

She found herself pulled back into his arms, the embrace so hard it threatened to cut off her breath, but she didn't care. Breathing hardly seemed necessary when Evan was holding her like this. She wanted to laugh and to weep at once, to throw back her head and shout with a free-flowing joy that sprang from her soul.

"We'll go to your parents' place," Evan said, "talk to them about Adison's response, and then I'll take you to dinner and from there—"

"Stop," Mary Jo said, breaking free of his hold and raising her right hand. "You'll take me to dinner? Do you honestly think we're going to escape my mother without being fed?"

Evan laughed and pulled her into his arms again. "I suppose not."

Evan was, of course, welcomed enthusiastically by both her parents. He and Norman Summerhill discussed the Adison situation, while Mary Jo helped her mother prepare a simple meal of fried chicken and a pasta-and-vegetable salad. Over dinner, the mood was comfortable and lighthearted.

As it turned out, though, the evening included a lot more than just conversation and dinner. Her brothers all played on a softball team. They had a game scheduled that evening, and one of the other players had injured his ankle in a fall at work. The instant Evan heard the news, he volunteered to substitute.

"Evan," Mary Jo pleaded. "This isn't like handball, you know. These guys take their game seriously."

"You think handball isn't serious?" Evan kissed her

on the nose and left her at her parents' while he hurried home to change clothes.

Her mother watched from the kitchen, looking exceptionally pleased. She wiped her hands on her apron skirt. "I think you did a wise thing breaking up with Gary when you did."

"I'm so happy, Mom," Mary Jo whispered, grabbing a dish towel and some plates to dry.

"You love him."

Mary Jo noticed it wasn't a question.

"I never stopped loving him."

Her mother placed one arm around Mary Jo's shoulders. "I knew that the minute I saw the two of you together again." She paused, apparently considering her next words. "I've always known you loved Evan. Can you tell me what happened before—why you broke it off?"

"I didn't believe I was the right woman for him."

"Nonsense! Anyone looking at the two of you would realize you're perfect for each other. Who would say such a thing to you?"

Mary Jo was intelligent enough not to mention Lois Dryden. "He's very wealthy, Mom."

"You can look past that."

Mary Jo's laugh was spontaneous. Her sweetheart of a mother saw Evan's money as a detriment—and in some ways, it was.

"His father's a senator."

"You think his money bought him that position?" Marianna scoffed. "If you do, you're wrong. He was elected to that office because he's a decent man with an honest desire to help his constituents."

Her mother could make the impossible sound plausible. Mary Jo wished she could be more like her.

"Now, freshen up," Marianna said, untying her apron, "or we'll be late for your brothers' game."

Evan was already in the outfield catching fly balls when Mary Jo and her parents arrived. He looked as if he'd been a member of the team for years.

The game was an exciting one, with the outcome unpredictable until the very end of the ninth inning. Mary Jo, sitting in the bleachers with her family—her parents, a couple of sisters-in-law, some nieces and nephews—screamed herself hoarse. Their team lost by one run, but they all took the defeat in stride—including Evan, who'd played as hard as any of them.

Afterward, the team went out for pizza and cold beer. Mary Jo joined Evan and the others, while her parents returned to the house, tired from the excitement.

Evan threw his arm over her shoulders and she wrapped her own arm around his waist.

"You two an item now or something?" her brother Rob asked as they gathered around a long table at the pizza parlor.

"Yeah," Rich chimed in. "You look awful chummy all of a sudden. What's going on?"

"Yeah, what about good ol' Gary?" Mark wanted to know.

Evan studied her, eyebrows raised. "What *about* Gary?" he echoed.

"You don't need to worry about him anymore," Jack explained, carrying a pitcher of ice-cold beer to the table. "M.J. broke up with him over the weekend."

"You did?" It was Evan who asked the question.

"Yup." Once more her brother was doing the talking

for her. "Said they were drifting in opposite directions or some such garbage. No one believed her. We know the *real* reason she showed Gary the door."

"Will you guys *please stop?*" Mary Jo insisted, her ears growing redder by the minute. "I can speak for myself, thank you very much."

Jack poured them each a beer and slid the glasses down the table. "You know M.J. means business when she says *please stop*. Uh-oh—look at her ears. Let's not embarrass her anymore, guys, or there'll be hell to pay."

Evan barked with laughter, and her brothers smiled approvingly. He fit in with her family as if he'd been born into it. This was his gift, Mary Jo realized. He was completely at ease with her brothers—as he would be with a group of government officials or lawyers or "society" people. With *anyone*. He could drink beer and enjoy it as much as expensive champagne. It didn't matter to him if he ate pizza or lobster.

But Mary Jo was definitely more comfortable with the pizza-and-beer way of life. Hours earlier she'd been utterly confident. Now, for the first time that night, her newfound resolve was shaken.

Evan seemed aware of her mood, although he didn't say anything until later, when they were alone, driving to her place. Reluctant to see the evening end, Mary Jo gazed at the oncoming lights of the cars zooming past. She couldn't suppress a sigh.

Evan glanced over at her. "Your family's wonderful," he said conversationally. "I envy you coming from such a large, close-knit group."

"You're close to your brother, too."

"True. More so now that we're older." He reached

for her hand and squeezed it gently. "Something's troubling you."

She stared out the side window. "You're comfortable in my world, Evan, but I'm not comfortable in yours."

"World? What are you talking about? In case you haven't noticed, we're both right here in the same world—the planet earth."

She smiled, knowing he was making light of her concerns. "If we'd been with your family, do you think we'd be having pizza and beer? More likely it'd be expensive French wine, baguettes and Brie."

"So? You don't like baguettes and Brie?"

"Yes, but…" She paused, since it wouldn't do any good to argue. He didn't understand her concerns, because he didn't share them. "We're different, Evan."

"Thank goodness. I'd hate to think I was attracted to a clone of myself."

"I'm an electrician's daughter."

"A lovely one, too, I might add."

"Evan," she groaned. "Be serious."

"I *am* serious. It'd scare the socks off you if you knew *how* serious."

He exited the freeway and headed down the street toward her duplex. As he parked, he said, "Invite me in for coffee."

"Are you really interested in coffee?"

"No."

"That's what I thought," she said, smiling to herself.

"I'm going to kiss you, Mary Jo, and frankly, I'm a little too old to be doing it in a car. Now invite me inside—or suffer the consequences."

Mary Jo didn't need a second invitation. Evan helped her out of the car and took her arm as they walked to her door. She unlocked it but didn't turn on the lights as they moved into her living room. The instant the door was closed, Evan maneuvered her in his arms so that her back was pressed against it.

Her lips trembled as his mouth sought hers. It was a gentle caress more than it was a kiss, and she moaned, wanting, *needing* more of him.

Evan's hand curved around the side of her neck, his fingers stroking her hair. His mouth hovered a fraction of an inch from hers, as if he half expected her to protest. Instead, she raised her head to meet his lips again.

Groaning, Evan kissed her with a passion that left her breathless and weak-kneed.

Mary Jo wound her arms around his neck and stood on the tips of her toes. They exchanged a series of long kisses, then Evan laid his head on her shoulder and shuddered.

Mary Jo was convinced that if he hadn't been holding her upright, she would've slithered to the floor.

"We'd better stop while I have the strength," Evan whispered, almost as if he was speaking to himself. His breathing was ragged and uneven. He moved away from her, and in the dark stillness of her living room, illumined only by the glow of a streetlight, she watched him rake his hands through his thick, dark hair.

"I'll make us that coffee," she said in a purposeful voice. They both squinted when she flipped on the light.

"I really don't need any coffee," he told her.

"I know. I don't, either. It's an excuse for you to stay."

Evan followed her into the kitchen and pulled out a chair. He sat down and reached for her, wrapping his arms around her waist, drawing her down onto his lap. "We have a lot of time to make up for."

Unsure how to respond, Mary Jo rested her hands on his shoulders. It was so easy to get caught up in the intensity of their attraction and renewed love. But despite her earlier optimism, she couldn't allow herself to ignore the truth. Except that she didn't know how to resolve this, or even if she could.

Evan left soon afterward, with a good-night kiss and the reminder that they'd be together again in the morning.

Mary Jo sat in her rocking chair in the dark for a long time, trying to sort out her tangled thoughts. Loving him the way she did, she was so tempted to let her heart go where it wanted to. So tempted to throw caution to the winds, to ignore all the difficult questions.

Evan seemed confident that their love was possible. Jessica did, too. Mary Jo desperately wanted to believe them. She wanted to overlook every objection. She wanted what she would probably never receive—his family's approval. Not Damian and Jessica's; she had that. His parents'.

Sometimes loving someone wasn't enough. Mary Jo had heard that often enough and she recognized the truth of it.

Too tired to think clearly, she stood, setting the rocker in motion, and stumbled into her bedroom.

Saturday, Mary Jo met Evan at the yacht club at noon. They planned to sail after a leisurely lunch. She'd been looking forward to this from the moment Evan had invited her on Wednesday.

The receptionist ushered her to a table outside on the patio, where Evan was waiting for her. There was a festive, summery atmosphere—tables with their striped red-yellow-and-blue umbrellas, the cheerful voices of other diners, the breathtaking view of the marina. Sailboats with multicolored spinnakers could be seen against a backdrop of bright blue sky and sparkling green sea.

Evan stood as she approached and pulled out her chair. "I don't think you've ever looked more beautiful."

It was a line he'd used a thousand times before, Mary Jo was sure of that, although he sounded sincere. "You say that to all your dates," she chided lightly, picking up the menu.

"But it's true," he returned with an injured air.

Mary Jo laughed and spread the linen napkin across her lap. "Your problem is that you're such a good liar. You'd be perfect in politics since you lie so convincingly." She'd been teasing, then suddenly realized how rude she'd been. His father was a politician!

"Oh, Evan, I'm sorry. That was a terrible thing to say." Mary Jo felt dreadful, reminded anew that she was the type of person who could offend someone without even being aware of it. She simply wasn't circumspect enough.

He chuckled and brushed off her apology. "Dad would get a laugh out of what you said."

"Promise me you won't ever tell him."

"That depends," he said, paying exaggerated attention to his menu.

"On what?" she demanded.

He wiggled his eyebrows. "On what you intend to offer me for my silence."

She smiled and repeated a line her brothers had often used on her. "I'll let you live."

Evan threw back his head and laughed boisterously.

"Evan?" The woman's voice came from behind Mary Jo. "What a pleasant surprise to find you here."

"Mother," Evan said, standing to greet Lois Dryden. He kissed her on the cheek. "You remember Mary Jo Summerhill, don't you?"

Chapter 7

"Of course I remember Mary Jo," Lois Dryden said cheerfully. "How nice to see you again."

Mary Jo blinked, wondering if this was the same woman she'd had that painful heart-to-heart chat with all those years ago. The woman who'd suggested that if Mary Jo really loved Evan she would call off their engagement. Not in those words exactly; Mrs. Dryden had been far too subtle for that. Nevertheless, the message had been there, loud and clear.

"I didn't know you two were seeing each other again," Lois continued. "This is a…surprise."

Mary Jo noticed she didn't say it was *pleasant* surprise. Naturally, Evan's mother was much too polite to cause even a hint of a scene. Not at the yacht club, at any rate. Now, if she'd been at Whispering Willows, the Dryden estate, she might swoon or have a fit of vapors, or whatever it was wealthy women did to convey their shock and displeasure. Mary Jo knew she was being cynical, but couldn't help herself.

Evan reached for her hand and clasped it in his own. His eyes smiled into hers. "Mary Jo's working for me this summer."

"I… I hadn't heard that."

"Would you care to join us?" Evan asked, but his eyes didn't waver from Mary Jo's. Although he'd issued the invitation, it was obvious that he expected his mother to refuse. That he *wanted* her to refuse.

"Another time, perhaps. I'm lunching with Jessica's mother. We're planning a first-birthday party for Andrew, and, well, you know how the two of us feel about our only grandchild."

Evan chuckled. "I sure do. It seems to me that either Damian or I should see about adding another branch to the family tree."

Mary Jo felt the heat of embarrassment redden her ears. Evan couldn't have been more blatant. He'd all but announced he intended to marry her. She waited for his mother to comment.

"That would be lovely, Evan," Lois said, but if Evan didn't catch the tinge of disapproval in his mother's voice, Mary Jo did. Nothing had changed.

The lines were drawn.

Lois made her excuses and hurried back into the yacht club. Mary Jo's good mood plummeted. She made a pretense of enjoying her lunch and decided to put the small confrontation behind her. Her heart was set on enjoying this day with Evan. She loved sailing as much as he did, and as soon as they were out in the bay, she could forget how strongly his mother disapproved of her. *Almost* forget.

They worked together to get the sailboat ready. Once the sails were raised, she sat next to Evan. The wind tossed her hair about her face, and she smiled into the warm sunshine. They tacked left and then right, zig-zagging their way through the water.

"Are you thirsty?" Evan asked after they'd been out for an hour or so.

"A cold soda sounds good."

"Great. While you're in the galley, would you get one for me?"

Laughing, she jabbed him in the ribs, but she went below and brought back two sodas. She handed him his, then reclaimed her spot beside him.

Evan slipped his arm around her shoulders and soon she was nestled against him, guiding the sailboat, with Evan guiding her. When she veered off course and the sails slackened, he placed his hand over hers and gently steered them back on course.

Mary Jo had found it easy to talk to Evan from the moment they'd met. He was easygoing and congenial, open-minded and witty. But this afternoon he seemed unusually quiet. She wondered if he was brooding about the unexpected encounter with his mother.

"It's peaceful, isn't it?" Mary Jo said after several long minutes of silence.

"I think some of the most profound moments of my life have taken place on this boat. I've always come here to find peace, and I have, though it's sometimes been hard won."

"I'm grateful you introduced me to sailing."

"I took the boat out several times after...three years

ago." His hold on her tightened. "I've missed you, Mary Jo," he whispered, and rubbed the side of his jaw against her temple. "My world felt so empty without you."

"Mine did, too," she admitted softly, remembering the bleak, empty months after their breakup.

"Earl Kress stopped by the office a while back, and I learned that you weren't married. Afterward, I couldn't get you out of my mind. I wondered what had happened between you and this teacher you loved. I wanted to contact you and find out. I must've come up with a hundred schemes to worm my way back into your life."

"W-why didn't you?" She felt comfortable and secure in his arms, unafraid of the problems that had driven them apart. She could deal with the past; it was the future that terrified her.

"Pride mostly," Evan said quietly. "A part of me was hoping you'd come back to me."

In a way she had, on her knees, needing him. Funny, she couldn't have approached him for herself, even though she was madly in love with him, but she'd done it for her parents.

"No wonder you had that gleeful look in your eye when I walked into your office," she said, hiding a smile. "You'd been waiting for that very thing."

"I wanted to punish you," he told her, and she heard the regret in his voice. "I wanted to make you suffer like I had. That was the reason I insisted you work for me this summer. I'd already hired Mrs. Sterling's replacement, but when I had the opportunity to force you into accepting the position, I couldn't resist."

This wasn't news to Mary Jo. She'd known the moment he'd offered her the job what his intention was. He'd wanted to make her as miserable as she'd made him. And his plan had worked those first few days. She'd gone home frustrated, mentally beaten and physically exhausted.

"A woman of lesser fortitude would have quit the first day, when you had me ordering roses and booking lunch dates."

"Those weren't any love interests," he confessed. "I'm related to each one."

"I know." She tilted back her head and kissed the underside of his jaw.

"How?" he asked, his surprise evident.

"Jessica told me."

"Well, I certainly hope you were jealous. I went through a great deal of unnecessary trouble if you weren't."

"I was green with it." She could have downplayed her reaction, but didn't. "Every time you left the office for another one of your dates, I worked myself into a frenzy. Please, Evan, don't ever do that to me again."

"I won't," he promised, and she could feel his smile against her hair. "But you had your revenge several times over, throwing Gary in my face. I disliked the man as soon as I met him. There I was, hoping to catch you off guard by showing up at your parents' for dinner, and my plan immediately backfires when you arrive with your boyfriend in tow."

"You really didn't like Gary?"

"He's probably a nice guy, but not when he's dating *my* woman."

"But you acted like Gary was an old pal! I was mortified. My entire family thought it was hilarious. You had more to say to Gary than to me."

"I couldn't let you know how jealous I was, could I?"

Mary Jo snuggled more securely in his arms. A seagull's cry came from overhead, and she looked up into the brilliant blue sky, reveling in the sunshine and the breeze and in the rediscovery of their love.

"Can we ever go back?" Evan asked. "Is it possible to pretend those years didn't happen and take up where we left off?"

"I... I don't know," Mary Jo said. Yet she couldn't keep her heart from hoping. She closed her eyes and felt the wind on her face. Those years had changed her. She was more confident now, more sure of herself, emotionally stronger. This time she'd fight harder to hold on to her happiness.

One thing was certain. If she walked out of Evan's life again, it wouldn't be in silence or in secrecy.

She remembered the pain of adjusting to her life without Evan. Pride had carried her for several months. She might not come from old Boston wealth, but she had nothing to be ashamed of. She was proud of her family and refused to apologize for the fact that they were working class.

But pride had only taken her so far, and when it had worn down, all she had left was the emptiness of her dreams and a life that felt hollow.

Like Evan, she'd forced herself to go on, dragging from one day to the next, but she hadn't been fully alive—until a few days ago, when he'd taken her in his arms and kissed her. Her love for him, her regret at what she'd lost, had never gone away.

"I want to give us another chance," Evan murmured. The teasing had gone out of his voice. "Do you?"

"Yes. Oh, yes," Mary Jo said ardently.

He kissed her then, with a passion and a fervor she'd

never experienced before. She returned his kiss in full measure. They clung tightly to each other until the sails flapped in the breeze and Evan had to steer them back on course.

"I love you, Mary Jo," Evan said. "Heaven knows, I tried not to. I became…rather irresponsible after we split up, you know. If it hadn't been for Damian, I don't know what I would've done. He was endlessly patient with me, even when I wouldn't tell him what was wrong. My brother isn't stupid. He knew it had something to do with you. I just couldn't talk about it. The only relief I found was here, on the water."

Turning, Mary Jo threw her arms around his middle and pressed her face against his chest, wanting to absorb his pain.

"When you told me you'd fallen in love with another man, I had no recourse but to accept that it was over. I realized that the moment you told me how difficult it was for you. Loving him while you were still engaged to me must have been hell."

A sob was trapped in her throat. This was the time to admit there'd never been another man, that it was all a lie….

"Can you tell me about him?"

"No." She jerked her head from side to side. She couldn't do it, just couldn't do it. She was continuing the lie—because telling him would mean revealing his mother's part in all of this. She wouldn't do that.

His free arm cradled her shoulders, his grip tight.

"I'd more or less decided that if I couldn't marry you," Evan said after a lengthy pause, "I wasn't getting married at all. Can't you just see me twenty or thirty years down the road, sitting by a roaring fire with my ever-faithful dog sleeping at my side?"

The mental picture was so foreign to the devil-may-care image she'd had of him these past few years that she laughed out loud. "Nope, I can't quite picture that."

"What about fatherhood? Can you picture me as a father?"

"Easily." After watching him with Andrew and her own nieces and nephews, she realized Evan was a natural with children.

"Then it's settled," he said, sounding greatly relieved.

"What's settled?" she asked, cocking her head to one side to look up at him. His attention was focused straight ahead as he steered the sailboat.

"We're getting married. Prepare yourself, Mary Jo, because we're making up for lost time."

"Evan—"

"If you recall, when I gave you the engagement ring, we planned our family. Remember? Right down to the timing of your first pregnancy."

Mary Jo could hardly manage a nod. Those were memories she'd rarely allowed herself to examine.

"We both thought it was important to wait a couple of years before we started our family. You were supposed to have our first baby this year. Hey, we're already behind schedule! It seems to me we'd better take an extended honeymoon."

Mary Jo laughed, the wind swallowing the sound the moment it escaped her lips.

"Two, three months at the very least," Evan went on, undaunted. "I suggest a South Pacific island, off the tourist track. We'll rent a bungalow on the beach and spend our days walking along the shore and our nights making love."

He was going much too fast for her. "Do you mind retracing a few steps?" she asked. "I got lost somewhere between you sitting by a roaring fire with your faithful dog and us running into Gauguin's descendants on some South Pacific beach."

"First things first," Evan countered. "We agreed on four children, didn't we?"

"Evan!" She couldn't keep from laughing, her happiness spilling over.

"These details are important, and I'd like them decided before we get involved in another subject. I wanted six kids, remember? I love big families. But you only wanted two. If you'll think back, it took some fast talking to get you to agree to a compromise of four. You did agree, remember?"

"What I remember was being railroaded into a crazy conversation while you went on about building us this huge mansion."

"Ah, yes, the house. I'd nearly forgotten. I wanted one large enough for all the kids. With a couple of guest rooms. That, my beautiful Mary Jo, isn't a mansion."

"It is when you're talking seven bedrooms and six thousand square feet."

"But," Evan said, his eyes twinkling, "you were going to have live-in help with the children, especially while they're younger, and I wanted to be sure we had a place to escape and relax at the end of the day."

"I found an indoor swimming pool, hot tub and exercise room a bit extravagant." Mary Jo had thought he was teasing when he'd showed her the house plans he'd had drawn up, but it had soon become apparent that he was completely serious. He was serious now, too.

"I still want to build that home for us," he said, his dark eyes searching hers. "I love you. I've loved you for three agonizing years. I want us to be married, and soon. If it were up to me, we'd already have the license."

"You're crazy." But it was a wonderful kind of crazy.

"You love me."

Tears filled her eyes as she nodded. "I do. I love you so much, Evan." She slid her arms around his neck. "What am I going to do with you?"

"Marry me and put me out of my misery."

He made it seem so easy and she was caught up in the tide of his enthusiasm, but she couldn't agree. Not yet. Not until she was convinced she was doing the right thing for both of them.

"Listen," Evan said, as though struck by a whole new thought. "I have a judge in the family who can marry us as soon as I make the necessary arrangements. We can have a private ceremony in, say, three days' time."

"My parents would be devastated, Evan. I know for a fact that my father would never forgive us if we cheated him out of the pleasure of escorting me down the aisle."

Evan grimaced. "You're right. My mother's the same. She actually enjoys planning social events. It's much worse now that my dad's a senator. She's organized to a fault." He grinned suddenly, as if he found something amusing in this. "My father made a wise choice when he married Mom. She's the perfect politician's wife."

The words cut through Mary Jo like an icy wind. They reminded her that she'd be a liability to Evan should he ever decide to run for political office.

Often the candidates' spouses were put under as

much scrutiny as the candidates themselves. The demands placed on political wives were often no less strenuous than those placed on the politicians.

"Evan," she said, watching him closely. "I'm not anything like your mother."

"So? What's that got to do with our building a big house and filling all those bedrooms with children?"

"I won't make a good politician's wife."

He looked at her as if he didn't understand what she was saying.

Mary Jo had no option but to elaborate. "I've heard, from various people, that you intend to enter politics yourself."

"Someday. I'm in no rush. My family, my mother especially, seems to think I have a future in that area, but it isn't anything that's going to happen soon. When and if the time comes, the two of us will decide together. But for now it's a moot point."

Mary Jo wasn't willing to accept that. "Evan, I'm telling you here and now I'd hate that kind of life. I'm not suited for it. Your mother enjoys arranging spectacular society events and giving interviews and living her life a certain way, but I don't. I'm uncomfortable in a roomful of strangers—unless they're five-year-olds."

"All right," Evan said with an amused air. "Then I won't enter politics. My mother has enough to keep her busy running my father's career. You're far more important to me than some elected position. Besides, I have the feeling Mother would've driven me crazy."

His words should have reassured her, but didn't. It seemed ludicrous to pin their future together on something as fleeting as this promise, so lightly made. Her greatest fear was that Evan would change his mind and regret ever marrying her.

"Let's go talk to your parents," Evan said, apparently unaware of the turmoil inside her.

"About what?"

His head went back and he frowned. "Making the arrangements for the wedding, what else? My mother will put up a fight, but I believe a small, private ceremony with just our immediate families would be best."

"Oh, Evan, please, don't rush me," Mary Jo pleaded. "This is the most important decision of our lives. We both need to think this through very carefully."

He gaze narrowed. "What's there to think about? I love you, and you love me. That's all that matters."

How Mary Jo wished that was true.

It took even more courage to drive over to Whispering Willows than Mary Jo had expected. She'd spent most of the night alternating between absolute delight and abject despair. She awoke Sunday morning sure that she'd never find the answers she needed until she'd talked to Evan's mother.

That was how Mary Jo came to be standing outside the Drydens' front door shortly before noon. With a shaking hand, she rang the bell.

She'd assumed one of the household staff would answer. Instead, Lois Dryden herself appeared at the door. The two women stared at each other.

Mary Jo recovered enough to speak first. "I'm sorry to disturb you, Mrs. Dryden, but I was wondering if I could have a few minutes of your time."

"Of course." The older woman stepped aside to let Mary Jo enter the lavish house. The foyer floor was of polished marble, and a glittering crystal chandelier hung from the ceiling, which was two-and-a-half stories high.

"Perhaps it would be best if we talked in my husband's office," Lois Dryden said, ushering Mary Jo to the darkly paneled room down the hall. This must be the room Evan had described in his absurd scenario of lonely old bachelor sitting by the fire with his dog.

"Would you like some something cold to drink? Or perhaps coffee?"

"No, thank you," Mary Jo answered. She chose the dark green leather wing chair angled in front of the fireplace. Mrs. Dryden sat in its twin.

"I realize you were surprised to see me with Evan yesterday."

"Yes," Lois agreed, her hands primly folded in her lap, "but who my son chooses to date is really none of my concern."

"That's very diplomatic of you. But I suspect you'd rather Evan dated someone other than me."

"Mary Jo, please. We got started on the wrong foot all those years ago. It was entirely my fault, and I've wished many times since that I'd been more thoughtful. I have the feeling I offended you and, my dear girl, that wasn't my intention."

"I'm willing to put the past behind us," Mary Jo suggested, managing a small smile. "That was three years ago, and I was more than a little overwhelmed by your family's wealth and position. If anyone's at fault, it was me."

"That's very gracious of you, my dear." Mrs. Dryden relaxed in her chair and crossed her ankles demurely.

"I love Evan," Mary Jo said, thinking it would be

best to be as forthright as possible. "And I believe he loves me."

"I'm pleased for you both." No telltale emotion sounded in her voice. They could've been discussing the weather for all the feeling her words revealed.

"Evan has asked me to marry him," she announced, carefully watching the woman who sat across from her for any signs of disapproval.

"I'm very pleased." A small and all-too-brief smile accompanied her statement. "Have you set the date? I hope you two understand that we'll need at least a year to plan the wedding. This type of event takes time and careful preparation."

"Evan and I have decided on a small, private ceremony."

"No," Lois returned adamantly. "That won't be possible."

"Why not?" Mary Jo asked, taken aback by the vehemence in the older woman's voice.

"My husband is a senator. The son of a man in my husband's position does not sneak away and get married in…in secret."

Mary Jo hadn't said anything about sneaking away or secrecy, but she wasn't there to argue. "I come from a large family, Mrs. Dryden. We—"

"There were ten of you or some such, as I recall." Her hands made a dismissive motion.

Mary Jo bristled. The woman made her parents sound as if they'd produced a warren of rabbits, instead of a large, happy family.

"My point," Mary Jo said, controlling her irritation with some difficulty, "is that neither my parents nor I could afford a big, expensive wedding."

"Of course," Lois said in obvious relief. "We wouldn't expect your relatives to assume the cost of such an elaborate affair. Walter and I would be more than happy to foot the bill."

"I appreciate the offer, and I'm sure my parents would, too, but I'm afraid we could never accept your generosity. Tradition says the bride's family assumes the cost of the wedding, and my father is a very traditional man."

"I see." Mrs. Dryden gnawed her lower lip. "There must be some way around his pride. Men can be such sticklers over things like this." For the first time she seemed almost friendly. "I'll come up with a solution. Just leave it to me."

"There's something you don't understand. An ostentatious wedding isn't what I want, either."

"But you must! I've already explained why it's necessary. We wouldn't want to create even a breath of scandal with some hushed-up affair. Why, that could do untold damage to my husband and to Evan's political future."

"Breath of *scandal?*"

"My dear girl, I don't mean to be rude, and please forgive me if I sound like an old busybody, but there are people who'd delight in finding the least little thing to use against Walter."

"But I'm marrying Evan, not Walter."

"I realize that. But you don't seem to grasp that these matters have to be handled...delicately. We need to start planning immediately. The moment the announcement is made, you and your family will be the focus of media attention."

Mary Jo's head began to spin. "I'm sure you're mistaken. Why should anyone care about me or my family?"

Lois was wringing her hands. "I don't suppose it does any harm to mention it, although I must ask you not to spread this information around. Walter has been contacted by a longtime friend who intends to enter the presidential campaign next year. This friend has tentatively requested Walter to be his running mate, should he garner the party's nomination."

Mary Jo developed an instant throbbing headache.

"My husband and I must avoid any situation that might put him in an unflattering light."

"We could delay the wedding." She'd been joking, but Evan's mother looked relieved.

"Would you?" she asked hopefully.

"I'll talk to Evan."

At the mention of her youngest son, Lois Dryden frowned. "Shouldn't he be here with you? It seems a bit odd that you'd tell me about your engagement without him."

"I wanted the two of us to chat first," Mary Jo explained.

"An excellent idea," Lois said with a distinct nod of her head. "Men can be so difficult. If you and I can agree on certain…concerns before we talk to Evan and my husband, I feel sure we can work everything out to our mutual satisfaction."

"Mrs. Dryden, I'm a kindergarten teacher. I think you should know I feel uncomfortable with the idea of becoming a media figure."

"I'll do whatever I can to help you, Mary Jo. It's a lot to have thrust on you all at once, but if you're going to marry my son, you have to learn how to handle the press. I'll teach you how to use them to your advantage and how to turn something negative into a positive."

Mary Jo's headache increased a hundredfold. "I don't think I've been clear enough, Mrs. Dryden. I'm more than uncomfortable with this—I refuse to become involved in it."

"Refuse?" She repeated the word as if unsure of the meaning.

"I've already told you about my feelings for Evan," Mary Jo continued. "I love your son so much…" Her voice shook and she stopped speaking for a moment. "I'm not like you or your husband, or Evan, for that matter. Nor do I intend to be. When Evan asked me to marry him, I told him all this."

A frown creased Lois Dryden's brow. "I don't understand."

"Perhaps I'm not explaining it well. Basically, I refuse to live my life seeking the approval of others. I want a small, private wedding and Evan has agreed."

"But what about the future, when Evan decides to enter politics? Trust me, Mary Jo, the wife's position is as public as that of her husband."

"I'm sure that's true. But I'd hate the kind of life you're describing. Evan knows that and understands. He's also agreed that as long as I feel this way, he won't enter politics."

His mother vaulted from her chair. "But you can't do this! Politics is Evan's destiny. Why, from the time he was in grade school his teachers have told me what a natural leader he is. He was student-body president in high school *and* in college. From his early twenties on, he's been groomed for this very thing. I can visualize my son in the White House someday."

His mother had lofty plans indeed. "Is this what Evan wants?"

"Of course it is," she said vehemently. "Ask him yourself. His father and brother have had countless conversations with him about it. If my son were to marry a woman who didn't appreciate his abilities or understand his ambitions, it might destroy him."

If the words had come from anyone other than Lois Dryden, Mary Jo would've thought them absurd and melodramatic. But this woman believed implicitly in what she said.

"Evan's marrying the right kind of woman is crucial to your plans for his future, isn't it?" Mary Jo asked with infinite sadness.

Mrs. Dryden looked decidedly uncomfortable. "Yes."

"I'm not that woman."

The older woman sighed. "I realize that. The question is, what do you intend to do about it?"

Chapter 8

"I love Evan," Mary Jo insisted again, but even as she spoke, she realized again that loving him wasn't enough. Although she'd matured and wasn't the skittish, frightened woman she'd been three years earlier, nothing had really changed. If she married Evan, she might ruin his promising career. It was a heavy burden to carry.

Mary Jo couldn't change who and what she was, nor should she expect Evan to make all the concessions, giving up his future.

"I'm sure you do love my son," Lois said sincerely.

"And he loves me," Mary Jo added, keeping her back straight and her head high. She angled her chin at a proud, if somewhat defiant, tilt, unwilling to accept defeat. "We'll work this out somehow," she said confidently. "There isn't anything two people who love each other can't resolve. We'll find a way."

"I'm sure you will, my dear." Lois Dryden's mouth formed a sad smile that contradicted her reassurances. "In any case, you're perfectly right. You should discuss this with Evan and reach a decision together."

The older woman smoothed an invisible wrinkle from her dove-gray skirt. "Despite what you may think, Mary Jo, I have no personal objections to your marrying my son. When the two of you separated some time ago, I wondered if it had something to do with our little talk. I don't mind telling you I suffered more than a few regrets. I never intended to hurt you, and if I did, I beg your forgiveness."

"You certainly opened my eyes," Mary Jo admitted. Evan's mother had refined that talent over the past few years, she noted silently.

"I might sound like a interfering old woman, but I do hope you'll take our little talk to heart. I trust you'll seriously consider what we've discussed." She sighed. "I love Evan, too. God has blessed me with a very special family, and all I want is what's best for my children. I'm sure your parents feel the same way about you."

"They do." The conversation was becoming more and more unbearable. Mary Jo desperately wanted to leave. And she needed to talk to Evan, to share her concerns and address their future. But deep down she'd caught a fearful glimpse of the truth.

Mary Jo stood up abruptly and offered Mrs. Dryden her hand. "Thank you for your honesty and your insights. It wasn't what I wanted to hear, but I suppose it's what I needed to know. I'm sure this was just as difficult for you. We have something in common, Mrs. Dryden. We both love your son. Evan wouldn't be the

man he is without your love and care. You have a right
to be proud."

Evan's mother took Mary Jo's hand in both of her
own and held it firmly for a moment. "I appreciate that.
Do keep in touch, won't you?"

Mary Jo nodded. "If you wish."

The older woman led her to the front door and
walked out to the circular driveway with her. Mary
Jo climbed into her car and started the engine. As she
pulled away, she glanced in her rearview mirror to find
Lois Dryden's look both thoughtful and troubled.

Normally Mary Jo joined her family for their Sunday get-togethers. But not this week. Needing time and
privacy to sort out her thoughts, she drove to the marina. She parked, then made her way slowly to the wa-
terfront. The wind coming off the ocean was fresh and
tangy with salt. She had to think, and what better place
than here, where she'd spent countless happy hours in
Evan's company?

How long she sat on the bench overlooking the water
she didn't know. Time seemed to be of little conse-
quence. She gazed at the boats moving in and out of
their narrow passageways. The day had turned cloudy,
which suited her somber mood.

Standing, she walked along the pier, once again re-
viewing her conversation with Evan's mother. Her steps
slowed as she realized no amount of brooding would
solve the problems. She had to talk to Evan, and soon,
before she lost her nerve.

She found a pay phone, plunked in a quarter and di-
aled his home number.

"Mary Jo. Thank goodness! Where were you?" Evan

asked. "I've been calling your place every fifteen minutes. I have some wonderful news."

"I...had an errand to run," she said, not ready to elaborate just then. He was obviously excited. "What's your good news?"

"I'll tell you the minute I see you."

"Do you want to meet somewhere?" she asked.

"How about Rowe's Wharf? We can take a stroll along the pier. If you want, we can visit the aquarium. I haven't been there in years. When we're hungry we can find a seafood restaurant and catch a bite to eat." He paused and laughed at his weak joke. "No pun intended."

"That'll be great," she said, finding it difficult to rouse the proper enthusiasm.

"Mary Jo?" His voice rose slightly. "What's wrong? You sound upset."

"We need to talk."

"All right," he agreed guardedly. "Do you want me to pick you up?" When she declined, he said, "I'll meet you there in half an hour, okay?"

"Okay." It was ironic, Mary Jo mused, that Evan could be so happy while she felt as if her entire world was about to shatter.

When she finished speaking to Evan, Mary Jo phoned her mother and told her she wouldn't be joining them for dinner. Marianna knew instantly that something wasn't right, but Mary Jo promised to explain later.

From the marina she drove down Atlantic Avenue and found a suitable place to park. It had been less than twenty-four hours, and already she was starved for the sight of Evan. It seemed unthinkable to live the rest of her life without him.

He was standing on the wharf waiting for her when

she arrived. His face lighted up as she approached, and he held out both hands to her.

Mary Jo experienced an immediate sense of comfort the moment their fingers touched. In another second, she was securely wrapped in his arms. He held her against him as though he didn't intend to ever let her go. And she wished she didn't have to leave the protective shelter of his arms.

"I've missed you," he breathed against her temple. "I've missed you so much." He threaded his fingers lovingly through her windblown hair.

"We spent nearly all of yesterday together," she reminded him lightly, although she shared his feelings. Even a few hours apart left her wondering how she'd managed to survive all those years without him. How she'd ever do it again...

"I love you, Mary Jo. Don't forget that."

"I won't." His words were an immense comfort. She buried her face in his neck and clung to him, wanting to believe with everything she possessed that there was a way for them to find happiness together.

"Now tell me your good news," she murmured. Evan eased her out of his arms, but tucked her hand inside his elbow. His eyes were shining with excitement.

"Damian and I had a long talk last evening," Evan said. "I phoned to tell him about the two of us, and he's absolutely delighted. Jessica, too. They both send their congratulations, by the way."

"Thank them for me," she said softly. "So, come on, tell me your news." She leaned against him as they walked leisurely down the wharf.

"All right, all right. Damian's been in contact with a number of key people over the past few weeks. The general consensus is that the time for me to make my move into the political arena is now."

Mary Jo felt as though a fist had plowed into her midsection. For a moment she remained frozen. She couldn't breathe. Couldn't think. She was dimly aware of Evan beside her, still talking.

"Now?" she broke in. "But I thought...you said..."

"I know it probably seems too early to be discussing next year's elections," Evan went on to say, his face alive with energy. "But we've got some catching up to do. I won't file for office until after the first of the year, but there're a million things that need to be done before then."

"What office do you intend to run for?" Her mind was whirling with doubts and questions. The sick feeling in the pit of her stomach refused to go away. She felt both cold and feverishly hot at the same time.

"I'm running for city council. There's nothing I'd enjoy more. And, Mary Jo," he said with a broad grin, "I know I can make a difference in our city. I have so many ideas and I've got lots of time, and I don't mind working hard." He raised her hand to his lips and kissed the knuckles. "That's one of the reasons I want us to get married as soon as it can be arranged. We'll work together, side by side, the way my father and mother did when he ran for the Senate."

"I—"

"You'll need to quit your teaching job."

So many objections rose up in her she didn't know which one to address first. "Why can't I teach?"

He looked at her as if the question surprised him. "You don't have to work anymore, and besides, I'm

going to need you. Don't you see? This is just the beginning. There's a whole new life waiting for the two of us."

"Have you talked this over with your parents?" Mrs.
Dryden must've already known, Mary Jo thought.

"Dad and I discussed it this morning, and he agrees
with Damian. The timing is right. Naturally, he'd like
to see me run for mayor a few years down the road, and
I might, but there's no need to get ahead of ourselves.
I haven't been elected to city council yet."

"What did your mother have to say?"

"I don't know if Dad's had the chance to talk to her
yet. What makes you ask?"

"I...visited her this morning," Mary Jo said, studying
the water. It was safer to look out over Boston Harbor
than at the man she loved.

"You spent the morning with my mother?" Evan
stopped. "At Whispering Willows?"

"Yes."

His eyebrows shot straight toward his hairline. "Why
would you go and visit my mother?"

Mary Jo heaved in a deep breath and held it until
her chest ached. "There's something you should know,
Evan. Something I should've told you a long time ago."
She hesitated, hardly able to continue. Eventually she
did, but her voice was low and strained. "When I broke
our engagement three years ago, it wasn't because I'd
fallen in love with another man. There was never anyone else. It was all a big lie."

She felt him stiffen. He frowned and his eyes narrowed, first with denial and then with disbelief. He
shook off her hand and she walked over to the pier,
waiting for him to join her.

It took him several minutes.

"I'm not proud of that lie," she told him, "and I apologize for stooping to such cowardly methods. You deserved far better, but I wasn't strong enough or mature enough to confront you with the truth."

"Which was?" She could tell he was making a strenuous effort to keep his voice level and dispassionate. But his fists were clenched. She could feel his anger, had anticipated it, understood it.

"Various reasons," she confessed. "I invented another love interest because I knew you'd believe me, and…and it avoided the inevitable arguments. I couldn't have dealt with a long-drawn-out debate."

"That makes no sense whatsoever." He sounded angry now, and Mary Jo couldn't blame him. "You'd better start at the beginning," he suggested after a long silence. "What was it we would have argued about?"

"Our getting married."

"Okay," he said, obviously still not understanding.

"It all began the evening you took me to meet your family," Mary Jo said. "I'd known you were wealthy, of course, but I had no idea how prominent your family was. I was naive and inexperienced, and when your mother asked me some…pertinent questions, I realized a marriage between us wouldn't work."

"What kind of 'pertinent' questions?" The words were charged with contained fury.

"Evan, please, it doesn't matter."

"The hell it doesn't!"

Mary Jo closed her eyes. "About my family and my background, and how suitable I'd be as a political wife. She stressed the importance of your marrying the right woman."

"It appears my mother and I need to have a chat."

"Don't be angry, Evan. She wasn't rude or cruel, but she brought up a few truths I hadn't faced. Afterward, I was convinced a marriage between us would never survive. We have so little in common. Our backgrounds are nothing alike, and I was afraid that in time you'd... you'd regret having married me."

He made a disgusted sound. "And so you invented this ridiculous lie and walked out of my life, leaving me lost and confused and so shaken it..." He paused as if he'd said more than he'd intended.

"I behaved stupidly—I know that. But I hurt, too, Evan. Don't think it was easy on me. I suffered. Because I loved you then and I love you still."

He sighed heavily. "I appreciate your honesty, Mary Jo, but let's put the whole mess behind us. It doesn't concern us anymore. We're together now and will be for the next fifty years. That's all that matters."

Tears blurred Mary Jo's eyes as she watched the airport shuttle boat cross Boston Harbor. The waters churned and foamed—like her emotions, she thought.

"It's quite apparent, however," Evan went on, "that I need to have a heart-to-heart with my dear, sweet, interfering mother."

"Evan, she isn't the one to blame. Breaking up, lying to you—that was *my* bad idea. But it isn't going to happen again."

"I won't let you out of my life that easily a second time."

"I don't plan on leaving," she whispered. He placed his arm around her shoulder, and Mary Jo slid her own arm around his waist. For a moment they were content in the simple pleasure of being together.

"Because of that first meeting with your mother, I

felt it was important to talk to her again," Mary Jo said, trying to explain why she'd gone to see Mrs. Dryden that morning. "She's a wonderful woman, Evan, and she loves you very much."

"Fine. But I will not allow her to interfere in our lives. If she doesn't understand that now, she will when I finish talking to her."

"Evan, please! She did nothing more than open my eyes to a few home truths."

"What did she have to say this morning?"

"Well…she had some of the same questions as before."

"Such as?" he demanded.

"You want us to be married soon, right?"

He nodded. "The sooner the better." Bending his head, he kissed a corner of her mouth. "As I said earlier, we have three years of lost time to make up for. Keep that house with all those empty bedrooms in mind."

Despite the ache in her heart, Mary Jo smiled. "Your mother told me that a small, private wedding might cause problems for your father."

"Whose wedding is this?" Evan cried. "We'll do this our way, sweetheart. Don't worry about it."

"It could be important, Evan," she countered swiftly. "Your father can't be associated with anything that… that could be misinterpreted."

Evan laughed outright. "In other words, she prefers to throw a large, gala wedding with a cast of thousands? That's ridiculous."

"I…think she might be right."

"That's the kind of wedding you want?" Evan asked, his eyes revealing his disbelief.

"No. It isn't what I want at all. But on the other hand, I wouldn't want to do anything to hurt your father."

"Trust me, Mary Jo, you won't." He gave her an affectionate squeeze. "Now you listen. We're going to be married and we'll have the kind of wedding *we* want, and Mother won't have any choice but to accept it."

"But, Evan, what if our rushed wedding did cause speculation?"

"What if it did? Do you think I care? Or my father, either, for that matter? My mother is often guilty of making mountains out of molehills. She loves to worry. In this day and age, it's ridiculous to get upset about such things."

"But—"

He silenced her with a kiss thorough enough to leave her feeling that anything was possible. "I love you, Mary Jo. If it was up to me, we'd take the next plane to Las Vegas and get married this evening."

"People might gossip." She managed to dredge up one last argument.

"Good. The more my name's in circulation, the better."

Mary Jo's spirits had lightened considerably. She so desperately wanted to believe him, she didn't stop to question what he was saying.

"It's settled, then. We'll be married as soon as we can make the arrangements. Mom can fuss all she wants, but it isn't going to do her any good."

"I... There are some other things we need to talk over first."

"There are?" He sounded exasperated.

She leaned against the pier, knotting and unknotting her hands. "You're excited about running for city council, aren't you?"

"Yes," he admitted readily. "This is something I want, and I'm willing to work for it. I wouldn't run for office if I wasn't convinced I could make some positive changes. This is exactly the right way for me to enter politics, especially while Dad's in the Senate."

She turned to study him. "What if I asked you not to run?"

Evan took a moment to mull over her words. "Why would you do that?"

"What if I did?" she asked again. "What would you do then?"

"First, I'd need to know exactly what you objected to."

"What if I reminded you I wasn't comfortable in the spotlight? Which, I might add, was something we discussed just yesterday. I'm not the kind of person who's comfortable living my life in a fishbowl."

"It wouldn't be like that," he protested.

Her smile was sad. Evan didn't understand. He'd grown up accustomed to having people interested in his personal life. Even now, his dating habits often provided speculation for the society pages.

"It *would* be like that, Evan. Don't kid yourself."

"Then you'll adjust," he said with supreme confidence.

"I'll adjust," she repeated slowly. "What if I don't? Then what happens? I could be an embarrassment to you. My family might be, as well. Let me give you an example. Just a few days ago, Jack and Rich were so upset over this investment problem my father's having that they were ready to go to Adison's office again and punch him out. If we hadn't stopped them, they'd have been thrown in jail. The press would have a field day with that."

"You're overreacting."

"Maybe," she agreed grudgingly, then added with emphasis, "but I don't think so. I told you before how I feel about this. You didn't believe me, did you? You seem to think a pat on the head and a few reassurances are all I need. You've discounted everything I've said to you."

"Mary Jo, please—"

"In case you haven't noticed, I—I have this terrible habit of blushing whenever I'm the center of attention. I'm not the kind of woman your mother is. She enjoys the spotlight, loves arranging social events. She has a gift for making everyone feel comfortable and welcome. I can't do that, Evan. I'd be miserable."

Evan said nothing, but his mouth tightened.

"You may think I'm being selfish and uncaring, but that isn't true. I'm not the right woman for you."

"Because my mother said so."

"No, because of who and what I am."

Evan sighed. "I can see that you've already got this all worked out."

"Another thing. I'm a good teacher and I enjoy my job. I'd want to continue with my kindergarten class after we were married."

Evan took several steps away from her and rubbed his hand along the back of his neck. "Then there's nothing left for me to say, is there? I'll talk to Damian and explain that everything's off. I won't run for city council, not if it makes you that uncomfortable."

"Oh, Evan." She was on the verge of tears. This was exactly what she'd feared. Exactly what she didn't want. "Don't you see?" she pleaded, swallowing a sob. "I can't marry you knowing I'm holding you back from your dreams. You may love me now, but in time you'd grow to resent me, and it would ruin our marriage."

"You're more important to me than any political office," Evan said sharply. "You're right, Mary Jo, you did tell me how you felt about getting involved in politics, and I did discount what you said. I grew up in a family that was often in the limelight. This whole thing is old hat to me. I was wrong not to have considered your feelings."

She closed her eyes in an effort to blot out his willingness to sacrifice himself. "It just isn't going to work, Evan. In the beginning you wouldn't mind, but later it would destroy us. It would hurt your family, too. This isn't only your dream, it's theirs."

"Leave my family to me."

"No. You're a part of them and they're a part of you. Politics has been your dream from the time you were a boy. You told me yourself that you believe you can make a difference to the city's future."

By now, the tears were running down her face. Impatiently she brushed them aside and forced herself to continue. "How many times are you going to make me say it? *I'm not the right woman for you.*"

"You *are* the right woman," he returned fiercely. His hands gripped her shoulders and he pulled her toward him, his eyes fierce and demanding. "I'm not listening to any more of this. We've loved each other for too long. We're meant to be together."

Mary Jo stared out at the harbor again. "There's someone else out there—from the right family, with the right background. A woman who'll share your ambition and your dreams, who'll work with you and not against you. A woman who'll...love you, too."

"I can't believe you're saying this." His grip tightened on her shoulder until it was almost painful, but she knew he didn't even realize it. "It's *you* I love. It's *you* I want to marry."

Mary Jo shook her head sadly.

"If you honestly think there's another woman for me, why didn't I fall in love with someone else? I had three whole years to find this phantom woman you mention. Why didn't I?"

"Because your eyes were closed. Because you were too wrapped up in your own pain to look. For whatever reasons... I don't know..."

"Is this what you want? To walk out of my life a second time as if we meant nothing to each other?" He was beginning to attract attention from passersby, and he lowered his voice.

"No," she admitted. "This is killing me. I'd give anything to be the kind of woman you need, but I can only be me. If I ask you to accept who I am, then... I can't ask you to be something you're not."

"Don't do this," he said from between clenched teeth. "We'll find a way."

How she wanted to believe that. How she wished it was possible.

Evan drew a deep breath and released her shoulders. "Let's not make any drastic decisions now. We're both emotionally spent. Nothing has to be determined right this minute." He paused and gulped in another deep breath. "Let's sleep on it and we can talk in the morning. All right?"

Mary Jo nodded. She couldn't have endured much more of this.

* * *

The following morning Evan phoned the office shortly after she'd arrived and told her he'd be in late. His voice was cool, without a hint of emotion, as he asked her to reschedule his first two appointments.

Mary Jo thought she might as well have been speaking to a stranger. She longed to ask him how he was or if he'd had any further ideas, but it was clear he wanted to avoid speaking to her about anything personal.

With a heavy heart, she began her morning duties. Around nine-thirty, the office door opened and Damian walked in. He paused as if he wasn't sure he'd come to the right room.

"Evan won't be in until eleven this morning," she explained.

"Yes, I know." For a man she'd assumed was utterly confident, Damian appeared doubtful and rather hesitant. "It wasn't Evan I came to see. It was you."

"Me?" She looked up at Damian, finding his gaze warm and sympathetic. "Why?"

"Evan stopped by the house yesterday afternoon to talk to both Jessica and me. He was confused and..."

"Hurt," Mary Jo supplied for him. She knew exactly what Evan was feeling because she felt the same way.

"My talking to you may not solve anything, but I thought I should give it a try. I'm not sure my brother would appreciate my butting into his personal business, but he did it once for me. I figure I owe him one." Damian's smile was fleeting. "I don't know if this is what you want to hear, but Evan really loves you."

A lump developed in her throat and she nodded. "I realize that." She loved him just as much.

"From what Evan said to us, I gather he's decided

against running for city council. He also told us why he felt he had to back out. Naturally, I support any decision he chooses to make."

"But..." There had to be a "but" in all this.

"But it would be a shame if he declined."

"I'm not going to let that happen," Mary Jo said calmly. "You see, I love Evan and I want what's best for him, and to put it simply, that isn't me."

"He doesn't believe that, Mary Jo, and neither do I."

She could see no reason to discuss the issue. "Where is he now?" she asked softly.

"He went to talk to our parents."

Their parents. If anyone could get him to face the truth, it was Lois Dryden. Mary Jo had approached the woman, strong and certain of her love, and walked away convinced she'd been living in a dreamworld. Lois Dryden was capable of opening Evan's eyes as no one else could.

"We both need time to think this through," Mary Jo murmured. "I appreciate your coming to me, Damian, more than I can say. I know you did it out of love, but what happens between Evan and me, well, that's our concern."

"You didn't ask for my advice, but I'm going to give it to you, anyway," Damian said. "Don't be so quick to give up."

"I won't," she promised.

Mary Jo was sitting at her desk sorting mail when Evan arrived shortly after eleven. She stood up to greet him, but he glanced past her and said tonelessly, "I can't fight both of you." Then he walked into his office and shut the door.

His action said more than his words. In her heart,

Mary Jo had dared to hope that if Evan confronted his parents and came away with his convictions intact, there might be a chance for them.

But obviously that hadn't happened. One look plainly revealed his resignation and regret. He'd accepted from his parents what he wouldn't from her. The truth.

Sitting back down, Mary Jo wrote her letter of resignation, printed it and then signed it. Next she phoned a temporary employment agency and made arrangements for her replacement to arrive that afternoon.

When she'd finished, she tapped on his closed door and let herself into his office.

"Yes?" Evan said.

She found him standing in front of the window, hands clasped behind his back. After a moment, he turned to face her.

With tears blocking her throat, she laid the single sheet on his desk and crossed the room to stand beside him.

His gaze went from the letter to her and back. "What's that?"

"My letter of resignation. My replacement will be here within the hour. I'll finish out the day—show her around and explain her duties."

She half expected him to offer a token argument, but he said nothing. She pressed her hand against the side of his face and smiled up at him. His features blurred as tears filled her eyes.

"Goodbye, Evan," she whispered.

Chapter 9

A week passed and the days bled into one another until Mary Jo couldn't distinguish morning from afternoon. A thousand regrets hounded her at all hours of the day and night.

Blessed with a loving family, Mary Jo was grateful for their comfort, needed it. There was, for all of them, some consolation in the news that came from Evan. Through his new personal assistant, he'd been in touch with her father regarding Adison Investments.

Mary Jo heard from him, too. Once. In a brief letter explaining that Adison would be forthcoming with the return of the original investment money, plus interest. Since he'd calculated his fee for an extended lawsuit, she owed him nothing.

Mary Jo read the letter several times, searching for a message. Anything. But there were only three short sentences, their tone crisp and businesslike, with no hidden meaning that she could decipher. Tears blurred her eyes as she lovingly ran her finger over his signature. She missed him terribly, felt empty and lost, and this was as close as she'd ever be to him again—her finger caressing his signature at the end of a letter.

Another week passed. Mary Jo was no less miserable than she'd been the first day after she'd stopped working for Evan. She knew it would take time and effort to accept the infeasibility of her love for him, but she wasn't ready. Not yet. So she stayed holed up in her apartment, listless and heartbroken.

The fact that the summer days were glorious—all sunshine and blue skies—didn't help. The least Mother Nature could've done was cooperate and match her mood with dark gray clouds and gloomy weather.

She dragged herself out of bed late one morning and didn't bother to eat until early afternoon. Now she sat in front of the television dressed in her nightie and munching dry cornflakes. She hadn't been to the grocery store in weeks and had long since run out of milk. And just about everything else.

The doorbell chimed, and Mary Jo shot an accusing glance in the direction of her front door. It was probably her mother or one of her sisters-in-law, who seemed to think it was up to them to boost her spirits. So they invented a number of ridiculous excuses to pop in unexpectedly.

The love and support of her family was important, but all Mary Jo wanted at the moment was to be left alone. To eat her cornflakes in peace.

She set the bowl aside, walked over to the door and squinted through the peephole. She caught a glimpse of a designer purse, but unfortunately whoever was holding it stood just outside her view.

"Who is it?" she called out.

"Jessica."

Mary Jo pressed her forehead against the door and groaned. She was an emotional and physical wreck. The last person she wanted to see was anyone related to Evan.

"Mary Jo, please open the door," Jessica called. "We need to talk. It's about Evan."

Nothing could have been more effective. She didn't want company. She didn't want to talk. But the minute Jessica said Evan's name, Mary Jo turned the lock and opened the door. Standing in the doorway, she closed her eyes against the painfully bright sun.

"How are you?" Jessica asked, walking right in.

"About as bad as I look," Mary Jo mumbled, shutting the door behind her. "What about Evan?"

"Same as you." She strode into the room, removed a stack of papers from the rocking chair and planted herself in it as if she intended to stay for a while.

"Where's Andy?" Mary Jo asked, still holding the doorknob.

Jessica crossed her legs, rocking gently. "My mother has him—for the *day*."

Mary Jo noted the emphasis. Jessica was going to stay here until she got what she wanted.

"I told Mom I had a doctor's appointment, and I do—later," Jessica said. "I think I'm pregnant again." A radiant happiness shone from her eyes.

"Congratulations." Although Mary Jo was miserable, she was pleased for her friend, who was clearly delighted.

"I know it's none of my business," Jessica said sympathetically, "but tell me what happened between you and Evan."

"I'm sure he's already explained." Mary Jo wasn't up to discussing all the painful details. Besides, it would solve nothing.

Jessica laughed shortly. "Evan talk? You've got to be joking. He wouldn't say so much as a word. Both Damian and I've tried to get him to tell us what happened, but it hasn't done a bit of good."

"So you've come to me."

"Exactly."

"Please don't do this, Jessica," Mary Jo said, fighting back the tears. "It's just too painful."

"But you both love each other so much."

"That's why our breakup's necessary. It isn't easy on either of us, but this is the way it has to be."

Jessica threw her hands in the air. "You're a pair of fools! There's no talking to Evan, and you're not much better. What's it going to take to get you two back together?"

"A miracle," Mary Jo answered.

Jessica took some time to digest this. "Is there anything I can do?"

"No," Mary Jo said sadly. There wasn't anything anyone could do. But one thing was certain: she couldn't continue like this. Sliding from one day to the next without a thought to the future. Immersed in the pain of the past, barely able to live in the present.

"You're sure?"

"I'm thinking of leaving Boston," she said suddenly. The impulse had come unexpectedly, and in a heartbeat Mary Jo knew it was the right decision. She couldn't live in this town, this state, without constantly being bombarded with information about the Dryden family. Not a week passed that his father wasn't in the news for one reason or another. It would only get worse once Evan was elected to city council.

Escape seemed her only answer.

"Where would you go?" Jessica pressed.

Anywhere that wasn't here. "The Northwest," she said, blurting out the first destination that came to mind. "Washington, maybe Oregon. I've heard that part of the country's beautiful." Teachers were needed everywhere and she shouldn't have much trouble obtaining a position.

"So far away?" Jessica seemed to breathe the question.

The farther the better. Her family would argue with her, but for the first time in two weeks, Mary Jo had found a reason to look ahead.

Her parents would tell her she was running away, and Mary Jo would agree, but sometimes running was necessary. She remembered her father's talks with her older brothers; he'd explained that there might come a day when they'd find themselves in a no-win situation. The best thing to do, he'd told them, was to walk away. Surely this was one of those times.

"Thank you for coming," Mary Jo said, looking solemnly at her friend. "I appreciate it. Please let me know when the baby's born."

"I will," Jessica said, her eyes sad.

"I'll have my mother send me the results of the election next year. My heart will be with Evan."

It would always be with him.

Jessica left soon afterward, flustered and discouraged. They hugged and, amid promises to keep in touch, reluctantly parted. Mary Jo counted Evan's sister-in-law as a good friend.

Mary Jo was filled with purpose. She dressed, made a number of phone calls, opened the door and let the sunshine pour in. By late afternoon, she'd accomplished more than she had in the previous two weeks. Telling her parents her decision wouldn't be easy, but her mind was made up. It was now Tuesday. Tomorrow she'd give the school her notice and let her landlord know, too. First thing next Monday morning, she was packing what she could in her car and heading west. As soon as she'd settled somewhere she'd send for her furniture.

Before Mary Jo could announce her decision, her father phoned her with the wonderful news that he'd received a cashier's check returning his investment. Not only that, Evan had put him in contact with a reputable financial adviser.

"That's great," Mary Jo said, blinking back tears. Hearing the relief in her father's voice was all the reward she'd ever need. Although it had ultimately broken her heart, asking Evan to help her parents had been the right thing to do. Her father had gotten far more than his investment back. In the process he'd restored his pride and his faith in justice.

"I need to talk to you and Mom," Mary Jo said, steeling herself for the inevitable confrontation. "I'll be over in a few minutes."

The meeting didn't go well. Mary Jo hadn't expected that it would. Her parents listed their objections for nearly an hour. Mary Jo's resolve didn't waver. She was leaving Boston; she would find a new life for herself.

To her surprise, her brothers sided with her. Jack insisted she was old enough to make her own decisions. His words did more to convince her parents than hours of her own arguments.

The Friday before she planned to leave, Mary Jo spent the day with her mother. Marianna was pickling cucumbers in the kitchen, dabbing her eyes now and then when she thought Mary Jo wasn't looking.

"I'm going to miss you," Marianna said, shaking her head.

Mary Jo's heart lurched. "I'll miss you, too. But, Mom, you make it sound like you'll never hear from me again. I promise to phone at least once a week."

"Call when the rates are cheaper, understand?"

Mary Jo suppressed a smile. "Of course."

"I talked to Evan," her mother said casually as she was inserting cloves of garlic into the sterilized canning jars.

Mary Jo froze, and her breath jammed in her chest.

"I told him you'd decided to leave Boston, and you know what he said?"

"No." The word rose from her throat on a bubble of hysteria.

"Evan said you'd know what was best." She paused as if carefully judging her words. "He didn't sound like himself. I'm worried about that boy, but I'm more concerned about you."

"Mom, I'm going to be fine."

"I know that. You're a Summerhill and we're strong people."

Mary Jo followed her mother, dropping a sprig of dill weed into each of the sparkling clean jars.

"You never told me what went wrong between you and Evan, not that you had to. I've got eyes and ears, and it didn't take much to figure out that his family had something to do with all this."

Her mother's insight didn't come as any surprise, but Mary Jo neither confirmed nor denied it.

"The mail's here," Norman Summerhill said, strolling into the kitchen. "I had one of those fancy travel agencies send us a couple of brochures on the South Pacific. When you're finished packing those jars, let's sit down and read them over."

Marianna's nod was eager. "We won't be long."

Her father set the rest of the mail on the table. The top envelope caught Mary Jo's attention. The return address was a bankruptcy court. She didn't think anything of it until later when her father opened the envelope.

"I wonder what this is?" he mumbled, frowning in confusion. He stretched his arm out in front of him to read it.

"Norman, for the love of heaven, get your glasses," Marianna chastised.

"I can see fine without them." He winked at Mary Jo. "Here, you read it for me." Mary Jo took the cover letter and scanned the contents. As she did, her stomach turned. The bankruptcy court had written her parents on behalf of Adison Investments. They were to complete the attached forms and list, with proof, the amount of their investment. Once all the documents were submitted, the case would be heard.

The legal jargon was difficult for Mary Jo to understand, but one thing was clear. Adison Investments hadn't returned her father's money.

Evan had.

"It's nothing, Dad," Mary Jo said, not knowing what else to say.

"Then throw it out. I don't understand why we get so much junk mail these days. You'd think the environmentalists would do something about wasting all those trees."

Mary Jo stuck the envelope in her purse, made her excuses and left soon afterward. She wasn't sure what she was going to do, but if she didn't escape soon, there'd be no hiding her tears.

Evan had done this for her family because he loved her. This was his way of saying goodbye. Hot tears burned in her eyes, and sniffling, she rubbed the back of her hand across her face.

The blast of a car horn sounded from behind her and Mary Jo glanced in the direction of the noise. Adrenaline shot through her as she saw a full-size sedan barreling toward her.

The next thing she heard was metal slamming against metal. The hideous grating noise blasted her ears and she instinctively brought her hands up to her face. The impact was so strong she felt as though she were caught in the middle of an explosion.

Her world went into chaos. There was only pain. Her head started to spin, and her vision blurred. She screamed.

Her last thought before she lost consciousness was that she was going to die.

"Why didn't you call me right away?" a gruff male voice demanded.

It seemed to come from a great distance away and drifted slowly toward Mary Jo as she floated, unconcerned, on a thick black cloud. It sounded like Evan's voice, but then again it didn't. The words came to her sluggish and slurred.

"We tried to contact you, but your personal assistant said you couldn't be reached."

The second voice belonged to her father, Mary Jo determined. But he, too, sounded odd, as if he were standing at the bottom of a deep well and yelling up at her. The words were distorted and they vibrated, making them difficult to understand. They seemed to take a very long time to reach her. Perhaps it was because her head hurt so badly. The throbbing was intensely painful.

"I came as soon as I heard." It was Evan again and he sounded sorry. He sounded as if he thought he was to blame. "How seriously is she hurt?"

"Doc says she sustained a head injury. She's unconscious, but they claim she isn't in a coma."

"She'll wake up soon," her mother said in a soothing tone. "Now sit down and relax. Everything's going to be all right. I'm sure the doctor will be happy to answer any of your questions. Mary Jo's going to be fine, just wait and see."

Her mother was comforting Evan as if he were one of her own children, Mary Jo realized. She didn't understand why Evan should be so worried. Perhaps he was afraid she was going to die. Perhaps she already had, but then she decided she couldn't be dead because she hurt too much.

"What have they done to her head?"

Mary Jo was eager to hear that answer herself.

"They had to shave off her hair."

"Relax." It was her father speaking. "It'll grow back."

"It's just that she looks so…" Evan didn't finish the sentence.

"She'll be fine, Evan. Now sit down here by her side. I know it's a shock seeing her like this."

Mary Jo wanted to reassure Evan herself, but her mouth refused to open and she couldn't speak. Something must be wrong with her if she could hear but not see or speak. When she attempted to move, she found her arms and legs wouldn't cooperate. A sense of panic overwhelmed her and the pounding pain intensified.

Almost immediately she drifted away on the same dark cloud and the voices slowly faded. She longed to call out, to pull herself back, but she lacked the strength. And this way, the pain wasn't as bad.

The next sound Mary Jo heard was a soft thumping. It took her several minutes to recognize what it meant. Someone was in her room, pacing. Whoever it was seemed impatient, or maybe anxious. She didn't know which.

"How is she?" A feminine voice that was vaguely familiar drifted toward Mary Jo. The pain in her head was back, and she desperately wanted it to go away.

"There's been no change." It was Evan who spoke. Evan was the one pacing her room. Knowing he was there filled her with a gentle sense of peace. She'd recover if Evan was with her. How she knew this, Mary Jo didn't question.

"How long have you been here?" The feminine voice belonged to Jessica, she decided.

"A few hours."

"It's more like twenty-four. I met Mary Jo's parents in the elevator. They're going home to get some sleep. You should, too. The hospital will call if there's any change."

"No."

Mary Jo laughed to herself. She'd recognize that stubborn streak of his anywhere.

"Evan," Jessica protested. "You're not thinking clearly."

"Yeah, I know. But I'm not leaving her, Jessica. You can argue all you want, but it won't make a damn bit of difference."

There was a short silence. Mary Jo heard a chair being dragged across the floor. It was coming toward her. "Mary Jo was leaving Boston, did you know?"

"I know," Evan returned. "Her mother called to tell me."

"Were you going to stop her?"

It took him a long time to answer. "No."

"But you love her."

"Jess, please, leave it alone."

Evan loved her and she loved him, and it was hopeless. A sob swelled within her chest and Mary Jo experienced a sudden urge to weep.

"She moved," Evan said sharply, excitedly. "Did you see it? Her hand flinched just now."

Mary Jo felt herself being pulled away once more into a void where there was no sound. It seemed to close in around her like the folds of a dark blanket.

When Mary Jo opened her eyes, the first thing she saw was a patch of blue. A moment later, she realized it was the sky outside the hospital window. A scattering of clouds shimmied across the horizon. She blinked, trying to figure out what she was doing in this bed, this room.

She'd been in a car accident, that was it. She couldn't remember any details—except that she'd thought she

was dying. Her head had hurt so badly. The throbbing
wasn't nearly as bad now, but it was still there and the
bright sunshine made her eyes water.

Rolling her head to the other side demanded a great
deal of effort. Her mother was sitting at her bedside
reading from a Bible and her father was standing on the
other side of the room. He pressed his hands against the
small of his back as if to relieve tired muscles.

"Mom." Mary Jo's voice was husky and low.

Marianna Summerhill vaulted to her feet. "Norman!
Norman, Mary Jo's awake." Having said that, she covered her face with her hands and burst into tears.

It was very unusual to see her mother cry. Mary Jo
looked at her father and saw that his eyes, too, were
brimming with tears.

"So you decided to rejoin the living," her father said,
raising her hand to his lips. "Welcome back."

Smiling required more strength than she had.

"How do you feel?" Her mother was dabbing at her
eyes with a tissue. She was so pale that Mary Jo wondered if she'd been ill herself.

"Weird," she said hoarsely.

"The doctor said he expected you to wake up soon."

There was so much she wanted to ask, so much she
had to say. "Evan?" she managed to croak.

"He was here," her mother answered. "From the moment he learned about the accident until just a few minutes ago. No one could convince him to leave."

"He's talking with some fancy specialist right now,"
her father explained. "I don't mind telling you, he's
been beside himself with worry. We've all been scared."

Her eyes drifted shut. She felt so incredibly weak,
and what energy she had evaporated quickly.

"Sleep," her mother cooed. "Everything's going to be fine."

No, no, Mary Jo protested, fighting sleep. Not yet. Not so soon. She had too many questions that needed answering. But the silence enveloped her once more.

It was night when she stirred again. The sky was dark and the heavens were flecked with stars. Moonlight softly illuminated the room.

She assumed she was alone, then noticed a shadowy figure against the wall. The still shape sat in the chair next to her bed. It was Evan, and he was asleep. His arms were braced against the edge of the mattress, supporting his head.

The comfort she felt in knowing he was with her was beyond measure. Reaching for his hand, she covered it with her own, then yawned and closed her eyes.

"Are you hungry?" Marianna asked, carrying in the hospital tray and setting it on the bedside table.

Mary Jo was sitting up for the first time. "I don't know," she said, surprised by how feeble her voice sounded.

"I talked to the doctor about the hospital menu," her mother said, giving her head a disparaging shake. "He assured me you'll survive on their cooking until I can get you home and feed you properly."

It probably wasn't all that amusing, but Mary Jo couldn't stop smiling. This was the first day she'd really taken note of her surroundings. The room was filled with fresh flowers. They covered every available surface; there were even half a dozen vases lined up on the floor.

"Who sent all the flowers?" she asked.

Her mother pointed toward the various floral arrangements. "Your brothers. Dad and I. Those two are from Jessica and Damian. Let me see—the teachers at your old school. Oh, the elaborate one is from the Drydens. That bouquet of pink carnations is from Gary."

"How sweet of everyone." But Mary Jo saw that there were a number of bouquets her mother had skipped. Those, she strongly suspected, were from Evan.

Evan.

Just thinking about him made her feel so terribly sad. From the time she'd regained consciousness, he'd stopped coming to the hospital. He'd been there earlier, she was sure of it. The memories were too vivid not to be real. But as soon as she was out of danger, he'd left her life once more.

"Eat something," Marianna insisted. "I know it's not your mama's cooking, but it doesn't look too bad."

Mary Jo shook her head and leaned back against the pillow. "I'm not hungry."

"Sweetheart, please. The doctors won't let you come home until you've regained your strength."

Evan wasn't the only one with a stubborn streak. She folded her arms and refused to even glance at the food. Eventually, she was persuaded to take a few bites, because it was clear her lack of appetite was distressing her mother.

When the tray was removed, Mary Jo slept. Her father was with her when she awoke. Her eyes met his, which were warm and tender.

"Was the accident my fault?" She had to know. She remembered so little of what had happened.

"No. The other car ran a red light."

"Was anyone else hurt?"

"No," he said, taking her hand in both of his.

"I'm sorry I worried you."

A slight smile crossed his face. "Your brothers were just as worried. And Evan."

"He was here, wasn't he?"

"Every minute. No one could get him to leave, not even his own family."

But he wasn't there now. When she really needed him.

Her father gently patted her hand, and when he spoke it was as if he'd been reading her thoughts. "Life has a way of making things right. Everything will turn out just like it's supposed to. So don't you fret about Evan or his family or anything else. Concentrate on getting well."

"I will." But her heart wasn't in it. Her heart was with Evan.

A week passed, and Mary Jo regained more of her strength each day. With her head shaved, she looked as if she'd stepped out of a science-fiction movie. All she needed were the right clothes and a laser gun and she'd be real Hollywood material.

If she continued to improve at this pace, she should be discharged from the hospital within the next few days. That was good news—not that she didn't appreciate the excellent care she'd received.

Mary Jo spent part of the morning slowly walking the corridors in an effort to rebuild her strength. She still tired easily and took frequent breaks to chat with nurses and other patients. After a pleasant but exhausting couple of hours, she decided to go back to bed for a while.

As she entered her room, she stopped abruptly. Lois Dryden stood by the window, looking out of place in her tailored suit.

Lois must have sensed her return. There was no disguising her dismay when she saw Mary Jo's shaved, bandaged head. She seemed incapable of speech for a moment.

Mary Jo took the initiative. "Hello, Mrs. Dryden," she said evenly.

"Hello, my dear. I hope you don't mind my dropping in like this."

"No, of course I don't mind." Mary Jo made her way to the bed and got in, conscious of her still-awkward movements.

"I was very sorry to hear about your accident."

Mary Jo adjusted the covers around her legs and leaned back against the raised mattress. "I'm well on the road to recovery now."

"That's what I understand. I heard there's a possibility you'll be going home soon."

"I hope so."

"Is there anything I can do for you?"

The offer surprised Mary Jo. "No, but thank you."

Lois walked away from the window and stood at the foot of the bed, the picture of conventional propriety with her small hat and spotless white gloves. She looked directly at Mary Jo.

"I understand Jessica has come by a number of times," she said.

"Yes," Mary Jo responded. "She's been very kind. She brought me some books and magazines." Except that Mary Jo hadn't been able to concentrate on any of them. No sooner would she begin reading than she'd drift off to sleep.

"I suppose Jessica told you she and Damian are expecting again."

Without warning, Mary Jo's heart contracted painfully. "Yes. I'm delighted for them."

"Naturally, Walter and I are thrilled with the prospect of a second grandchild."

It became important not to look at Evan's mother, and Mary Jo focused her gaze out the window. The tightness in her chest wouldn't go away, and she knew the source of the pain was emotional. She longed for a child herself. Evan's child. They'd talked about their home, planned their family. The picture of the house he'd described, with a yard full of laughing, playing children flashed into her mind.

That house would never be built now. There would be no children. No marriage. No Evan.

"Of course, Damian's beside himself with happiness."

Somewhere deep inside, Mary Jo found the strength to say, "I imagine he is."

"There'll be a little less than two years between the children. Andrew will be twenty months old by the time the baby's born."

Mary Jo wondered why Mrs. Dryden was telling her all this and could think of nothing more to say. She found the conversation exhausting. She briefly closed her eyes.

"I... I suppose I shouldn't tire you anymore."

"Thank you for stopping by," Mary Jo murmured politely.

Lois stepped toward the door, then hesitated and turned back to the bed. Mary Jo noticed that the older woman's hand trembled as she reached out and gripped the foot of the bed.

"Is something the matter?" Mary Jo asked, thinking perhaps she should ring for the nurse.

"Yes," Evan's mother said. "Something is very much the matter—and I'm the one at fault. You came to me not long ago because you wanted to marry my son. I discouraged you, and Evan, too, when he came to speak to his father and me."

"Mrs. Dryden, please—"

"No, let me finish." She took a deep breath and leveled her gaze on Mary Jo. "Knowing what I do now, I would give everything I have if you'd agree to marry my son."

Chapter 10

Mary Jo wasn't sure she'd heard Evan's mother correctly. "I don't understand."

Instinctively, she knew that Mrs. Dryden was someone who rarely revealed her emotions. She knew the older woman rarely lost control of a situation—or of herself. She seemed dangerously close to losing it now.

"Would...would you mind if I sat down?"

"Please do." Mary Jo wished she'd suggested it herself.

Lois pulled the chair closer to the bed, and Mary Jo was surprised by how delicate, how fragile, she suddenly appeared. "Before I say anything more, I must ask your forgiveness."

"Mine?"

"Yes, my dear. When you came to me, happy and excited, to discuss marrying my son, I was impressed by your…your courage. Your sense of responsibility. You'd guessed my feelings correctly when Evan brought you to dinner three or so years ago. Although you were a delightful young woman, I couldn't picture you as his wife. My son, however, was enthralled with you."

Mary Jo started to speak, but Mrs. Dryden shook her head, obviously determined to finish her confession. "I decided that very night that it was important for us to talk. I'd never intended to hurt you or Evan, and when I learned you were no longer seeing each other, I realized it might have had something to do with what I'd said to you."

"Mrs. Dryden, please, this isn't necessary."

"On the contrary. It's very necessary. If you're to be my daughter-in-law, and I sincerely hope you will be, then I feel it's vital for us to…to begin afresh."

Mary Jo's pulse began to hammer with excitement. "You meant what you said earlier, then? About wanting me to marry Evan?"

"Every word. Once we know each other a little better, you'll learn I almost never say what I don't mean. Now, please, allow me to continue."

"Of course. I'm sorry."

Mrs. Dryden gave her an ironic smile. "Once we're on more familiar terms, you won't need to be so apprehensive of me. I'm hoping we can be friends, Mary Jo. After all, I pray you'll be the mother of my grandchildren." She smiled again. "Half of them, anyway."

Mary Jo blinked back tears, deeply moved by the other woman's unmistakable contrition and generosity.

"Now…where was I? Oh, yes, we were talking about three years ago. You and Evan had decided not to see each other again, and frankly—forgive me for this,

Mary Jo—I was relieved. But Evan seemed to take the breakup very badly. I recognized then that I might have acted too hastily. For months, I contemplated calling you myself. I'm ashamed to tell you I kept putting it off. No," she said and her voice shook, "I was a coward. I dreaded facing you."

"Mrs. Dryden, it was a long time ago."

"You're right, it was, but that doesn't lessen my guilt." She paused. "Evan changed that autumn. He'd always been such a lighthearted young man. He still joked and teased, but it wasn't the same. The happiness had gone out of his eyes. Nothing held his interest for long. He drifted from one brief relationship to another. He was miserable, and it showed."

In those bleak, lonely months, Mary Jo hadn't fared much better, but she said nothing about that now.

"It was during this time that Walter decided to run for the Senate, and our lives were turned upside down. Our one concern was Evan. The election was important to Walter, and in some ways, Evan was a problem. Walter discussed the situation with him— Oh, dear. None of this applies to the present situation. I'm getting sidetracked."

"No. Go on," Mary Jo pleaded.

"I have to admit I'm not proud of what we did. Walter and I felt strongly that Jessica Kellerman was the right woman for Evan, and we did what we could to encourage a relationship. As you know, Damian and Jessica fell in love. You'd think I'd have learned my lesson about interfering in my sons' lives, but apparently not."

Mary Jo wished she could say something to reassure Lois.

"Early this summer, Walter and I noticed a...new

happiness in Evan. He seemed more like he used to be. Later we learned that you were working for him. I decided then and there that if you two decided to rekindle your romance, I'd do nothing to stand in your way."

"You didn't," Mary Jo said quickly.

"Then you came to me and insisted on a small, private wedding. It was obvious you didn't understand the social demands made of a husband in politics. I could see you were getting discouraged, and I did nothing to reassure you. At the time it seemed for the best."

"Mrs. Dryden, you're taking on far more blame than you should."

"That's not all, Mary Jo." She clutched her purse with both gloved hands and hung her head. "Evan came to speak to Walter and me about the two of you. I don't believe I've ever seen him so angry. No other woman has ever held such power over my son. You see, Evan and I've always been close and it...pains me to admit this, but I was jealous. I told him that if you were willing to break off another engagement over the first disagreement, then you weren't the woman for him.

"I must've been more persuasive than I realized. Later Evan told me he couldn't fight both of us and that he'd decided to abide by your wishes."

"He said that to me, too," Mary Jo murmured.

"It's been several weeks now, but nothing's changed. My son still loves you very much. After your accident, he refused to leave the hospital. I came here myself early one morning and found Evan sitting alone in the hospital chapel." She paused and her lower lip trembled. "I knew then that you weren't some passing fancy in his life. He loves you as he's never loved another woman and probably won't again."

Mary Jo leaned forward. "I'll never be comfortable in the limelight, Mrs. Dryden," she said urgently. "But I'm willing to do whatever it takes to be the kind of wife Evan needs."

Mrs. Dryden snapped open her purse, took out a delicate white handkerchief and dabbed her eyes. "It's time for another confession, I'm afraid. I've always believed Evan would do well in politics. I've made no secret of my ambitions for my son, but that's what they were—*my* ambitions. Not his. If Evan does decide to pursue a political career, it should be his decision, not mine.

"In light of everything that's taken place, I'm determined to stay out of it entirely. Whatever happens now depends on Evan. On you, too, of course," she added hurriedly, "but I promise you, I won't interfere. I've finally learned my lesson."

Unable to speak, Mary Jo reached for the other woman's hand and held it tightly.

"I'd like it if we could be friends, Mary Jo," Lois added softly. "I'll do my damnedest to stop being an interfering old woman."

"My mother learned her lessons with my oldest brother, Jack, and his wife. You might like to speak to her sometime and swap stories," Mary Jo suggested.

"I'd like that." She stood and bent to kiss Mary Jo's cheek. "You'll go to Evan, then, when you're able?"

Mary Jo grinned. "As soon as I look a bit more presentable."

"You'll look wonderful to Evan now, believe me." The older woman touched her hand softly. "Make him happy, Mary Jo."

"I'll do my best."

"And please let me know when your mother and I

can talk. We have a million things to discuss about the wedding."

Mary Jo ventured, a bit hesitantly, "The wedding will be small and private."

"Whatever you decide."

"But perhaps we could have a big reception afterward and invite the people you wouldn't want to offend by excluding them."

"An excellent idea." Lois smiled broadly.

"Thank you for coming to see me."

A tear formed in the corner of Lois's eye. "No. Thank *you,* my dear."

From the day of Lois Dryden's visit, Mary Jo's recovery was little short of miraculous. She was discharged two days later and spent a week recuperating at her parents' home before she felt ready to confront Evan.

According to Jessica, he was frequently out on his sailboat. With her friend's help, it was a simple matter to discover when he'd scheduled an outing.

Saturday morning, the sun was bright and the wind brisk—a perfect sailing day. Mary Jo went down to the marina. Using Damian's key, she let herself in and climbed aboard Evan's boat to wait for him.

She hadn't been there long when he arrived. He must've seen her right away, although he gave no outward indication that he had.

She still felt somewhat uncomfortable about her hair, now half an inch long. She'd tried to disguise it with a turban, but that only made her look as if she should be reading palms or tea leaves. So she left it unadorned.

"Mary Jo?"

"It's hard to tell without the hair, right?" she joked.

"What are you doing here?" Evan wasn't unfriendly, but he didn't seem particularly pleased to see her.

"I wanted to talk, and this is the place we do our best talking. Are you taking the boat out this morning?"

He ignored the question. "How are you?" The craft rocked gently as he climbed on deck and sat down beside her.

"Much better. Still kind of weak, but I'm gaining strength every day."

"When were you released from the hospital?"

Evan knew the answer as well as she did, Mary Jo was sure. Why was he making small talk at a time like this?

"You already know. Your mother told you, or Jessica." She paused. "You were at the hospital, Evan."

His mouth tightened, but he said nothing.

"There were periods when I could hear what was going on around me. I was awake, sort of, when you first got there. Another time, I heard you pacing my room, and I heard you again when Jessica came by once." She took Evan's hand and threaded her fingers through his. "One of the first times I actually woke was in the middle of the night, and you were there, asleep."

"I've never been more frightened in my life," he said hoarsely, as if the words had been wrenched from his throat. He slid his arms around her then, but gently, with deliberate care. Mary Jo rested her head against his shoulder, and his grip on her tightened just a little. He buried his face in the curve of her shoulder; she felt his warm strength. After a moment, he let her go.

"I understand my parents' investment was returned to them—with interest," she said, her tone deceptively casual.

"Yes," he admitted. "They were among the fortunate few to have their money refunded."

"*Their* money?" She raised his hand to her mouth, kissing his knuckles. "Evan, I know what you did."

He frowned. He had that confused, what-are-you-talking-about expression down to an art.

"You might've been able to get away with it but, you see, the papers came."

"What papers?"

"The day of my accident my parents received a notice from the bankruptcy court—as I'm sure you know. If their investment had been returned, how do you explain that?"

He shrugged. "Don't have a clue."

"Evan, please, it's not necessary to play games with me."

He seemed to feel a sudden need to move around. He stood, stretched and walked to the far end of the sailboat. Pointedly, he glanced at his watch. "I wish I had time to chat, but unfortunately I'm meeting a friend."

"Evan, we need to talk."

"I'm sorry, but you should've let me know sooner. Perhaps we could get together some other time." He made an elaborate display of staring at the pier, then smiling and waving eagerly.

A tall, blond woman, incredibly slender and beautifully tanned, waved back. She had the figure of a fashion model and all but purred when Evan hopped out of the boat and met her dockside. She threw her arms around his neck and kissed him, bending one shapely leg at the knee.

Mary Jo was stunned. To hear his mother speak, Evan was a lost, lonely man, so in love with her that his world had fallen apart. Clearly, there was something Mrs. Dryden didn't know.

In her rush to climb out of the sailboat, Mary Jo practically fell overboard. With her nearly bald head and the clothes that hung on her because of all the weight she'd lost, she felt like the little match girl standing barefoot in the snow. Especially beside this paragon of feminine perfection.

She suffered through an introduction that she didn't hear, made her excuses and promptly left. When she was back in her car, she slumped against the steering wheel, covering her face with both hands.

Shaken and angry, she returned to her parents' place and called Jessica to tell her what had happened. She was grateful her parents were out.

Mary Jo paced the living room in an excess of nervous energy until Jessica came to the house an hour later, looking flustered. "Sorry it took me so long, but I took a cab and it turned out to be the driver's first day on the job. We got lost twice. So what's going on?" She sighed. "I don't know what I'm going to do with the two of you."

Mary Jo described the situation in great detail, painting vivid word pictures of the other woman.

Jessica rolled her eyes. "And you *fell* for it?"

"Fell for what?" Mary Jo cried. "Bambi was all over him. I didn't need anyone to spell it out. I was mortified. Good grief," she said, battling down a sob, "look at me. Last week's vegetable casserole has more hair than I do."

Jessica laughed outright. "Mary Jo, be sensible. The man loves you."

"Yeah, I could tell," she muttered.

"Her name's Barbara, not that it matters. Trust me, she doesn't mean a thing to him."

The doorbell chimed and the two women stared at each other. "Are you expecting company?"

"No."

Jessica lowered her voice. "Do you think it could be Evan?"

On her way to the door, Mary Jo shook her head dismally. "I doubt it."

"Just in case, I'd better hide." Jessica backed out of the room and into the kitchen.

To her complete surprise, Mary Jo found Lois Dryden at the door.

"What happened?" the older woman demanded.

Mary Jo opened the door and let her inside. "Happened?"

"With Evan."

"Jessica," Mary Jo called over her shoulder. "You can come out now. It's a Dryden, but it isn't Evan."

"Jessica's here?" Lois said.

"Yes," Jessica said. "But what are *you* doing here?"

"Checking up on Mary Jo. I got a call from Damian. All he said was that he suspected things hadn't gone well with Evan and Mary Jo this morning. He said Mary Jo had phoned and Jessica had hurried out shortly afterward. I want to know what went wrong."

"It's a long story," Mary Jo said reluctantly.

"I tried calling you," Lois explained, "then realized you must still be staying with your family. I was going out, anyway, and I thought this might be an excellent opportunity to meet your mother."

"She's out just now." Mary Jo exhaled shakily and gestured at the sofa. "Sit down, please."

Her parents' house lacked the obvious wealth and luxury of Whispering Willows, but anyone who stepped inside immediately felt welcome. A row of high-school graduation pictures sat proudly on the fireplace mantel. Photos of the grandchildren were scattered about the room. The far wall was lined with bookcases, but some shelves held more trophies than books.

"So you went to see Evan this morning," his mother said, regarding her anxiously. "I take it the meeting was…not a success?"

"Evan had a *date,*" Mary Jo said, glancing sharply at Jessica.

"Hey," Jessica muttered, "all you asked me to do was find out the next time he was going sailing. How was I supposed to know he was meeting another woman?"

"Who?" Lois asked, frowning.

"Barbara," Mary Jo said.

Lois made a dismissive gesture with her hand. "Oh, yes, I know who she is. She's a fashion model who flies in from New York every now and then. You have nothing to worry about."

"A fashion model." Mary Jo's spirits hit the floor.

"She's really not important to him."

"That may be so," Mary Jo pointed out, "but he certainly seemed pleased to see her." Depressed, she slouched down on the sofa and braced her feet against the edge of the coffee table.

Lois's back stiffened. "It seems to me I'd better have a chat with that boy."

"Mother!" Jessica cried at the same moment Mary Jo yelped in protest.

"You promised you weren't going to interfere, remember?" Jessica reminded her mother-in-law. "It only leads to trouble. If Evan wants to make a fool of himself, we're going to have to let him."

"I disagree," Lois said. "You're right, of course, about my talking to him—that would only make matters worse—but we can't allow Mary Jo to let him think he's getting away with this."

"What do you suggest we do?" Jessica asked.

Lois bit her bottom lip. "I don't know, but I'll think of something."

"Time-out," Mary Jo said, forming a *T* with her hands—a technique she often used with her kindergarten class. "I appreciate your willingness to help, but I'd really like to do my own plotting, okay? Don't be offended, but…" Her words trailed off, and her expression turned to one of pleading.

Jessica smiled and took for her hand. "Of course," she said.

Mary Jo looked at Lois, and the woman nodded. "You're absolutely right, my dear. I'll keep my nose out." She reached over and gave Mary Jo a hug.

"Thank you," Mary Jo whispered.

Mary Jo didn't hear from Evan at all the following week. She tried to tell herself she wasn't disappointed—but of course she was. When it became clear that he was content to leave things between them as they were, she composed a short letter and mailed it to him at his office. After all, it was a business matter.

Without elaborating, she suggested she work for him the next four summers as compensation for the money he'd given her parents.

Knowing exactly when he received his morning mail, she waited anxiously by her phone. It didn't take long.

His temporary personal assistant phoned and set up an appointment for the next morning. By the time she hung up the receiver, Mary Jo was downright gleeful.

The day of her appointment, she dressed in her best suit and high heels, and arrived promptly at eleven. His personal assistant escorted her into his office.

Evan was at his desk, writing on a legal pad, and didn't look up until the other woman had left the room.

"So, is there a problem?" she asked flatly.

"*Should* there be a problem?"

She lifted one shoulder. "I can't imagine why you'd ask to see me otherwise. I can only assume it has something to do with my letter."

He leaned back in his chair and rolled a gold pen between his palms. "Where did you come up with this harebrained idea that I forked over fifty thousand dollars to your mother and father."

"Evan, I'm not stupid. I know exactly what you did. And I know why."

"I doubt that."

"I think it was very sweet, but I can't allow you to do it."

"Mary Jo—"

"I believe my suggestion will suit us both nicely. Mrs. Sterling would love having the summers free to travel. If I remember correctly, her husband recently retired, and unless she has the freedom to do as she'd like now and then, you're going to lose her."

Evan said nothing, so she went on, "I worked out all right while I was here, didn't I? Well, other than losing that one file, which wasn't my fault. Naturally, I hope you won't continue trying to make me jealous. It almost worked, you know."

"I'm afraid I don't know what you're talking about."

"Oh, Evan," she said with an exaggerated sigh. "You must think I'm a complete fool."

He arched his thick brows. "As it happens, I do."

She ignored that. "Do you honestly believe you could convince me you're attracted to…to Miss August? I know you better than you think, Evan Dryden."

His lips quivered slightly with the beginnings of a smile, but he managed to squelch it immediately.

"Are you agreeable to my solution?" she asked hopefully.

"No," he said.

The bluntness of his reply took her by surprise and her head snapped back. "No?"

"You don't owe me a penny."

At least he wasn't trying to get her to believe the money came from Adison Investments.

"But I can't let you do this!"

"Why not?" He gave the appearance of growing bored. Slumped in his chair, he held the pen at each end and twirled it between his thumb and index finger.

"It isn't right. You don't owe them anything, and if they knew, they'd return it instantly."

"You won't tell them." Although he didn't raise his voice, the tone was determined.

"No, I won't," she admitted, knowing it would devastate her parents, "but only if you allow me to reimburse you myself."

He shook his head. "No deal."

Mary Jo knew he could be stubborn, but this was ridiculous. "Evan, please, I *want* to do it."

"The money was a gift from me to them, sent anonymously with no strings attached. And your plan to substitute for Mrs. Sterling—it *didn't* work out this summer. What makes you think it will in the future? As far as I'm concerned, this issue about the money is pure nonsense. I suggest we drop it entirely." He set the pen down on his desk, as if signaling the end of the conversation.

Nonsense. Mary Jo reached for her purse. "Apparently we don't have anything more to say to each other."

"Apparently not," he agreed without emotion.

Mary Jo stood and, with her head high, walked out of the office. It wasn't until she got to the elevator that the trembling started.

"Are you going to tell me what's bothering you?" Marianna asked Mary Jo. They were sitting at the small kitchen table shelling fresh peas Marianna had purchased from the local farmers' market. Both women quickly and methodically removed the peas from their pods and tossed them into a blue ceramic bowl.

"I'm fine," Mary Jo insisted, even though it was next to impossible to fool her mother. After years of raising children and then dealing with grandchildren, Marianna Summerhill had an uncanny knack of recognizing when something was wrong with any of her family.

"Physically, yes," her mother agreed. "But you're troubled. I can see it in your eyes."

Mary Jo shrugged.

"If I was guessing, I'd say it had something to do with Evan. You haven't seen hide nor hair of him in two weeks."

Evan. The name alone was enough to evoke a flood of unhappiness. "I just don't understand it!" Mary Jo cried. "To hear his mother talk, you'd think he was fading away for want of me."

"He isn't?"

"Hardly. He's dated a different woman every night this week."

"He was mentioned in some gossip column in the paper this morning. Do you know anything about a Barbara Jackson?"

"Yes." Mary Jo clamped her lips together. If he was flaunting his romantic escapades in an effort to make her jealous, he'd succeeded.

"I imagine you're annoyed."

"'Annoyed' isn't it." She snapped a pea pod so hard, the peas scattered across the table like marbles shooting over a polished hardwood floor. Her mother's smile did nothing to soothe her wounded pride. "What I don't get," she muttered, "is *why* he's doing this."

"You haven't figured that out yet?" Marianna asked, her raised voice indicating her surprise. The peas slid effortlessly from the pod to the bowl.

"No, I haven't got a clue. Have *you* figured it out?"

"Ages ago," the older woman said casually.

Mary Jo jerked her head toward her mother. "What do you mean?"

"You're a bright girl, Mary Jo, but when it comes to Evan, I have to wonder."

The words shook her. "What do you mean? I *love* Evan!"

"Not so I can tell." This, too, was said casually.

Mary Jo pushed her mound of pea pods aside and stared at her mother. "Mom, how can you say that?"

"Easy. Evan isn't sure you love him. Why should he be? He—"

Mary Jo was outraged. "Not sure I love him? I can't believe I'm hearing this from my own mother!"

"It's true," Marianna continued, her fingers working rhythmically and without pause. "Looking at it from Evan's point of view, I can't say I blame him."

As the youngest in a big family, Mary Jo had had some shocking things said to her over the years, but never by her own mother. And never this calmly—as if they were merely discussing the price of fresh fruit.

Her first reaction had been defensive, but she was beginning to realize that maybe Marianna knew something she didn't. "I don't understand how Evan could possibly believe I don't love him."

"It's not so hard to understand," Marianna answered smoothly. "Twice you've claimed to love him enough to marry him, and both times you've changed your mind."

"But—"

"You've turned your back on him when you were confronted with any resistance from his family. You've never really given him the opportunity to answer your doubts. My feeling is, Evan would've stood by you come hell or high water, but I wonder if the reverse is true."

"You make it sound so…so simple, but our situation is a lot more difficult than you understand."

"Possibly."

"His family is *formidable*."

"I don't doubt that for an instant," came Marianna's sincere reply. "Let me ask you one thing, though, and I want you to think carefully before you answer. Do you love Evan enough to stand up to opposition, no matter what form it takes?"

"Yes," Mary Jo answered heatedly.

Marianna's eyes brightened with her wide smile. "Then what are you going to do about it?"

"Do?" Mary Jo had tried twice and been thwarted by his pride with each attempt. One thing was certain—Evan had no intention of making this easy for her.

"It seems to me that if you love this man, you're not going to take no for an answer. Unless, of course..." Her mother hesitated.

"Unless what?"

"Unless Evan isn't as important to you as you claim."

Chapter 11

Mary Jo pushed up the sleeves of her light sweater and paced the floor of her living room. Her mother's comments about the way she'd treated Evan still grated. But what bothered her most was that her mother was right.

No wonder Evan had all but ignored her. He couldn't trust her not to turn her back and run at the first sign of trouble. After all her talk of being older, wiser and more mature, Mary Jo had to admit she was as sadly lacking in those qualities as she'd been three years before. And she was furious.

With herself.

What she needed now was a way to prove her love to Evan so he'd never have cause to doubt her again. One problem was that she had no idea how long it would take for that opportunity to present itself. It might be months—maybe even another three long years. Mary

Jo was unwilling to wait. Evan would just have to take her at her word.

But why should he, in light of their past? If he refused, Mary Jo couldn't very well blame him. She sighed, wondering distractedly what to do next.

She could call Jessica, who'd been more than generous with advice. But Mary Jo realized that all Jessica could tell her was what she already knew. Mary Jo needed to talk to Evan herself, face-to-face, no holds barred.

Deciding there was no reason to postpone what had to be done, she carefully chose her outfit—a peach-colored pantsuit with gold buttons, along with a soft turquoise scarf and dangly gold earrings.

When she arrived at his office, Mary Jo was pleasantly surprised to find Mrs. Sterling.

"Oh, my, don't you look lovely this afternoon," the older woman said with a delighted smile. She seemed relaxed and happy; the trip had obviously done her good.

"So do you, Mrs. Sterling. When did you get back?"

"Just this week. I heard about your accident. I'm so pleased everything turned out all right."

"So am I. Is Evan in?"

"I'm sorry, no, but I expect him any time. Why don't you make yourself at home there in his office? I'll bring you some coffee. I don't think he'll be more than a few minutes."

"Thanks, I will." Mary Jo walked into the office and sank onto the sofa. In her determination to see this through, she naively hadn't considered the possibility of Evan's being out of the office. And she was afraid that the longer she waited, the more her courage would falter.

She was sipping the coffee Mrs. Sterling had brought her and lecturing herself, trying to bolster her courage, when she heard Evan come in. Her hands trembled as she set the cup aside.

By the time Evan strolled into the room, still rattling off a list of instructions for Mrs. Sterling, Mary Jo's shoulders were tensed.

His personal assistant finished making her notes. "You have a visitor," she announced, smiling approvingly in Mary Jo's direction.

Evan sent a look over his shoulder, but revealed no emotion when he saw who it was. "Hello, Mary Jo."

"Evan." She pressed her palms over her knees, certain she must resemble a schoolgirl feeling the principal after some misdemeanor. "I'd like to talk to you, if I may."

He frowned and glanced at his watch.

"Your schedule is free," Mrs. Sterling said emphatically, and when she walked away, she closed the door.

"Well, it seems I can spare a few minutes," Evan said without enthusiasm as he moved behind his desk and sat down.

Mary Jo left the sofa and took the chair across from him. "First I'd like to apologize."

"No," he said roughly. "There's nothing to apologize for."

"But there is," she told him. "Oh, Evan, I've nearly ruined everything."

His eyebrows rose, and his expression was skeptical. "Come now, Mary Jo."

She slid forward in her seat. "It all started the summer we met when—"

"That was years ago, and if you don't mind, I'd prefer to leave it there." He reached for his gold pen, as if he needed to hold on to something. "Rehashing it all isn't going to help either of us."

"I disagree." Mary Jo would not be so easily discouraged this time. "We need to clear up the past. Otherwise once we're married—"

"It seems to me you're taking a lot for granted," he said sharply.

"Perhaps, but I doubt it."

"Mary Jo, I can't see how this will get us anywhere."

"I do," she said hurriedly. "Please listen to what I have to say, and if you still feel the same afterward, then…well, I'll just say it another way until you're willing to accept that I love you."

His eyebrows rose again. "I have a date this evening."

"Then I'll talk fast, but I think you should know you aren't fooling me."

"Do you think I'm lying?"

"Of course not. You may very well have arranged an evening with some woman, but it's me you love."

His handsome features darkened in a frown, but she took heart from the fact that he didn't contradict her.

Mary Jo studied her own watch. "How much time do I have before you need to leave?"

Evan shrugged. "Enough."

He wasn't doing anything to encourage her, but that was fine; she knew what she wanted, and she wasn't going to let a little thing like a bad attitude stand in her way.

It took her a few mintes to organize her thoughts

and remember what she'd so carefully planned to say. Perhaps that was for the best. She didn't want to sound as if she'd practiced in front of a mirror, although she'd done exactly that.

"You were saying?" Evan murmured.

She bit her lip. "Yes. I wanted to talk to you about the house."

"What house?" he asked impatiently.

"The one with the seven bedrooms. The one we've discussed in such detail that I can see it clear as anything. The house I want to live in with you and our children."

She noticed that his eyes drifted away from hers.

"I've been doing a lot of thinking lately," Mary Jo continued. "It all started when I was feeling sorry for myself, certain that I'd lost you. I...found the thought almost unbearable."

"You get accustomed to it after a while," he muttered dryly.

"I never will," she said adamantly, "not ever again."

He leaned forward in his chair as if to see her better. "What brought about this sudden change of heart?"

"It isn't sudden. Well, maybe it is. You see, it's my mother. She—"

"Are you sure it wasn't *my* mother? She seems to have her hand in just about everything that goes on between you and me."

"Not anymore." This was something else Mary Jo wanted to correct. "According to Jessica, your mother's been beside herself wondering what's going on with us. We have to give her credit, Evan—she hasn't called or pressured me once. She promised she wouldn't, and your mother's a woman of her word."

"Exactly what did she promise?"

"Not to meddle in our lives. She came to me when I was still in the hospital, and we had a wonderful talk. Some of the problems between us were of my own making. Your mother intimidated me, and I was afraid to go against her. But after our talk, I understand her a little better and she understands me."

She waited for him to make some comment, but was disappointed. From all outward appearances, Evan was merely enduring this discussion, waiting for her to finish so he could get on with his life.

"I'm not Lois's first choice for a daughter-in-law. There are any number of other women who'd be a far greater asset to you and your political future than I'll ever be."

"I'm dating one now."

The information was like a slap in the face, but Mary Jo revealed none of her feelings.

"Above and beyond anything else, your mother wants your happiness, and she believes, as I do, that our being together will provide that."

"Nice of her to confer with me. It seems the two of you—and let's not forget dear Jessica—have joined forces. You're all plotting against me."

"Absolutely not. I've talked to Jessica, but not recently. It was my mother who helped me understand what was wrong."

"And now *she's* involved." He rolled his eyes as if to say there were far too many mothers interfering in his life.

"All my mother did was point out a few truths. If anything, we should thank her. She told me you've got good reason to question the strength of my love for you.

I was floored that my own mother could suggest something like that. Especially since she knew how unhappy and miserable I've been."

The hint of a smile lifted his mouth.

"Mom said if I loved you as much as I claim to, I would've stood by your side despite any opposition. She…she said if our situations had been reversed, you would've stood by me. I gave up on you too easily, and, Evan, I can't tell you how much I regret it." She lowered her gaze to her hands. "If I could undo the past, step back three years—or even three weeks—I'd do anything to prove how much I love you. I believe in you, Evan, and I believe in our love. Never again will I give you cause to doubt it. Furthermore—"

"You mean there's more?" He sounded bored, as if this was taking much longer than he'd expected.

"Just a little," she said, and her voice wavered with the strength of her conviction. "You're going to make a wonderful member of city council, and I'll do whatever's necessary to see that it happens. It won't be easy for me to be the focus of public attention, but in time, I'll learn not to be so nervous. Your mother's already volunteered to help me. I can do this, Evan, I know I can. Another three or four years down the road, I'll be a pro in front of the cameras. Just wait and see."

He didn't speak, and Mary Jo could feel every beat of her heart in the silence that followed.

"That's all well and good," Evan finally said, "but I don't see how it changes anything."

"You don't?" She vaulted to her feet. "Do you love me or not?" she demanded.

He regarded her with a look of utter nonchalance. "Frankly, I don't know what I feel for you anymore."

In slow motion, Mary Jo sank back into her seat. She'd lost him. She could see it in his eyes, in the way he looked at her as if she was nothing to him anymore. Someone he'd loved once, a long time ago, but that was all.

"I see," she mumbled.

"Now, if you'll excuse me, I have some business I need to attend to."

"Ah…" The shock of his rejection had numbed her, and it took her a moment to get to her feet. She clutched her purse protectively to her stomach. "I… I'm sorry to have bothered you." She drew on the little that remained of her pride and dignity to carry her across the room.

"No bother," Evan said tonelessly.

It was at that precise moment that Mary Jo knew. She couldn't have explained exactly how, but she *knew*. Relief washed over her like the warm blast of a shower after a miserable day in the cold. *He loved her.* He'd always loved her.

Confident now, she turned around to face him.

He was busily writing on a legal pad and didn't look up.

"Evan." She whispered his name.

He ignored her.

"You love me."

His hand trembled slightly, but that was all the emotion he betrayed.

"It isn't going to work," she said, walking toward him.

"I beg your pardon?" He sighed heavily.

"This charade. I don't know what you're trying to prove, but it isn't working. It never will. You couldn't have sat by my hospital bed all those hours and felt nothing for me. You couldn't have given my parents that money and not cared for me."

"I didn't say I didn't care. But as you said yourself, sometimes love isn't enough."

"Then I was wrong," she muttered. "Now listen. My mother and yours are champing at the bit to start planning our wedding. What do you want me to tell them? That the whole thing's off and you don't love me anymore? You don't honestly expect anyone to believe that, do you? *I* don't."

"Believe what you want."

She closed her eyes for a moment. "You're trying my patience, Evan, but don't think you can get me to change my mind." She moved closer. There was more than one way of proving her point. More than one way to kick the argument out from under him. And she wasn't going to let this opportunity pass her by.

She stepped over to his desk and planted both hands on it, leaning over the top so that only a few inches separated their faces. "All right, Dryden, you asked for this."

His eyes narrowed as she edged around the desk. His head followed her movements. He turned in his chair, watching her speculatively.

Just then she threw herself on his lap, wound her arms around his neck and kissed him. She felt his surprise and his resistance, but the latter vanished almost the instant her mouth settled over his.

It'd been so long since they'd kissed. So long since she'd experienced the warm comfort of his embrace.

Groaning, Evan kissed her back. His mouth was tentative at first, then hard and intense. His hold tightened and a frightening kind of excitement began to grow in-

side her. As she clung to him, she could feel his heart
beating as fast as hers, his breathing as labored.

Cradling his face with her hands, she spread eager,
loving kisses over his mouth, his jaw, his forehead. "I
love you, Evan Dryden."

"This isn't just gratitude?"

She paused and lifted her head. "For what?"

"The money I gave your family."

"No," she said, teasing a corner of his mouth with
the tip of her tongue. "But that *is* something we need
to discuss."

"No, we don't." He tilted her so that she was practically lying across his lap. "I have a proposition to
make."

"Decent or indecent?" she asked with a pretended
leer.

"That's for you to decide."

She looped her arms around his neck again, hoisted
herself upright and pressed her head against his shoulder.

"You'll marry me?" he asked.

"Oh, yes—" she sighed with happiness "—and soon.
Evan, let's make this the shortest engagement on record."

"On one condition. You never mention that money
again."

"But—"

"Those are my terms." He punctuated his statement
with a kiss so heated it seared her senses.

When it ended, Mary Jo had difficulty breathing normally. "Your terms?" she repeated in a husky whisper.

"Do you agree, or don't you?"

Before she could answer, he swept away her defenses

and any chance of argument with another kiss. By the time he'd finished, Mary Jo discovered she would have concurred with just about anything. She nodded numbly.

Evan held her against him and exhaled deeply. "We'll make our own wedding plans, understood?"

Mary Jo stared at him blankly.

"This is our wedding and not my mother's—or your mother's."

She smiled and lowered her head to his shoulder. "Understood."

They were silent for several minutes, each savoring the closeness.

"Mom was right, wasn't she?" Mary Jo asked softly. "About how I needed to prove that my love's more than words."

"If you'd walked out that door, I might always have wondered," Evan confessed, then added, "You wouldn't have gotten far. I would've come running after you, but I'm glad I didn't have to."

"I've been such a fool." Mary Jo lovingly traced the side of his neck with her tongue.

"I'll give you fifty or sixty years to make it up to me, with time off for good behavior." He paused, then said, "You've made a concession to my career, and I'm going to do the same. I know you love teaching and if you want to continue, it's fine with me."

The happiness on her face blossomed into a full smile. She raised her head and waited until their eyes met before she lowered her mouth to his. The kiss was long, slow and thorough. Evan drew in a deep breath when it was over.

"What was that for?"

"To seal our bargain. From this day forward, Evan

Dryden, we belong to each other. Nothing will ever come between us again."

"Nothing," he agreed readily.

The door opened and Mrs. Sterling poked her head in. "I just wanted to make sure everything worked out," she said, smiling broadly. "I can see that it has. I couldn't be more pleased."

"Neither could I," Mary Jo said.

Evan drew her mouth back to his and Mary Jo heard the office door click shut in the background.

Epilogue

Three years later

"Andrew, don't wake Bethanne!" Jessica called out to her four-year-old son.

Mary Jo laughed as she watched the child bend to kiss her newborn daughter's forehead. "Look, they're already kissing cousins."

"How are you feeling?" Jessica asked, carrying a tall glass of iced tea over to Mary Jo, who was sitting under the shade of the patio umbrella.

"Wonderful."

"Evan is thrilled with Bethanne, isn't he?"

"Oh, yes. He reminded me of Damian when you had Lori Jo. You'd think we were the only two women in the world to ever have given birth."

Jessica laughed and shook her head. "And then the grandparents…"

"I don't know about you," Mary Jo teased, "but I could become accustomed to all this attention."

Jessica eyed her disbelievingly.

"All right, all right. I'll admit I was a bit flustered when the mayor paid me a visit in the hospital. And it was kind of nice to receive flowers from all those special-interest groups—the ones who think Evan is easily influenced. Clearly, they don't know my husband."

Jessica sighed and relaxed in her lounge chair. "You've done so well with all this. Evan's told Damian and me at least a hundred times that you as much as won that council position for him."

Mary Jo laughed off the credit. "Don't be silly."

"You were the one who walked up to the microphone at that rally and said anyone who believed Evan wasn't there for the worker, should talk to you or your family."

Mary Jo remembered the day well. She'd been furious to hear Evan's opponent state that Evan didn't understand the problems of the everyday working person. Evan had answered the accusation, but it was Mary Jo's fervent response that had won the hearts of the audience. As it happened, television cameras had recorded the rally and her impassioned reply had been played on three different newscasts. From that point on, Evan's popularity had soared.

Bethanne stirred, and Mary Jo reached for her daughter, cradling the infant in her arms.

A sound in the distance told her that Evan and his brother were back from their golf game.

"They're back soon," Jessica said when the men strolled onto the patio. Damian poured them each a glass of iced tea.

Evan took the seat next to his wife. "How long has

it been since I told you I love you?" he asked in a low voice.

Smiling, Mary Jo glanced at her watch. "About four hours."

"Much too long," he said, kissing her. "I love you."

"Look at that pair," Damian said to his wife. "You'd think they were still on their honeymoon."

"So? What's wrong with that?" Jessica reached over and squeezed his hands.

He smiled at her lovingly. "Not a thing, sweetheart. Not a damn thing."

* * * * *

A FAMILY FOR EASTER

Lee Tobin McClain

To my dad,
because we always visited his family at Easter, and
because I know he's singing in the heavenly choir.

For God so loved the world,
that he gave his only begotten Son, that
whosoever believeth in him should not perish,
but have everlasting life.
—*John* 3:16

Chapter 1

Fiona Farmingham clutched the edge of Chez La Ferme's elegant tablecloth and wished she were home on the couch with her kids, eating popcorn and watching movies. Wearing sweats and slippers rather than heels and a dress and shapewear.

Based on tonight, at least, dating was way overrated.

"You should come see me in Cleveland," Henry said loudly, forking braised lamb shank into his mouth. "We have restaurants that would put this place to shame. *Really* fancy."

She forced her face into something resembling a smile and pushed her roasted vegetables around her plate, not daring to look around at all the Rescue River customers and waitstaff Henry had probably just offended.

A throat cleared a couple of tables away, and she glanced up. A soccer-dad friend, Eduardo Delgado, was looking over his date's shoulder, smiling at Fiona with what looked like sympathy.

Her tight shoulders relaxed a little. Eduardo's warm, friendly face reminded her of school parent nights and carpools and kids' league games. Her normal life.

She was a little surprised to see Eduardo, a single parent who worked as a groundsman at Hinton Enterprises, dining at their small Ohio town's only upscale restaurant. He never even bought himself nachos or a hot dog at the school concession stand, always relying on a cooler from home for himself and his two kids instead. She'd thought that meant he was economizing, but maybe he was just into eating healthy.

"Did you hear me?" Henry scooted his chair closer. "I have a nice big house. Six bedrooms and three-and-a-half bathrooms. You should come visit!"

Like *that* was going to happen. She channeled her society-perfect mother, who could out-polite the Queen of England, even managing a small smile. "With my kids, it's hard for me to get away."

"Yeah, four kids, that's a lot!" Henry shook his head and attacked his spring pea risotto with vigor. She turned her chair half away and pretended to hear a sound from the evening bag she hadn't used since attending society events with her late husband three years ago. She pulled out her cell phone and studied its blank screen. "Henry, I'm so sorry, but I think my kids need me." Not a lie; kids always needed their parents, hers in particular. Right now, though, it was *she* who needed her kids.

"I thought you said you had a sitter. I was hoping we could spend more time together."

"Thanks, but no, thanks. I really do have to go."

Fiona tried to keep her voice low, even though half the restaurant's patrons had surely heard their discussion.

Why, oh, why had she let her friends Daisy and Susan talk her into online dating? But they'd both approved Henry's profile, and he'd sounded nice on the phone.

She knew why: because she thought her kids might benefit from having a man in their lives. And, maybe a tiny bit, because she wished for a male companion who would care for her, even love her, just as she was.

Fat chance of that, *fat* being the operative word.

"Look, Fiona." He gulped his drink and wiped a napkin across his mouth. "I wouldn't have sprung for this expensive dinner if I'd known…"

Fiona stood and grabbed her purse, thankful she'd driven there in her own car. "Henry, it's been…*interesting* to meet you."

"Hey! You can't just leave in the middle of—"

"Actually, I can." She fumbled for her wallet. Why had she thought, for one minute, that she should try a relationship again?

"Can I help you?" Their waitress, a college-aged girl Fiona knew slightly, touched her forearm. Her curious expression made Fiona's stomach twist.

She swallowed and lifted her chin, her mother's training once again coming to her aid. "Thanks, yes, Mia. Separate checks, please, and I'm sure this will cover mine." She extracted two twenties and handed them to the waitress. Then she turned, keeping her eyes on the front door. If she didn't look to the right or the left, she could avoid the pitying stares that were surely coming her way.

"Oh, Mrs. Farmingham," Mia called after her, "that's

way too much. You just had an appetizer and salad, and you didn't even order a drink!"

Let the world know I'm dieting, would you? "It's fine, keep the change."

"Just hang on a minute." It sounded like Henry's mouth was full. "How much was it?"

Father God, please just let me get home, and I'll forget about dating and just be happy being a mom. I'll delete my online profile. I'll avoid the matchmakers at the Senior Towers. She hurried away from the sound of Henry's bargaining with poor Mia, toward freedom.

Outside, the spring breeze cooled her cheeks. With just an hour of daylight left, the setting sun was nestled in the clouds, turning the sky pink and gold.

She took deep breaths of the rich, fragrant farm-town air and reminded herself that she'd been through far worse than a bad date and had survived.

Behind her, she heard the restaurant door opening and the sound of voices, including Henry's calling for her to wait.

She quickened her pace and stumbled a little. *Slow down. This is embarrassing enough without you falling on your face.* She reached her SUV, and the sight of her kids' car seats, the snack bags scattered across the floor, reminded her once again of her priorities.

Her kids were what was important. Not a man. Men ridiculed and cheated on women like her.

She was opening the door when Henry caught up with her. "Hey, come on, what did I say wrong?" He grabbed her arm. "I like big gals!"

Seriously bad pickup line, buddy. She jerked away and started to climb into the driver's seat. Not as easy in a dress and heels as in her usual mom uniform of jeans and sneakers, but she managed.

He didn't let go of her forearm, and his fingertips pushed deeper into her skin. "What are you waiting for?" he asked, leaning in, standing on tiptoe. "You're not getting any younger, and in a cow town like this, you're never going to meet anyone— Hey!" Suddenly, his hand was off her. There was a low rough exchange of words, and then Henry was gone.

In his place stood Eduardo Delgado, the sunset glowing golden behind him. "Everything okay, Fiona? I got worried when he followed you out."

She let her head rest on the steering wheel for just a few seconds. "Thank you. I... He didn't want to leave me alone."

"He will now." A smile tweaked up the corners of Eduardo's mouth as he gestured toward Henry, sliding into a silver Jaguar and slamming the door behind himself. The car started with a powerful roar and then backed out too fast, tires squealing. A moment later, Henry was gone.

"Wow. What did you say to him?"

"I explained how we treat women here in Rescue River. He decided he didn't fit in."

A surprised chuckle escaped her. Eduardo without his kids was...different.

She wondered if he'd heard that comment about *big gals*. She hoped not. Not because she especially cared what Eduardo thought. It was just...mortifying. "Thanks for taking time out of your date to rescue me."

"It's no problem. My date was a bust, too." His mouth twisted a little to one side as he leaned back against her open car door. He was a big man, his muscles visible even in his suit jacket. Which made sense, given the kind of work he did.

"Where *is* your date?" she asked, looking around the parking lot.

"She left. Bad match."

Fiona lifted an eyebrow. "Don't tell me you're on-line dating, too."

"No. No way. But I did some work at the Senior Towers, and…" He looked down at the ground, shaking his head as a grin tugged at the side of his mouth.

"You let the ladies get to you!" Fiona laughed out-right. "Nonna D'Angelo, right? She's relentless."

"They triple-teamed me. Nonna and Miss Minnie and Lou Ann Miller. Apparently, their matchmaking business is taking off, and they needed more men to participate."

"And you started at Chez La Ferme?"

"That's how they do it. They worked with the res-taurant to cut first-time couples a special deal." He was studying her curiously. "How well did you know your date?"

"Not at all. This was our first meeting." She wrin-kled her nose. "And our last."

They smiled at each other, that eye-rolling sympa-thetic smile of fellow sufferers.

Eduardo's phone pinged, and he pulled it out of his pocket and studied the face of it. Then he spun away and raced toward the other side of the parking lot.

"What's wrong?" She climbed out of the SUV.

"Fire at my place!" he called over his shoulder.

"Oh, no! What can I do to help?" She ran a few steps toward him, then stopped. If he needed her, she should take her own car.

"Sitter says kids are okay!" he called as he climbed into a truck with the logo *Delgado Landscaping* on the side.

An unrelated thought—*I didn't know he ran his own landscaping business in addition to working for Hinton Enterprises*—distracted her. Par for the course. "Fiona brain," her brother had called it. She shook her head, refocused in time to see Eduardo pulling out of the parking lot, his phone to his ear.

Fiona started her car and pulled out. She'd run home and check on the kids, get them into bed and see if the sitter could stay late. Then she'd go check on Eduardo. Even though he'd said his kids were fine, a fire could be devastating. They might need some help she could offer.

Eduardo slammed on the brakes in front of his rented duplex. No flames, but there were flashing lights, caustic smoke and men's voices registered as he looked around, fixated on just one thing: finding his kids.

"Papa!" Sofia called.

Eduardo turned toward the voice. When he saw Sofia and Diego running toward him, he knelt, opened his arms and clutched them to him, his throat tight.

His children had been at risk. He could have lost them.

Through his own negligence, just like with their mother. He had no plans to get involved with someone else, so why had he left his children with a sitter so he could go on a silly date?

He felt a hand on his shoulder. "They've had a scare, but they were never in danger," said Lou Ann Miller, his babysitter. In her late seventies, she was sharper and more agile than a lot of people half her age.

Her words calmed him and he stood, keeping a hand on each child's shoulder. "You're all right, Lou Ann? What happened?"

"We're all fine, and the fire seems to be contained to the bathroom," she said. "But no thanks to a smoke alarm, and you really ought to talk to your landlord about that."

"*I* was the one who smelled the smoke," Diego announced.

"And I ran out in the hall and saw fire!" Sofia leaned close to Eduardo. "It was scary, Papa. Miss Lou Ann made us run across the street to the Silvases' house and call 911."

"And she broke the door of the new neighbors to get them out!" Diego's voice sounded impressed. "She used a hammer!"

Eduardo's heartbeat was returning to normal, and he looked up at Lou Ann.

"They weren't answering the door, and since it's a duplex…" She shrugged apologetically. "I broke a window and reached in to unlock their door. They'd fallen asleep and didn't hear the doorbell or the knocking."

He looked at her quizzically. "They were sleeping heavily this early in the evening?"

"Very," she said, meeting his eyes with meaning in her own. "Pretty much passed out."

From what Eduardo had seen of the new neighbors, drinking or drugs had probably been involved. "They're okay?"

She nodded. "The fire turned out to be small and the firefighters contained it quickly. They interviewed me and the kids already, but they'll probably want to talk to you as well."

"Of course." As he made arrangements for Lou Ann

to take the kids to her house and gave them more hugs and praise, his mind chewed on one pressing problem.

He *had* to get his kids into a safer home.

He'd chosen this place because it was inexpensive, in a decent neighborhood with a good-sized yard. When would he learn that his instincts were terrible when it came to keeping his family safe? Hadn't Elizabeth's death proved that?

A busy hour later, Eduardo sat on a concrete wall outside his wet, smoking home. They were fortunate that it was unseasonably warm for mid-March. As he watched firefighters and a police inspector finish examining the smoke and water damage, he tried to think about what to do next.

The firefighters had kept the flames from spreading to the shared attic, limiting the damage to just the Delgados' bathroom. Apparently, when the men had pulled the ceiling down, they'd found insulation smoldering around an exhaust fan.

Eduardo clenched his fists, then consciously took a couple of deep breaths. The most important thing was that no one had been injured.

Police Chief Dion Coleman, who lived the next street over and seemed to know everything happening in the town, sat down beside him. "You okay, man?"

"Not really." Eduardo looked blankly as neighbors gathered near the fire truck in the deepening twilight. On the other side of the yard, their landlord was still talking to an inspector, gesticulating wildly.

"I spoke with one of the firefighters, and he says damage looks minimal. You could probably move back in within a couple of weeks, and insurance would pay—"

"No." Even the thought of taking his kids back inside the duplex appalled Eduardo. "We'll be looking for somewhere else to live. Somewhere safe."

"I understand." Dion leaned forward, elbows on his knees, weaving his fingers together. "Rental market around here is tight, though. Where are your kids now?"

"Lou Ann Miller took them in for the night." Eduardo gestured down the street toward the older woman's house. "She was babysitting when it happened. I'm going to crash on her couch later, too, if I can even sleep."

"This kind of thing can prey on your mind," Dion said. "But you know the good Lord's got you in His hand, right? Your kids, too."

"Right." Eduardo didn't want to go into his fear that if Lou Ann and the kids hadn't been awake and alert, the Lord might not have seen fit to save them. Not to mention the fact that the Lord *hadn't* had Elizabeth in His hands when she'd struggled with cancer.

Or maybe it was just Eduardo himself who excelled at letting his family down.

Dion stood. "If you need anything, you know where to find me." And he was gone.

Eduardo rubbed a hand across his face, and all of a sudden, Fiona Farmingham was in the spot Dion had vacated beside Eduardo on the concrete wall. "Eduardo, is there anything I can do to help?"

He squinted at her pretty features framed by long wavy red hair. "What are you doing here?"

"I was worried. After I got my kids settled, I came over to see if there was anything I could do."

"You have a sitter?" he asked inanely. He was still

trying to process everything that had happened tonight. His brain seemed to be running at reduced speed.

"Yes, and I talked to her. She's fine with staying later, and she put the kids to bed. But you have bigger things on your mind. Is there anything you and the kids need?"

He lifted his hands, palms up. "No. I'm just trying to figure out what to do. I have to find a new place to live."

"It's a total loss?"

"No, not much damage. But this happened because of an electrical issue." He slammed his fist into his hand, shaking his head. "I *knew* there were maintenance problems, that the landlord wasn't keeping the place up. I should have moved us out months ago."

Hesitantly, she put a hand on his arm. "That must make you really mad. But the kids are okay. And you're okay." She squeezed his arm lightly and then pulled her hand back. "You can figure out who's to blame later, even think about legal action. For now, you need to decide about the day-to-day stuff, what to do."

Her voice was husky, calm, soothing. A little of the tension left his shoulders, chased away by the strange feeling that he had someone at his side, shoulder to shoulder. "Yeah. That's right."

She nodded briskly. "Your kids are settled for the night? And you have a place to sleep?"

"Lou Ann Miller's house," he said, nodding.

"Do you need clothes, toiletries, pajamas?"

"I don't think so. I think they're going to let me back in pretty soon, take me around and let me gather up some stuff. There'll be an investigation, but it's pretty clear the problem started with some faulty wiring in the bathroom exhaust fan. The smoke alarm malfunctioned, too, apparently." He shook his head. "I've got to find a new place to live."

She looked thoughtful for a moment, and then she nodded as if she'd made a decision. "You could stay in my carriage house."

"What?" He cocked his head at her and frowned.

"It's a complete three-bedroom little home. Used to be where people kept their carriages, and then it was a spare garage, but the previous owners modified it into a space that could work as an office or a rental. I was using it for... Doesn't matter." She waved her hand. "I've been planning to advertise for a tenant, anyway."

Eduardo looked at Fiona. Her eyes held concern and the desire to help. The woman was kind and good, but he didn't feel comfortable with the spur-of-the-moment offer. "I don't see... We probably can't make that work," he said. "You have your own plans for the place. And anyway, I'm looking for something really safe, up to code, after what happened here."

She glared at him. "Do you think I'd offer you a place that was dangerous or unsound?"

Oh, man, now he'd upset this kind woman who was only trying to help. "Of course not. I'm sorry. I'm a mess."

"Understandable." She stood up, something like insecurity creeping into her eyes. "I'm sure you have other options, but if you want to talk more about the place, I'll be at church tomorrow."

She bent down, put her arms around his shoulders for an awkward hug and then disappeared into the darkness.

Exhausted as he was by the events of the evening, Eduardo was awake enough to feel a particular warmth where she'd touched him.

Chapter 2

The next day, Fiona and her four kids walked—or in Ryan's and Maya's case, ran—out of the little white clapboard church on the edge of Rescue River.

"Careful!" Fiona called. "Stay on the sidewalk!" But she couldn't help smiling at her middle two children's joy. Maya's exuberance didn't surprise her—at seven, Maya was her wild child—but Ryan, though only two years older, tended to be way too serious. It was good to see him run and play.

Beside Fiona, ten-year-old Lauren walked with more decorum, as befitted the dignity of the eldest child. Little Poppy nudged in between Fiona and Lauren and then reached up to grab their hands. "Swing me," she ordered with the confidence of a three-year-old, and Fiona and Lauren held her hands tight while she jumped up, swinging her legs.

"Hey," Ryan called back to them, "there's Diego and Sofia!"

Fiona's heart gave a tiny little leap as she looked ahead and saw Eduardo and his two kids walking in the same direction Fiona was heading. She always parked near the church's little play area, and today Eduardo's truck was next to her SUV.

Had he decided to take her up on her offer of the carriage house?

She'd seen Eduardo dressed up once before, on his date at Chez La Ferme, but he looked happier and more comfortable today, in his dark suit and open-collared blue shirt, laughing with his kids.

"Sofia! Hey!" Lauren dropped Poppy's hand and ran toward the Delgados. Ryan followed suit. They played on the same coed soccer team with Sofia and Diego, and the four children were becoming friends.

A moment later, all of them were on the grass next to their vehicles. Ryan, Diego and Maya darted back and forth, burning off energy by throwing around the cotton-ball lambs they'd made in Sunday school.

"Is that sacrilegious, to play with the Easter lamb?" Fiona asked, half-joking.

"Is it, Dad?" Diego clutched his lamb to his chest, his expression anxious.

Eduardo looked amused. "Not really. In some cultures, kids raise a lamb for Easter. I'm sure they play with it."

"That would be fun!" Maya danced over to Fiona. "Can we get a lamb, Mom?"

"No." Fiona tried to tuck Maya's hair back into its ponytail holder without much success. "But we're thinking about a dog when summer comes, and you kids can all help pick it out."

"Yes!" Maya pumped her arm in the air and ran back to the game of toss-the-lamb.

Fiona glanced over at Eduardo. "I don't think the kids would like what happens to the pet lamb at Easter."

"Easter dinner?" He winced. "Good point."

"Mom, can me and Sofia swing Poppy?" Lauren asked.

Poppy threw her arms around Lauren. "Please, Mommy? I wanna swing with LaLa!"

"If you're careful. Not too high."

"I *know*, Mom. Come on, Sofia." Lauren picked Poppy up easily and carried her toward the swing set. At ten, she was tall and broad-shouldered, often mistaken for a teenager.

"Poppy's cute," Eduardo said, looking a little wistful. "I remember those days."

"They go by too fast." Fiona didn't want to think about how she wasn't going to get another baby, how Poppy was her last. So, she watched as Lauren set her little sister on a swing, giving her a stern lecture about holding on tight. Lauren liked to show off her childcare skills, and Sofia was a new audience.

Which was fine. To a pair of ten-year-olds, a toddler seemed like a doll, and Poppy was glad to play that role if it got her some big-girl attention.

Fiona and Eduardo stood together, watching their happy kids. Was the question of the carriage house hanging between them, making things awkward, or was it just her being silly?

She focused her attention on a robin pecking at the newly turned earth, pulling out a fat earthworm.

It was a beautiful spring day and the service had been uplifting, and there was no need to feel uncomfortable with family friends. If he didn't want to take her up on her offer, that was perfectly fine. He probably had lots of friends to reach out to.

"If you were serious about renting to us," Eduardo said to Fiona, "could we stop over and check out the carriage house sometime soon? I've been online and in the paper, and there's not much out there to rent. I have an appointment to look at a trailer out on County Line Road, but it's a little more isolated than I'm comfortable with."

"Sure!" Fiona heard the enthusiasm in her own voice and toned it down. "Come out this afternoon, if you'd like. And you know, I also have a landscaping project I need done. Maybe you could take a look."

"Are they coming over?" Maya had overheard, and a big smile broke out on her face.

"Maybe," Fiona said.

"They might come over!" Maya rushed over to the big girls with her important news, followed by Diego and Ryan.

"They're obviously on board," Fiona said. "In fact, you're welcome to come for some lunch. I have plenty of hot dogs and burgers—"

"No, thank you," Eduardo interrupted, a shadow crossing his face. "That's a nice invitation, but we have other plans."

Heat rose in Fiona's face, and she was sure it showed in her cheeks. The disadvantage of being a fair-skinned redhead.

The rebuff was so definite. He didn't want to come. "I just thought... It's always hard to figure out what to do for lunch after church, at least it is for me, and so if you needed…" *Stop talking. He doesn't want to be your friend.*

"As far as helping with your landscaping…" He trailed off.

"It was just an idea. I know you have a lot going on."

He looked at the ground and then met her eyes with a forthright gaze. "You didn't suggest it to be charitable?"

"*Charitable?* What you do mean?"

"I just thought… Since we're going to struggle a little, given what's happened, maybe you were trying to help. And that's not necessary." His chin lifted.

"I'm sorry to say that didn't even occur to me," she admitted. "I've been meaning to look for a landscaper, but I haven't gotten around to it. When I saw from your truck that you do landscaping, it seemed providential. If you're not interested, it's no problem."

He opened his mouth to answer. But the kids had been conferring over by the swings, and before he could say anything, they ran over in a group.

"Are Sofia and Diego coming over?" Ryan was obviously the designated speaker.

Fiona glanced up at Eduardo, eyebrow lifted. His call.

"Yes, I think so," he said. "A little later."

"Well, we were wondering…" Ryan glanced at his big sister.

"We figured out a plan." A winning smile broke across Lauren's face. "Can Sofia ride with us?"

"And can I ride with Diego?" Ryan asked. "Please, Mom? I like their truck."

"That won't work." Fiona looked over at Eduardo. "They're coming over later in the afternoon. Right?"

"We have a stop to make," Eduardo said, putting a hand on Diego's shoulder and another on Sofia's.

"Oh, yeah. I forgot," Sofia said. "We're going to the cemetery."

"How come?" Ryan asked.

"Our mom is there," Diego explained.

"Well, her grave is," Sofia clarified. "Mama's in heaven."

"I *know* she's in heaven. I'm not a dummy." Diego's face reddened, and he opened his mouth as if to say more. But Eduardo squeezed his shoulder and, when Diego looked up, shook his head.

Diego's shoulders slumped.

"Our dad's in heaven, too." Ryan bumped against Diego's arm in a friendly way and then dug up a pebble with his toe, booting it down the sidewalk. That was Ryan, kindhearted and empathetic. "C'mon!"

Diego pulled away from his father and jogged alongside Ryan, kicking a stone of his own.

"If she's in heaven," Maya said, looking up at Sofia and Eduardo, "then why are you going to the cemetery?"

Fiona blew out a breath and squatted down beside her inquisitive seven-year-old. "Every family does things differently. A lot of people like to put flowers on a loved one's grave."

"I'll show you," Sofia said, tugging the truck key out of her father's hand. She clicked open the vehicle and pulled a pot of hyacinths from the passenger side. "Today, we're gonna put these on Mama's grave."

"They're pretty." Maya stood on tiptoe to sniff the fragrant blossoms. "I never saw a cemetery."

Fiona didn't correct her. Of course, Maya had been

at her father's funeral, together with the other kids, including Poppy, who'd been just two months old.

"Some of the graves have tricycles on them, or teddy bears," Sofia announced. "That's kids who died."

"Sofia." Eduardo gestured toward Poppy, obviously urging silence in front of a little one.

"Sorry," Sofia whispered and then squatted down on her haunches, holding out the flowers to Poppy. "Want to smell?"

Poppy did and then giggled as the flowers tickled her nose. Distraction accomplished.

"Can we go with them?" Lauren asked unexpectedly.

Fiona opened her mouth and then closed it again. She knew it was important to deal with kids' questions about death, but really? "We don't want to intrude," she said, putting a hand on Lauren's shoulder. "It's their private family time."

"We don't care," Diego said as he passed by, chasing the rock he was kicking. "We go all the time."

They *did*? Fiona couldn't help glancing at Eduardo curiously. He must still be grieving hard for his wife.

"We go once every month," Sofia corrected her little brother.

"Why don't we go to our daddy's grave, Mom?" Maya asked.

"Because our daddy was bad," Lauren said before Fiona could put together a response.

Poppy tugged at Fiona's hand. "Was our daddy bad?"

Pain and concern twisted Fiona's stomach, along with anger at Reggie. He'd hurt her, badly, but even worse was how he'd hurt his children.

Nonetheless, she knew what she had to do: keep her own feelings inside and be positive about the children's father, lest they grow up worrying that they themselves carried something bad inside them. "He was your daddy who loved you and there was lots that was good about him," she said, making sure her voice was loud enough for all the kids to hear. "But his grave is back in Illinois, where we used to live."

"Our mom was the best," Diego said. "Daddy has a picture." He tugged the keys out of his sister's hands and showed the photo attached to the ring.

Fiona squinted down at it, and Lauren and Maya leaned in to see as well. A petite dark-haired woman held a baby, with a little girl who must be Sofia leaning into her. Eduardo stood behind the woman, arms protectively around his whole family.

"She's really pretty," Maya said.

"*Was* pretty," Lauren corrected in her automatic big-sister mode, then reddened and looked over at Sofia. "I'm sorry your mom died."

Sofia nodded and leaned back against her father, who knelt and put an arm around her. Taking back the key ring from Diego, he held it so Sofia could see. "She was very pretty. Just a tiny little thing, but strong. You look a lot like her."

"I don't," Diego said, obviously parroting what he'd heard before. "I look more like you."

"Your mother loved both of you very much." Eduardo squeezed Sofia's shoulders, let her go and then patted Diego on the back. "She loved to cook for you, and play with you, and read to you. We'll talk about her at the cemetery, like we always do."

Fiona's throat tightened. Helping kids through the loss of a parent was an ongoing challenge.

"Do we have a picture of our daddy?" Maya asked.

"Because..." She looked up at Fiona, her face uncertain. "I don't really remember what he looks like."

"Back home in our albums, stupid," Lauren said.

"We don't call each other stupid," Fiona said automatically. "And, speaking of back home, we should get going and leave the Delgados to do what they were planning to do." Maya still looked unhappy—rare for her—so Fiona stooped down and grasped her hands. "Do you want to look at our albums when we go home? There are some good pictures of you and Daddy."

"Okay." Maya nodded, her momentary distress gone.

"Are we still having hot dogs?" Ryan asked. "I'm starving!"

"Yes. Come on, everyone in the car." Fiona clicked open the door locks and then looked at Eduardo. "I'm sorry for your loss."

He nodded, his eyes unreadable. "And I'm sorry for yours as well."

As Fiona drove home, her mind kept going back to Eduardo's family picture. Obviously, he wasn't over his tiny, beautiful, loving wife.

She had no right to feel jealous just because *she'd* struck out in the marriage game. It was nothing more than what her mother had always predicted—at her size, and not being the brightest woman around, attracting any man at all had been unlikely. The chances of him being a good, responsible, trustworthy person? Just about nil.

She had more than she deserved in her four wonderful children, and she was content with her life now, as it was.

Later that Sunday afternoon, Eduardo pulled up in front of Fiona's house, stopped the truck and waited. He knew exactly what his kids were going to say.

"*That's* their house?" Sofia asked. "It looks like it's from a movie!"

"It's cool," Diego said. "Is that where we'd live?"

"No. Mrs. Farmingham is looking to rent the carriage house, out back. I haven't seen it, but I'm sure it's nothing fancy."

Diego shrugged, then poked his sister in the side. "C'mon, let's go! There's Ryan!"

"Wait." Eduardo turned in his seat to face both of his kids. "We need to remember some things."

"I know. Good manners." Diego had his hand on the door handle.

"Like what?" he prompted.

"Wipe your feet, and say please and thank you, and be quiet inside the house." Sofia recited the list with an eye roll that previewed the teen she would soon become.

"Good." From the glove box, Eduardo pulled out two bags of *mazapán*, a round and chewy Mexican candy one of his aunts always sent them in quantity. He handed a bag to each child. "These are to share with everyone after we check with Mrs. Farmingham. She and I are going to be talking about work before we check out the carriage house, so I need you to be self-reliant. You can interrupt us if it's an emergency."

"Like fire or blood," Diego said, and Eduardo let out a short laugh. He should never have said that to the kids, but one night when he'd been working on the books for his landscaping business, he'd ordered his whining kids to watch TV and only disturb him under those circumstances.

Of course, that's what they remembered. "Right," he said, "or anything else that you think is important. You both have good judgment."

"Can we go now?" Sofia asked, and Eduardo looked at the house and saw that Fiona had come out onto the porch, holding Poppy on her hip. The other three kids were already on the stairs.

"Go ahead," he said, taking his time about gathering up his tablet and a couple of plant catalogs.

He climbed out slowly. Fiona stood listening to his kids, and he saw her smile and nod. Sofia and Diego distributed pieces of candy all around and gave the rest of the bags to Fiona; then all of the kids took off for the big side yard.

Fiona was wearing jeans and a puffy kind of blouse, light green, that made her red hair glow. Behind her, the old two-story Victorian mansion rose in splendor.

It was exactly the kind of house he'd have bought himself if he'd had the money. The yellow paint with green trim was nice, but best of all were the wraparound porches, one on the first floor and one on the second. A couple of redbrick chimneys indicated fireplaces inside and a turret at the top, with windows all around, would make a great playroom for kids.

Or a relaxing spot for parents to kick back and watch the sunset.

He straightened his shoulders and glanced down at his *Delgado Landscaping* shirt. He'd debated wearing just ordinary casual clothes, but that would have misrepresented the relationship.

He was aiming to rent a place from her and maybe to do some work for her, too. She was a potential client and landlord, not a friend.

He walked briskly up the sidewalk and held out a hand to shake hers. "Hey, Fiona. Thanks for letting us

see the carriage house. And for considering me for a
landscaping job, too."

She lifted an eyebrow and shook his hand. "Of
course."

Heat rose in the back of his neck. Why did he feel
so awkward with her?

And her hand—which, he noticed, he was still grasping in his, and he let it go like a hot potato—wasn't
the well-manicured, callus-free one he'd expected, but
strong, with plain short-cut nails.

Long delicate fingers, too.

"So," he began.

"Would you like something—" she started at the
same time.

They both laughed awkwardly. "Ladies first," he said
and then wondered if that had sounded stupid.

"Um, okay." Her cheeks went pink. "What was I…
Oh, yeah. Would you like something to drink? Coffee,
soda, iced tea?"

"No, I'm fine. Thanks. And thanks for letting the
kids come along. It's a big help."

"Sure. They're all having fun." She gestured across
the yard.

The kids were running toward a play set situated
near a tidy little outbuilding that must be the carriage
house. Poppy couldn't keep up and called out to the
others. Sofia turned, went back to the little girl and
picked her up.

His heart did a funny little twist at the sight of his
daughter holding a toddler. Sofia would *love* to have
a little sister. He and Elizabeth had hoped for that,
planned for it.

Plans don't always work out. "Does somebody live in your carriage house now?" he asked to distract himself.

"No. I was using it for my dog-walking business, but now..." She shrugged, looking away. "I just want to rent it out."

"You're not thinking of trying another business?"

"Well... I'd like to. But...no. Not for now." She crossed her arms over her chest.

Clear enough. None of my business. "Why don't you show me what you're thinking of doing in the yard first, since that'll take more time. I can look at the carriage house after."

"Okay, sure." She wiped her hands down the sides of her jeans. As she headed to the side yard, he fell into step beside her. It was nice that she was so tall. Easy for them to walk in step.

Unbidden, a memory of Elizabeth, scolding him for his tendency to outpace her, came to mind.

Fiona was talking, and he forced himself to focus. "So over here," she said, "I'm thinking about digging up this whole section and planting vegetables. Corn and tomatoes and squash and peppers. I'd like to maybe slope it south? To catch the sun?"

"That makes sense." He looked around the yard, measured it in his mind, pictured some ways it could look, "You thinking about raised beds?"

"Yes, if it's possible."

He nodded. "I think we could put in three small terraces. It would look good." He bent down, pinched up some soil and squeezed it between his thumb and forefinger. Thick and hard; too much clay. "You're going to need some soil amendments. In future years you can compost, if you're into that, but you'll probably have to shell out for commercial stuff this year. Peat moss, humus, maybe some mushroom compost. It'll cost you."

"That's not a problem," she said, and then a blush rose up her cheeks again and she looked away. "I...inherited some money. Nothing I earned myself."

He'd known she was wealthy. A lot of his customers were. As a professional, he could look at it as a good thing. "Hey, it's great you can afford to do that. It'll get your garden off to a strong start. Mind if I take some measurements?"

"That would be great. And here's the key to the carriage house. Go ahead and look around when you're done."

She checked on the kids while he measured and sketched. By the time they'd gotten around to the other side of the yard and discussed fruit trees and blueberry bushes, they were more at ease with each other. And when the kids came running up, thirsty, he helped her get drinks for everyone and accepted one himself.

While Fiona bandaged Ryan's scraped knee and helped Poppy change into a clean outfit—some kind of a mud puddle accident—Eduardo went out onto the porch and tried to get started on an estimate.

He found himself thinking about Fiona instead.

Specifically, about her past.

It was common knowledge in town that Fiona had been married to a wealthy man. And that her husband had turned out to have a double life, but Eduardo didn't know any of the details. Now he found himself curious and sympathetic. How did you explain something like that to your kids? How did you deal with it yourself?

And why on earth would anyone who was married to Fiona have felt the need for someone else?

Eduardo did another walk-around, checked a couple of measurements and looked up costs online. By the time he'd finished, the afternoon sun was sinking toward the horizon.

Dinnertime. He needed to take a look at the carriage house, collect his kids and go back to the motel where they were staying. He'd finalize the estimate tonight and email it all to her, and mull over renting the carriage house if it seemed suitable. It would mean a late night, but the job would be great for his bottom line, and the fact that he could work on it basically from home, if the rental worked out, meant that he could get to it quickly.

Sofia was running across the lawn and he called to her. "Get your brother," he said. "I'm going to take a quick look at the carriage house and then go inside to talk to Mrs. Farmingham. After that, we'll head home."

"But we're having fun!"

"Sofia…" He lifted an eyebrow. She was just starting to question his authority, and he understood it was a stage. But she needed rules and boundaries, and she needed to obey.

"I…" She seemed to read the firmness in his eyes. "Okay." She gave him a little hug and then ran toward her brother.

Eduardo looked after her, bemused. How long would she keep giving him spontaneous hugs?

He walked through the carriage house. It was small but pretty and sturdy, well built. He checked the smoke alarms and found them all working. Three small bedrooms, a kitchen with space for a table, a sunny front room with hardwood floors.

If Fiona was charging a reasonable price, this place would be perfect.

He went to the front door of Fiona's house, tapped on it, and when there was no answer, he walked inside. "Fiona?"

He heard her voice from the kitchen, so he headed in that direction. "Hey, I'm about done—" He broke off, realizing she was on a video call.

The image on her big laptop computer screen was blurry, an older woman, but the voice was perfectly clear. "You really need to watch what you're eating, honey."

"Mom, we've talked about this." Fiona's voice was strained.

"But you've gained so much weight, and at your height…"

"Heard and understood, Mother. I'll get the kids." Fiona turned away, stepped out of the computer camera's range and buried her head in her hands. Her shoulders started to shake.

Eduardo backed away—nobody wanted a witness to their breakdown—but despite the fact that the old house had been beautifully renovated, you couldn't eliminate creaky floors. He felt the loose board beneath his feet at the same moment he heard a loud squeak.

Fiona looked up and saw him, and her face contorted even more. "Get out," she whispered through tears. "Just get out."

Chapter 3

"He has to hate me." Fiona pushed up the sleeves of her sweatshirt and picked up the pace, glancing over at her friends Susan and Daisy. She'd tried to back out of their planned morning walk, but they must have heard something in her voice, because they'd come over anyway and insisted that she join them. And they were right: it *did* feel good to get out and move in the fresh spring air.

"I doubt he *hates* you," Daisy said. "Okay, it sounds like it was awkward, and maybe you hurt his feelings, but Eduardo's an understanding guy." She looked slyly over at Fiona. "Handsome, too."

"Daisy!" Susan fake-punched her. "Remember what Pastor Ricky said last week. We need to focus on what's inside people, not what's outside. Although," she said, her voice thoughtful, "Eduardo *is* one of the best-looking workers at Hinton Enterprises. Almost as handsome as the boss."

"Biased much?" Daisy teased. "Sam's my brother, and I love him, but even I think judging a beauty contest between Eduardo and Sam would be a tough job."

"Would you guys stop?" Fiona dug in her pocket for a ponytail holder. "How Eduardo looks is the least of my worries. I kicked him out in a mean way after he'd come over to my house to make a landscaping estimate. I didn't even show him the carriage house. I'm an idiot." Her cheeks heated at the memory of looking up during her meltdown to see Eduardo's concerned face, of blurting out something, anything, to make him go away.

She'd regretted it only moments later, but by then he'd collected his kids and left. "I wasn't just rude to him. I disappointed and confused his kids, too. They were expecting to look at the carriage house. I'm sure he's decided to rent something else, now that he realizes what a loon I am."

"You're *not* a loon," Susan said. "You're a human being with emotions."

"Don't be so hard on yourself," Daisy added. "We all make mistakes."

"I guess."

Daisy squeezed her arm and Susan patted her back, and the tightness in Fiona's chest relaxed just a little bit. A woman out weeding her garden called a greeting, and two mothers with babies in strollers waved from the other side of the street. In a fenced front yard, a toddler squatted to pet a puppy while his father talked on the phone.

Life went on.

"If it makes you feel any better, I'm the queen of saying the wrong thing, and most people forgive me for it," Susan added. "I'm sure Eduardo will forgive you if you apologize nicely."

"I can't apologize. I'm too embarrassed that he heard my mom calling me fat." Fiona could barely squeak the words out in front of her friends. "I mean, it's out there for everyone to see, but still…"

"You're not even close to fat!" Daisy sounded indignant.

"That's ridiculous," Susan said. "When you came to town, everyone talked about how you looked like a model. I was totally jealous when Sam's old mother-in-law tried to fix him up with you."

"I remember." Fiona thought back to that Fourth of July picnic almost two years ago. "I was such a mess then. Reggie had died earlier that year, and then I found out about his second family. I'd just moved here, and the kids were really struggling." She sighed. "But at least I was thin."

"Listen to yourself!" Susan scolded. "Would you trade where you are now for where you were back then, just to wear a smaller pants size? I mean, look at me." She patted her rounded stomach. "I've got baby weight I need to lose, sure, but I wouldn't trade it for the figure I used to have, no way."

"Of course you wouldn't." Daisy sounded just a little wistful. "And Sam wouldn't, either. He claims Sam Junior is the perfect child, and you're the perfect wife for producing him."

Susan snorted. "If he said *I* was perfect, he's delusional."

They reached Rescue River's small downtown and walked down Main Street. Early on a Monday morning, pedestrian traffic was light and most businesses were still closed. There was Mr. Love, though, sweeping the sidewalk in front of Love's Hardware, whistling a quiet tune. At eightysomething, he had more energy than most twenty-year-olds.

"Hey, Mr. Love," Daisy called.

The stooped dark-skinned man stopped sweeping and looked slightly to the left of them, leaning on his broom. "Who's that now? Is that you, Daisy Hinton?"

They came to a halt to chat with the man whose visual impairment didn't stop him from doing anything and everything.

"Me, and Susan, and Fiona Farmingham. Do you know Fiona, Mr. Love?"

"Oh, we've met," the old man said before Fiona could answer. "I'm blessed to get a morning greeting from the three prettiest ladies in Rescue River. Excepting my Minnie, of course."

Daisy arched an eyebrow at Fiona and Susan. "Are you two finally out in the open?" she asked Mr. Love.

"Thinking about shopping for an engagement ring. At my age!" He shook his head, a big smile creasing his face. "God's been smiling on me in my golden years."

"That's wonderful news." Daisy gave him a gentle hug while Susan and Fiona offered their congratulations.

"Don't rush into congratulating me. She hasn't said yes." Mr. Love put a hand on Daisy's arm. "You listen to what I'm saying now. Life's short. Too short for avoiding love due to fear."

Daisy's cheeks went pink. "You're not giving me advice on my love life, are you?"

"My name *is* Love, after all," he said with a chuckle.

"And at my age, I think I can claim a little wisdom. Now, you ladies get on. I know you've got more exercising to do on this fine day."

As they walked on through the downtown, the old man's words echoed in Fiona's mind. Was *she* avoiding love due to fear?

Well…yeah. She was. But in her case, she had every reason to.

"Fiona! Listen to me." Susan glared at her.

"Sorry, I was spacing out," Fiona said. "What did I miss?"

"I was saying that it's important for those of us raising girls, especially, to help them grow up with a healthy body image."

"That's true," Fiona said, thinking of Susan's stepdaughter, Mindy, as well as her own three. "I wouldn't want to do to my girls what my mom does to me on a regular basis."

"Kids learn by example as much as by words," Susan said. "I've learned that during ten years of teaching elementary school. If you put yourself down in front of them, or if you're always on some crazy diet, they'll notice."

"Exactly," Daisy said. "Besides, some men like women who enjoy their food. Dion says—" She broke off, blushing.

Susan cocked her head. "Is there something you want to tell us, about you and the police chief?" she asked Daisy.

"No. Anyway, today isn't about me." Daisy turned away from Susan and looked at Fiona. "What are you going to do about Eduardo?"

What *was* she going to do? She couldn't let the discomfort between them fester—if for no other reason than that they'd see each other at kids' events all the time. "I guess I could text him an apology."

"Text him? Really?" Daisy stepped in front of Fiona, making her stop. Susan came to her side, blocking Fiona's way.

"Call him?" Fiona asked weakly.

"God didn't give us a spirit of fear," Daisy said.

"And how about if you're offering a gift at the altar, and you remember someone is mad at you?" Susan added.

"Yes!" Daisy nodded vigorously. "The Bible doesn't say *text* them or *call* them. It says go to them."

"But that's because they didn't have that technology back then..." Fiona trailed off as her friends crossed their arms and shook their heads at the same time.

"Do I *have* to apologize in person?"

At that, Daisy and Susan turned to continue walking, each grabbing one of Fiona's arms. "Come on," Susan said. "We'll help you figure out what to say."

The next afternoon, Eduardo noticed two of the younger workers putting equipment away without doing the daily maintenance.

It would be easier to finish the jobs himself, but then the new guys wouldn't learn. "Tommy. Duke." He gestured toward the machinery the men had just put away. "You're not done."

"Man, don't you ever lighten up?" Duke grumbled good-naturedly as he grabbed a cloth and knelt beside the mower's grassy blades.

"He's got nothing else to do," Tommy joked. "He

needs a social life. Good work there, my man," he added to Duke.

"That skid-steer loader you brought in needs its fluid levels checked," Eduardo said mildly.

"Sorry, man." Tommy turned toward the small vehicle and started the daily inspection. "I'm in a hurry. I've got to go get cleaned up and take my woman out on the town."

"On a Tuesday?"

"Anniversary," Tommy explained. "My aunt's taking the kids."

A warm band tightened around Eduardo's heart. He remembered the days when he'd scrambled to get a sitter, had scrimped and saved to take Elizabeth out for a special occasion. She'd argued against the expense, but she'd always given in and they'd had fun, usually ending the evening with dancing.

"Need the place swept out?" Tommy asked Eduardo.

"Nah, go on. Have fun. I'll finish up."

"Thanks!"

As the two men left, a text message buzzed, and Eduardo pulled his phone out of his pocket.

It's Fiona. Can you meet me at the Chatterbox?

Instead of answering, he started pushing a broom across the floor of the storage shed. What did she want to talk to him about? If she wanted to see the estimate on her landscaping job—even after she'd booted him out of her home—he supposed he should give it. But at the café? Why not at her house?

He pushed debris into a heap and looked for a dustpan. Another message buzzed.

My treat. I want to apologize.

No need to apologize, he texted back. But I can meet you and give you your estimate if you'd like.

Great. Half an hour?

See you there.

He pocketed his phone and tamped down the small surge of excitement in his chest. He liked Fiona, found her attractive, if the truth be told, but he wasn't sure about renting her carriage house. What if she decided to use it as an office again? Or decided to kick them out for reasons he couldn't understand, as she'd done the other night?

On the other hand, the situation at their little motel was deteriorating. After Diego and Sofia had spent several noisy hours kicking around a soccer ball outside yesterday, the manager had let Eduardo know that they couldn't stay much longer. "We just aren't set up for kids," the man had said apologetically. "Couple more days, fine, but I'd like to see you move on soon."

Which meant he needed to find another place today or tomorrow; easier said than done in the limited rental market of Rescue River.

Again, the thought of Fiona's carriage house came to mind.

Thirty minutes and one speed-shower later, Eduardo reached the Chatterbox. The place wasn't crowded midafternoon, and Fiona wasn't there yet.

He sat down at a table where he could watch the door,

waving to a few coworkers from Hinton who were at the counter eating.

A moment later, Fiona flew into the restaurant, her purse swinging. He stood and she hurried over. "I'm sorry I was late!"

He glanced at the clock above the door as he moved to pull out her chair. From the corner of his eye, he saw the Hinton workers nudging each other. One of them gave Eduardo a thumbs-up.

Heat rose in the back of his neck as he sat down across from her. "You're not late. I was early. Are you hungry?"

"I am, but I'm not going to get anything. Just coffee. You go ahead, though. It's my treat."

Not in this universe.

"Are you ready to order?" Their waiter arrived with an order pad.

"Coffee for both of us, and a piece of cherry pie for me," Eduardo said.

"Ice cream?"

"Absolutely," he said and looked at Fiona. "You're sure you don't want to join me?"

She bit her lip. "Well... No. No, thank you."

After their server walked away, Eduardo pulled out his tablet. "I have your estimate right here."

"Wait." Fiona touched his arm and then pulled her hand back. "I invited you here so I could apologize. I'm sorry I was so rude when you were at my house the other day."

"No need to apologize. We all have bad days." The question was did she make a practice of it? If she did, he probably shouldn't rely on renting her place.

"I was having a difficult conversation with my

mother," she went on, "but that's no excuse. It wasn't your fault."

Ah. Mother-daughter issues. "No problem. Don't give it another thought. Should we talk about the estimate?"

"Yes, and the carriage house rental, too."

"Okay, sure." But he *wasn't* sure. He didn't think he wanted to move his family onto Fiona's property. She was a lovely lady, and kind, but was she reliable?

Unfortunately, though, he had no viable alternative.

He pulled out the tablet computer and started explaining his estimate for the landscaping job, crunching numbers, talking measurements, offering possibilities and alternatives based on price. Usually, the client was right with him on this kind of thing, but Fiona didn't seem to be paying attention. Was it because she was so wealthy she didn't care what she spent? Or was she not liking what he was proposing?

The third time she spaced out, he confronted her. "Look, would you rather I just give you the bottom line? Or are you uninterested? If you don't want to hire me, you can say it right out."

"Oh, no, it's not that!" Her hands twisted together in a washing motion. "I'm sorry, Eduardo. I just..." She trailed off.

"I'm in business. I know I'm not right for every potential client."

"I'm very interested. I'm just not good with numbers." She looked embarrassed.

Funny, he hadn't pegged Fiona as the ditzy careless type, but that was how she was acting. "No problem," he lied. He started from the beginning and went through it again, more slowly.

All the same, he lost her.

Something tickled at his brain, and before he could stop himself, he blurted it out. "Do you have something like dyslexia?"

"No!" She looked shocked. "Why would you even say that?"

"Sorry, crazy idea. It's just…" He trailed off and then shook his head. "I'm out of line. I shouldn't have said anything. I apologize."

She drew in a breath and visibly composed herself. "It's okay."

But it clearly wasn't, so he blundered on. "I just noticed… You're obviously a smart woman. But talking to you about math is a little bit like talking to my son, Diego, about letters and reading. He has dyslexia."

She let out a short harsh laugh. "I *wish* there was that kind of explanation for my weaknesses."

Compassion squeezed his heart as he studied her. She was wealthy and carefree on the surface, but there were layers upon layers to uncover in her, that much was clear.

Also, it was clear that he was a little too interested in exploring those layers.

"Here you go, sir." The waiter placed a large piece of cherry pie in front of him. Gooey, rich with fruit, the ice cream melting down the sides of the large triangle.

Fiona eyed it. "Wow, that looks delicious."

"Want a taste?" Without waiting for an answer, he cut her a small slice and slid it onto her saucer.

"I shouldn't, but…twist my arm." She took a tiny bite and her eyes widened. "This is fabulous!"

He felt absurdly happy to have given her something that brought her pleasure, however small.

"Let me look at the figures while you eat," she said. "Maybe I can get it through my thick skull."

He scrolled to the cover sheet and handed her the tablet. "That's the overview of what I'd recommend. I should've started with that, anyway, rather than bombarding you with a million details and choices."

She took another tiny bite of pie and smiled. "*So* good. Thank you." And then she focused on the tablet, frowning, asking the occasional question.

As he finished his pie, she nodded decisively. "I like what you've recommended. I'd be interested in hiring you if you're still willing."

"I'm willing and honored." Then his neck heated. *Honored?* That wasn't the kind of thing he'd normally say to a new client.

An elderly couple who'd been sitting at a table in the corner of the restaurant stood and headed toward the door. The white-haired woman used a walker, and the African American man who followed her held her shoulder. And they seemed to be arguing.

"Is that Mr. Love from the hardware store?" Eduardo asked, glad for a change of topic.

Fiona twisted to see, and then her face broke out in a smile. "Yes, and he's with Miss Minnie Falcon. I wonder…" She trailed off as the couple neared.

"I don't want to hear one more word about it," the woman said.

"Now, Minnie, don't shut me down cold. Hear me out."

Fiona stood and reached out a hand as the older couple started to pass by. "Miss Minnie. Mr. Love. It's nice to see you."

Eduardo stood, too, interested to see that Fiona was

acquainted with the pair. He was grasping for signs that she was a good person to work for and rent from, and he needed to weigh the situation carefully. His kids deserved that.

"Well, well, is that Miss Fiona Farmingham?" Mr. Love asked.

"Yes, it is, and I'm with Eduardo Delgado, who works at Hinton. Do you both know him?"

"I certainly do," Mr. Love said. "I believe you stopped in two weeks ago for some crabgrass treatment, didn't you?"

"I'm impressed that you remember." Eduardo stepped closer, which brought him close enough to Fiona to notice that she was wearing perfume.

"Not all senior citizens are forgetful," the older woman said, her voice tart.

"Now, now, Minnie," Mr. Love soothed. "That's not what the young man meant."

"I was just surprised he remembered my order better than I did when he has so many customers," Eduardo said truthfully.

"Miss Minnie, have you met Eduardo Delgado?" Fiona asked, the tiniest hint of a smile in her voice. "He works at Hinton Enterprises."

"And he does some work at the Senior Towers. We've met," Miss Minnie said, "but the two of us can't stop to chat. We've seen quite enough of each other today, and our ride is waiting outside."

Mr. Love grasped Fiona's hand, then Eduardo's, smiling apologetically as Miss Minnie hurried him away.

Fiona sat back down, watching the two seniors depart. "I guess the marriage proposal didn't go well."

"They're contemplating marriage?" Wow. Amazing that two elderly people had that much faith in the future.

"Love is ageless, or so they say." She turned back to face him. "I don't suppose you were able to look at my carriage house the other day."

"I did take a look. It seems like a great place." He tried to keep his ambivalence from showing in his voice.

"It's cute. I love the front porch." She shrugged. "It's not much. It's small, but it's solid and clean."

"You'd mentioned before that you were using it for your business. Won't you need it for that again? Are you sure you want a tenant?"

"I might give entrepreneurship another go if…well, if I can get someone to help with the numbers part." She laughed self-deprecatingly, gesturing toward the tablet that had confused her. "But that won't happen for months. If ever."

"Then… I think we'll give the place a try."

"Great!" She smiled at him. "You can move in anytime. We'll deal with the lease then."

That smile was dazzling. Way too dazzling. "I have references if you'd like to check them."

She waved a hand. "I don't need references. I know you."

"Yeah, but you don't know whether I pay my bills."

She blushed. "I'm really not much of a businesswoman, am I?"

"Nothing wrong with being trusting."

Her expression darkened. "Believe me, there is."

The stories he'd heard about her husband came immediately to mind. How could a man have two separate families, deceiving both of them? What a jerk. Hard to fathom anyone so lacking in honor and morals.

The waiter brought their check, and Eduardo took it and reached for his wallet.

"I'll take that," she said. "It's on me." She fumbled in her purse.

"Fiona, I'm paying."

"No, really, it's no problem. I have plenty—"

Heat rose up the back of his neck. "I may not be at your level of affluence," he gritted out, "but I'm not going to let a lady pay the check." He extracted a bill and handed it to the server.

They both watched him walk away, not looking at each other.

"I'm sorry, Eduardo," she said after a moment, quietly. "I didn't mean to insult you."

And of course, she hadn't. It was just that he needed to keep in mind their relationship: landlord/tenant. Employer/employee. They lived on different planets, economically speaking.

And even if that barrier hadn't existed, he needed to remember how vulnerable Fiona was. She'd been hurt badly. She didn't need any more problems in her life.

Especially not a problem like him. Because despite her wealth—yeah, and her beauty, too—Fiona seemed like a woman who needed protection and support. And if he hadn't been able to provide that to Elizabeth, he definitely couldn't provide it to Fiona and her four kids.

Chapter 4

"Hey, Mom, they're here already!" Ryan burst into the kitchen, where Fiona was making Saturday-morning pancakes. "And they're carrying stuff inside. Can we help them move in?"

Maya slid off her chair and headed toward the window. Lauren shoved away her plate. "Can we, Mom?"

Fiona glanced up at the clock. Eight o'clock, a full hour before she'd expected Eduardo and his mover-friends to arrive. Briefly, she regretted her makeup-free face, ancient concert T-shirt and ripped jeans.

She went to stand behind Maya, looking out into the sunny yard. Sure enough, a midsize rental truck sat in front of the carriage house beside Eduardo's overloaded pickup. A couple of unfamiliar cars were parked along the edge of the alley road, and six or seven people milled around, along with Sofia and Diego.

Two men opened the back of the rental truck while another fumbled with the hinges of the carriage house's front door. Eduardo climbed into the back of the truck, then emerged a moment later holding a long metal ramp. He set it down, leaped nimbly to the ground and moved it so it made a walkway from the back of the truck. Diego and Sofia pulled boxes from the piled-high back of Eduardo's pickup.

Standing easily a head taller than the other men, Eduardo called out instructions as he moved to take a too-heavy box from Diego and steady a tall plant Sofia was carrying.

Even from here, Fiona could see his wide smile. Her mouth suddenly felt dry.

"Can we go out, Mom?" Now all three of her older kids clustered around the window.

Poppy banged her sippy cup on the table and pointed at her empty plate. "More pancakes first!"

Fiona clapped her hands. "Back to your seats, everyone." She hurried to the stove to flip pancakes that had gotten just a shade too brown. "We'll give the Delgados a chance to get started moving in. Once we've finished breakfast…"

The kids all started shoveling pancakes into their mouths.

"…*and* cleaned up, we'll stroll over there and see how they're doing. It looks like they have a lot of helpers, so maybe Sofia and Diego could come play here while the men work." She brought the last plate of pancakes to the table and sat down. She considered pouring herself a bowl of low-calorie cereal, but the pancakes smelled way too good.

Half an hour later, she followed the kids over to the

carriage house. As they greeted Sofia and Diego, Eduardo approached her. Though the morning was still cool, sweat had gathered on his brow.

"We got started early," he said. "Hope we didn't wake you guys up. Some of the men have to work this afternoon."

"No, it's fine. We were up," she said. "In fact, the kids were ready to come out and offer their assistance the minute you pulled up. It's exciting for them."

"For us, too."

Diego and Ryan dodged in front of a pair of guys lifting a couch, and both Fiona and Eduardo spoke simultaneously with words of caution.

"Hey, careful there."

"Stay out of the men's way."

The men set the couch down in front of the carriage house's little porch and conferred, pointing at the door, obviously discussing how to get the couch inside.

"Come over here and meet my buddies," Eduardo said and started over toward the two men.

Fiona followed, feeling self-conscious in her Saturday-morning finest. She'd considered changing into better clothes, but that would have evoked notice from her kids. And she had to get used to the idea of being herself around Eduardo, who was, after all, renting her carriage house, not taking her out on a fancy date.

The men greeted her and one of them lifted an eyebrow and grinned, then said to Eduardo, "I see why you liked this place."

Eduardo opened his mouth, but before he could say anything, Fiona gave the man a wide vacuous smile. "Tim! I remember you. I've done some of the food banks with your wife."

"Right." The man's expression changed to bland friendliness.

"I'm Tony," said another man. "Pleased to meet you. I'd shake your hand, but mine's pretty dirty. I think I've seen you at the soccer field."

"That's right, you're Hailey and Kaylee's dad, aren't you?" The presence of another parent eased her discomfort.

"Hey, you guys letting me do all the work? How's that fair?" A young woman, pretty and muscular and dressed in Hinton groundskeeper garb, put down a box and marched over. "That's what you get, working with a bunch of guys," she said to Fiona with mock-disgust. "I'm Angie, and I'm guessing you and I could finish this move-in in half the time while these guys stand around shooting the breeze." She gave Eduardo a friendly nudge.

Fiona's senses went on high alert. Was Angie Eduardo's girlfriend?

And what business was *that* of Fiona's? Why did she care?

Angie grabbed the other two men's arms. "Come on, I don't know about you, but he's paying me by the hour. And not to stand around."

"Fine, fine." The others grumbled and left.

Which left her alone with Eduardo.

"Sorry about Tim," he said.

"I know him. It's not your fault. Look, how about if your kids come play at our house? They'd be out of your hair, and my kids would love it."

"That would be a huge help," he said gratefully. "Just while we're moving the big stuff. But, Fiona," he added as she started to turn, "I don't expect you to babysit my kids on a regular basis. It's a nice offer for today, but in the future, I'll either return the favor or keep the kids over here. That's not part of the contract."

"Um, okay." She felt unaccountably hurt. Was that what this was? A contract?

Late in the afternoon, Eduardo stretched as he watched the truck drive away. Between his friends and his coworkers, they'd finished the move on schedule. Not only that, but the beds were all set up and the furniture in place. Someone had even unpacked some of his kitchen boxes so there were dishes, pots and silverware ready to use. He sent up a prayer of thanks for the good people in his life.

Fiona being one of them now. She'd kept his kids busy and happy all day, fed them lunch and snacks, shown them kids' room decorating ideas on her computer. He had to be careful not to take advantage of her kindness, because she was obviously a caregiver to the core and great with kids. He grabbed his phone and called for pizza, enough for all of them.

Forty-five minutes later, he texted Fiona.

Pizza's on me. Come on over and bring your kids.

The kids consumed the pizza in record time, and the older four ran upstairs for the great task of room arrangement. Eduardo got the TV set up, and Fiona settled Maya and Poppy in front of a movie.

It was all very homey and too, too comfortable. Having Fiona and her kids here made Eduardo realize how lonely he'd been.

The problem was that in his loneliness there was the

dangerous possibility he'd lead this wonderful woman on, make her think he was interested in a relationship when he wasn't. Or shouldn't be, anyway. He cast about for something to talk about, something serious and businesslike and impersonal.

It didn't take long for him to think of a safe topic. "Stay here," he said, "I found something in one of the closets."

A moment later he was back at the dining room table with a box in hand. "This was on the shelf in the room you said you were using for an office. Up high, pushed back. I took a peek and realized it might be important. Don't worry, I didn't read anything."

Fiona reached for the box with an expression of extreme distaste. "Is that what I think it is?" she murmured as she opened the lid.

Inside was a mess of receipts and envelopes and papers. "Ugh," she said as she shuffled through the papers aimlessly, then closed the lid. "Thanks for finding it."

"Sounds like you'd rather it had stayed lost."

"No," she said, "it's a good reminder, in case I ever get serious about starting another business. I can just pull this out and all those ideas will go away."

"That's from your business?" Eduardo tried to keep any kind of judgment out of his voice, but in truth, the jumble of paperwork horrified him. He thought of his own carefully organized spreadsheets, his neatly labeled file folders, the app he used to keep track of small receipts.

"Yeah." She sighed. "I... Well, like I mentioned, I'm not too great at math. Or at being organized. So I kept putting off getting the money side of things straightened out. That was one of the factors that led to the dog-walking business failing."

He nodded. "A lot of people hire a bookkeeper if numbers aren't their thing."

"I tried. She quit!" Fiona rolled her eyes. "I had too many kids, too much going on. I got overwhelmed and botched the details."

"Don't get down on yourself," he said, putting a hand over hers. "It's hard enough running a business with two kids, and I can't imagine doing it with four." Then, when his hand wanted to squeeze hers tighter, he pulled it back. *None of that*, he told himself sternly.

"Mama?" Poppy came over and leaned against Fiona's leg, and Fiona pulled her up onto her lap.

"How's it going, kiddo? Where's Maya?"

"She went upstairs." Poppy stuck her thumb in her mouth, which seemed like a young thing for a three-year-old to do. But she was awfully cute. And she provided a good distraction, wiping the sadness off Fiona's face.

"I remember when Sofia was that age," he said. "And then Diego. They grow up so fast."

"I know. I want to cling on to my baby as long as I can. But she's getting big." As proof of that, Poppy wiggled hard to get down and started to slide to the floor.

Eduardo reached over and caught her, hands around her upper arms. "Careful there, young lady," he said, steadying her.

She wiggled away and grabbed Fiona's leg, looking back fearfully at Eduardo.

"I'm sorry." He looked from Poppy to Fiona. "I didn't realize..."

"She's not much used to men, that's all." She pulled

Poppy up onto her lap. "Mr. Delgado is a very nice man."

Poppy shook her head. "Not nice."

Oh, great. Now Fiona would think there was something wrong with him. Because kids and dogs always know, right?

Fiona tapped Poppy's lips gently and shook her head. "We use kind words," she said and then reached out to Eduardo and patted his forearm. "She wasn't around her father much at all, and… Well, we were in a lot of turmoil shortly after she was born. It's had its impact."

"I understand. Diego went through a phase where he was nervous around strangers."

"I thought she'd have outgrown it by now." Fiona looked out the window, seeming to see something disturbing through the deepening twilight. Absently, she stroked Poppy's head until it rested against her chest. The little girl's eyes were barely able to stay open.

Eduardo wanted nothing more than to comfort Fiona, but that wasn't his place…was it?

He'd been fortunate enough to have a good marriage, with a wonderful woman. But he hadn't been able to keep her safe.

Yes, it had been bad timing. When the small landscaper he'd been working for had gone bankrupt, the minimal medical coverage he'd had for his family had been gone. It had taken time to get replacement coverage. To get a new job, too, what with a sick wife and two little kids. Once he'd finally found work, his new job had provided great benefits, even covering Elizabeth's preexisting condition. But the three-month gap had meant spotty treatment at a crucial stage of Elizabeth's illness, and although a couple of doctors had told him it wouldn't have made a difference, he knew better.

He'd never forget the feeling: three pairs of eyes looking to him for protection and help he couldn't give.

He'd vowed after Elizabeth died that he would never marry again, never have more kids. His job was to take care of his own kids, raise them to adulthood in safety and security. *Not* to take on additional responsibilities he wouldn't be able to fulfill.

The fact that Fiona had her own money, could afford all the insurance and medical help she needed, didn't change one thing. Because challenges weren't only financial. There were all kinds of ways a man was supposed to take care of his family, and his confidence in his ability to do so had been broken.

He coughed and took a swig of soda, trying to wash away the depressing thoughts.

Fiona shifted the now-dozing Poppy to a more comfortable position and stroked her hair. "Sorry about that," she said.

"Sorry for what?"

"For spacing out on you. I got a little distracted, thinking about the past."

"Me, too," he admitted.

"Good thoughts?" She shifted Poppy against her shoulder. The little girl's eyes kept closing.

He shrugged. "Mostly. I had a wonderful marriage, but…"

"But what?"

"But I made mistakes." He looked into those caring eyes and felt a terrible urge to reveal everything. He even opened his mouth to do it, but he stopped himself.

"We all make mistakes," she said, glancing down at

Poppy and then back at Eduardo. "I was a fool not to see what was going on with my husband. Maybe you've heard that he had a whole other family."

"I did hear that." He shook his head. "Must have been rotten."

"And we didn't find out until after he died. Do you know how frustrating that is?" Poppy raised her head, and Fiona bit her lip and started rocking and soothing her again. "There's no one to be mad at. No way for me to ask him all the questions I have. I'll never understand why he did what he did."

"Stinks." Again, Eduardo felt the urge to comfort her, to go over and put his arms around her. But aside from the fact that it would totally freak out little Poppy, it would be the mistake of starting something he couldn't finish.

"And you're not supposed to speak ill of the dead," she continued. "And anyway, I don't want the kids to grow up thinking there's something wrong with them because of what their father did. They already hear enough gossip and negativity from other kids."

"Even here in Rescue River?"

She leveled her hand and rocked it slightly back and forth in a so-so gesture. "A little. Not so much as back in Illinois, of course. And I hope that as we become more and more established in the community, people will judge us on the merits of what we are now, rather than on our history."

"I think they will. I, for one, already do."

Their eyes met and held just a second too long. Eduardo couldn't look away from that gorgeous face, disturbed with memories from the past.

She broke eye contact first. "Yeah, well, you're getting to see the worst of me. You can see firsthand the mess I made of my business." She looked down at the box of receipts. "And you can see me in my Saturday finest."

Fiona in her old jeans and T-shirt still looked incredible.

"Anyway," she said, touching his arm in a friendly way that burned right through him, "thanks for the pizza. I'm glad you guys are going to be living here."

"Speaking of living here, I'd better pull my home together and get my kids ready for bed." He stood, knowing it was abrupt and rude to push a guest out this way, but it was better than the alternative of pulling her into his arms, tiny sleeping darling and all.

On Monday morning, after getting the kids on the bus and dropping Poppy off at preschool—literally kicking and screaming—Fiona led Miss Minnie Falcon up the stairs of her porch and leaned her folding walker against the railing.

"Thank you for coming over," she said as she offered the older woman a comfortable rocking chair. "I needed the company."

"I could see that." Miss Minnie looked around appreciatively. "My, you have a lovely home, dear."

Fiona surveyed her sunny porch, satisfied that it was a bright, comfortable spot for people to gather. At the bottom of the steps, crocuses bloomed purple and gold. Chirping birds in the nearby apple trees created a lively chorus. "I'll get you some tea," she said and headed inside.

She hadn't been kidding about needing the company, not only because she worried about Poppy's separation anxiety but because Eduardo's truck was still in the driveway of the carriage house. She didn't know why he hadn't gone to work, but he was the last person she wanted to see.

They'd gotten a little too close on the day he'd moved in, or at least, it had felt like closeness to her. Apparently, he hadn't liked it, because he'd sent her and the kids away with an abruptness that wasn't like him. It had hurt, but she'd understood. Just because they were living on the same grounds didn't mean they should share every moment together. It was best not to get the kids into that pattern. So, yesterday, she'd hurried her kids out after church without even greeting Eduardo and his kids, and they'd done a day trip to a nearby nature reserve.

Now she finished making tea, put lemon and sugar on a tray and carried the lot out to the porch. Miss Minnie smiled as Fiona poured her a cup. "Now, this is nice," she said. "I've come to like living at the Senior Towers, but there are times when it's good to be in a real home."

"I was feeling blue when I ran into you at the church. You probably heard Poppy screaming. It's tough to walk away, even though everyone says preschool is good for her."

"The church preschool is wonderful," Miss Minnie declared. "And she's your fourth child. Surely, you know she's going to be okay."

Fiona stirred sugar into her own tea. "Poppy is different from the others. She's shy. Anxious."

"She'll grow out of it." Miss Minnie rocked gently. "You give her plenty of love. Opportunities to socialize, like the church preschool, are just what she needs."

"Do you think? She just started last month, three days per week. It's a battle to go every time, but the teachers say she settles down within fifteen minutes." Fiona shook her head. "My others were all eager to go to school and see their friends. Still are."

"Any idea why she's different?" The older woman studied her over the rim of her teacup, eyes piercing.

"It's my fault." Fiona sighed. "She must've picked up on my anxiety. I should have seen the signs sooner, but I was...going through a tough time." She picked up her tea and sipped it. "You probably know all about my family's history. Seems like everyone in Rescue River does."

Miss Minnie put down her cup with a little clatter. "Rise above it, young lady! You did nothing wrong."

"I suppose," Fiona said. "Still, after three years, I feel like an idiot for what happened."

"Because you were misled by a man?" Miss Minnie made a *pfft* sound. "We've all been there."

That surprised Fiona. "You, too?"

"Oh, my, yes." Miss Minnie rocked and looked out toward the road. "I thought I knew someone," she said, "and I didn't. My fiancé, to be exact."

"You were engaged?" Fiona was surprised, because Miss Minnie seemed like a confirmed and happy spinster.

Miss Minnie nodded but didn't offer more details. "We can all be fooled by love."

Seeing that she wanted to change the subject, Fiona obliged. "I'm bad at choosing. The last date I went on was a mess." She told Miss Minnie the story of her date with Henry and, to her surprise, she was able to make it funny enough that Miss Minnie laughed…and then Fiona did, too.

"Oh, my, the stories we get at the Senior Matchmakers. To say nothing of our own stories." Miss Minnie's face wrinkled with amusement. "Lou Ann Miller and her love triangle are the stuff of many a legend here in Rescue River."

The idea of the elders still going through romantic shenanigans gave Fiona an odd sort of hope. Maybe, when her kids were grown and she'd truly gotten over her past, she'd find love…or at least, have fun looking for it. "What about you?" she asked the older woman. "Any chance that you and Mr. Love might take your friendship to the next level?"

A blush crept up Miss Minnie's papery cheek and she waved a hand. "It would be so ridiculous at my age. To get engaged. To get married!"

"You volunteer at church and you started a business just last year," Fiona pointed out. "Age doesn't stop you in any other area. Why should it stop you from falling in love?"

"Oh, well." Miss Minnie rocked faster, her cheeks still pink.

"Nice to see you ladies taking advantage of this fine morning!" The deep male voice thrummed along Fiona's nerve endings as Eduardo approached and put down the bag of fertilizer he was carrying, wiping his forehead with a bandanna.

"I'm surprised you're not at work." Then Fiona felt her cheeks warm. She didn't want Eduardo to think she was keeping track of his movements.

Miss Minnie's sharp, observant eyes flashed from one face to the other. "Yes, indeed. Mr. Sam Hinton can barely run Hinton Enterprises without you from what I hear."

Eduardo's already-tan skin went a shade darker. "Not the case. I keep the outside of the property running so Sam can do the hard stuff inside. And the folks on my shift are pretty well trained. They get along just fine when I'm not there to supervise."

"I'm sure. Sam speaks highly of your teaching abilities, too."

Fiona studied him with interest. She'd known he was a supervisor, but Miss Minnie was making it sound like he headed the entire grounds operations. Most men tended to brag about their work, but Eduardo was always humble.

"Thank you for telling me that, Miss Minnie," he said now and then looked at Fiona. "I'm taking the day off to get the house in order, but I'd also like to get a start on your garden project if that's okay with you."

"Of course, that would be wonderful."

"I'm planning to dig out the grass where the raised bed will go. That'll help drainage and weed control. And then sometime this week, I'll pick up the boards to build the terrace walls. Sound good?"

"Perfect." She watched him walk away, noticing the way the sun shone on his dark hair.

When she came back to herself, Miss Minnie was looking at her, one eyebrow lifted.

"So it's like that, is it?" the older woman asked.

"Like what?" What had Miss Minnie seen in her expression? Had Eduardo seen the same thing, now or earlier? Was that why he'd kicked them out of the carriage house on Saturday?

Miss Minnie was still studying her and she didn't

answer Fiona's question. "Do you have a Bible?" she asked unexpectedly.

"Of course!"

"Would you get it, please?"

"Um, sure." She stood and headed into the house. What was *this* all about? Miss Minnie was, after all, a Sunday school teacher from way back. But Fiona, discombobulated as she was by Eduardo's presence, didn't feel like being preached at.

She schooled her expression before returning to the porch and handing Miss Minnie her Good News Bible. Miss Minnie ran her hands over the cover. "I love this translation," she said. "And I think it has something to say to both of us." She flipped the pages with the ease of long familiarity and then ran a weathered finger down a page. "Ah, here we are. Second Corinthians 5:17. Do you know it?" She looked up at Fiona expectantly.

"I'm sorry. I don't." Fiona felt inadequate.

"I'm going to read it to you," Miss Minnie said, her voice taking on a teacher's firm tone. "Verse 17: 'Old things are passed away; behold, all things are become new.' In other words, anyone who is joined to Christ is a new creation." She looked up at Fiona.

Fiona nodded, processing the words.

"Sit down, dear. I have the sense that you're focusing on the past and what went wrong in it. With your children, Poppy in particular. And that it's hindering any possible connection with that handsome young man there."

"Eduardo isn't interested—" She stopped. "Anyway, I *did* make huge mistakes in the past."

Miss Minnie held up a hand. "The point is, you're joined to Christ, and you're a new creation. You can put all that behind you. The old is gone, and the new has come." Her face broke into a crinkly smile.

Fiona couldn't help smiling back. "If it's true for me, Miss Minnie, then it's true for you, isn't it? You need to open your mind to all the new possibilities ahead of you."

Miss Minnie's smile went wry. "So a certain gentleman keeps telling me," she said.

As if on cue, a sedan pulled up. "I believe that's my ride," Miss Minnie said, color blooming in her cheeks.

Mr. Love got out of the passenger's side, and a younger woman emerged from the driver's seat. "That's his granddaughter," Miss Minnie said. "Could you help me up, dear? She claims she's driving him around as a charitable act, but I suspect she wants to keep an eye on us as well."

"Keeping you out of trouble?" Fiona couldn't help smiling as she helped the older woman down the stairs and unfolded her walker for her.

"And rightly so," Miss Minnie said tartly as she made her way down the sidewalk. "Men never change. Thank you for the tea and conversation, dear. You think about what we discussed."

"I will." Fiona watched as Mr. Love helped Minnie into the back seat and then climbed in beside her.

"Is it any wonder I feel like a chauffeur?" the granddaughter asked with good-natured exasperation. With a wave and a honk, they were off.

Fiona checked the time. Another hour and a half before she had to pick up Poppy. And there was Eduardo, working up a sweat, creating the garden of her dreams.

She grabbed a pair of gloves and a shovel from the

shed and approached him. "Need a hand?" she asked. "I hate to sit and watch while you're slaving away."

He stopped, leaning on his shovel. "Truthfully? No."

She'd already lifted her shovel to start digging. She froze in midair and looked at him. "How come?"

"You hired me to do the job. If you're going to be uncomfortable with me working for you, we should call it off right now."

"I didn't say I was uncomfortable with you working for me," she said, although she kind of *had* said that. "I said I wanted to help. Does that make *you* uncomfortable?"

He hesitated and then looked away across the yard, still leaning on his shovel. Which gave Fiona the time to analyze his answer and come up with the unpleasant truth.

"Look," she said, "if you don't want me to help, if it's too much togetherness, that's fine. I didn't even consider that you might enjoy having your day off to work by yourself, without having to talk to someone else all the time." She was babbling. Totally babbling, because she felt so mortified and embarrassed to have forced herself on him.

What was that Bible verse Miss Minnie had insisted on reading to her? Something about how she was a new creation.

She wasn't the same person who'd been betrayed, rejected and made to look ridiculous by a man who had vowed to cherish her. No, she'd grown beyond that... sort of.

But that still didn't make her the type of woman most men wanted to spend time with. She pulled off her gardening gloves and turned away.

A hand on her shoulder stopped her. "Fiona." Eduardo's voice was closer than she expected behind her. "It's not that I don't want to be with you."

She half turned back, not meeting his eyes. "It isn't?"

"No," he said, "it's that I want to be with you too much."

"You don't have to say that, Eduardo. I'll get out of your hair." And she hurried off toward the house, before he could say more painfully kind but empty things.

Chapter 5

The next Saturday, Eduardo was washing dishes when Sofia and Diego burst into the carriage house. "Dad!" Diego cried. "Lauren and Ryan and Maya and Poppy got a dog!"

Eduardo turned, his hands soapy, as both of his kids crashed into him. "Hey, slow down."

"It's a hound-pointer mix, like, *this* big." Sofia held her hands a yardstick apart.

"They got him at A Dog's Last Chance and his name is Brownie, 'cause he's mostly brown!"

"He has the softest floppy ears," Sofia said.

"Come out and see!"

Their excitement made him smile. "You go ahead. I'll be right out."

"Hurry!" They rushed outside, letting the screen door slam.

Eduardo rinsed the last of the dishes and dried his hands. If he had any sense, he'd stay inside and ignore the feelings that roiled in his chest whenever he thought of the family across the yard. Particularly the family's mother.

He needed to focus on work and his own kids, like he'd been doing for the past week, ever since he'd made his idiotic pronouncement about wanting Fiona around too much.

Why had he gone and done such a foolish thing?

Because he *didn't* have any sense, obviously. And because it was the truth.

But it also had to do with the vulnerability in her eyes as she'd said he probably didn't want her around. He couldn't let her keep assuming that, putting herself down, believing that all men were like her ridiculous, deluded husband who'd betrayed her.

Except who had appointed him caretaker of the world? He was the *worst* candidate for that job.

Maybe Fiona wouldn't be outside with her kids. Maybe he could come out and meet the new pup and skulk back inside without encountering the tall red-headed beauty who'd been haunting his dreams.

But of course, that wasn't how it played out. When he crossed the lawn to the side yard near Fiona's house, she was right there on the ground with her kids and an ecstatic brown-and-white hound, who was bounding from one kid to the next, barking madly.

She glanced up at him, gave a brief wave and then focused on the dog. "Ryan, let your sister have a turn," she said to her son, who'd grabbed the new dog by the collar.

Maya scooted over and wrapped her arms around

the dog's neck, fearlessly, and stuck out her tongue at her brother.

"Poppy needs a turn, too," Lauren said, looking up at her mother for approval, as the dog bounded away again.

"That's a kind thought, Lauren." Fiona brushed a hand over her daughter's reddish-brown hair. "But I'm not sure Poppy wants a turn just yet."

"Yes, she does! C'mere, Brownie!" Ryan had knelt beside Poppy, and Maya ran to squat on her little sister's other side.

Gamely, the dog bounded their way, placed oversize paws on Poppy's lap and proceeded to lick her face.

Poppy jerked back and wailed.

In a flash, Fiona was there, picking Poppy up and frowning at Ryan and Maya. "We never force people to play with the dog. You know it takes your sister some time to warm up."

"Aw, Mom, she liked him at the farm," Ryan said.

Fiona just raised an eyebrow at him, holding Poppy on her hip and stroking her hair.

"I'm sorry, Pop," Ryan said.

"Me, too. C'mon, let's throw a ball for him!" Maya matched word to action, grabbing a ball and throwing it surprisingly far for a child her age.

All three of Fiona's older kids, plus Eduardo's two, ran after the dog, leaving Fiona, Eduardo and Poppy to watch.

Eduardo blew out a sigh and tried not to notice the way the sun set fire to Fiona's hair. Or the curve of her smile as she watched her kids play. Or the unconsciously warm and motherly way she made little sounds in her throat to soothe her youngest, who still rested her head on Fiona's shoulder.

He didn't want to notice what a deep-down good person Fiona was. But being around her so much made that reality impossible to ignore.

Maybe he needed to start looking for a new place to live. Before he did something crazy again, such as tell her how much he liked being around her.

"Five more minutes, kids," she called, clearly oblivious to his inner turmoil. Then she turned to him. "I told them they needed to let him rest today. Even though he's having a good time, making a move is stressful on an animal. He's not used to this kind of craziness."

"He sure is cute." There. That was an innocuous comment anyone would make, right?

Abruptly, the kids' voices rose in unhappy tones, shouting back and forth. "Uh-oh," Fiona said, and they both started walking toward the noise.

Around the corner of the house, Fiona's kids knelt, holding the dog.

Eduardo's two stood shoulder to shoulder six feet away, faces stormy.

"He's *our* dog!" Lauren was saying.

"We *know* that, but you could at least let us pet him."

Ryan squeezed the dog against his chest. "You don't know how to take care of a dog like we do."

"Oh, like you have *all this* experience with dogs," Sofia said cuttingly. "You only got one this morning."

Maya sat on the ground and wrapped her arms around the dog, half tugging it out of Ryan's lap. The dog responded with a plaintive yelp.

Fiona marched over to her kids and Eduardo to his. Behind him, Eduardo heard Fiona remonstrating.

"They're being selfish, Dad." Diego was almost crying. "I just want to play with him. I wasn't trying to steal him."

"He's an ugly dog, anyway," Sofia said, just loud enough to set off another wave of outrage among Fiona's kids. "And he runs around like he's crazy."

"Hey." Eduardo knelt and gripped a forearm of each of them, not tight, but firm, so they couldn't escape. "When our friends get something new, we celebrate with them. We don't try to take it away." He frowned at Sofia. "And we don't talk it down. That's unkind and it's uncalled for."

"I'm sorry," Sofia said, looking away.

"I'm not the one you need to apologize to."

She pressed her lips together and glared at Eduardo. He glared right back.

She yanked her arm out of his grip and crossed her arms over her chest. "Sorry," she yelled over toward the Farmingham kids. Then she spun and ran toward the house.

"I'm sorry, Dad," Diego said, sounding much more sincere than his sister. "Can I go tell them?"

"First tell me how you're going to act toward the new dog."

"I'm going to watch him and talk to him and only pet him if they say I can."

"And not argue?"

"Yeah." Diego was practically bouncing, looking over at the four kids, who were sitting around their mother while she held the dog at her side and patted it gently.

"Go ahead," he said.

Eduardo watched as Diego approached the Farmingham kids, said something and was welcomed to join the little group. A minute later, Lauren ran toward the carriage house, where Sofia had disappeared.

Eduardo busied himself pulling a few early weeds, keeping his ear tuned toward his place for any signs of an argument. But a few minutes later, Lauren came back out with Sofia, the two of them talking like old friends. And the next minute, all six kids were running and playing with the dog and each other.

"Disaster averted," Fiona said, coming to stand beside Eduardo. "I'm sorry. I should have warned you we were getting a dog, but this little trip came up suddenly. Once we were there, seeing all the dogs who needed homes…" She shrugged and lifted her hands. "What can I say, I'm a sucker for big brown eyes." Then she looked at him and clapped a hand over her mouth.

Eduardo couldn't resist smiling a little, enjoying the way her cheeks were going pink. Of course, she hadn't meant anything by it. No way had she been flirting with him. She wasn't the type.

"I didn't mean… I meant, a *dog's* brown eyes… Oh, wow. I'd better stop talking."

"No, don't worry. I understand. I didn't think you meant anything." Wasn't there some yard work he could do, rather than trying to hold an intelligible conversation with the most gorgeous woman he'd ever seen?

The unbidden thought shocked him. Was Fiona more gorgeous than Elizabeth had been?

Guilt rose, but he firmly tamped it down. Every woman was beautiful in her own way; he truly believed that. Elizabeth had been, and Fiona was.

It was just that Fiona was right here, smelling like hyacinths…

"Hey, Dad!"

"Mom!"

The six kids came running toward them, Lauren carrying Poppy, the dog bounding alongside. "We want to talk to you," Sofia said, offering him a winning smile.

"Okay." Eduardo could tell some kind of con job was coming, but he still welcomed the interruption.

"Families are important, right?" Sofia said.

"Yes, of course," Eduardo said, cocking his head to one side and looking skeptically at his daughter.

"And it's important to be with your family, to be all together," Diego said. "That's why we go visit Mexico sometimes."

"Right."

"But *this* dog—" Sofia indicated Brownie "—this dog was taken away from his mother."

Eduardo frowned. "He's not a little puppy. It's okay for him to be taken away."

"But, Dad, Brownie's mom is still at A Dog's Last Chance," Diego said. "And she was really sad to be left behind. Right?" He turned, and all four Farmingham kids nodded solemnly. Even the dog seemed to agree, eyes fixed on Eduardo, tongue lolling.

"And she's old, Mr. Delgado," Ryan said. "She has grey hair on her nose."

Eduardo was starting to see where this was going. Automatically, he shook his head.

"So we were wondering..." Diego started and trailed off.

Sofia put a hand on her brother's shoulder. "Could *we* get Brownie's mother and have her be our dog?"

"No." Eduardo drew in a breath. "No, we're not ready for a dog."

"Aww, Dad!" Diego's face crinkled into a pout.

"Come on, my kids," Fiona said. "Lunchtime, and time for Brownie to have a rest."

The kids complained, but they did as Fiona said. She gave him a little wave and a rueful look—perhaps an apology for stirring up his kids' desire for a dog—and then followed them toward her house.

She didn't invite them to join in. Not that he wanted to, not that he would have, but he noticed the omission because she was usually quick to offer hospitality.

She was guarded around him now. As well she should be, but it was hard. "Go on inside," he told his sulky kids. "I'll be along in a minute. I need to pull the rest of these weeds." In reality, he needed to collect his thoughts before entering into the get-a-dog fray.

When he did go inside, the kids were already pulling peanut butter and jelly out of the cupboard and arguing. He started into the kitchen to break it up and then heard what they were saying and froze.

"That wasn't why she died, Diego. It didn't have anything to do with you knocking over that lamp."

Diego didn't speak. His head was bowed over the sandwich he was making.

"*I'm* the one who made her sicker. I wanted her to come to school like the other moms, and she didn't, and I yelled at her about it. She went to the hospital the next day, and she never came home."

A tight band circled Eduardo's chest and squeezed tight. He hadn't known his kids still felt guilty about Elizabeth's death. The concerns they'd raised had been addressed long ago, or so he'd thought. But maybe, unintentionally, he'd brushed them aside.

Just like the doctors had brushed aside his own feelings of guilt about not having good insurance when Elizabeth had first gotten sick.

He hadn't just said "Oh, okay" and dropped his own guilt instantly. Why would he expect that his kids could do that?

He came up behind his son and daughter, who were facing the counter, and put a hand on each shoulder. Leaned close and inhaled the sweaty-kid smell of their hair. "Mom died because she had cancer," he said firmly. "Not because of anything you did."

Two pairs of hands froze in their work, then started up again. "We know, Dad," Sofia said.

"But from what I heard you both say," he persisted, "it sounds like you're still blaming yourselves."

Diego looked up at him. "I know you said it's not my fault, but I wish I didn't break the lamp. I remember she yelled at me, and then she cried. And before that, people were always telling me to be quiet and not upset Mom. So when I did..."

Eduardo shook his head and pulled Diego to him, enveloping him in a hug that was as much for himself as for his son. He reached out his other hand and pulled Sofia into the embrace. "Kids are supposed to be kids," he explained. "She knew that you were young, and she wanted you to have fun and play. She knew things could break."

"But she cried," Diego said.

"And she cried when I yelled at her," Sofia added. "Her face got really red."

Eduardo pulled them over to the kitchen table and sat them down in their chairs, then knelt between them. "It's true she got upset sometimes," he said. "Because Mom was a real human being, with real feelings. She cried a lot toward the end because…" He swallowed the tight knot in his throat. "Because she knew she didn't have much time left with us. She knew how sick she was long before you broke the lamp and yelled at her. It made her sad. Mad, even, sometimes."

"I was mad at her," Sofia said cautiously, "when she didn't come to Muffins-for-Moms day. I told her about it, but she forgot. How could she forget?"

Eduardo sighed. "The drugs the doctors gave her made her forget things sometimes. But you know what? I should have remembered Muffins-for-Moms, but I forgot, too." He should have found a friend or relative to attend, but life had been so crazy at that awful time. "The thing is… I'm not perfect and neither was Mom. And you don't have to be perfect, either. Everybody makes mistakes."

"And everybody sins," Diego said thoughtfully. "We talked about it in Sunday school, and kids told what they'd done wrong. But I made something up, because I didn't want to tell about the lamp." Tears stood in his brown eyes, and his concerned expression was the exact replica of his mother's. The sight made Eduardo's own eyes burn.

"Breaking the lamp wasn't even a sin, Diego. It was just an accident," Sofia said. "But me yelling at her was a sin."

Eduardo swallowed. One was never ready for these big discussions with kids. They came suddenly, over peanut butter sandwiches on a Saturday afternoon, and they just had to be handled as best as possible. "Feelings are feelings," he told Sofia. "They're not right or wrong. It was okay to feel mad at Mom for forgetting. Even for being sick."

Both kids' heads snapped around to stare at him.

Ah. That was the core, then. "Sometimes," he told them, "I felt angry at Mom for being sick. I wished she could have fun and do things like she used to do." The admission made him ashamed, but he could see that his kids were eating up every word. "Sometimes, she got mad at me for being so healthy, I think."

"Did she get mad at us for that?" Sofia asked.

"No," he said, filling his voice with the certainty that he felt. "The most she ever got was annoyed with you for the same things parents always get annoyed about. She loved you both so much, and she was glad you were healthy and strong. Her biggest hope was to get to see you grow up, to be your mom and do everything moms do." His throat closed then, and he couldn't say any more. He just pulled them both close and held them until he could get himself under control.

Showing emotions was okay—good, even; that was what the social worker and the grief counselor had said right after Elizabeth's death. But still, he had to be strong for his kids. Had to be their rock. They needed to know that he wouldn't fall apart on them.

So he drew in a deep breath, then another, and then he pulled back from them and stood. They both looked at him, eyes round and teary and serious.

"I'm pretty hungry," he lied. "I'm hoping you made one of those sandwiches for me."

"We did, Dad," Diego said. "The one with the most jelly, because—"

Sofia slapped a hand over her brother's mouth and glared at him. "Just sit down, Daddy, and we'll bring you a sandwich and milk."

Which meant they were still trying to butter him up

about the dog. But after the conversation they'd just had, arguing about a dog seemed so simple and happy and normal. He had to be careful, or he'd let himself make an emotional decision that wouldn't be good for any of them. Something he seemed to be tempted to do a lot of these days, he thought, looking over at Fiona's house.

He had to be careful about her, too. Because given his history, the way he'd failed Elizabeth and the long-lasting repercussions for his kids, getting too close to Fiona would put both her *and* her kids at risk.

Chapter 6

The next day, after they'd all changed out of their church clothes, Fiona and the kids got in the car and headed for the park. Brownie bounced from one side of the middle seat to the other, trying to get his head out the window, his long brown ears blowing in the breeze. The kids weren't bickering, the day was bright and sunny, and Fiona's strange feelings about Eduardo had settled down.

"Wasn't this a good idea, Mom?" Lauren asked as she helped Fiona pull out the picnic basket, a blanket and a bunch of yard toys.

Poppy squatted down to examine a dandelion. Maya grabbed Brownie's leash and took off across the field, Ryan chasing behind.

"Yes, honey, good idea. Hey, kids, back here right now!" Fiona called after her middle two.

Poppy tugged at Fiona's leg. "Look, Mommy, it's a

lion flower!" she crowed, holding up a dandelion. "Cuz it's like a lion's mane, right?"

Fiona's heart tugged and she shared a smile with Lauren as she bent down and picked Poppy up, settling her on her hip. Nothing was as sweet as a small child's view of the world. She wanted to hold her youngest tight and beg her to stay little.

Ryan jogged back, Maya and Brownie trailing behind. Fiona waited until all the kids clustered around her. "Okay, first rule—Brownie stays on the leash all the time, and you hold him with your hand through the strap like they showed us out at the rescue farm. Understand?"

They all nodded quickly.

"Second—before you play, everyone helps carry stuff to the picnic table. Maya, you're on toys. Ryan, the picnic basket. Lauren, you're going to help me carry the cooler, and I want you to hold Brownie's leash."

Sighs and groans.

"I wanna help, too," Poppy protested.

"I need you to carry the..." Fiona looked around.

"This Frisbee, because it's a little bit broken and you have to be careful with it." Maya reached into a basket and produced a Frisbee with a tiny flaw on the side. She handed it to Poppy. "Be careful, okay?"

"Okay!" Still in Fiona's arms, Poppy nodded seriously and held the Frisbee as if it were made of delicate glass.

Fiona smiled her thanks at Maya. She loved it when the kids were sweet with each other. *They really were obedient and helpful a lot of the time*, she thought gratefully as everyone picked up their assigned items. She turned toward their usual table.

"Can we have our picnic over there instead?" Ryan pointed toward a cluster of tables near the park's north side.

"Well…it's a little farther from the playground."

"But there's more room for Brownie to run," Lauren pointed out.

"And we're tired of going to the same picnic table all the time," Ryan added.

"Yeah, let's do something new." Lauren smiled brightly as she picked up her side of the cooler.

Fiona narrowed her eyes as she looked from the suggested spot to her two eldest kids. Something told her they'd agreed on this location change beforehand. The only question was why.

"Let's go *somewhere*! I want to play!" Maya jumped up and down, the Frisbees and balls bouncing in her basket.

"Please, Mom?" Lauren begged. "I'm tired of sitting by the little kids' playground."

"What do you think, Miss Poppy?" Fiona asked, rubbing noses with her youngest until she giggled.

"I'll give you piggyback rides and let you have my cookie," Lauren said.

"Yay!"

More and more suspicious. But Fiona couldn't think of a reason *not* to set up in a different section of Rescue River's large downtown park, so she nodded consent and followed her excited kids to the cluster of picnic tables they'd chosen. The distant sound of barking dogs gave her a moment's concern, but Lauren had Brownie tight on his leash, and the dog was too engrossed in sniffing every tree and chasing every butterfly to give the faraway dogs any notice.

"Put your basket by that tree," she directed Maya, "and then you can go play. Stay where you can see me, though."

"I will, Mom." Maya dropped the basket of toys and took off toward a couple of girls Fiona recognized from her school.

Ryan placed the food basket carefully on the table. "Do you want me to help get things out?" He glanced longingly toward an apple tree with low sturdy branches.

"No, it's okay," Fiona said. "Go climb. You, too, honey," she said to Lauren. "Go play. Just keep an eye on your sister."

"I will. Come on, Poppy." Lauren took her little sister's hand and they headed off across the grass.

As Fiona spread the tablecloth and started pulling out potato salad and plastic-wrapped sandwiches, the sound of barking caught her attention again, louder and closer this time.

"Hey, Fiona!" Troy Hinton's booming voice rang out behind her. "Coming back for more?"

She turned to see the tall veterinarian and shelter manager carrying a crate with a small terrier inside, yapping madly. In his other hand, upside down, was a sign that said *A Dog's Best Friend: Animal Rescue... A Day in the Park*.

Troy reached her side and set down the small dog's crate on the picnic table beside hers. "How's Brownie working out?" he asked.

"We love him. The kids are over there playing with him right now. What's..." She waved her hand toward the small dog, the sign and the two other workers she now saw headed in their general direction, with large dogs pulling at their leashes.

"It's our annual adoption-day-in-the-park. We like to get the dogs out in front of the public, see if we can find homes for some of the hard-to-place ones."

"Nice," she said, beginning to see the plan behind her kids' insistence on coming to this side of the park.

"Stop over if you get a chance. Angelica's coming later, with the kids, and she'd love to see you." He grabbed the crate and walked over toward a young volunteer who was practically being dragged along by a large boxer.

Fiona pulled drinks out of the cooler and put them on the edges of the tablecloth to weigh it down. If the kids thought she'd get another dog for them, they were out of their collective minds. She'd been very clear about that, and given how high-energy Brownie was, she'd been right. No way could they handle more than one. She wasn't going to give in to their ganging up on her.

"Fiona?"

She turned, and the sight of Eduardo sent a peculiar sensation down her spine. She turned, reclosable bag of chocolate chip cookies in hand. "Eduardo? What are you…" She stopped herself. He had every right to come to the park, but…

He glanced around at her picnic supplies and then back at her. He frowned. "Did your kids suggest coming today?"

She nodded slowly. "And they insisted we sit over here. Right by where Troy Hinton's setting up his adopt-a-dog event."

Eduardo scrubbed a hand over his face. "My kids begged me to bring our lunch here, too. They've been on me all morning, trying to talk me into getting a dog."

She pushed out a laugh. "Sorry about that. When

we brought Brownie home, I wasn't thinking about the pressure it would create for you."

He shrugged. "Not your fault. You can't run your family life based on not upsetting mine."

"True, but... I'm still sorry." She shaded her eyes to look over toward the dog rescue setup. Sure enough, her own kids and Eduardo's—along with a few others— were clustering around the caged and leashed adoptable dogs. Brownie bounced around hysterically barking, almost pulling Maya off her feet.

"I'd better go over there," she said. "I don't know what my kids are thinking. We already have all the dog we can handle."

"I think I might have an inkling," Eduardo said. "I'll come along, too, if you don't mind."

Eduardo's presence distracted Fiona from her annoyance with her kids. It was nice to walk beside a man several inches taller than she was. She didn't feel like a giant, as she sometimes did. It would be easy for him to put his arm around her. She'd actually fit beneath his shoulder.

And then she caught herself. Was she seriously daydreaming about cuddling up to Eduardo? That was about as smart as standing in front of the bakery window when you were dieting. She couldn't have a man like Eduardo, and there was no use torturing herself by imagining she could.

Except it was hard to resist her feelings. When his kids spotted them coming and ran over, he reached out muscular arms and caught one in each, kneeling down to mock-bang their heads together. His teeth flashed white in his deeply tanned face, and the care and fun in his eyes took her breath away. His kids seemed to know how special they had it, too; they both clung onto him for an extra few seconds, their love for their father obvious. For a moment, she ached at the thought that her own children had no such manly protector.

Ryan ran toward the trio and then stopped a few feet away from them, watching until the group hug broke up. His face held a mix of longing and jealousy. Of course, he was getting to the age where a mom wasn't enough. He needed a father figure, and Fiona was going to work on it. Maybe the husbands of some of her friends—Susan Hinton, Fern from the library—would be willing to spend a little male bonding time with Ryan. Or maybe it was time to get him into Boy Scouts, something he could do without his sisters always nearby.

"Dad, you gotta come see this!" Diego tugged at his father's hand, and a moment later, Ryan joined in. "Yeah, Mr. Delgado, come and see!"

The two boys pulled him toward the dogs and he let them, flashing an eye roll Fiona's way.

Sofia looked up at Fiona. "Do you want to come, too?" she asked hesitantly. "It's Brownie's mother who's here today. We hope Dad will let us get her."

Fiona didn't want to condone the behind-the-scenes manipulation that had obviously gone on between the kids. But the little wrinkle between Sofia's brows, the plaintive expression on her face, touched Fiona's heart. "I'll come look," she said. "But your dad will have to make the decision that's right for your family."

"I know." Sofia walked beside her. "He will. He'll pray about it."

Fiona smiled and impulsively ran a hand over Sofia's hair. "That's what I did, too."

"And God told you to get a dog?" Sofia reached up and took Fiona's hand, her eyes full of hope.

The affectionate gesture from the motherless little girl tugged at Fiona's heartstrings. "Not exactly. But I got a sense of peace about it, like if the right dog was there we'd know it, and we'd know if we were ready to handle the responsibility."

"And then you got Brownie!" Sofia took an extra skip, still clinging to Fiona. "I hope we can get Brownie's mom. I think our mom would have wanted us to."

"Really?" Fiona wondered whether that was true. "What's the dog's name? I don't think I met her at the shelter. I was too busy filling out paperwork for Brownie."

"She's called Sparkles." The little girl looked up at Fiona. "She had cancer, like my mom, but she didn't die from it. She just had to have her leg taken off, but she's still really pretty and nice. And I think—" She broke off.

Fiona swallowed the sudden lump in her throat. "What, honey?"

"I think she'd like to be with her son, Brownie. Just like our mom would like to be with us, if she could."

They were approaching the raucous collection of dogs and kids, so Fiona was spared having to answer. But her heart twisted into an impossible knot.

Of course, given Sofia's logic, she wanted the Delgado kids to get Brownie's mother. Except that the Delgado's residence near her own wasn't going to last forever. The kids and the dogs would be separated, maybe in a month, maybe several. They had to be careful about mingling their families, tightening the connections between them.

Eduardo's sweet children had already endured a terrible loss. Her own kids had as well.

Letting them get closer, having them share pets in common and become better friends, was a risk to young hearts that had already been broken.

Not to mention the risk to her own heart.

That evening, Eduardo sat outside on the grass, warm in the setting sun, watching his two kids and Fiona's four play with Brownie and Sparkles.

The grey-muzzled mama dog barked from a seated position, and Brownie kept bounding in circles around his mother. When he got close enough, she sniffed and licked him. Their obvious happiness about being together made Eduardo glad he'd given in to his kids' pleas.

Fiona approached, looking in the same direction and then smiling down at him.

He started to get to his feet, but she waved a hand and sat down beside him. "Sorry you caved?" she asked, a dimple tugging at the corner of her mouth.

He dragged his gaze away from it and shook his head. "Once I saw how excited Sparkles was to see Brownie, I was a goner."

"She gets around well on three legs." She hesitated, then added, "Did you know Sofia is making a connection between Sparkles and your wife?"

"What do you mean?"

"She had cancer and was separated from her child. Sofia told me she thought Sparkles wanted to be with Brownie the way your wife would have wanted to be with her and Diego, if she could."

The words hit him unexpectedly hard, and he couldn't speak.

Fiona seemed to read his emotions. She touched his hand and then shifted into a more comfortable position. "You okay?"

He nodded and swallowed the lump in his throat. *Boys don't cry.* He could remember his father saying it, but it was a lie and one he'd never repeated to Diego.

Still, he didn't want to break down in front of her just because his daughter had compared a hurt mama dog to Elizabeth. He was relieved when she changed the subject. "Sparkles is a sweet dog. If you hadn't adopted her, I might have done it myself. So, I'm *really* glad you did."

"I didn't know I could have shifted the burden onto you." He smiled at her and she smiled back, and they were just two parents sharing the humor and the challenges of raising kids.

It was lighthearted. And then it wasn't.

Fiona's eyes were green with gold flecks, and as he held her gaze, they seemed to darken.

His heart stirred in ways it hadn't since he was courting Elizabeth.

She must have detected the intensity, because she looked away. "I... I shouldn't take on any more responsibility, like another dog, because I need to think about what to do next," she said quickly. "After the dog-walking business failed, I thought I would never start another one, but all of a sudden now, I've been considering it again." She still wasn't looking at him.

"What..." He cleared his throat. "What would you do?"

"I keep looking at that barn back behind us. I'm

wondering... Could I buy it and make it into a wedding venue? Barn weddings are so popular now, and I love weddings." She met his eyes, looked away and blushed furiously.

He pushed out a chuckle. "Most women do. Have you researched the business side of it?"

A muscle twitched in the side of her face, the same side where the dimple had been. "Yes, but probably not enough. It's not my strong suit."

"Hey." He leaned a little closer, just to try to make her feel better. "No entrepreneur loves the research side of it, at least nobody I know. You have to do it, but that's not the most important skill."

"You think not?" She looked past him toward the old barn behind her property. "I like the idea of a wedding business because I could manage the hours. Do the prep work when I have time, or when the kids are in bed. Slow it down when things are busy at home. So, it would work with raising the kids. And it's a lot of the skills I *am* good at—organizing parties, decorating, caterers and food."

"And romance?" he asked teasingly, and then he could have kicked himself. What kind of a joker said something like that to a lady?

She didn't take it badly, though; she just snorted out a little laugh. "That, I'm not so good at. But I'm not the one who has to be romantic. I'd leave that to my clients."

"Wise."

She leaned back on her elbows. "I don't have much patience, though. Never been able to pay a whole lot of attention to details. So..." She shook her head. "I really shouldn't be planning another business endeavor."

"It takes time," he said. "When I started doing landscaping on the side, it seemed to take forever to get from two clients to five. I must have given out hundreds of business cards. I put up flyers everywhere. I came close to giving up, cashing in the equipment I'd bought and just taking more overtime at Hinton instead."

"How'd you stick with it?" She actually sounded interested.

He leaned over and plucked a blade of grass, held it up to the sun. "I started to realize a business is like a garden. You can't just put in the seeds and expect to be harvesting tomorrow. There's a growth process. Plants need sun and air and water. And time."

"Yeah." She looked over at her terraced vegetable garden, sat up straight to look again and then jumped up and ran over there. "Hey! Eduardo, c'mere!"

He followed, bemused to see her squatting in the grass in front of the terraces, studying the soil like a little kid. "Look! Something's coming up already!"

He studied the ground. "Yep. That's the lettuce. We planted it, what, nine days ago? And it's been nice and warm."

"I'm so excited!" She laughed up at him, her smile broad, eyes dancing.

"What's that, Mommy?" Poppy ran and banged into Fiona, then crouched to stare at the ground. The two of them looked so cute together, like the cover of a seed catalog.

An impression that was instantly broken when Brownie came loping over and ran carelessly through the garden, taking out a good six inches of lettuce seedlings just on the one pass.

He put his fingers to his lips and gave a loud whistle.

Brownie stopped, and Sparkles, who'd been following her son, froze as did all the kids.

"Okay, everyone. I need your help keeping the dogs out of the garden until we get a fence up."

"We need a fence?" Fiona frowned. "I'd rather have it be open."

"We weren't anticipating two active dogs," he said.

"Yeah, that's true, I guess." She studied the ground Brownie had torn up, picked up a tiny broken seedling. "Guess these little babies aren't going to make it."

"A fence will fix it," he reassured her. "It'll keep the critters out, too."

"Okay," she said with instant trust in his judgment. Then Ryan and Maya tugged at her hands and she followed them across the yard, laughing at some story they were telling. Sofia ran over, and Fiona reached out an arm to include his daughter in with her kids.

He watched them in the twilight, in the guise of replanting a couple of seedlings. Couldn't stop himself, not really.

He only wished he could put up a fence around his heart to keep out the uncomfortable feelings he was having toward the very pretty mother who grew more appealing the more time he spent with her.

Chapter 7

"Are you sure it's okay to leave all four of them with you?" Fiona asked Daisy the next Saturday. Colorful kids' crafts lined the tables in the activity room of the Senior Towers. Fiona's four kids had never been here before, but Maya had already sat down with a couple of other kids, clearly intrigued by their egg-painting project. A woman with short, stylish white hair and a colorful caftan held up an egg and demonstrated how to paint it.

"Absolutely," Daisy said. "We want kids. That's what this is all about. Right, Adele?"

"Right," the caftan-clad woman said, smiling. "Come on over."

Poppy clung to Lauren and Ryan looked from Fiona to the tables, his brow wrinkled.

"Go ahead, guys," Fiona encouraged them, walking

over to the tables with Daisy. Her kids followed. Moments later, Adele had them all set up with materials and she was showing them different ways they could color their eggs.

"They'll be fine," Daisy assured Fiona. "A couple of other kids are coming, I think. We'll keep them entertained, and you can help decorate the lobby and cafeteria. They really need some adult volunteers out there."

"Okay, if you're sure." Truthfully, a couple of hours working and talking with adults sounded blissful.

Behind them, a deep chuckle. "Well, well. Look who's here."

Chief Dion. Fiona looked over at Daisy and saw her friend suck in a breath, her face reddening.

Fiona extended a hand in greeting. "Hey, Chief Dion, what are you doing here?" she asked. "Are you going to paint Easter eggs?"

"If I'm needed," he said, then looked at Daisy. "I didn't know you were volunteering today."

"I didn't know *you* were." Daisy crossed her arms over her chest.

Wanting to ease the awkwardness between the two of them, Fiona cast around in her mind for conversation. "I didn't know you liked working with kids. You don't have any, do you?"

Something flashed in the police chief's eyes. "I... No. No, I don't."

Way to muck things up, Fiona. "I'm sorry, that was a rude question." She glanced over at Daisy, who gave her a half smile and a rueful shrug.

Dion patted Fiona's shoulder. "Don't you worry," he said. "There's a reason I keep getting invited. Every year, I say I won't do it—" he held open a large bag to display a fuzzy costume "—and every year, they talk me into it."

Fiona held back a laugh at the idea of the tall manly police chief in a bunny suit. "The kids will love it."

"Yes, they will," Daisy said, her voice unusually flat.

The sound of more kids' voices made them all turn toward the door, where Sofia and Diego were coming in. "Hey," they both said to the adults and then hurried to the table where Fiona's kids were already deep into wax pencils and egg dye.

Fiona looked to the doorway, and sure enough, there was Eduardo still dressed in the Hinton Enterprises polo shirt and work pants. "Sorry we're late," he said and then looked past Daisy and Dion to focus on Fiona. One dark eyebrow lifted a fraction. "Let me guess," he said slowly, "you're here to decorate the cafeteria."

Dion touched Daisy's arm and nodded toward the kids' table. "Want me to help you supervise?"

"That would be…great." Daisy sounded just a little breathless.

Eduardo's eyes narrowed a little as he looked after them.

"There you are!" Nonna D'Angelo came into the room, her eyes sparkling behind thick glasses. "Come on, the cafeteria decorating is getting started and we need some youngsters to climb ladders and lift heavy boxes." Slyly, she reached up and patted Eduardo's biceps. "I think you're almost as strong as my Vito."

"I doubt that." Eduardo smiled down at the much shorter woman. "But I'm a hard worker. Lead on."

Fiona followed, musing about the interactions she'd just witnessed. Daisy and Dion were rumored to be a couple, but they both claimed to be nothing but friends.

Something about the sparkle in Nonna D'Angelo's eyes, though, suggested that the matchmaking seniors had been involved in making sure the two volunteered together.

Was there a similar effort going on with Fiona and Eduardo?

In the cafeteria, chairs had been moved aside to allow those using wheelchairs to access the tables. A group of three women and a man in a red flannel shirt worked on what looked like centerpieces, consisting of low narrow baskets with colored grass, small figurines of rabbits and hens, and colorful ribbons. As they worked, they argued loudly.

"An Easter decoration isn't an Easter decoration without candy," the man said. "We oughta put chocolate eggs all through that grass."

"Kirk, you know that half the people here have diabetes, and the kids who are visiting shouldn't be getting all sugared up." The woman who spoke wove ribbon through a basket's rim and held it up for the others to see. "Do it like this, only with all different colors, and tie it in a pretty bow. I can help if you're not on board," she said to the red-shirted man.

"Kids are *supposed* to get sugared up at Easter," he grumbled, but he obediently took a ribbon and cardboard and followed the woman's lead.

"Over here." Nonna bustled over to a tall stepladder and a couple of baskets of crepe paper, with scissors and tape beside the baskets. She beckoned to Fiona and Eduardo. "Could you two be in charge of making streamers?"

"Sure," Eduardo said. "Right?" He looked at Fiona.

"Right." Her sense of being pushed together with

Eduardo was increasing. The disconcerting thing was the little jump in her pulse at the thought of working with him. She clenched her teeth, trying to get back to business.

"Eight or ten of them, meeting at the middle and then back to the opposite wall. And maybe some kind of backdrop for the dessert table." Nonna patted Fiona's arm, then Eduardo's. "Take your time."

Fiona picked up a bright pink roll of crepe paper. "Do you want to climb or twist?" she asked Eduardo. Contrary to Nonna's advice to take their time, she wanted to get this over with as soon as possible. She couldn't believe that she was now volunteering with Eduardo, in addition to living on the same property and working on the garden together. Attending the same church. Was there a day of the week when they didn't see each other?

And unfortunately, the more she saw of him, the more she liked him. He'd spoken truthfully—he *was* a hard worker, and she admired that. But he was never too busy to listen to a child's story or clean up the pews after services or help carry a heavy package. He had a ready laugh that drew people to him. His faith didn't just show up on Sundays but was an integral part of his life, as she'd seen in the way he talked to Sofia and Diego, guiding them toward being good Christians and good people.

Not to mention that the man was gorgeous. As he climbed the ladder, reached up to examine the ceiling and then looked down at her, eyes sparkling, she had to restrain herself from simpering like a middle schooler on her first crush.

"So," he said, "if I twist it around these braces, do you think it'll hold? I'm not exactly an expert at crepe paper streamers. In school, it was the girls who decorated for the prom."

"I'd say tape it." She handed him up the crepe paper and the roll of tape. "Did you go? To your prom, I mean?" Then she felt heat rise in her face. Why had she asked that question? Was it any of her business?

"I did," he said. "I took Elizabeth. It was one of our first dates." His hands went still for a moment, and then he smiled down at her. "Good times."

"That's nice. Nice to know high school sweethearts can make it last." She'd been awkward in high school and hadn't had a real boyfriend.

"We were together since age fifteen," he said. "Not that our parents let us date that young, but we ate lunch together at school and held hands in the hallways when we could get away with it." He shook his head as if shaking off the memories. "How about you? Did you go to prom?"

She nodded. "I went. With a boy who was at least a foot shorter than me. I wore flats and tried to hunch down for the photos, and he was practically on tiptoe. We got ourselves closer to the same height for the picture, but the expressions on our faces!" She gave a fake wince. "Totally miserable."

He chuckled. "I had the same problem. I was already six-three in tenth grade, and Elizabeth was a foot shorter. Dancing was a little awkward." He smiled. "But we figured it out."

And they'd been very happy together, from the sound of things.

"Was your husband tall?" he asked. "Not that it's any of my business," he added quickly, attaching the paper on one end and handing the streamer down to her. "Here. You twist, and I'll move the ladder to the center."

"He was about my height," she said, walking backward beside him, twisting the paper. "He didn't like for me to wear heels."

Eduardo laughed. "We men. We get our egos caught up in all the wrong things."

Miss Minnie Falcon approached, pushing her walker. She watched as they attached the next loop of crepe paper to a crossbar in the center of the ceiling.

"Do you think it looks okay?" Fiona asked her.

Miss Minnie waved a wrinkled hand. "It's fine. As long as the residents see some color, they'll be happy, and the same with the children. They'll all be busy playing games and eating candy."

"No candy, Minnie," said the same woman who'd restricted the man from adding it to the centerpieces.

Miss Minnie waved a hand and turned away. "There'll be candy, don't you worry," she said quietly to Fiona and Eduardo. "Your kids will have a wonderful time. They're coming, aren't they?"

"Our kids are here now," Eduardo said, climbing down from the ladder. "I think they're part of the practice drill for the big party next week. Daisy and Adele are in charge."

"And Dion," Fiona reminded them. "He's dressing up as the Easter bunny later. I would guess he'll at least have a few jelly beans to pass around."

"Sugar-free," said the woman at the table.

"Sugar-free candy gives me gas," said Kirk, the red-shirted man.

Fiona looked at Eduardo. His dark eyes twinkled with the same suppressed laughter that threatened to bubble up inside of her. He jerked his head sideways toward the next corner of the room and she nodded and took the roll of crepe paper from him, twisting it as she backed away from the now-lively altercation between Miss Minnie and the table decorators.

"I'm glad we're just on ceiling duty," he said as soon as they were out of the elders' earshot. "Wouldn't want to get in the middle of the sugar versus sugar-free debate."

"Me, either." She waited while he set up the ladder and then handed him the roll. "I do my best to keep a balance with my kids, food-wise, but Easter is no-holds-barred candy at my place. Hope that won't be a problem for you, because I'm sure our kids will want to share the wealth."

"Just as long as you don't steal all the peanut butter eggs," he said, pulling his face into a mock-serious expression. "Those are *mine*, lady."

"No way, they're my favorites, too! You won't be seeing any from the Farmingham household."

"Wait a minute." He narrowed his eyes at her. "You're a basket thief, too?"

"Of course!"

"Openly or stealth?"

"Oh, stealth, for sure. But I think Lauren's onto me. She took her basket to her room and hid it in the closet last year."

"You need to perfect your approach."

They were both laughing, gazes locked, standing close together. Something arced between them, a connection of humor and empathy and, maybe, something more.

Maybe if Eduardo were to bend a little closer and kiss her, she wouldn't pull back.

But what was she thinking? Women like Fiona didn't get men like Eduardo.

Not only that, but they were standing at the edge of a retirement center cafeteria, all tile floors and Formica tables, laughter and small talk drifting over from the few groups of people at the tables.

They were still looking at each other. She needed to pull back, and quickly.

"I used to decorate like that for all the school dances," said a shaky voice behind them.

Just in time. Fiona turned and saw a tiny woman in a wheelchair. "Miss Elsie! I haven't seen you in church lately."

"Can't do anything much now." The woman looked down at her own body with what seemed to be disgust.

Eduardo knelt beside her and took her tiny hand. "Hey, Miss Elsie. We could use some help with the decorating if you're up for it."

"I don't know what use I could be. Can't walk since I broke my hip. Don't have much energy."

Eduardo took the crepe paper roll from Fiona and placed it in the older woman's hands. "If you do the twisting while Fiona rolls you along and I get the ladder set up, it'll go a lot faster. Fiona can get on the step stool beside me, and you can hand it up to her. I won't have to keep climbing up and down."

The woman narrowed her eyes at him. "Don't you patronize me, Eduardo Delgado."

"We could use the help, but it's up to you," he said with a shrug and climbed the ladder.

Fiona hurried over to the wall and grabbed the step stool, setting it up between the tall ladder and the wheelchair.

Miss Elsie began twisting the crepe paper, and when it was ready, she handed it to Fiona, who handed it to Eduardo.

It was, in fact, a quicker and easier way to work.

Had Eduardo *wanted* to get the job over with quickly? Did he dislike working alone with Fiona? Or was he just being kind to an old woman who seemed in need of cheering up?

Fiona blew out a breath, and with it, her childish thoughts. What mattered was that the cafeteria began looking more and more festive, and a woman who'd been complaining of uselessness felt useful.

"How much of that crepe paper do you have?" Miss Elsie asked.

"Lots. Why?"

"It looks nice if you twist two together," Miss Elsie said. She took a pink strand, held it together with a white one and demonstrated. "And if you loop the ends around, like so, it covers the tape." As she spoke, she added a couple of twists and folds to the end of the streamer to make a flower effect.

"Wow, that's pretty!" Fiona studied the flower. "Can you show me how?"

"It does look better." Eduardo took the paper flower from Fiona and climbed the ladder to affix it to the spot where the streamer was taped to the ceiling.

"We're obviously rank amateurs," Fiona said. "Do you think we need to redo the ones that are done?"

Elsie waved her hand. "Goodness, no. It's a party for kids and old people. No one needs or wants perfection."

"Well," Eduardo said as he carried the ladder to the next location, Fiona pulling Elsie backward so she could twist the strands, "we're a little bit closer to perfection because of you. Thank you."

Elsie beckoned for Fiona to bend closer as Eduardo climbed the ladder. "He's a charmer, that one," she said. "Hold on to him."

"I'm not..." Fiona broke off. She wasn't *with* Eduardo, and she didn't want anyone to think she was; on the other hand, making a big deal out of how they *weren't* together didn't seem like the right move, either.

She set up her stepladder, took the twisted paper from Elsie and climbed up to Eduardo.

They were taping up the last streamer when a man spoke up behind her. "Where you from, honey?"

Fiona turned on the stepladder and looked down to see Kirk, the red-shirted man who'd complained about candy and gas, pointing at her. "I'm from Illinois," she said.

His bushy grey eyebrows lifted. "They grow 'em tall out there, don't they?"

Heat rose in her face as she descended the stepladder, wanting to get out of the spotlight. Talk about embarrassing! Would her size *always* be the first thing people noticed about her?

"Kirk Whittaker, you shut your mouth." Nonna D'Angelo said. "Fiona just needs a taller man than you are, that's all." She pulled herself to her full height of, at most, five foot three and glared at Mr. Whittaker, who wasn't much bigger.

The old man's face turned as red as his shirt. He glanced around, stiffened his back and squared his shoulders.

As she stood beside the stepladder, her face still warm, a thought struck Fiona: in addition to being about the same height as she was, Reggie had been slender, not muscular like Eduardo.

Maybe that was why he'd always told her to wear low heels and lose weight. Maybe he'd just felt small around her.

Another man, even shorter than Mr. Whittaker and sporting ancient-looking baggy blue jeans, strolled over. "What's that you say about tall women?"

Fiona groaned inwardly.

"Now, me," the jeans-clad man said around the toothpick he was chewing, not waiting for an answer, "I like a tall gal. My Lulu was six foot and did some modeling. I was proud to be at her side, even when she wore those high spike heels."

Miss Minnie Falcon shook her head and looked directly at Fiona but spoke loudly enough for all to hear. "We're God's workmanship, and that's the important thing. And all this focus on appearances takes away from what's truly important. What's in our hearts." She frowned sternly at the two men.

Obviously understanding the reprimand, they looked away from the stern former Sunday school teacher and got very busy cleaning up from the centerpiece-decorating project.

Still up on the ladder, Eduardo cleared his throat. "We'd better finish up," he said and climbed down. The elders, with the exception of Elsie, started carrying supplies to the boxes that lined one side of the room.

Fiona partially turned to find Eduardo standing closer than she'd expected. "I'm with Miss Minnie," he said in a half whisper. "We're all God's workmanship. And he did a particularly fine job on you."

Heat rose in her face again and she turned toward him. "Eduardo…"

"Inside and out," he added, looking directly into her eyes.

And then he backed up and moved the ladder to the next location, leaving Fiona to push Elsie's wheelchair. Meanwhile, Fiona's heart was pounding like Ryan's snare drum, way too hard and loud. Was it her imagination, or did handsome Eduardo feel something romantic toward her? And if he did…was he likely to do anything about it?

Be careful. Don't get sucked in.

She liked Eduardo and thought him to be a good person, but he was a man. And in her experience, men were genetically predisposed to betray women.

Especially women like her.

Chapter 8

Eduardo berated himself as he carried a ladder toward the storage room, Fiona walking in front of him.

Why'd you tell her how good she looks? Why would you want to say a thing like that? Why do you keep half hitting on her when you know you can't take it anywhere?

Fiona paused at the window, and the sunlight set her red hair on fire. She glanced back at him, wariness in her eyes. She knew he was interested, all right.

And that was bad. Because no matter how interested he was, he couldn't act on it. He kept walking past her, ignoring her magnetic pull.

"Looks like the kids are outside," she said as he passed.

"Go ahead. I'll be out in a minute." Or more. However long it took to calm his fool self down.

Ten minutes later, he'd put the ladders away, washed

his hands and splashed water on his face. At the same time, he gave himself a lecture about how he was committed to his kids, and only his kids, and how he wasn't in the market for a relationship.

Still, when he walked outside to see his children and Fiona's all clustered around a long bench with a giant white Easter bunny, with Fiona watching from across the wide deck, his resolve started to melt away.

Why was it, again, that he couldn't take a stab at forming a family with Fiona?

Poppy sat on the bench off to one side, a good six or eight feet away from the crowd around the bunny. She had a basket in her hands and was rhythmically putting candy into her mouth. Chocolate, if the smears on her hands and face were any indication.

As he approached, Fiona half turned.

"Poppy's okay?" he asked.

Fiona smiled fondly at her youngest child. "She's scared of the Easter Bunny," she said, "but not too scared to take the basket of chocolate eggs he offered her."

"Smart kid." And she was cute, too, with her flyaway blond hair and big serious eyes.

The bunny held out a basket to the other kids, and they all took pieces of paper out of it. The two older girls read theirs and ran off quickly. Maya, Ryan and Diego, slower readers, stood studying theirs.

Diego's forehead wrinkled and the color heightened in his cheeks. All of a sudden, he flung the paper back at the bunny. "This isn't the right way to do an egg hunt," he yelled.

Maya grabbed the fluttering sheet of paper. "If you don't want to find your surprise, I'll take it."

"Gimme that!" Diego grabbed the paper roughly out of Maya's hand.

"Hey!" Ryan said, stepping protectively in front of Maya. "Don't be mean to my sister!"

Instantly, without looking at each other, Fiona and Eduardo both headed toward the kids.

Eduardo reached the small group first and gripped Diego's shoulder firmly. "What's going on? You know better than to talk to people that way."

"I hate this egg hunt," Diego muttered, looking away.

"He was mean to Maya." Ryan glared at Diego.

"Diego, do you need to apologize?" Eduardo asked.

"It's no big deal." Maya shrugged and turned toward the lawn where colorful eggs peeped through the grass. "I'm gonna go hunt for eggs."

"Sorry," Diego grunted after her.

"And I'm gonna find my surprise," Ryan said. He looked at Fiona and Eduardo and held up his square of paper. "The Easter Bunny made it like a treasure hunt, and every kid gets a special surprise." Then he added in a whisper, "I *think* the Easter Bunny is Police Chief Coleman."

From inside the bunny, a low chuckle sounded. "Oh, no, no, no. Nobody knows the true identity of the Easter Bunny, young man."

Eduardo held out a hand for Diego's paper, then studied its small closely printed letters and immediately understood the problem. He turned to Diego. "Come on, let's sit down and look at your clue sheet together."

"I don't want to do it."

The Easter Bunny had been quiet, but now he stood. "Time for the old EB to go cool off," he said. Leaning toward Fiona, he whispered, "This suit is as hot as wearing a plastic bag in the desert at high noon."

She laughed and touched the bunny's arm. "You poor thing. You're enjoying every minute of this, and you know it."

The bunny chuckled again, and Eduardo felt jealousy knife through his chest.

"I might enjoy it," Dion added, quietly enough that the kids didn't hear, "except it smells like every other sweaty guy that ever rented it." He patted Diego's and Ryan's heads with a giant paw and headed toward the door into the Towers.

Eduardo was glad to see him go, which was ridiculous. Was he seriously jealous of a man in a bunny suit? He squatted in front of his son with the clue sheet. "You know what to do when you start getting frustrated, right?"

"Oh, Dad…" Diego's lower lip stuck out a little, his face still reminiscent of the toddler he'd been.

Eduardo clenched his teeth to keep from reading the page aloud to his son. "You know the steps to take."

"I just want to find my egg! I don't wanna go slow and sound it out."

That made sense. Again, Eduardo fought the urge to just do the work for his son. "Is there another way you could get it done?"

Diego sighed and turned to Ryan. "I'm sorry I was mean to Maya," he said. "You want to look for our eggs together? I have dyslexia, and it's hard for me to read this." He took the clue sheet from his dad and held it up.

"Sure, I'll help," Ryan said. "Let's go!"

And they ran off together.

Fiona stared after them and then sat down on the

steps of the deck. Her forehead wrinkled and she cocked her head to one side.

He shouldn't sit down next to her, and there wasn't much room on the step. He'd have to sit close.

Plus, the deck's fences and surrounding bushes gave them privacy. The last thing they needed.

But he was curious about what put that thoughtful expression on her face, so he sat down against his better judgment. "What?" he asked her.

"Diego has dyslexia," she said slowly, "and he does just fine. He takes steps to get help when he needs to."

"He gets embarrassed sometimes," Eduardo said. "But his teachers and I drill into him that it's not his fault. He learns differently, and sometimes he needs a different kind of help." He looked after his son and pride welled in his chest. "He's getting better about dealing with it."

"Eduardo," she said, gently grasping his arm, "do you think I could get help with my math thing, even though I'm an adult? Learn strategies to work around it?"

He tried to ignore the way her touch seemed to radiate through his body. "Of course you could."

"How?"

"Well… I'm no expert, but I do get a magazine from a national organization about learning disabilities. They have a whole section for adults with LD."

"Can I look at it sometime? Soon?"

"Of course. I'll get you a couple of copies tonight. I'm sure there are online resources, too."

"Because, the way Diego acted just then?" She spoke rapidly, her cheeks pink. "That's how I used to feel. Still do, sometimes."

"Like when we were looking at spreadsheets at the Chatterbox?"

She nodded. "Exactly. I've learned to cover it up under a ditzy-female routine, but I'm not laughing on the inside. Except now, I am. Or smiling, at least. Because maybe I can get help with it."

"I'm sure you can." *Why hadn't her parents gotten her help long ago?*

"And maybe," she went on, her eyes glowing, "maybe I can even get to where I can have a business again." Her hand tightened on his arm. "Oh, Eduardo, that would be so fantastic. It's been my dream, ever since I became a mom, to have a part-time business and stay home with the kids. I have dozens of ideas."

She was so pretty that he was tongue-tied. He just nodded like an idiot and kept staring at her.

She let go of his arm, maybe misinterpreting his silence. "I'd better not get too excited about this, right? I mean, who knows whether I'm one of those people who can be helped? I'm a whole lot older than Diego." She slid away from him, as much as possible on the narrow step. "I'm sorry to go so crazy on you, just because I saw your son figure something out."

Seeing her get so excited about the future and about new possibilities had warmed Eduardo's heart. Seeing her back off made it hurt. He didn't want her to retreat into fear and shame again.

He wanted to help her blossom.

Like it had a will of its own, his hand reached out to brush back a strand of hair that had fallen over her cheek. Once there, his thumb decided to stroke her jawline, just a little.

And now, a whole different kind of emotion came into her gold-flecked eyes, in fact, a mixture of them:

fear and worry, but also that awareness he'd seen a time or two before.

He drew in a breath and tried to smile reassuringly. "It's nice to see you excited about the future." Which would have worked as an excuse for his touching her, except that his hand was still up there, cupping her face.

Her own hand came up to his. To pull it away? No. Just to rest on top of his. Her breath was a little ragged, too, almost as ragged as Eduardo's own.

He knew he shouldn't kiss her. There were reasons, lots of reasons. It was just that, right now, he couldn't exactly remember what they were.

"We shouldn't..." she began. But her hand clutched his, convulsively, holding it to her face.

"I know." He leaned closer. "Tell me no."

Her eyes were wide. Slowly, she shook her head. "No."

"No, don't kiss you? Or no, you're not going to tell me no?"

"No," she said in a husky whisper, "I'm not going to tell you no."

Fiona felt her heart turn to butter as Eduardo's lips brushed hers, then came back to linger, warm against her mouth. She yielded to him, dizzily, and tightened her hand over his to steady herself. After a moment he pulled away and rubbed his cheek against hers, rough as sandpaper against her softness.

Voices echoed in her mind: *Why would someone like him kiss someone like you? You should be thankful to get any man. Does he mean it, or is it a lie like Reggie's kisses were?*

She pulled back, trying to shake the thoughts out of her head the way you'd shake away a buzzing insect.

Eduardo's warm brown eyes held concern along with caring. "Hey. What's going on in that head of yours?" His tone was deeper than usual.

"Nothing," she said in defiance of the voices. She leaned fractionally closer and Eduardo brushed his lips over hers again.

"Dad!" Sofia's voice was close.

Fiona and Eduardo pulled instantly apart.

"My mommy's kissing your daddy!" Poppy giggled from Sofia's arms.

Fiona's heart pounded as she stood quickly. "We're good friends," she said, uncomfortable with the breathless sound of her voice. She reached out to take Poppy from Sofia.

But Poppy struggled down and ran across the lawn toward the other kids. Her stomach knotting, Fiona hurried after her. But not before she caught a glimpse of Sofia's mistrustful expression and heard her say, "Dad? You're not supposed to kiss anybody but Mom."

Poppy reached the other children. "Our mommy kissed Mr. Delgado!" she crowed, obviously thrilled to be the one with the news for once.

Four heads snapped in her direction. Four pairs of eyes went rounder.

Fiona felt sick inside. What kind of parents were they, to share a stolen kiss practically in full view of their children?

A kiss that couldn't go anywhere, ever?

Eduardo sat in his pickup truck in the parking lot of the Senior Towers, trying to do damage control with his kids.

What had possessed him to kiss Fiona? And to do it there, where any of their kids could come around the corner and see them…as Sofia and Poppy in fact had done? How selfish they'd been to risk hurting innocent young children whose hearts had already been broken once before.

Fiona walked by on the way to her SUV, her kids surrounding her like a brood of chicks with a mother hen. They were all talking excitedly, but Fiona's face was drawn tight.

They glanced at each other, but all he could see in her eyes was regret.

"Why *did* you kiss Mrs. Farmingham, Dad?" Diego sounded confused, like he was trying to work out a new math problem in his head.

"Because he *likes* her, dummy." Sofia's arms were crossed over her chest.

Eduardo shot up a prayer for guidance. How did you protect young minds and hearts while being honest with them about life?

"I kissed her because…" Eduardo sought for the truth. "Because I like her very much."

"We like her, too, Dad," Sofia said in the snarky voice she hadn't been using as often lately. "But we don't hide behind bushes *kissing* her."

"Does it mean you're going to get married?" Diego asked.

Eduardo blew out a sigh and shook his head. "No. I've told you before, I don't have any plans to get married again. You two are my focus."

"And Mom was your wife," Sofia said.

"But Mom's gone," Diego pointed out, "and maybe Daddy wants another wife now."

Eduardo hated the way that sounded. "You kids know how much I loved your mother," he said through a tight throat. "How much I miss her. I wish she could be here with us right now."

"But she can't," Sofia said flatly, "so you're kissing Mrs. Farmingham now."

"That...that was a onetime thing," he told them. "I don't think we'll be kissing each other again." Not with the expression he'd seen on Fiona's face.

But, oh, that moment had been sweet. He'd felt like a bear coming out of hibernation after a long, long winter. Coming alive again in the spring. Waking up to a new world.

He wasn't a good choice for any woman, he reminded himself. He'd made a commitment to his kids, no one else.

"Mr. Hinton was married before and his wife died," Diego pointed out. "And then he married Mrs. Hinton, and now Mindy has a mom again. And a little brother." Diego sounded a little wistful.

"That's true," Eduardo admitted.

But Sam Hinton also had a stellar record of taking care of his first wife. She'd lived in luxury throughout her cancer treatments, with visits to specialists around the world.

And it still didn't save her, a voice inside reminded him.

"It would be weird having the Farmingham kids as brothers and sisters." Sofia sounded slightly intrigued by the possibility. "I'd have a sister my exact age, like a twin."

"Look, guys," Eduardo said, "let's stop talking about that like it's going to happen. Let's stop at..." He cast about for something that might distract them. "Let's stop at Taco Nation and pick up dinner and watch movies all night."

"All *night*?" Diego said.

At the same time, Sofia said, "Taco *Nation*?"

"All night until bedtime, and yes. Just this once."

"We haven't gone to Taco Nation since the night after Mom died," Sofia said.

Eduardo let his head sink back against the headrest. He'd forgotten about that miserable last-minute trip. Would hitting the fast-food Mexican place bring back bad memories for all of them?

He wanted to stop thinking. To stop making mistakes. "Buckle up," he said and started to pull out of the Senior Towers parking lot.

But the sound of sirens made him hit the brakes. An ambulance squealed into the parking lot and headed to the front door of the Towers. The sirens clicked off and the paramedics rushed inside.

He, Sofia and Diego sat watching. Nobody told Eduardo to hurry up. Nobody spoke.

Were they all three remembering the ambulance that had come for Elizabeth multiple times? Until the last time when there'd been no more need for speed?

He didn't want to stick around the Senior Towers watching to see who the patient was. Which friend. Whether the ambulance would fly off with lights and sounds or drive at a slow, sedate pace into the night.

He didn't want his kids to see it, either.

Swallowing hard, he put the truck into gear. "Taco Nation, here we come," he said, wondering whether his voice sounded as fake to his kids as it did to him.

"I'm not actually that hungry," Sofia said.

"Me, either," Diego said. "Where's my handheld?"

Eduardo felt around for the small gaming device and handed it back to Diego. Without her even having to ask, he handed his phone to Sofia so she could play her games on it. And he drove home slowly. For a day that had started out so promising, he definitely felt beat-up now.

After finally getting her overexcited kids into bed, Fiona collapsed back onto the couch at her house.

She lay there, flicking channels on the television; but when she finally recognized that she couldn't distract herself from her thoughts, she clicked the power off.

He'd kissed her. Eduardo had kissed her.

He'd kissed *her*. The woman who had to shop at the tall women's clothing store in Cleveland. Who'd repeated third grade and barely passed the math competency test required for high school graduation. Whose business had failed and whose husband had betrayed her.

We are God's workmanship, Miss Minnie had said.

Eduardo had said… What was it? *He did a particularly fine job on you.*

And then he'd kissed her. Her fingers rose to touch her lips as she remembered.

Maybe, just maybe, there was something new and wonderful in her future.

She thought of Diego and his frustration and grabbed her phone to look up *adult learning disabilities*. She was reading about something called "dyscalculia," with a sense of amazed recognition, when a text came in.

Kids in bed? Meet out by the garden?

Eduardo wanted to see her! She hugged herself and rushed into the bathroom to comb her hair. She checked the bedrooms and found all four kids sleeping soundly. Only then did she text back.

For a little bit, can't stay.

Should she put on a different shirt? No, that would seem like she was trying too hard. But definitely a little perfume. And she should brush her teeth. Just in case.

She forced herself to walk at a slow pace toward the garden. In the moonlight, there was Eduardo—tall muscular Eduardo.

A sense of hope and possibility made her heart knock around wildly in her chest.

He didn't walk to meet her but stood beside the fence post he'd just pounded into the ground yesterday. His face was somber.

Something was wrong.

She stopped a full four feet away from him and cocked her head, studying his face.

No, this didn't seem like a kissing-type encounter after all.

"Are you okay?" he asked. "Are your kids okay?"

She nodded, a couple quick jerks of her head up and down. "Yeah. We're fine. Um, you and yours?"

He shook his head. "Lots of questions."

"From you, or from them?"

"Both." He looked up at the starry sky as if seeking guidance and then looked at her straight on and met her eyes. "Look, Fiona…"

She lifted a hand to stop his speaking. She didn't want to hear it. Not from Eduardo.

"I know," she said rapidly. "I know, it's not… It was nothing. It's not going anywhere."

"It wasn't nothing," he said, "but you're right. It can't."

"Is…is that what you wanted to tell me?" Her voice sounded a little shrill. "Because I knew that, Eduardo. What did you think, that I'd take it all seriously? That I'd expect a marriage proposal because we shared a little kiss?"

Who *was* this woman talking so lightly about the most amazing kiss of her life?

"My kids asked if we were going to get married," he said, his voice serious.

"Oh, mine did, too." They'd bugged her about it, actually. They *wanted* her to marry Eduardo, wanted Sofia and Diego to be a part of the family. They were already talking about how they'd rearrange their bedrooms to fit them in.

Now she pushed out a laugh. "Kids. No sense of perspective."

"Right." Eduardo looked off to the side. "I just wanted to make sure, to see if you… Well, to see if you were okay. That was pretty intense for a minute there."

She waved a hand. "I'm fine. Fine! We're friends who got a little carried away, that's all. It wouldn't work between us, anyway. I'm sorry you wasted a minute worrying about it."

Her mouth continued to talk. She was fine. They were all fine. They'd reassure their kids that they were just friends. No upsets, no changes, nothing to worry about.

Her heart curled up in a tiny little ball in her chest, weeping.

"Okay, Fiona," Eduardo said finally. "That's all good, then. I should get back to the kids."

"Me, too," she said quickly. "I should get back to my kids, too."

"Good night, then." He gestured toward her house. "Go on. I'll watch until you get inside."

"It's Rescue River." She forced a cheerful smile. "I'm totally safe."

"I'll watch," he said gently. "See you safe inside."

"Okay. Good night." She turned and nearly ran toward the door of her house, eyes blurring.

Because she was anything but safe inside. Not when Eduardo had shoved her away, just as she'd known, in her heart, that he would.

Chapter 9

When Eduardo pulled his truck into the parking lot by the pond the next morning, he wasn't surprised to see Fiona and her kids pulling gear from her SUV.

Of course they were coming to today's fishing derby. Everyone in town was here.

In fact, he was late. As the person supervising the fishing of the eight-to ten-year-olds, he should have arrived half an hour early. But getting out of bed had proved to be a chore.

He'd tossed and turned most of the night, his mind cycling restlessly through particular moments. Sofia's accusation: *you're not supposed to kiss anyone but Mom.* Little Poppy's glee as she ran off to tell the other kids—and anyone else in earshot, presumably—about the romantic moment she'd seen. Fiona's stricken face last night in the garden before she'd brushed off his remarks with a carelessness that had surprised him.

And most of all, the bittersweet rightness of holding Fiona in his arms.

"There's Lauren and Ryan," Diego said. "Let's go with them."

He was opening his mouth to respond when he saw Fiona tug her eldest two back toward her and walk in the opposite direction from where he stood with his kids.

He dawdled at his truck until the Farminghams were out of sight and then headed toward the pond, where organized chaos reigned.

On one side was a large wading pool set up with toy fishing lines. A sign read *Two-to Three-year-olds*. Rowdy toddlers darted around while parents tried to keep them from plunging into the pool.

Many residents of the town, those who had grandkids or kids here and those who didn't, had set up lawn chairs. He walked by Mr. Love and Miss Minnie among some other residents of the Senior Towers. Kirk, the man who'd been complaining about sweets and gas yesterday, was at it again, saying, "You mark my words, there's a storm coming. I always feel it in my left knee."

"You and your left knee," muttered Nonna D'Angelo as her grandson, Vito, helped her into her seat.

On a small podium, Lou Ann was setting up chairs and a stand for first-place, second-place and third-place winners. Two older gentlemen stood arguing, one overdressed for the occasion and one underdressed. Mr. Hinton, Senior, and old Gramps Camden had been rivals for Lou Ann's affections for many years. As usual, she was ignoring their blustering and getting things done.

Farther down the shoreline, little Mercedes Camden held a group of kids rapt. As Eduardo and his kids got closer, he saw that Fiona's brood had stopped to listen.

"When I was little, I got lost here," Mercedes was saying proudly. "It was winter, and it was cold! I hid under this boat, right here."

"Didn't you freeze?" a girl asked.

"How'd you get found?" That was Ryan, sounding worried.

"My daddy found me," Mercedes said proudly. "And he carried me back to Mama Fern, and now we all live together."

"C'mon, Dad!" Diego was tugging at his arm. "They're about to tell the rules!"

Sure enough, there was a megaphoned explanation of the age groups and prizes for most fish and biggest fish. "We have buckets for everyone, so fill yours with water and keep your fish in it until one of the officials can come measure them. They're the ones in the red hats."

Eduardo looked around to see Vito and Lacey D'Angelo, Buck Armstrong and Troy Hinton all wearing red hats and waving.

After more discussion of safety rules and bait, the officials directed the kids to their places, starting with the youngest and organized by age group.

"The only thing I don't like about fishing," Diego said as they waited their turn, "is killing things."

"It's catch and release, buddy," Eduardo explained. "The fish don't die."

"But the worms do."

"You're weird," Sofia scoffed. "Come on, let's get our buckets!"

The next hour was a blur of helping all the eight-to ten-year-olds bait fishhooks, attach bobbers and throw lines into the water. Amid much tangling and arguing, there was thankfully only one volatile moment when Vito D'Angelo's son, Charlie, landed a hook in the newly curled hair of Paula Camden, the little girl Fern and Carlo Camden had adopted a couple of years ago—a crisis quickly averted by some expert parental intervention. Little Mindy Hinton was the first to catch a fish, and no one begrudged her the honor. Reeling it in had been a challenge with her prosthetic arm, but she'd insisted on doing it herself and she'd succeeded.

Parents watched and helped, and Vito and Lacey stood nearby to measure the fish. The kids laughed and yelled, trying their best to win. The day had gone slightly overcast, perfect for fishing.

But Eduardo didn't feel good. Didn't feel right. Didn't like the distance between him and Fiona, even though he knew that he'd done the right thing, and the only thing he could.

It must have shown, too, because Dion came over and slapped him on the back, then nodded sideways, urging Eduardo away from the group. "Gotta talk to you, man," he said. "They've got it under control. Right?" With a stern look, he recruited two fathers who'd been standing idly by to go over and help the eight-to ten-year-olds.

In an area sheltered from the increasing wind and from prying eyes, Dion glared at Eduardo. "What did you do to Fiona?"

Guilt beat at Eduardo, but he got in front of it with his annoyance at the man's tone. "Not your business what goes on between me and her."

"She's usually a happy person, but she's moping. Not saying a word, even though she's doing concessions with her two best friends."

"Did Daisy send you over here to ask me?" Eduardo demanded.

Dion opened his mouth, closed it and looked to the side. Maybe he was trying to fight a smile. "She and Susan, yeah. But it's true Fiona's upset. Even a lunk like me can see it." He studied Eduardo. "Come to think of it, you're not looking so good yourself. Those bags under your eyes make you look older than me."

Eduardo didn't answer, just turned to walk along the wide woodland trail, and Dion fell into step beside him.

Birds sang overhead and the smell of damp earth rose from the forest floor. For a few minutes, they just walked through the trees, and Eduardo felt a small dose of peace seep into his troubled heart.

"I kissed her," he said finally.

Dion looked over, lifted an eyebrow. "That usually makes people happy, not miserable."

"It did, until our kids caught us."

Dion made a sound suspiciously like a laugh.

Eduardo could see how it could be funny on a sitcom, but in real life, it was more complicated. "Sofia's upset."

"Because…"

"I'm not supposed to kiss anyone but Mom."

"Oh." Dion nodded thoughtfully. "She's not used to it because you've never dated much. How about Diego?"

Eduardo shook his head. "He's more thinking about how it'll be when Fiona and I get married."

"Boy moves fast." Dion clapped Eduardo on the back. "I'm sure they'll get accustomed to the idea soon enough. And kids aren't likely to be traumatized by a kiss. How'd Fiona's kids react?"

He wondered the same thing. "I don't know."

Dion stopped, turned to him. "You don't *know*? What did she say about it?"

"We didn't talk. Not really. I… I felt like that was best."

Dion turned to start walking again. "If you didn't have the sense to… Come on, help me understand it. You kissed her but didn't talk to her afterward? What's going on?"

"I'm a working-class landscaper who let down his first wife when she needed me. Fiona's got a million more appropriate opportunities."

"What if she likes *you*, though?"

"It's a mistake she'll get over soon enough."

Dion shook his head. "You're a bigger fool than I thought. Don't you know who you are in Christ?"

Eduardo stared at him. "What does Christ have to do with it?"

"You're kidding, right?"

"Well, sure, I know Christ has to do with everything, but specifically?" He shrugged. "I don't know how He plays into my love life. Or lack thereof."

Dion threw his hands in the air. "I'm dragging you back to Bible study next week. But seriously. If you made mistakes in your past relationship, you're forgiven. And as for money?" He shrugged. "Just not important. Not to a Christian. Not to Fiona, I'm guessing."

"Come on."

"I mean, sure. You've got to pay your way. No slackers in the Kingdom. But anything beyond that doesn't matter."

"When she could afford to take me on twenty luxury vacations for every camping trip I can offer her?" Eduardo shook his head. "Uh-uh. I'm too old-fashioned for that."

"Maybe she likes camping," Dion said mildly as they came out of the woods. "Ever think of that, my man?"

In front of them, the pond was still lively with groups of kids, families and community people. Golden sun slanted through the darkening clouds. Hard to know if it was going to rain or be warm and sunny.

"I'd better get back to my kids," Eduardo said. "Thanks for the talk."

"Anytime. Think about that Bible study."

"I will." Eduardo started to walk away and then turned back. "You listening to your own advice about women?"

A half smile creased Dion's dark face. "Touché," he said. "Get to work."

Fiona served up two more hot dogs from the concession stand and was about to turn away when she saw Sofia approaching, her forehead wrinkled.

She leaned out and smiled at the sweet child. No matter what differences Fiona and Eduardo had, the kids were innocent. "What's wrong, honey?"

Sofia held out the front of her white T-shirt to display a bright red spot. "I got ketchup on my favorite shirt, and Daddy said it's going to make a stain."

"Let's see." Fiona came outside the concession stand and knelt to study the stain. "He's right, although if we worked on it fast…"

Sofia's face lit up. "Can we? Please? Daddy's not good with stains."

How many men were? "Come on inside," she said, "and put on one of the derby T-shirts. I'll see what I can do."

Sofia changed in a corner, and Fiona went to work

on the stain while Daisy and Susan handled the counter, fetching chips and drinks. A couple of minutes later, Sofia came up beside Fiona. "Is it going to come out?"

"I think so," Fiona said. "See, you rinse it from the back with cold water. That keeps it from setting. And then we rub in some dish soap, like this. And then—" she looked around and located a clean bucket "—we'll let it soak in cool water for a while. I'm pretty sure we got it just in time."

Sofia hugged her. "Thank you sooo much," she said, letting her head rest against Fiona's side for an extra moment.

Fiona wiped her soapy hands and hugged the little girl close. "Sure, honey," she said, her throat tightening.

Like all little girls, Sofia needed a mother's love. A mother's guidance as she grew toward womanhood and started to face a woman's issues.

But Fiona couldn't let herself get too attached to the child. Or the reverse. Especially the reverse. It would be a disaster if Eduardo's kids got attached to her. "Go on out, catch some more fish," she urged. "Look, there's Lauren, and she wants to show you something, it looks like."

As Sofia ran down toward the pond, Dion came back to the grill and immediately he and Daisy started bickering. Susan was fretting because her husband had insisted on taking charge of Sam Junior, who, at four months, hadn't spent a lot of time away from his mama's side.

As for Fiona, after a sleepless night, she wanted nothing more than to go home, plunk the kids in front of some engrossing movie and block out the previous evening.

She'd been so happy, so sure that something wonderful was going to happen with Eduardo. His kiss had been tender and strong, everything a first kiss should be. And despite the semi-disaster of their kids discovering them, she hadn't been too worried. Her kids liked Eduardo and his kids, and the idea of the two families getting closer and spending more time together made them happy.

It had made Fiona happy, too.

But his kind, sober rejection in the garden had swept the rug out from under her, restored her idea of her own romantic future to the same unhappy condition she'd always known it was.

Dion brought in a plate of burgers. "Voilà, ladies! Perfection from the grill."

Daisy leaned over to study them. "Are you sure they're done?"

"Of course I'm sure. I've been grilling since you were in primary school!"

Daisy lifted her hands, palms up. "I was just asking! Why do you always have to bring it back to the age difference?"

Susan lifted an eyebrow at Fiona as she took the burgers from Dion and nodded toward the lake. "Thanks, Dion," she said. "This might be enough for the rest of the day. People are starting to pack up and go home."

"I may just do the same." Dion eyed Daisy. "It's feeling kind of cold in here."

"Fine." Daisy started wiping up the counter with unnecessary vigor. "Do what you want."

"Ladies." Dion gave a mock-salute to the three of them, spun on his heel and walked out of the concession stand, his back straight.

Daisy watched him go, her mouth twisted to one side. Fiona put an arm around her friend.

Eight-year-old Mindy came running in and tugged Susan's arm. "Mama, listen!"

Susan bent down, and Mindy whispered into her ear.

Susan's eyebrows lifted almost into her dark hair. "Is that so?"

"That's what Ryan and Lauren and Sofia and Diego said!"

Susan looked over at Fiona.

Fiona's heart sank. "What's wrong?"

Susan knelt in front of Mindy. "I want you to go on back outside, but don't talk about other people's business again. That's called gossip, and we don't do it."

Mindy stole a glance toward Fiona, looking stricken. "I'm sorry, Mama."

"Run and show Daddy the picture of you and your fish. I know he'll want to get copies for all the relatives."

"Yeah!" Mindy dashed out.

The moment she was gone, Susan grabbed a sign that said *Be Right Back!* and closed the front of the concession stand. Then she turned to Fiona. "You *kissed* him?"

"What?" Daisy squeaked. "Who? Eduardo?"

"Of course Eduardo," Susan said. "And in front of the kids, apparently."

"That part was a mistake," Fiona said as anxiety squeezed at her stomach. "But I'm sure the whole town knows about it by now."

Daisy opened a couple of folding chairs in the darkened end of the concession stand and gently pushed Fiona into one of them. "Sit."

Susan perched on the counter. "Tell us everything."

So, Fiona did. When she'd said it all, even the humiliating rejection in the garden last night, she found herself grim and dry-eyed. "So, it was nothing to him. He's so horribly *kind*, and he wanted to let me down easy. Keep me from making a fool of myself. Which would be fine if my kids weren't set on telling the whole town we're getting married."

"Zero to one hundred, that's kids," Susan said, frowning.

"That conversation in the garden was weird." Daisy reached out to squeeze Fiona's arm. "I'm sorry, hon, I can tell you're upset. But think about it. Could he really have meant it as bad as it sounded?"

"Judging from the way he's avoided me today, yes." Tears pushed at the back of her eyes and a couple escaped, which was ridiculous. Angry at herself, she brushed them away.

Susan grabbed a napkin and handed it to her, just as wind gusted through the half-open window of the booth, blowing over the cardboard stand that held candy and bags of chips.

A father and daughter peeked inside. "Any burgers left?" the man asked.

Susan threw a couple together in record time and shoved them toward the customers. "Donate what you want. Condiments over there." And she hurried back down to the spot where Daisy and Fiona were sitting. "What are you going to do?"

Fiona blotted at her eyes. "What *can* I do? He's made his decision, apparently."

Daisy scooted closer to put an arm around her. "I'm so sorry, honey. How do you feel about Eduardo?"

"How was it, kissing him?" Susan asked, waggling her eyebrows.

"Stop it!" Daisy scolded. "This is serious."

Fiona blew her nose and waved a hand, half laughing. "It's fine. To answer your question first," she added to Susan, "it was…fabulous, sadly."

"Sad because…" Daisy prompted.

"Because I was starting to like him, and kissing him made me like him even more. And so—" She raised a hand to keep Susan from interrupting. "So it's good he stopped me in my tracks. I should have known a guy like Eduardo wouldn't go for someone like me. I *did* know that, but I… I kind of forgot."

Susan and Daisy glanced at each other. "What do you mean 'someone like you'?" Susan asked.

Fiona gestured at herself. "Tall. Carrying extra weight. Not the sharpest…" She cut off the words, frowning. Maybe it wasn't that she was stupid, as she'd always thought. The moment of insight she'd had watching Diego and the things she'd read last night online came back to her mind for the first time since the miserable talk in the garden.

She was going to pursue that, she vowed to herself. She was going to find out if she had a learning disability and see if she could get help. And *that* was one good outcome of the whole Eduardo fiasco.

"You're totally insane, thinking that you aren't attractive," Daisy was saying. "Do you know what most of us would give to have your height and your looks?"

"Oh, well—" Fiona waved a hand. Women always said things like that. Women looked at the world differently than men did, looked for different things in people.

She was going to stick to women friends and not venture into the world of romantic love again.

"I'm not even going to dignify the whole extra-weight thing with a response," Susan said hotly. "I've *told* you and *told* you about our culture's crazy fixation on women being ultra slim, how it impacts us and hurts our self-esteem. You have three daughters, woman! You've got to stop!"

"You're right. I'll try." Fiona drew in a deep breath and reached out a hand to each of her friends. "You guys are the best. I don't know what I'd do without—"

But her words were cut off by the loudest clap of thunder she'd ever heard. There was a simultaneous flash of lightning, and then rain drummed sudden and hard against the concession stand's metal roof.

"My kids!" Fiona jumped up and ran to the window, peering out through the wall of pelting rain.

"Go, find them." Susan was texting and didn't look up from her phone. "I'm sure Sam has Sammy Junior. We'll clean up here. Go!"

"Bring that shirt from the bucket, would you?" Fiona ran out of the concession stand and was instantly soaked.

Eduardo shepherded the last of six soaking wet kids into the cab of his pickup and scanned the nearly empty parking lot. He'd been mildly worried as the skies had darkened and people had started to pack up and leave, but now... Where was Fiona?

"That came out of nowhere!" One of the remaining dads was throwing buckets and fishing tackle into the back of his truck. "So much for the awards ceremony."

"I wanted to get my award!" Diego's mouth compressed into a thin line. "I earned it and I want it."

Eduardo gave him a warning look. "The awards will

be figured out later. Right now, we need to focus on staying safe and getting dry and finding Fiona."

"I hope she has my shirt," Sofia said. "She's good at fixing stains."

"It's more important that she's okay," Lauren said from the crowded back seat.

"Yeah!" Ryan added. Then Poppy started to cry.

"I need for all of you to be very mature." Eduardo got in the driver's seat and wiped a hand across his wet face. "I'm going to pull over to your car. Maybe she's inside." Although, she wouldn't be. She'd be looking for her kids rather than trying to keep herself dry.

"There's Mom!" Ryan shouted.

Eduardo screeched to a halt beside Fiona's SUV. "Where?" But even as he asked, he saw her, or a flash of her. Running, but down toward the pond rather than toward the nearly empty parking lot. And then he lost sight of her in the dark downpour.

"I'm gonna go get her," Ryan said.

"Me, too." Lauren reached for the door handle.

"No." He turned in the front seat to make eye contact with all the children. "You need to stay here. Lauren and Sofia—" he eyeballed the two older girls "—you're in charge. You make sure everyone stays inside the truck. Sing songs or something. Got it?"

They both nodded, eyes wide.

"Is our mommy going to die like our daddy did?" Maya asked.

Poppy started crying louder.

"No way," Eduardo said. "She'll be fine." He jumped out and slammed the door, then started running toward the spot he'd last seen Fiona. Rain pelted his head and shoulders and ran into his eyes.

Fiona *would* be fine. She was probably just looking for the kids. They'd have a good laugh about how wet they'd all gotten.

"Eduardo!"

He blinked and saw someone running in his direction. Two people. Susan and Daisy.

He pressed the keys into Daisy's hands. "Can you watch the kids? They're in my truck. I'm looking for Fiona."

"Will do." She ran in the direction of his truck.

"Did you see Sam and my kids?" Susan sounded half-hysterical.

His impulse to help a woman in distress conflicted with his desire to find Fiona. He hesitated, automatically putting an arm around Susan's shoulders, and squinted around the parking lot. The rain stung his eyes.

A pair of headlights cut through the rain. There was a flash of red. Sam Hinton's Lexus?

"That's our car! I have to—"

"Go." He pushed her lightly toward the car that held her family. And then he turned toward the pond. "Fiona! Fiona, I have the kids!"

No answer. Where *was* she? He ran, his heart pounding, eyes scanning to the right and the left. His feet splashed in instant puddles and he nearly lost his balance. Had she fallen, too? "Fiona!"

Why had she been running toward the pond?

He zigzagged down that way, searching. And then a flash of lightning illuminated the area.

He saw Fiona lifting the rowboat the kids had clustered around earlier, the one Mercedes had said she'd hidden under when she'd gotten lost.

How was she strong enough to lift it by herself? She was going to hurt her back. He sped up.

"Fiona!"

A sickening pop, a flash and a large tree exploded into flying limbs and branches. Lightning!

He didn't see Fiona anymore. Had she been struck?

He ran faster than he'd ever ran in his life, arms and legs pumping, water and mud splashing up into his face.

Steam rose from the tree, but all Eduardo could think of was how hard and fast those branches had flown— like a bomb. "Fiona!"

He got to the spot where the rowboat lay half in the pond. Debris from the lightning-struck tree covered the surrounding mud.

His heart thudding, he lifted the boat. She wasn't under it. He ran along the shore to the right but didn't see her.

Ran to the left. Looked at the now-murky water and felt a moment's pure terror.

The thought of her four kids losing another parent warred with his own fear. He shoved it all away. *Focus. Find her.*

He spun and ran in the other direction, past the rowboat, scanning both the shoreline and the water now. "Fiona!"

He almost tripped over a large branch but caught himself. Saw a slim white hand.

And then he was lifting the giant tree branch off the pale, still form of Fiona Farmingham.

Chapter 10

Fiona woke to a jolting, dizzying world with someone holding her impossibly foggy head. Rain, a crash and then awful pain surged in her memory, and she struggled to sit up. "Kids," she rasped, opening her eyes and trying to focus.

"They're fine," said a woman's voice. "They're safe."

"Daisy?" She looked up at her friend's blurry face. Why was Daisy here?

Where *was* here?

"Shh. Lie still." Daisy glanced at someone off to the side. "Go straight to the emergency room. They're waiting for us."

Emergency room? But Fiona couldn't go to the emergency room. She had four kids to care for. Again, she tried to sit up, but a sharp pounding pain in her head made her collapse back down, gasping for air.

There was a screech and jolt, the too-loud bang of a door opening, voices.

"Lightning—"

"Tree branch—"

"Lost consciousness—"

"Head injury—"

Somehow, she was lying down flat, zooming along surrounded by people in scrubs. Clenching her teeth against the nausea, she looked around for someone familiar. "My kids..."

"Your kids are fine," came Daisy's soothing voice. "Safe and dry. Your friends are taking care of them."

But they needed *her*. Especially Poppy. She forced herself up onto her elbows, but pain knifed through her forehead and she collapsed back down again.

More shouts and then the stretcher stopped in a cubicle with beeping machines and too-bright lights and a whole crowd of people.

Daisy's face came into view, directly above Fiona's own. "Do. Not. Worry." Her reassuring smile didn't reach her eyes. "You hear? We're all taking care of your kids and they're fine. And you'll be fine, too." She glanced to the right where a masked doctor was doing something to Fiona's arm. "Right?"

"We'll do everything we can to take care of her. Are you a relative?"

"Her sister."

Fiona blinked at the skill with which Daisy told the lie, but it reassured her, too. Daisy would take care of things. Her kids were okay.

She started to sink back into fog again. If only they'd stop poking and prodding her.

Where was Eduardo? She wanted him. But there was

some reason—she couldn't think of it now—why she didn't get to have him.

And suddenly, overwhelmingly, she needed to sleep.

Eduardo sat in the ER waiting room, elbows on knees, hands clasped tight. The disinfectant-heavy hospital smell made him queasy, and a heaviness in his chest weighted him down. In his experience, hospital visits didn't end well.

Around the waiting room, a few family clusters sat, talking and looking at their phones. A television, sound off, showed talking heads. A low, well-modulated voice sounded from the hospital intercom: "Smythe family? Smythe family to the reception desk, please." A teenage boy went to the drinking fountain with a uniformed police officer a few feet behind him.

Everyone here had a story, but Eduardo couldn't rouse any curiosity about anyone's but Fiona's.

If he hadn't been having a stupid fight with her, she wouldn't have gone running off alone to find her kids. They'd have been in good communication, and when that sudden rain came up, they'd have gotten their kids into their respective vehicles and driven home like every other family at the fishing derby.

He'd have texted her to let her know he had her kids in his truck.

Why hadn't he taken the time to text her?

If he had, they'd be safe and dry inside one of their homes right now.

Instead, the kids were terrified, back at Fiona's house with Sam, Susan and Lou Ann. Of course, they didn't believe the adults' assurances that everything would be okay. All of them knew, way too young, that things didn't always turn out okay, no matter what the grown-ups said.

He should have protected them from this new worry, but he hadn't.

To his own surprise, he was including Fiona's kids in his slate of mishandled responsibilities. Since when had he started thinking of them as his own?

When you fell in love with Fiona, you idiot.

That thought stopped him. He wasn't really in love with Fiona. Was he?

He blew out a sigh as his heart twisted and turned. Yeah. In that moment when he'd lifted the branch off her lifeless-looking body, he'd realized it for certain: he was in love with her. Which was a disaster for him, personally, and was potentially a disaster for her.

The double doors to the back of the ER opened and Daisy came out. Instantly, he was on his feet and walking toward her, his heart pounding, trying to read her expression. "How is she?"

"She'd be better if you hadn't made her feel bad about herself yesterday," Daisy snapped. She sank into a chair.

Yesterday. Yesterday had started with a wonderful time decorating the cafeteria at the Senior Towers, and then there'd been that unwise but very delightful kiss. But next had come the kids and the guilt and the memory that he shouldn't be starting up a relationship with her at all. He'd been trying to ease her away from him, disentangle them so she wouldn't be hurt.

Not knowing what else to do, he sat down beside Daisy.

She glared at him. "If you hadn't been fighting, Susan and I wouldn't have had her holed up in the back of the concession stand with the window shut. This would never have happened!"

Guilt washed over him, a crashing wave. It wasn't anything he hadn't already told himself, but hearing it from Daisy—

He let his head sink into his hands. Familiar remorse pressed him down. He should never have moved into the carriage house, should have known that something would go wrong. The bleakness was an echo and a reminder of how he'd failed Elizabeth.

He turned his head sideways to face Daisy. "I know. I take responsibility. But is she going to be okay?"

She bit her lip, gripped his arm, shook it. "I'm sorry, Eduardo. Cancel everything I just said."

"No, you're right. If I'd only let her know I had her kids—"

"It's not your fault. I should never have said that," Daisy interrupted. "Or if it is, I'm just as much to blame. I'm feeling guilty because I kept her inside the concession stand instead of paying attention to how that storm was kicking up."

"You were trying to help."

"Sure, I was. But it was about me, too, because I wanted to talk about female self-esteem and I was having trouble with Dion, and..." Her voice started to crack. "And she has those four kids, those poor kids..."

"Wait." Eduardo's heart beat much too fast and he knelt in front of her. "Daisy. Is she going to be okay? What do the doctors say?"

"I don't know," she choked out. "They're acting weird. Or I think they are. I don't know." She paused. "They're asking her all kinds of questions about stuff like dates and math problems and current events.

They're testing her reflexes. And they said they want her to have..." Her voice broke and she took a deep breath. "A CT scan. They want to do a CT scan."

That didn't sound good.

He grabbed a tissue box from an end table and handed it to Daisy. "Do you think they'll let me in? I saw what happened. Maybe there's information I could give..."

Daisy wiped her eyes and shook her head. "I said I was her sister, but it's only a matter of time until they find out I'm not even a relative. I guess we should call her mom, but that'll be more of a problem than a help, from what I understand of their relationship, so I'm holding off. But I know they'll ask for next of kin..."

Eduardo's heart was a giant heavy stone.

"Attention," said the intercom. "Would the party accompanying patient Fiona Farmingham please come to the desk?"

Daisy stood and hurried toward the reception desk. Eduardo followed her.

"You're Fiona's sister?" asked a doctor in scrubs, standing behind the receptionist.

Daisy hesitated fractionally and then nodded. Eduardo stepped off to the side, hoping the doctor would talk openly if he didn't appear to be eavesdropping.

It worked. "Looks like she dodged a bullet," the doctor said cheerfully. "Of course, we'll do a few more tests. CT scan as a precaution. But it looks like a very mild concussion. She has a few contusions, but we were able to patch her up. It could have been much worse."

"Can she go home tonight?"

The doctor frowned. "What's the home situation?"

"She has four kids."

"Then definitely not. She needs as much rest as possible, not a bunch of kids hanging on her. Besides, we need to do those tests. But she should be good for tomorrow." The doctor turned and hurried back into the ER.

"Thank you!" Daisy called after the doctor, sounding jubilant.

"You can go back and see her now," the receptionist said. "Just push the button to the right of the doors."

Daisy went over and pressed the button. The doors opened.

She looked back at him. "Come on," she said. "You can say you're my husband."

Reflected in the metallic doorway, he could see the flashing lights of an ambulance. Medics jogged in beside a stretcher holding a small dark-haired woman.

The beeps of medical machinery shrilled over the low hum of voices, artificially calm doctors and nurses.

Behind him, in the waiting room, a child began to cry.

A roaring started in his head. *Your fault. Your fault. Your fault.*

That crying child sounded just like Sofia had sounded all those years ago, crying for the mommy who would never return.

What had he been doing, getting involved with Fiona and her family? Why would he risk replicating that kind of misery? What had possessed him, thinking he'd changed?

He'd come to care for Fiona and her kids way too much. Which was exactly why he needed to stay out of their lives.

He stepped back from Daisy's beckoning arm. "It's okay. Uh, you'll take care of her. Right?"

Daisy cocked her head to one side and looked at him hard. "Right, of course. I'm her *friend*."

"That…that's great. You let me know if you need anything. Right now, I'm… I have to go. Go home."

He turned and practically ran out of the hospital.

Three days later, Fiona pushed herself up to a sitting position and readjusted her pillows behind her back. She was in her own sunny front room, waiting for the kids to come home from school, while Lou Ann Miller prepared dinner in the kitchen. The nanny, temporarily rehired, was playing with Poppy upstairs.

She looked out the window, relieved that the light didn't hurt her eyes today. The tests had all come back clear, and her slight dizziness had subsided. A faint lingering headache and some blue-green bruises up one arm were the only reminders of the fright she'd had last weekend. If she got lots of extra rest this week, and resumed her normal life slowly, she'd be fine, according to the doctors.

She was still a little hazy on the details of the accident. She remembered running out into the storm, not seeing her kids, thinking there was movement down by the water. Poppy had been so fascinated with Mercedes's story about hiding under the boat, and Fiona had feared that Poppy, or all her kids, were playing there or hiding from the lightning. Exactly the most unsafe thing to do.

She remembered looking around frantically, seeing the rowboat and then…just a big blank.

Sometimes, she got a mental glimmer of strong arms

lifting her up and carrying her through the rain. It must have been Eduardo. She knew he'd driven her to the hospital while Daisy had held her steady in the back seat. Sam and Susan had taken all the kids home, got them dry clothes and food and reassurance. Other than Poppy being a little more clingy than usual, there were no ill effects.

Every time she thought about the near disaster, she closed her eyes and sent up a prayer of thanks and gratitude for the help of her friends.

The only thing missing now was Eduardo.

The school bus chugged up and her older three ran inside. She could hear the thuds and clinks of supplies as they threw down their backpacks and lunchboxes and then all three burst into the front room, Lauren importantly hushing everyone else.

Fiona hugged each one of them fiercely and made them sit around her and tell her about their school days. Maya had a drawing that had gotten two gold stars, Ryan had aced his spelling test and Lauren's oral report had gone "okay, better than Tiffany Winthrop's." Fiona listened and breathed in the sweaty smell of her kids, and again her heart expanded with thanks.

So easily, things could have gone a different way. She could have gotten a much worse concussion. *Even been killed.* The doctors had impressed on her the dangers of being outside in a lightning storm, and Fiona took it all seriously. More than ever, she felt grateful for each moment with her children and was determined to give them everything she had to help them grow up strong.

She wanted to get up and fix them a snack right now, as she usually did, but Lou Ann called out for them to come to the table. One mention of fresh-made brownies and Ryan and Maya ran toward the kitchen. Lauren stayed behind, leaning against Fiona.

Fiona held her hand as the others raced away, smiled at her eldest and brushed her hair back from her forehead. There were two vertical wrinkles between Lauren's eyebrows, a sure sign that something was wrong. "Come sit on the porch with me after you have your snack, if you want to."

Lauren glanced toward the kitchen, from which a rich chocolaty smell was wafting.

"Go ahead. Eat your snack and I'll meet you on the porch."

Lauren leaned down and gave Fiona a gentle hug. "Thanks, Mom."

Moments later, they were on the porch in the sun, both sipping iced tea, Lauren's watered-down with a significant amount of lemonade.

"Mom," she asked, "how come Mr. Delgado hasn't been over to visit like all your other friends?"

Fiona looked involuntarily in the direction of the carriage house. That was the million-dollar question, but she couldn't say that to her daughter. "I'm sure they've had a lot to do," she said. "And remember, Mr. Delgado has a landscaping business. Spring is his busiest season."

"Sofia says he's *moody*." Lauren looked rather impressed with her ten-year-old friend's observation. "She says he stares off into the distance. And he keeps looking at pictures of their mom, who died."

Fiona's heart was open and emotional and the idea of Eduardo, sad and suffering, pained her. But she'd sent him a note thanking him for rescuing her and for helping with the kids, along with Sofia's stain-free shirt.

The ball was in his court now, but apparently he wasn't going to hit it.

"Sometimes grown-ups go through hard times, just like kids do," she said, feeling her way. "He could be feeling extra sad about losing his wife. Just like you sometimes get sad about Daddy, right around Christmas or your birthday."

"Yeah, because he used to get me lots of presents and call me his little lady." Lauren looked wistful.

"He loved you very much." Lauren, more than the others, had memories of Reggie. Sometimes Fiona speculated that Reggie hadn't yet started up his other family when Lauren was small, so he'd been more attached to her.

A car pulled up in front of the house and a petite dark-haired woman emerged. Fiona waved a greeting and started to stand, but the woman was looking past the house, where Eduardo soon appeared. He walked to meet the woman and they embraced.

Then they walked back toward the carriage house, arms around each other. Neither one glanced in the direction of the porch.

Lauren looked over at Fiona. "Does Mr. Delgado have a new girlfriend?" she asked.

Fiona's own automatic thought as well. She took a couple of deep breaths and thought about Eduardo, the man she knew him to be. Thought about how he'd expressed feelings for her and kissed her not even a week ago. "I don't think so, honey," she said. "That might be a relative."

And tried to hold on to her reasoning in the face of some very nasty jealousy.

"Oh, good," Lauren said matter-of-factly, "because we want you and Mr. Delgado to get married."

Fiona sighed, reached out and stroked Lauren's hair. "That's not going to happen, I'm pretty sure," she said softly.

"But you kissed him—"

"I know. We like each other. But when you're a grown-up with jobs and kids and…and hard things that happened in the past, it's complicated to go on dates and to, well, be together." She chose her next words carefully, wanting to reassure Lauren and avoid making her feel somehow responsible or guilty. "I can only take care of so much. You and your sisters and brother fill up my world. You're my priority, and I wouldn't have it any other way. Do you understand?"

Lauren frowned. "That lady is really small and skinny. Do you think he likes her because she is littler than you?"

Fiona's breath caught as her daughter articulated the ugly notion that had stabbed at her the moment she'd seen Eduardo put his arm around the dark-haired woman. "What makes you think that, honey?"

"I know you go on diets, and in pictures, you hunch down to be smaller. So I thought…" She trailed off, looking at the floorboards of the porch.

Fiona lifted her eyes to the ceiling and tried to channel Daisy and Susan. "Sometimes, in magazines and on TV, women and girls look skinny and small. But that's not real life, is it? We come in all sizes."

Amazing how calm she was able to sound, as if she had complete confidence in these ideas that she was only now starting to internalize.

Amazing how important it felt now to correct her

daughter's misperceptions, when she'd suffered under the same ideas herself for so many years.

"Tiffany Winthrop is the littlest girl in the class, and the prettiest, too. She teases me about being the biggest." Lauren studied the floor as if something very interesting was down there.

Hot anger rose in Fiona and she took a couple of breaths, then scooted over on the porch swing and put an arm around Lauren. "I'm sorry that's happening. It can't feel good."

"It doesn't. And now some of the other kids are saying it, too, and I'm afraid I won't have any friends." She looked up at Fiona. "Do you think I could go on a diet?"

Fiona swallowed a knot in her throat and tightened her arm around her daughter. "No way. You eat a normal amount, and you're a normal size. That's healthy." She focused on what Lauren had said, thought of how important Susan and Daisy were in her own life. "Let's think of all the good friends you have."

"Well, there's Dana. She's my best friend."

"I like Dana." And Fiona resolved to invite the girl over within the next week. "Who else?"

"Valerie and Danica and Annalisa and Beth. We all sit together at lunch."

"And they all came to your birthday party last year. They seem to really like you."

"And Sofia. She's not in my class, but we're friends at soccer. And at home." Lauren's face was brightening. "And David. He's a boy, but he's nice and fun. And he's a *lot* taller than I am."

"Boys can be good friends, too."

"He yelled at the boys who were teasing me. And Annalisa told the teacher."

Where had *she* been while her eldest was going through mean-girl misery? "I'm sorry all this has been happening. Why didn't you tell me?"

"Because I knew you'd get upset and talk to the school," Lauren said truthfully. "And anyway, you have to stay in bed."

Bad mother. Bad mother. The usual negative voices rose inside her, but alongside them, there was a core of strength that told her to look at the whole situation before she blamed herself.

Lauren and her friends were handling the name-calling. And Lauren was telling Fiona all about it now.

"You have some really good friends, it sounds like. Did you speak up to Tiffany when she said mean things?"

Lauren looked down again. "Yeah, but..."

"But what, honey?" She stroked Lauren's hair gently.

"I said mean things back to her. I called her a pipsqueak and I teased her about her bad grades."

Fiona nodded, watching emotions play across Lauren's face. Let her think it through.

"What should I do, Mom?"

"Would you feel better if you apologized?"

Barely, almost imperceptibly, Lauren nodded.

"Tomorrow?"

"Okay, Mom."

"Good." Fiona squeezed Lauren's shoulders again. "And I think it's time you started having more sleepovers. You and your friends are big enough to clean up after yourselves and fix your own snacks. Would you like to have two or three girls over? Not this week, since it's going to be Easter, but maybe next?"

"I'd love that!" Lauren hugged Fiona. "Can we make

s'mores?" Then her face fell. "Oh, wait, are they fattening?"

Fiona took a breath. "Do you care? Since you're a normal weight and treats are part of good healthy eating?"

"We could have s'mores and strawberries," Lauren decided. "Okay?"

"Sure, as long as you share with the other kids." She smiled at her thoughtful eldest daughter. "And me. I love strawberries *and* s'mores."

"Can I go call the girls now?"

"Sure thing." After Lauren ran inside the house, Fiona sat rocking and wondering whether she could take to heart her own wise words to her daughter.

"So what's this I hear about a new girlfriend?" Sara, Eduardo's sister-in-law, grinned at him and crushed her empty soda can before tossing it into the trash. They were sitting in Eduardo's little kitchen, catching up on the latest news about each other, the kids and their relatives. Except for her short hair and boyish T-shirt and jeans, she looked almost exactly like Elizabeth. Seeing her always provoked a mixture of joy and sadness in Eduardo.

"No new girlfriend," he said.

Sara raised an eyebrow. "Then who were you kissing on the street? Some random stranger?"

Eduardo let his head fall back against his chair and stared up at the ceiling. "How do you hear all the Rescue River gossip when you're living in Toronto?"

"I have my sources." She smiled. "And I want you to know that I think it's time. Elizabeth would, too."

"No." He watched the ceiling fan blades going

around. Was that a cobweb up there in the rafters? He'd have to get out a long-handled broom and get it down.

At the screen door, there was a scratching sound, and Sparkles stood up with a little lurch and made her way over. Outside, Brownie whined an invitation. Sparkles looked back over her shoulder at Eduardo, as if asking permission to go play.

He stood, glad for a reason to move away from Sara's intensity, and opened the door. "Go ahead," he said, running a hand along the dog's bony back as she went out. Brownie lowered his front half into a play bow and barked, then dashed away, and Sparkles followed at a more sedate lope.

He returned to the kitchen table to find Sara looking at him steadily. "Why not start dating? You're a normal man with normal feelings and needs. And those kids in there—" she gestured toward the living room, where Sofia and Diego had reluctantly gone to start their homework "—they would benefit from a woman's influence, especially now. Sofia's turning into a young lady."

Maybe it was because of Fiona's accident and his subsequent realization that he had fallen in love with her. Or maybe it was how much he missed talking to her. Something, at any rate, took away his usual filters. "Truth?" he said. "I'd like to date. And there's someone I have in mind, yeah. But after what happened with Elizabeth—"

"You're afraid of losing another wife?"

"I'm afraid of *letting down* another wife." He propped his elbows on his knees and leaned forward, staring at the floor. "You know all the troubles we had with insurance and doctors. If I'd had a better job, gotten her better care..." He trailed off and let out a sigh.

"Then what?" Sara asked gently.

"If I'd gotten better care for her, she might have survived."

Sara didn't say anything. What could she say?

After a minute, he hazarded a glance at her and saw that she was frowning and biting her lip.

"What?" he asked. "You can say it." He waited for the recriminations he'd always expected but had never received from Elizabeth's closest sister.

"I really shouldn't," she said. "But..." She looked away.

Diego came and knocked on the kitchen door frame. "Can Aunt Sara come play with us now?"

"In a minute, *chico*," she said. She got up and handed him two cookies from the plastic container she'd brought. "One for you and one for your sister," Sara said and ruffled his hair. For a minute, she looked so much like Elizabeth that Eduardo's throat tightened up.

But there was a surprising bit of happiness there, too. For once, he flashed on a memory of Elizabeth's life, not her terrible death—a time when she'd mussed up Sofia's hair in the exact same way, before she'd gotten sick.

"Thanks, Aunt Sara." Diego clearly didn't have any such complicated reaction. He just hugged her hard and then ran into the other room.

Sara turned back to Eduardo, leaned against the counter and crossed her arms. "I'm going to tell you something I wasn't supposed to tell you."

"About Elizabeth?"

She nodded. "I think you need to hear it. And I think Elizabeth would agree, if she knew how much you're beating yourself up."

He should tell her not to break Elizabeth's confidence, but the chance to hear something new about his wife was too intriguing. "Go on."

Sara drew in a breath and let it out in a big sigh. "She knew she was terminal from the very beginning."

Eduardo frowned, shook his head. "No, she didn't."

Sara walked over and sat down across the table from him. "She just didn't want you and the kids to know."

"But the doctors never told me—"

"She didn't give permission," Sara said. "Medical records are private."

"She wouldn't have lied to me." Heat rose in him. He looked out the window and then back at Sara. "Would she?"

Sara reached out and clasped his hand. "Only if she thought it was the best for you. She knew how hard you'd take it. She knew you needed to fight."

Eduardo shook his head, trying to sort out the conflicting information. All the months of trying so hard to get her the best healthiest food, to enroll her in clinical trials, to research alternative treatments... Elizabeth had *known* it wasn't going to work, and she'd let him do it?

Painful anger battered at his heart. "But she told you? You, and not me?"

Sara sighed. "She had to talk to someone. I was the only person she told, and she made me promise not to tell you." She looked heavenward. "I'm sorry, *mi hermana*, but I have to break that promise. He needs to know."

"She couldn't talk to her own husband?"

Sara shook her head, shrugged and lifted her hands, palms up. "Some things you can only tell a sister. But the point is, Eduardo, you're not at fault for some imagined mistake you made in providing care for her. She wasn't going to beat her cancer."

She wasn't going to beat her cancer. She hadn't beat it. And she'd known she wouldn't from the beginning.

"Daddy," came Sofia's wheedling voice from the doorway, "can I go out and play with Lauren? I got almost all my homework done. And she said she needs to talk to me."

"Sure. Go. Your brother can go out, too." Normally, he would've looked into her claim further before letting her go, but he was still reeling from Sara's revelation.

After Sofia and Diego were outside, he scraped a hand across his face and looked at Sara. "How could Elizabeth have lied to me, even when she was so sick?"

She stood up instantly, came over and wrapped her arms around him from behind. "She agonized about it. Prayed about it. She didn't want to lie to you, but she loved you so much and she truly thought it was what would help you get through." She released him and sat back down. "For the record, I thought she should tell you the truth. But she felt like it was the last gift she could give you and the kids. Hope."

He shook his head. "Wow."

"She loved you so much. You know that, right?"

"Yeah." But processing what his sister-in-law had told him might take some time.

Sara hopped up and tugged at his hand. "Come on. Let's sit outside and watch the kids play and talk about something else. I've only got an hour before I have to get back on the road for my rally, and I want to take some pictures of those beautiful kids."

"I'm coming, I'm coming." He stood up and forced his attention out of the past and into the present, this sunny day, the opportunity for his kids to see the aunt they loved.

"Who's the older lady talking to Sofia and her friend?" Sara asked from the doorway. "They look like they're plotting something."

Eduardo glanced out the window. "That's Lou Ann Miller. She babysits for a lot of the kids in town when she can find the time between her athletics and her coursework." And she was helping Fiona while she recovered from her concussion. As he should have been doing, if he were more of a friend than a coward.

"Impressive. She's no spring chicken." Sara was still looking out the screen door. "FYI, it looks like Diego and another boy his age are getting involved in the plotting. You're probably going to be asked to spring for pizza, at the very least."

But as it turned out, the plot wasn't anything to do with pizza.

Chapter 11

Fiona sighed and stretched and looked at her watch. Cleveland's Gribshaw House Bed-and-Breakfast was beautiful, and she'd gotten lots of rest, but she didn't like being away from her children for more than twenty-four hours.

She shouldn't complain. The group of elders from the Senior Towers had been lovely to go together and get her this escape, all because they'd heard from Lou Ann that it was hard for her to rest when she was at home with four kids. What they didn't understand was that she didn't want to rest anymore. She felt fine. She wanted to go about her normal activities, cook and garden and take care of her children.

Even though the doctors said she should still take it easy, she was ready to jump into her life again.

She carried her overnight bag downstairs and said

goodbye to Mrs. Gribshaw, the proprietor, who'd been very kind…and extremely interested in everything about Fiona.

"You get help with those four children, you hear? Don't let them run all over you. When my kids were young, I traded mornings with my neighbor so I could get things done. You should try that."

"What a good idea," Fiona said. "Thank you for everything."

"You're welcome. You ought to think about eating more for breakfast, too, dear. There's nothing like a good breakfast to get you started in the morning. Gives you energy and pep. It's the most important meal of the day!"

"You're right," Fiona said, "and the breakfast was delicious." And massive. There had been only a few guests in the B and B last night, but Mrs. Gribshaw seemed to have cooked for a battalion. In point of fact, Fiona had eaten a big plate of eggs, bacon, toast and fruit for brunch and still felt full even though it was midafternoon. "Thank you again. I'd better get outside. My friend Susan is picking me up, and she's always in a hurry."

"Of course, dear," Mrs. Gribshaw said, a broad smile creasing her friendly face.

Fiona escaped into the cool morning air to the garden that surrounded the B and B. The treetops were filled with birdsong, and green hedges sat on either side of benches and along flagstone paths, and the flower beds were overflowing with what seemed like hundreds of daffodils.

She sank down onto a stone bench and lifted her face to the sunshine and thanked God, again, for all His blessings: health and safety for herself and her children; friends who cared enough to provide her with a vacation day; and a beautiful, natural oasis in the midst of a bustling city.

"Fiona?"

The familiar voice sounded a little disbelieving.

"Eduardo?" She turned, and there he was, framed in the arbor-style gateway to the garden. Involuntarily, she stood and walked toward him. "What are you doing here?"

"I could ask you the same question," he said slowly, his eyes narrowing. "Were the Senior Matchmakers involved in your being here?"

"Yes, they were," she said slowly. "They raised money for me to have a night off from mothering. I got a lot of rest last night, and it was great, but… Susan was supposed to come and pick me up today."

"And I was supposed to be picking up Susan here, because she was stranded."

Mrs. Gribshaw hurried out. "Oh, mercy, he's just as handsome as the ladies told me he'd be. Dear me, but I had a hard time keeping this a secret. Here. I was to give this to you when your ride arrived." She held out a small gift bag to Fiona.

"What?" Fiona took the bag and stared at it, then at Mrs. Gribshaw, then Eduardo. "Who gave you this?"

"A whole carload of senior citizens from your small town. My, what fun they were having!" She looked a little wistful. And then she clapped a hand to her forehead. "And they specifically told me to leave you two alone while you opened it. Enjoy yourselves! Come back again soon!" She turned and practically scurried into the guesthouse.

Fiona watched her go and then looked at Eduardo, who was shaking his head.

"You'd better open it," he said, his voice resigned.

She did. "It's a gift card for dinner out at… Let's see. Ever heard of Bocca Felice in Little Italy?"

His eyebrows lifted. "Sure have. It's one of the best Italian restaurants in Cleveland. Is there a card?"

She took it out and read aloud, "'All of your kids are safe and happy with Lou Ann, Susan and Daisy. They'll be sound asleep when you get home. Enjoy a lovely evening.'" She looked at him helplessly. "What should we do?"

He shrugged. "Use it, I guess." He reached out for her overnight bag. "We'll put your bag in the car, and…" He checked the time on his phone. "It's a little early for dinner. Do you feel like walking?"

She was rapidly shedding her eagerness to get home in the face of spending time with Eduardo, even if it was togetherness forced by interfering friends. "I'd love to walk off Mrs. Gribshaw's breakfast if we're going to have a big Italian dinner."

"How are your shoes?" he asked, and she held out her foot to display her eminently practical rubber-soled canvas slip-ons.

"We'll drive over to this trail I know around the Lake View Cemetery. It's right by Little Italy. Have you been there?"

She shook her head, feeling a bit dizzy at how this day was shaping up. "Actually, beyond a little shopping, I haven't spent much time in Cleveland."

"You haven't seen the grave of the man who invented Salisbury steak?" he asked and held out a hand. "Come on. You're in for a cultural experience."

A wave of warmth toward him washed over her. He was such a good sport, and so much fun. But was he just being kind? His day had been just as disrupted as hers had been. "Don't you have to work?"

"Normally, yes," he said, touching the small of her back to urge her toward his car. "But... Oh, man. Sam gave me the afternoon off so I could help Susan." He rolled his eyes and shook his head.

"They're all in on it!" Heat rose in her face. "Eduardo, I'm really sorry they're trying to push us together. Believe me, I had nothing to do with this."

"Nor did I. We have some interfering friends, for sure." He opened the car door for her. "Come on. Since they've gone to all this trouble, let's have some fun. We can pick up with our at-home lives at midnight."

"Like Cinderella," she said.

"Like Cinderella." He flashed her a smile as he closed the door, and all of a sudden, it felt like a real date.

Don't get carried away, Fiona.

They strolled the trail that looped around the historic cemetery, weaving through woods and low hills, and he regaled her with tales of life in the landscaping business. He'd had many funny customers and he was a good storyteller.

"Are you going to tell stories about the job on my garden once it's all over?" she asked. "About this crazy lady with four kids who couldn't even understand the estimate you made?"

He reached out and took her hand, squeezed it, his face going serious. "I would never make fun of you for a disability."

"Guess what!" She turned to him, excited to remember her news. "I made an appointment to get tested. I'm coming back to Cleveland next week to meet with the specialist."

"Good for you."

"I know, and I owe it to you for bringing it up to me. So thank you."

"I'm glad I could help."

They were being polite and friendly with each other. It felt like they were on a first date. Not like they'd ever kissed...

Fiona looked across the trees to Lake Erie in the distance, and she tried to keep hold of the strength she'd found in her talks with her girlfriends and in her prayers.

I don't have to be defined by a man's views of how I should be. I'm strong in myself.

But her heart and mind kept skittering back toward Eduardo.

He was so very attractive. And kind and good-natured, getting into the spirit of a forced date planned not by him but by their friends. A lot of men would have been irritated at the unexpected change to their work schedule, but Eduardo cheerfully pointed out landscapes and held back branches and helped her over rough spots in the trail.

It was almost hard to remember that he'd been clear about what he wanted, and it wasn't her.

She was going to enjoy this one night with him, though. It had been kind of their friends to set this up, even if it wasn't going to go the way her heart wanted it to. She was going to live every day fully—that was one of the revelations she'd had in last night's solitude.

They came to a stretch of trail that ran through the woods, cool and refreshing. "I've been doing all the talking," Eduardo said. "Tell me about the B and B. How was it, getting a night away from the kids?"

"I miss them like crazy," she admitted. "But I took advantage of the time. Brought my Bible and did a lot of thinking and praying."

He glanced over at her as they walked side by side on a wide stretch of the trail. "About what, if you don't mind my asking?"

Fiona wasn't one to talk a whole lot about her faith. She'd grown up in a family that was private and restrained. But what did she have to lose? If nothing else, Eduardo was a member of her faith community and she knew they shared the same basic values.

"Death and resurrection," she said. "Don't laugh! I know it sounds super deep."

"I wouldn't laugh at your faith! Why do you think I would?"

Why *did* she think so? Immediately, the answer came to her: Reggie. "My husband was a churchgoer—liked to have me and all the kids dressed up nice and sitting in a row beside him—but when it came to talking about real faith, he brushed my ideas aside."

"That was wrong of him," Eduardo said sharply. "What's more, death and resurrection are the core of Christianity."

"True, but I didn't come up with the concept on my own. I've been doing a Lenten devotional... Well, when I have time...and I caught up on it last night. And it's one of those you apply to your own life, so... I did."

"Figure anything out?"

She looked at him shyly. "A couple of things. You sure you want to hear this?"

He squeezed her hand. "I want nothing more than to hear it," he said. And the look in his warm brown eyes told her he was being truthful.

What would it be like to be with a man who welcomed discussions that went beyond life's surface?

Be in the moment, Fiona. "Okay, here goes. Sometimes, I feel sorry for myself."

"You make that sound like such a bad thing. Who doesn't?"

"Well, you lost your wife…"

"And you lost your husband."

"But you had a great marriage. That must make it harder."

"In some ways," he said. "But your burden has been pretty heavy. You struggled through a tough marriage and then found out you'd been betrayed. You kept it together with four kids, and you're a fantastic mother to them."

She started to protest and he touched a finger to her lips, just one tiny touch, but it stole her breath. "No. Uh-uh," he said. "You're a fantastic mother, and I know that doesn't come easy. You end up sacrificing a lot of your own time and interests."

"Nothing could be more worth it."

"Agreed. But that doesn't mean it's easy." He dropped her hand and she felt bereft, but then he put an arm around her. "Is this okay?"

Her heartbeat skittered, then settled into a faster-than-usual rhythm.

Her cautious side told her to cool it. But this was just

for one night. She could enjoy the dream for one night, right? She smiled up at him. "I like it."

He tightened his grip marginally, held her gaze for a moment and then smiled a little and looked away, shaking his head.

What was he thinking?

"I interrupted you," he said after a moment. "You were starting to say you felt sorry for yourself. I had to argue, but I shouldn't have cut off your story."

She had to pause a moment to even remember what they were talking about. "It's fine. It's just that I was reading the Easter story. I always avoid it, you know. I hate to hear about how horribly everyone treated Jesus. And it just hurts that He was scared, and His disciples wouldn't stick by Him. But last night, I read it. I did what my devotional said and read it in all four gospels."

"Tough material."

"Yes, it was. But it brought something home to me. In addition to the fact that nothing I've suffered has any comparison to what He endured."

"That's true," he said quietly.

"But I also really took it in, for the first time, that even though He suffered horribly, the outcome was greater. It was greater because of His pain. And then that led me to the book of Romans, and the part about how suffering produces endurance and... Well, anyway, I'm talking too much."

"Fiona." His hand squeezed her shoulder. "I really want to hear it."

Around them, squirrels darted from branch to branch, and birds sang a quiet accompaniment. A rich pine scent rose from the forest floor. Now that they were deeper into the trees, there was a chill in the air, and Fiona was glad for Eduardo's warm arm around her.

Don't focus on that. "It's just... I realized that all my family went through, all the dark nights, all the tears... they're for some kind of purpose. They're a crucible, you know? They make us who we are. And they make us strong."

He tightened his arm around her shoulders, and this time, he didn't loosen his grip. "You're a very insightful person," he said.

"I'm not." She waved a hand and then looked up at him. "Do you think any of that applies to you?"

"That suffering's a crucible? I don't know." He frowned. "I spent a lot of time wondering why Elizabeth had to die. Listening to my daughter crying for her mama, knowing there was nothing I could do to help. It's hard to maintain your faith in that situation."

"Did you lose it?"

"For a time," he said. "I was really angry at God. Elizabeth was so good. She didn't deserve to suffer. But lately..." He trailed off.

"What?"

"Lately, I've been picturing her actually in heaven. She loved to sing, and so... Well, I've been imagining her singing in the heavenly choir. Is that weird?"

"I think it's beautiful." And it actually choked her up a little. She cleared her throat. "Does it make you feel better?"

He nodded. "My anger is really sort of selfish. It's about me. Because she's fine. She's happier than ever, filled with joy."

She nodded, and just for a moment, she felt sad for Reggie. "I'm sorry to say I don't have that confidence about my husband." She took a breath. "But my pastor back in Illinois said to leave it in God's hands, that maybe Reggie had turned it around in the last moments. I hope he did."

"That's because you're a good person."

She looked off into the trees and shook her head. "No. Not really. But I'm glad you're figuring out how to deal with losing your wife. Did you share the choir image with Diego and Sofia?"

"No, I didn't. But maybe I will."

They'd come out of the park and into Little Italy, a colorful old street full of turreted brick buildings, restaurants, shops and a beautiful church as an anchor. The sun shone gold through a partly cloudy sky. Couples and clusters of young people, talking and laughing, gave the street a bustling air.

It's just for this one night, Cinderella, she reminded herself. Eduardo was honorable, trustworthy, able to talk about his feelings, a great father, a faithful Christian. He was still a man, though, and she couldn't quite shake the notion that men weren't to be trusted, that she wasn't good enough for a man like Eduardo.

Just for this one night, though, she'd enjoy the fairy tale.

As they walked into Bocca Felice, Eduardo had a moment of misgiving. This was the type of restaurant he'd been to maybe twice in his life—all white tablecloths, attentive waiters and well-dressed people talking quietly. He appreciated the seniors' gesture, but he felt out of place.

Fiona, on the other hand, lived in this world. She

could probably write a check tonight to buy the whole building if she wanted to.

Sure enough, she looked perfectly at ease as they waited to be seated. "The food smells fabulous. Let's ask if we can sit by the window and watch the people." Which they proceeded to do and discovered they both liked imagining the lives of the various groups, individuals and couples passing by. Fiona was friendly with the waiter, happy to try what he recommended, and she ate with gusto, which Eduardo found incredibly appealing.

The whole thing was pleasing. He was out on a date with Fiona Farmingham. He'd somehow gotten up the courage to put his arm around her, and she'd let him! The feel of her shoulders beneath his hand and arm seemed burned in his memory.

His usual warning to himself—that he shouldn't get close, that he was a bad risk—nudged at him. But suddenly, now, he questioned the concept.

If Elizabeth's death hadn't been his fault...and if, as Dion had said, they were saved and forgiven by Christ, which was what the cross was all about...then he was free.

Free to live without the horrible weight that had been pressing down on him for so many years.

Free to look at his kids without feeling responsible for the death of their mother.

Free to court Fiona, if she'd have him.

But why *would* she have him? He was still just a landscaper. He was in awe of a restaurant this expensive. He lived in the little carriage house behind her big house, which seemed to symbolize their relationship.

Except...she never ever made him feel like he was

less than her. She was a good person and didn't put so much stock in material things.

If she wasn't putting up barriers, then why should he?

After dinner, they strolled slowly through Little Italy. Streetlights and colorful signs lit up as the sun glowed red gold on its way into night. *Almost the color of Fiona's hair*, Eduardo thought and then half smiled to himself. He'd never been much of a romantic, but maybe, just maybe, that was changing.

"Why did you let me order the tiramisu?" Fiona groaned. She was holding his arm with one hand and her stomach with the other.

"Wasn't it delicious?" he asked. "Mine was."

"Yes, it was fantastic, but I overdid it."

"You didn't finish your lasagna," he said, holding up their doggie bag as evidence. "Besides, I like a woman who enjoys her food."

She glanced over at him, narrowing her eyes. "You don't have to say that."

He didn't look away. "Why shouldn't I say the truth?"

Color rose in her cheeks and she laughed a little. "Come on, let's walk."

Ahead of them, on the steps of the stately Holy Rosary Church, at least ten white-gowned brides stood around while two more posed on the steps. Photographers called out orders and assistants scurried about.

"We have twenty minutes of decent light, max!" yelled a man in a suit. "I want everyone in position."

Fiona and Eduardo looked at each other, nodded agreement and joined the small crowd of onlookers.

"What's going on?" Fiona asked a woman next to her. "Not a group wedding, surely."

"Photo shoot for some bridal website," another man

informed them. "They've been here for an hour and everyone's getting cranky."

One of the brides, along with a photographer, came to a railing in front of the small crowd.

"Folks, I'll need you to move away, please," an assistant said, tossing a cigarette butt to the ground.

In a jostling, unorganized way, the little crowd moved to get out of the camera's line of sight.

"Could ya hurry, Theo?" the bride said. "I'm starving and this dress is squeezing me like a sausage!"

Fiona laughed, along with several of the women. "I wouldn't wear such a tight dress if you paid me," a twentysomething woman said. "I want to enjoy my own wedding."

"When I got married," said a white-haired woman, "poufs and ruffles were the style. They covered a multitude of sins."

"High-waisted prairie style for me," said a fiftysomething woman with long hair and a lot of turquoise jewelry. "Much more comfortable."

"You guys are killing me," the model called over. "Just whatever you do, don't start talking about food."

"Best ravioli in the world just up the street!" called a man with an Italian accent. "DeNunzio's Family Restaurant. You should come on up after."

"DeNunzio's *is* good," the white-haired woman agreed. "Served with that wonderful bread, isn't it?"

"You bet." The round balding man who'd brought up the restaurant was out of the crowd now, edging closer to the model. "Dripping with butter. All you can eat."

"You're cruel!" the model cried.

"And...shoot," the photographer said. "Turn. Chin up. Smile!"

"I'm there for you afterward," the balding man said.

"You're old enough to be her father!" someone cat-called.

The model laughed and pointed at the Italian man. "Just wait for me to change into sweats, and I'd love to go to dinner with you."

The man pumped his fist in the air and the crowd laughed.

Fiona was laughing along with everybody else and Eduardo loved watching her, so he was sorry when she turned to him with an expression of regret. "We should go, I guess," she said. "Though the romantic in me would love to stay and see whether they end up together."

"What was *your* wedding dress like?" he asked as they strolled on toward the car. Then, because he was feeling brave, he took her hand. He held his breath as he did it, but she gave his hand an answering squeeze and smiled over at him.

"I could identify with that model," she said. "I was a lot thinner then, but my mom still talked me into a dress that was a half size too small. Let's just say, there wasn't room for wedding cake."

"But you love dessert. Right?"

"Yep. And it shows." She glanced down at herself.

"You know what?" he said. "Men don't like women who are the size of those models, not really. Most of us like normal women who enjoy food. And life."

"You didn't see any plus-size models at that photo shoot, did you?"

"Those magazines and websites are for women, not men. Women are the ones who focus on the skinny. It's not an issue for men." He smiled at her. "Not for me. Believe me. And besides," he said, "you talk like you're overweight, but you must be comparing yourself to a time when you were thin as a rail. You look wonderful now."

Two pink spots appeared on her cheeks. She looked at him and then away. "Thanks for saying that."

He pulled her to face him. "I'm not just saying it. It's true."

For a minute, he wanted to kiss her right there on the street, but she gave a tiny smile and tugged him to start walking again. "It's late. We should be getting home."

Their drive back to Rescue River was quiet. When they got to Fiona's property, he pulled into the parking space by the carriage house. "I'll walk you home."

"That would be nice," she said. "It's a lovely night."

And it was. Moonlight shone silver over the stone path that wound from the carriage house to the walkway of the big house. Apple blossoms and spring flowers released their scent to the warm night air. "Let's stop by the garden," he suggested. "I want to show you something."

"Yes! I haven't been out since my accident."

They got there, and Eduardo knelt and showed her the inch-high sprouts. "Your peas and kale and chard are coming in now," he said, looking up at her.

She crouched beside him. "That was so fast!"

"Good soil and air and sunshine. That's all a plant needs to grow."

She met his eyes and studied him thoughtfully.

Could their relationship grow, too? Did they have what was needed to make it thrive?

He reached for her, moved closer. "I don't want this evening to end," he admitted.

"It's been lovely," she said, her voice guarded. "The seniors were so sweet to set it up."

He reached for her face, ran a finger down her smooth cheek and leaned closer. But she pulled back a little.

"Come on, Eduardo. You're getting caught up in the date and the romance, but I know you don't want to take this further. You made it very clear."

"I've done some thinking since then," he said.

"Is that right?" Her voice was husky.

"Yeah." He leaned closer, but far enough that he could see her eyes. "I had a barrier related to some past baggage, but it's recently gotten knocked over."

She just looked at him, her eyes speculative.

"So I was wondering...if I can kiss you."

"Well..." She took a step back and looked up at the star-filled sky. "I don't want it to turn out badly again."

"I won't..."

"Because, Eduardo," she said in a low, intense voice, "that really hurt."

"I'm sorry." He cupped her cheek in his hand gently. "That's the last thing I want to do, hurt you. And if you're not interested, that's okay, too."

"I'm interested. But cautious."

"Understandable." He stood up and held out his hand to pull her to her feet.

"Come on, I'll walk you home."

"You're not mad?"

He shook his head. "How could I be? I want the best for you. And I respect your feelings."

They strolled slowly toward the house, holding hands. They weren't talking, but the silence was comfortable. And it wasn't really silence, because the crickets' chorus serenaded them, rising and falling. Freshly plowed earth from the field next door mingled with blossoms Fiona had planted around the base of her flowering trees.

The aroma of spring.

They were almost to her house now, and he dropped her hand to slide an arm around her back. He couldn't help wanting to be closer to her.

Her steps slowed, then stopped. She turned to face him.

"Too much?" he asked, lifting his hands away from her. The last thing he wanted to do was to push her or overstep her boundaries.

"No, not too much." She stepped closer and put her arms around him, so he let himself hold her. It felt like a precious gift.

She lifted her face to his. "About that kiss..."

He looked down at her and lifted an eyebrow. "Yeah?"

She slid a hand up into his hair and pulled his face down to hers. And then he was kissing her soft lips, and the emotion of it, the closeness, the sense of possibility almost knocked him out.

Until he heard a door open behind him.

"Fiona!" said a high female voice. "What on earth are you doing?"

Chapter 12

"You're making macaroni and cheese for lunch?" Fiona's mother swept into the kitchen the next day in a swirl of her trademark perfume.

"Uh-huh." Automatically, Fiona sucked in her stomach. She wished her mother hadn't decided to surprise them by visiting early.

"What are *we* going to eat?"

Fiona stirred cheese into the white sauce. "I can make extra salad if you don't want the carbs, Mom."

Poppy ran into the room and Fiona welcomed the distraction. "My mommy!" her youngest crowed and flung herself against Fiona's leg.

"My Poppy!" Fiona echoed, sweeping her up.

Poppy chortled gleefully. It was a game she never tired of.

"You're going to hurt your back, picking up a three-year-old like that," her mother said.

Fiona cuddled Poppy closer and then set her down so she could stir the sauce. 'Believe me, after four kids, my back is strong."

Poppy ran to Fiona's mother. "My grammy!" she shouted and hugged her grandmother's leg.

"Oh, sweetie, I've missed you so much." Her mom's eyes softened as she cuddled Poppy against her leg. "Guess what? Grammy brought each of you kids a present. You can open them after lunch."

Poppy's eyes widened. "Really?"

"Really."

"Can I tell?"

"Of course you can, honey."

Poppy raced out of the room.

"That was nice of you, Mom." Her mother really did love her grandkids and missed them since they'd moved out of state. Even though Fiona had felt the move necessary for herself and her kids, being away from one of their only living relatives was a huge disadvantage. She vowed to plan a family trip to visit her mother once school was out.

In the den, Fiona could hear the kids laughing, balls bouncing and toys beeping and ringing, and her heart swelled with gratitude. She was so glad to be home and feeling better, taking care of her kids. It just took a little accident sometimes to remind you how precious every moment of daily life actually was.

Last night had been precious, too. Every time she thought of her evening with Eduardo, warm excitement expanded in her chest. The walk, the dinner, their conversation...his compliments...the way he accepted her as she was...the feeling of holding his hand. All of it filled her with such sweet promise.

The kiss had been wonderful, too. Until the unfortunate interruption by her mother.

To his credit, Eduardo hadn't seemed upset. He'd squeezed her shoulders and whispered, "Need me to stay?" And when she'd shaken her head, he'd quickly introduced himself to Fiona's mother, waved and headed home.

He was a grown-up. Which couldn't be said of some men she'd known.

"Is there something you're not telling me?" her mother asked. She was holding up a large hardback book, *Stage a Beautiful Barn Wedding.*

Fiona laughed. "It's not what you think, Mom." She checked the pasta. "Actually, I'm considering starting a business. I'd like to make the barn in the back field into a wedding venue."

Her mother's thin eyebrows rose to her perfectly coiffed hair. "Really?" She managed to put a world of skepticism and doubt into that single word.

Shouldn't have told her. Fiona straightened her shoulders and refocused on the food. "Yes, really." She turned off the cheese sauce and carried the pot of pasta over to the colander in the sink.

"You know, honey, it's great that you keep trying. But you have to acknowledge your limitations." Her mother's voice was quiet, worried.

The words made her think of a poster she'd seen in Daisy's social work office, festooned with butterflies and flowers. Something about learning to fly despite your limitations.

Her mother was from another generation. She didn't understand learning disabilities. And Fiona didn't have to buy into her mom's old-fashioned assessment.

Once the food was on the table and they'd said grace and started eating, Fiona's mother kept the conversation rolling with her grandkids, asking them questions about school and activities and friends. The kids ate up the attention, along with big plates of food.

Her mother picked at her salad and turned down the macaroni and cheese. "I don't dare. It does smell good, though."

Fiona didn't have much of an appetite, either. She was thinking about Eduardo and about starting her business, and anxiety nudged at her despite her efforts to avoid it. Was she smart enough to start a wedding business? Was she just making excuses, thinking she might have a learning disability?

Had Eduardo really felt something for her yesterday, or was he just being nice?

She tuned back into the conversation when her mother's tone changed. "My," she said, "you certainly do spend a lot of time with these Delgado children. Isn't that the man who was, ahem, *here* last night?"

"They're our best friends!" Maya said.

"Um-hum." Then her mother focused in on Lauren. "You don't have to finish all that," she said, pointing to Lauren's nearly empty plate. "It's never too soon to start watching your weight."

Fiona put her fork down. "Lauren is a healthy girl with a healthy appetite. She knows how to listen to her body. That's what we all try to do, right, kids?"

"Right, Mom," they chorused dutifully.

Lauren looked at Fiona, her face anxious.

"Go ahead, honey," she said to Lauren. "Eat what you're hungry for. There's plenty."

Lauren looked at the remaining food on her plate. "No, it's okay. I'm getting full."

"Good for you," Fiona's mother said.

"Mom." Heat rose in Fiona's face. She was used to her mother's jabs, had grown up on them, but no way was she going to let her mom start on her girls.

Her mother just took another small bite of salad.

"Hey, I'm done eating, too," Maya said.

"Me, too!" Poppy's fork fell with a clatter. "Presents, presents!"

Ryan blinked and pushed his own plate away. "Can we open them, Grammy?"

"Of course! Will you come help me carry them in?"

"Yeah!" He jumped up and ran toward the guest bedroom, then stopped to wait for his grandmother. Moments later, they were back in the kitchen, each carrying two wrapped presents.

"Youngest first, or oldest?" Lauren asked, looking at Fiona. Her voice sounded a little unhappy, probably because her gift was much smaller than the other three.

"Alphabetical order this time," Fiona said. She liked to try to mix it up. "Who goes first?"

"I do!" Lauren ripped into her present and her eyes widened. She pulled out the latest cell phone model. "Wow! Thank you, Grandma! Wow!" She ran around the table to hug her, then turned to Fiona. "Am I allowed to have this?"

"We'll talk about it," Fiona said, trying to conceal her inner groan. She'd had no intention of letting her kids have cell phones this young, but how was she supposed to retract a gift like that?

"I'll be the first girl in my class to have this model,"

Lauren crowed. "Even Tiffany doesn't have one! And I can't wait to show Sofia."

Fiona supposed they could load games onto the phone and put some kind of parental controls on it. "We'll have to figure out how you can use that," she warned. "There are going to be limits."

"I know. I'm just going to set it up to try it out. A little. Thank you, Grandma." Lauren kissed her grandma's cheek and then started playing with the phone, pressing buttons and studying the screen.

"Who's next in the alphabet?" Fiona smiled at Maya.

"*L*, then *M*! Me!" Maya ripped into her large package, but her forehead creased as she opened the box. Billows of taffeta burst out. She pulled out a long tutu, two leotards and ballet practice shoes. "But I don't dance, Grammy."

"Keep looking," her grandmother said, and Maya pulled out an envelope and opened it. "Gift…"

"Certificate," Lauren read over her shoulder. "For Miss Josephine's School of Dance. Where's that, Mom?"

"It's in Creeksville." Which was forty-five minutes away. Her mother must have forgotten Maya was anything but a ballet type of kid. "That was nice of you, Mom."

Maya shrugged. "I can try it," she said and hugged her grandmother. "Hurry up, you guys. I want to go out and play!"

"Poppy, it's your turn," Lauren said. "The big one's for you. Want me to help you?"

Poppy nodded, and they ripped into a giant fully stocked dollhouse. "Aww, look at all the little furniture," Lauren said. "This is so cool!"

Even Ryan and Maya came over to see. "Poppy, that's

great," Maya said, squatting down to examine the furniture wrapped up inside. "Can I help you set it up later?"

Poppy looked around and seemed to realize that her present was desirable to everyone. She smiled broadly. "You can all play, but I'm the boss!"

"Tell Grammy thank you," Lauren coached, and Poppy ran over to fling herself into her grandmother's lap.

"Thank you, Grammy! I love my dollhouse!"

Fiona's mother smiled and hugged Poppy close. "I'm glad, sweetie."

Ryan ripped open his present next and his eyes went wide. "Look, Mom!"

Fiona came over and squatted to look at the enormous building kit. "That's a very generous gift," she said, knowing Ryan adored the movie series it was based on. "You'll love playing with that, buddy."

He thanked his grandmother and then ran back to study the carton.

The gift had surely cost several hundred dollars. All of them had. Fiona blew out a breath.

She tried not to emphasize money to her kids, had always done her best to keep the gifts modest at Christmas, focusing on the reason for the season. But you couldn't control what relatives wanted to give, and her children would enjoy what her mother had provided.

She'd figure out how to limit the phone use and handle the unwanted dance lessons after her mother left town.

"Isn't that the one Diego is always talking about?" Lauren sank down to her knees beside Ryan to look at the building kit.

"Yeah, he really wants one. But they don't have

enough money to buy it. Hey, maybe I'll share this with him!"

Fiona's heart swelled with pride for her thoughtful son.

"That's the way to get the toy broken," her mother said. "Those people aren't careful with their things."

Fiona opened her mouth, but before she could speak up, Ryan did. "Do you know the Delgados, Grammy?" He sounded puzzled.

"Sofia and Diego are *really* careful with their toys," Lauren said.

"More careful than me," Maya added.

Before her mother could say anything else, Fiona started clearing dishes from the table. Lauren picked up a load, too, and Ryan reluctantly put aside his new treasure to pick up his plate and Poppy's.

"Thank you," she said. "If you kids will finish clearing the table and wipe it off, your grandma and I will do the dishes. You can play with your toys."

When she reached the sink, Fiona looked out the window and saw Eduardo working on the garden, putting up the fences he'd promised to keep unwanted critters out. His dark hair shone in the sunlight, and his muscles strained the sleeves of his shirt as he put the pickets into place. She felt a surge of happiness just seeing him.

Her mother came up beside her. "He's your *gardener*?"

"No, Mom," she said patiently. "He's an independent contractor. He does landscaping for people all over town."

"Do you think he's here legally? So many immigrants who don't have their papers work in landscaping."

"Mom! Of course he—"

"Oh, my goodness," her mother interrupted, "I wonder if he's after a green card, romancing you."

Fiona frowned and looked pointedly toward the children, going in and out with dishes and sponges.

And ears tuned to adult conversation.

"I mean, that would make more sense of why he's paying attention to you," her mother said in a lower voice once the kids were out of the kitchen. "He's very good-looking."

Fiona wanted to put her hands over her ears to push out her mother's words, but even more, she wanted to correct the misperceptions. "Look, Mom, the Delgados are second-generation. Yes, they're of Mexican descent, but they're American citizens. And Eduardo isn't the type to use anyone, anyway."

"Hmm." Her mother opened the dishwasher. "Still, you'd think he'd want someone…smaller," she mused.

"I need a break from this conversation." Fiona let the pan she was washing slide into the soapy water, marched to the unoccupied front room and leaned against the wall.

She's always like this.

She's not going to change.

She doesn't define you.

The prejudice was unfortunate and meant she'd have to sit down with the kids and explain that their grandmother had some blind spots, that they should treat all people the same.

The idea of Eduardo preferring a tiny woman… That remark dug at her.

Eduardo had told her he liked the way she looked. They'd laughed together at the bride show and the model's complaints about being hungry.

But then again, his first wife had been tiny. He'd said so himself. *Tiny and pretty*, his kids had said.

But he likes me, he said so!

Of course, he'd say that. He's kind and gentle. He doesn't want to hurt anyone.

She sank down into a chair and looked absently at the bookshelves, trying to postpone the moment when she had to go back to her mother's company.

Her eyes settled on a diet book she'd bought a year ago during one of her low self-esteem periods. It was one of those fad diets, promising speedy weight loss. Not very healthy, and she'd never tried it. She should have thrown the book away.

Maybe it would work, though. And if she lost weight, she'd feel so much better about herself. Her mother would get off her case, and men wouldn't treat her the way her husband had.

She pulled it off the shelf.

Paperwork day. Eduardo didn't love it, but nobody wanted their landscaping done on Easter weekend, so it was a good time to catch up. Trouble was, the weather was gorgeous and he'd always rather be outside. The kids were already running around, and from the sounds of it, they'd connected with Fiona's kids, who were also out enjoying the beautiful spring weather.

Fiona. He'd texted her a *hello* this morning and had gotten no response. But she was probably busy with her surprise guest.

How had it happened that they'd kissed only two

times, and they'd been caught on both occasions? Once by the kids, and once by her mother, and he didn't know which was worse. He hoped Fiona's mom hadn't been too hard on her.

After a few minutes of daydreaming about yesterday, he decided to take his laptop outside. Maybe he could concentrate better there, push aside the warm feeling that grew in him when he thought of spending yesterday with her, holding her hand, sharing stories that drew them ever closer as they got to know each other.

He'd barely settled himself on the front porch with his laptop and a glass of iced tea when he heard several of the kids come around the side of the house.

"Are you guys Mexicans?" Ryan was asking.

"Kind of," Diego said. "We're Americans, but our grandparents moved here from Mexico, so that's why we have darker skin and hair."

"Our grandma says *you people* don't take care of your things, but we told her you do," Maya said. "Hey, are you guys poor?"

Heat rose in Eduardo's neck, but he forced himself to stay seated and let Diego handle it.

"No!" Diego said, and then there were murmurs Eduardo couldn't make out. "I don't want to play with your building set, anyway," Diego said sharply. "I don't like it anymore."

More murmurs, then Diego spoke again. "He could buy it for me if he wanted to, but he doesn't want to."

From the opposite direction, Sofia came up onto the porch and sat by Eduardo. "Lauren got a phone," she said.

"Really?" That surprised him. He wouldn't have pegged Fiona as a person who'd buy her ten-year-old a cell phone, but maybe he didn't know her as well as he thought.

"I wish I could have one," Sofia said, "but it's okay, Dad. I know you don't have enough money for it."

He blew out a breath. His happy mood was rapidly disappearing.

A little later, after Sofia had taken off, Poppy came to the bottom of the porch steps and stood looking at him. That was surprising. She wasn't usually off on her own apart from the others.

And although she'd become more comfortable with him, he didn't want to scare her, so he stayed in his seat. "Hey, Poppy," he said, keeping his voice casual.

Slowly, she came to the top of the stairs and again stood still, looking at him. It was a little creepy.

"Anything wrong, honey?" he asked her. "Where's your mom?"

"It's okay if she marries you," Poppy said, taking a step closer, but holding on to the porch railing.

He couldn't help smiling. "We're not planning on that," he said, and then something made him add, "right now, anyway."

"If you marry Mommy, you won't have to go away," she explained seriously.

"We don't have to go away, sweetheart."

"Yes, you do, to Mex-i-co," she said in a singsong voice and moved closer until she was right by his side. "Lauren and Ryan 'splained it to me. But if you marry Mommy, you and Sofia and Diego can stay." She studied him. "You can be my daddy."

The acceptance in that sweet smile warmed his heart, but the implications of what she'd said, in all innocence, annoyed him thoroughly. Who had been telling Poppy that Eduardo and his family were illegal immigrants?

"Thank you, Poppy," he said. "Now, you'd better run home."

As she went down the steps, Diego came running up, his face stormy.

"Whoa, son, what's wrong?"

"Leave me alone!" Diego hurried into the house.

Eduardo tried to focus on his work, to give Diego some space, but he'd never been very good at that, especially when one of his kids was obviously hurting. And the things Poppy had said kept playing in his mind. *Poor...you people...can't afford...not Americans...*

Sofia came up the steps again, looking glum.

"Hey, Sof, what's wrong?"

"Nothing."

"Come on." He patted the chair beside him. "Tell me."

She sat down and shrugged. "Now that Lauren has a phone, she's texting with all these other girls in our grade. She doesn't want to just, you know, hang out."

"That's a problem with cell phones." And it was one reason why he didn't think children should have them.

"I just wish we weren't poor," Sofia burst out. She stood and flounced into the house.

This had gone too far. Eduardo followed her, shaking his head, and called for Diego to come downstairs. Once they were both sitting on the couch, he nudged his way between them and put an arm around each.

"I love you both," he said, feeling his way, "and I can't stand it when other people say things to hurt you."

"We know, Dad." Diego tried to shift away.

"It sounds like someone has been talking about us being Mexican."

Sofia rolled her eyes. "Duh, Dad. I mean, it's obvious from how we look."

Eduardo frowned. Those didn't sound like words Sofia would have come up with on her own. But probing for details wasn't the answer. "I'm proud of my Mexican heritage, and so was your mom. So many artists and businesspeople and athletes come from—"

"We *know*, Dad!"

Okay. So now wasn't the time for a history lesson, but he still had more to say to his kids. "The other thing to remember is that it's not what you have that makes you good and important. It's what's in your hearts."

"Uh-huh," Diego said.

"Can we turn on the TV?" Sofia asked.

He sighed and took a good look at Sofia, then at Diego. Not only did they look upset, but they both looked weary.

It was tiring when people took swings at your self-image. And maybe something he'd said would sink in later.

"Sure, okay," he said, standing up. "I'll be out on the porch if you want to talk."

No answer. As he walked outside, the TV blared behind him.

Eduardo sat, looking out over the grass, thinking.

Obviously, a lot of this new talk and negativity came from Fiona's mom. He couldn't blame Fiona for what her mother thought or said. He didn't know whether she agreed with any of it or not.

But he *did* know that Fiona could buy her kids anything they wanted.

If they blended their families, Fiona's mother would be a part of his life, and more important, a part of his kids' lives. They'd be exposed to attitudes he tried to protect them from. Exposed on a frequent basis, from an actual relative.

And there was another problem: his own kids would have far less materially than Fiona's kids would. And no matter how hard you tried to instill the right values in your kids, they were still kids. They wanted what other children had, especially those in their own families.

Other people would look at him and Fiona the way her mother did. Thinking he'd married her for money, or for a green card. The very idea made heat rise through his body, made his head feel like it was going to explode.

He couldn't live like that. Couldn't expose his kids to the poison. He had to protect his family; he'd vowed that he would.

He sat another half hour, thinking.

And then he got on the phone with the manager of the motel they'd stayed at before. Negotiated a good rate for an end room, where they wouldn't bother the other guests.

Now that he had an alternative place to live, though, something nagged at him. Some feeling that he wasn't doing the right thing.

Chapter 13

Fiona had just started to recover from her mother's digs when Brownie went crazy with barking, and Fiona opened the front door to find Susan and Daisy, both wearing workout clothes. Their friendly faces looked like sunshine after a morning of grey clouds.

"Ready for our walk?" Susan asked.

"Shh, Brownie!" Fiona grabbed the dog's collar, looked back into the house and then frowned out at her friends. "I'd love to come," she said, "but Mom's visiting. I can't make it today. Didn't you get my text?"

"We *need* you." Daisy gave her a winning smile.

"Go find your walking shoes," Susan said and then added in a whisper, "I'll take care of your mom."

"Who is it, Fiona?" Her mother came into the foyer, and her standard social smile appeared on her face. "Hello, ladies."

"Hi, Mrs. Farmingham!" Susan gently shoved Fiona to the side as she walked in, holding out a hand. "I didn't get a chance to chat with you when you got here last night."

"Oh, yes. The babysitter." Mom didn't hold out her hand, which was unusual for her. "Susan, right? I remember meeting you a while back, but I'm sorry I don't remember your last name. I have such trouble pronouncing... Well, it was a bit *unusual*, I think."

Susan didn't retract her hand, although her smile widened into something of a grimace. "That's right. Hayashi was my maiden name. But I'm married to Sam Hinton now. You know, the *head of Hinton Industries*. So I'm Susan Hinton now."

"Oh!" Now Fiona's mother's smile became more genuine, and she shook Susan's hand with warmth.

"Get your shoes!" Daisy nudged Fiona toward the stairs and then walked up to Fiona's mother. "And I'm Daisy *Hinton*, Sam's sister," she said sweetly. "I was babysitting the kids last night, too, but in the confusion I don't think we really exchanged names."

Fiona jogged upstairs, grabbed her workout shoes and sat at the top of the stairs to put them on. If her friends could get her an hour away from her mother's negative commentary, she'd buy them both enormous pastries at the Chatterbox.

And one for herself as well.

"I know how much you love your grandkids," Daisy was enthusing. "Fiona has said so much about all the nice gifts you send."

"So we thought we'd give you a little time alone with them, away from Fiona." Susan's voice was firm. "She has a hard time letting anyone else take charge."

"Come on, Fiona!" Daisy called gaily up the stairs. "We won't take no for an answer. Your mom wants the kids to herself."

Blinking, Fiona walked down the stairs. No way was her mom going to let herself be manipulated like this. But it would be *so* nice to escape…

Susan grabbed her arm. "Let's go. Bye, Mrs. Farmingham!"

"Mom?" Fiona looked over her shoulder at her mother as Susan pulled her out the door."

"Thanks so much for letting us steal her away!" Daisy had her hand on the doorknob. "Your grandkids are going to be thrilled!"

Her mother looked a little befuddled. "Well…"

"We'll be back by dinnertime," Susan called. "In fact, we'll *bring* dinner. Don't want you to have to cook. Just enjoy the kids."

By *dinnertime*? Fiona looked at her phone. It was only two o'clock. Her mom couldn't…

"That'll be fine, I guess," her mom said in a faint voice.

"You're such a sweetheart!" Daisy said and closed the door behind them with a sharp click.

They walked down the porch steps and around the side of the house in silence, but once they were safely out of sight and earshot of Fiona's mother, Susan and Daisy high-fived each other.

"You guys, I can't go for a walk without telling the kids."

"I saw Lauren with a phone when we came in," Daisy said. "Why don't you just text her?"

"I don't want to encourage…"

"What's her new number?" Susan asked.

"I don't remember. I don't even want her to have a…"

"Did you put it in your phone?" Susan asked as they walked past the carriage house. She took Fiona's phone out of her hand and started scrolling.

Sparkles loped over on three legs, nudged Fiona's hand and whined.

"Are you looking for Brownie?" Fiona asked. She gestured toward her house. "He's back there. Go get him."

Sparkles cocked her head as if trying to understand.

"Go get Brownie," Fiona said again, waving an arm toward her house.

The dog's tongue lolled out in a sort of smile, hanging to one side, and she ambled toward Fiona's house.

"Here, I found Lauren's number and I'm texting her," Susan said. "I'm saying, 'It's Mrs. Hinton. Congrats on new phone.'"

A few seconds later, Susan's phone buzzed and she read out Lauren's text:

So excited! Put you in my contacts!

"But I haven't even decided if I'm going to allow…" Fiona protested.

"Hey, there." Eduardo's voice sounded from the direction of the carriage house. Fiona's heart pumped harder as she looked over to see him jump nimbly off the side of the steps and walk toward them. "We need to talk," he told her.

Daisy grabbed Susan's arm. "No problem," she said to Eduardo. And to Fiona: "We'll wait out by the alley. Go talk."

When Fiona saw the tight expression on Eduardo's

face, though, a sense of dread rose in her. "Can we talk" never meant anything good.

It was how her mother often started critical conversations. It was how her ex had informed her he'd be out of town for another business trip… Business trips that, she'd later learned, hadn't even existed but had served as cover for his life with his second family.

"I'm not happy about some things I heard this morning," Eduardo said. His voice wasn't kind and gentle like usual. It was sharp, almost angry.

It's happening again.

"My kids came home spouting misconceptions about our economic status and our Mexican heritage." He warmed to his topic. "Someone even gave your kids the notion that we're illegal immigrants, which is absolutely ridiculous. My kids and I are American citizens."

Somehow, her mother's words had gotten back to him. She opened her mouth to try to explain.

He didn't give her the chance. "I can't have that, Fiona. I want my kids to be proud of who they are and comfortable with the life I'm able to provide. What I heard this morning put that at risk."

What was the use of trying to discuss it? It had never done any good in the past. Arguing with her mom, pleading with her ex…all of it was basically useless.

"I don't… I didn't mean to… I mean, I'm sorry…" Her words tangled and she gave up, her shoulders slumping.

"Do you actually agree with the things my kids heard?" His voice was angry, accusatory. As if he'd already made up his mind, judged her and found her wanting.

She looked down to hide her distress. How could she argue back intelligently and convince him he was wrong about her especially when her heart was shattering into a thousand pieces? When the bright new hope she'd been nurturing was fading to black?

"Fiona, I thought we had something here. I was really starting to care for you." Anger and confusion clouded his eyes.

She had to speak up, to explain. But the words were stuck in her throat. She felt the same way as when she'd taken hard tests at school. The pressure was on, and she knew she was going to fail. Her heart pounded. It was hard to catch her breath.

She should have known it wasn't going to work with Eduardo. He was a wonderful, caring, appealing man.

And women like Fiona didn't get to have wonderful, caring, appealing men.

Words continued to fail her.

"I'd never have guessed you were on board with what was said." His chin lifted and his shoulders squared. "My kids and I will be moving out."

The sudden declaration made her gasp. Images of their time together—working in the garden, helping their kids learn to be responsible dog owners, sharing a tender kiss—flashed through her mind in a steadily darkening kaleidoscope. She looked down so he wouldn't see the tears gathering in her eyes, nodded because she couldn't speak. And even if she could finally find the words, what would be the point now?

She turned and forced herself to walk toward Susan and Daisy rather than collapsing into a sobbing heap on the ground.

Up ahead, her friends stood at the gate that separated the carriage house's yard area from the alley. "You ready?" Susan asked, glancing up from her phone.

Daisy was waving at a couple of kids who were carrying fishing poles toward the creek.

Good, they weren't paying attention to her. Because no way could she talk about what had just happened without breaking down.

"Let's go!" Daisy said.

Fiona nodded and followed them blindly to their usual walking route.

Susan was pecking her fingers rapidly at her phone and nearly bumped into a parked car. Daisy caught her elbow on one side and Fiona automatically took the other.

"Thanks," Susan said, still without looking up. "I said, 'Taking your mom for a walk. Your grandma's in the house, but you're in charge. K?' She'll be thrilled."

Fiona's mother-brain kicked in and she swallowed her tears. "But I didn't even talk to her..."

Susan's phone buzzed again, and Susan looked, smiled and held it out for Daisy and Fiona to see.

"KK?" Daisy asked. "How'd she learn texting shortcuts when this is her first day with a new phone?"

"Don't question it, just come on."

They headed through the residential section of Rescue River. But the beauty of the blooming redbuds and dogwoods, the sound of a lawn mower and the smell of fresh-cut grass had no power to lift Fiona's spirits.

He was leaving. It was over.

"We want to hear about your date with Eduardo last night," Daisy said.

"The date we helped set up," Susan added. "Man, did we do well or what?" She fist-bumped Daisy. "Tell us every single detail."

How could she begin to tell her friends what had happened in the past twenty-four hours? How she'd reached the heights of hope and excitement—maybe even love—with Eduardo.

And how it had all come crashing down.

Her phone buzzed and automatically she pulled it out.

The text was from Lauren.

Mr. Delgado says they're moving out on Monday. <frowny face> Can we take care of Sparkles until they find a new house?

She hadn't known she could feel worse, but the heaviness of a thousand stones pressed down on her. She hadn't just imagined it. It was really happening.

Her steps slowed, then stopped.

"What?" Daisy asked.

"What's wrong?" Susan put her hand on Fiona's arm.

She texted back.

Sure.

And then she looked from Susan to Daisy. "He's moving out of the carriage house. On Monday." Slowly, she started walking again.

"Why would he do that?" Daisy asked. "I thought they were staying through the end of the school year, at least."

"Maybe he found a house," Susan said. "Wasn't he looking to buy something?"

"They haven't found a place yet. He wants us to take care of his dog until they do." She felt like a robot, saying the words in a monotone. "It's because…because he's mad at me."

Amid her friends' questions and concerned glances, Fiona kept hearing her mother's voice: *Why would he choose you?*

She didn't know she'd said it aloud until Daisy and Susan tugged her to a halt. "He would choose you because you're wonderful," Daisy said.

"And beautiful and a good person and fun," Susan added.

Fiona shook her head. Her girlfriends would always staunchly defend her, but she knew her deficits.

"You have to talk to him," Susan said. "Confront him with it. Find out what's really going on."

"I already know what's going on," she said miserably. "I froze under pressure and didn't get a chance to explain before he walked away. Besides, he could have any woman in town. One with no baggage or a mom who would make him and his kids feel like less. He doesn't want anything more to do with me."

"Talk to him some more," Daisy urged.

Fiona shook her head. "I just don't think I can handle another rejection. Not this weekend. Not now."

Daisy and Susan glanced at each other. "I'm texting Dion," Daisy said.

"And I'm texting Sam."

"No, don't." But she didn't have the energy to stop them. To talk anymore. She just wanted to go home and crawl into bed.

But of course, that wasn't to be. When she got home, the place was in chaos. Kids crying, her mother ineffectually trying to force them to behave, the dog barking.

"Do you want us to…?" Daisy and Susan both asked in unison.

"No. I'll handle it." And she waved goodbye to them and waded in, feeling like a hundred-pound weight sat on her shoulders.

Mechanically, she hugged Poppy, who was crying. Got her a stuffed animal and some semi-healthy chips, and told Maya to sit with her and watch a princess movie. Maya was the only one who didn't seem upset— which was par for the course, and Fiona thanked God she had one nonsensitive child—but even she seemed to welcome a chance to relax and settle down.

"Mom," Fiona said wearily. "Get yourself a cup of coffee. I'm going to talk to Lauren and Ryan." And she led her two eldest out to the porch.

She didn't feel like talking, didn't want to confront this. But that was what you did as a single parent. You carried on even when you felt like you couldn't, because there was no one else to shoulder the load.

For a brief bright moment, she'd thought she and Eduardo might go forward together. But clearly, she'd been deluded. She was alone, and she'd better get used to it.

The cheerful blooms along her front sidewalk sent their fragrance to them on a warm breeze, and Fiona tried to take in their message. Rebirth. Redemption. Life springing forth from cold, frozen ground.

She was learning. Trying to, anyway.

Amid her sadness, a little righteous anger surfaced toward Eduardo. He'd pushed her away again, just as he'd done after they'd kissed.

By now, he should know her better. He should have given her a chance to explain. And, she acknowledged to herself, she should have used her newfound strength and self-understanding to insist on it.

When Lauren sniffled, Fiona's attention snapped back to the present moment. No matter what happened to her own dreams, her commitment to her kids' well-being was ironclad. "So what happened, exactly?" she asked Lauren.

"I hate this thing." Lauren pulled out her cell phone and handed it to Fiona. "Tell Grandma I don't want it."

"You don't have to use it, but sure, we can give it back." Fiona pocketed the phone. "What's got you so upset?"

"Sofia's mad at me because she doesn't have one," she said. "And I was texting Tiffany and this girl named Raquel, and they wanted me to download these apps that you're not supposed to use until you're thirteen. I told them I wasn't allowed, and they called me a baby."

"You did the right thing," Fiona soothed her, a tiny sliver of light piercing the darkness in her heart. If Lauren could make a choice like that, against peer pressure, then Fiona had done something right as a mother, at least. She hugged Lauren. "I'm proud of you."

"Thanks, Mom. I want to make up with Sofia, but they're moving away."

"So I hear." Pain started to rise up in her again, but she stifled it down for her kids' sakes. She couldn't fall apart.

She looked at Brownie, who'd come outside with them. "So Brownie is going to have his mom visiting us for a little while, huh?"

"I don't know why they're moving. I wish they weren't," Lauren said.

Ryan cleared his throat. "I think I might know why. I hurt Diego's feelings."

"What happened?" She put an arm around her sensitive boy.

"We were talking about how his family didn't have as much money as ours. He was kind of jealous of my building set, and I told him he could play with it, even though Grammy said his kind of people weren't careful."

"You told him what Grammy said?"

Ryan nodded miserably. "And he got mad. And said he didn't want to play with it, anyway, or with me."

Poppy banged out through the screen door and squatted down to give her brother and sister hugs. "I told Mr. Delgado he didn't have to go back to Mex'co. Told him to marry Mommy and stay here."

"You did?" Lauren asked.

"You did?" Ryan's eyes widened.

"You did?" Fiona echoed, trying to wrap her mind around the umpteen ways this day had gone wrong. "Um...what did he say?"

"He didn't answer me," Poppy said.

Anger at her blunt, hurtful mother blazed in Fiona, but she tamped it down and beckoned to Maya, who'd been listening from inside the house. "All four of you, listen to me. What Grammy said was wrong. People come from all different places. Some have lots of money and some don't have very much, but God values us all the same, do you hear me? We're all the same in God's eyes. And He wants all of us to get along. We don't treat people differently based on where they're from, or what they look like, or how much money they have."

All four kids looked at her, eyes round, nodding. Of

course, they knew all of that; she'd raised them that way, and where she'd fallen short, Sunday school had filled in and expanded on that basic lesson.

Unfortunately, her mother hadn't gotten the memo.

"I want you to stay out here while I talk to Grandma," she said. She couldn't fix things with Eduardo, but she could make sure her kids didn't suffer any more damage. She *wasn't* a weak woman who'd fall apart because of a man. She'd stayed strong for her kids before, and she could do it again.

"Are you mad at us?" Ryan asked.

"No. I'm not mad at you." She hugged each of them quickly and then went inside.

In the kitchen, she yanked out a chair across from her mother, who was drinking coffee. "I have something to discuss with you."

"My goodness, you sound angry."

"I am," she said. "First of all, the comments about weight have to stop. To me, but most of all, to my daughters."

"What comments about weight?" Her mother's eyes opened wide.

"Comments like 'You're not cooking that, are you?' and 'It's never too early to watch your weight.'"

"I can understand why you've always been sensitive about your weight," her mother said. "You're so tall, and when you put on the pounds…"

"That. Comments like that. I want you to say nothing at all about size or weight. To me or to the girls. Or to Ryan, for that matter."

"Nothing? That's a little extreme."

"Nothing. But even more important, I don't want to

hear any more remarks about a person's ethnicity or financial status."

"I don't talk about those things!" her mother said indignantly. "And I don't appreciate you making me feel like some sort of bad person. What kind of a way is that to treat your mother?"

"My children repeated some of what you said this morning to the Delgado family."

"Oh, dear. Is that why they're leaving?" Her mother looked down, but the corners of her mouth turned up just a little.

Until this moment, Fiona had never thought her mother's negative comments had ill intent. She'd thought her remarks—the weight ones, at least—were a misguided way of trying to help.

But her smirk now made it seem like she'd been *hoping* the kids would repeat her stereotypes to the Delgados.

"You're my mother," she said evenly. "And you're my children's grandmother, and I know you love us. I hope you'll stay for the rest of the weekend. But if you make one more remark that suggests that stereotyping and racism are okay, you're going to need to leave."

"Are you threatening your own mother?"

Fiona cocked her head to one side and studied the woman who'd raised her. She'd done so much for Fiona…and so much *to* Fiona as well. "I'm setting the conditions for you to be in my home, Mom," she said, gentling her voice. "I can't have toxicity here, harming me and my children. But if you're willing to take the high road in your conversations with us, you are welcome to stay." She blinked away the sudden tears that rose to her eyes. "I love you, Mom. I hope we can have a better relationship."

"I just care about you! I've worked so hard to be slim all my life and you just don't even... Do you *know* how long it's been since I ate macaroni and cheese?"

Fiona swallowed the lump in her throat and shook her head.

"And if you cared about yourself, you wouldn't go out with a Mexican!"

Anger heated Fiona's face and made her breath come fast. "Out."

"What?" Her mother's voice rose an octave.

Dry-eyed, Fiona found her phone and looked for the number of Ralph Montour, a man in town who ran a car service. "Go get your things together," she said to her mother while the phone was ringing.

"But...it's Easter weekend."

That gave Fiona a pang.

"Hello?" Ralph said.

"Would you be able to drive my mother to the airport?" she asked.

"Sure thing. Today?"

"Yes. Today."

"My flight's not until Monday!" her mother protested.

"I'll call the airport and pay to get it changed." She gave Ralph the address. "She'll be ready in an hour."

"Fiona!" Her mother's voice rose into hysteria and tears came into her eyes. "You can't do this to me! You're all I have!"

Fiona drew in a breath. "I can't have poison in my kids' lives."

"I'm sorry!" Her mother grabbed her hand. "Please. Don't send me away."

Looking at her mother's hand—perfectly manicured, yes, and sporting several expensive rings, but still wrinkled and age-spotted—Fiona's resolve faltered. Slowly, she pulled out a chair and sat back down, facing her mother, knee to knee. "Do you understand what it is I don't want you to say? Or imply? To me, or the kids, or anyone else in Rescue River?"

Her mother's chin shook and big tears stood in her eyes. "I understand."

"Do you? Do you really understand that it's what's in a person's heart that matters, rather than a dress size or a bank account?"

She nodded. "I… I suppose so. It's just not…" She trailed off, then met Fiona's eyes. "It's not how I was raised, and it's not how I've thought about things. Looks are important. Money is important."

Fiona shook her head. "No, Mom. They're not. And putting priority on those things will only lead to misery."

Her mother stared at the ground, her throat working.

"And there's more."

Her mother took a tissue and wiped her eyes. "What more do you want from me?"

"I want a promise that you won't comment about people from other ethnic backgrounds or races. Not to them, not to me and especially not to, or in front of, the kids." She leaned forward to emphasize her point. "God made the world with all types of people in it, and our job is to love each other, not put each other down."

Her mother nodded. "I know," she said very quietly.

"I mean it, Mom. All kinds of people live in Rescue

River. You're going to see different skin colors and hear different languages, see different styles of dress. It's not okay to disparage them. If you do, you'll have to leave."

"Fine." Her mother let out a windy sigh.

Fiona's indignation was fading. "I'll call Ralph back and let him know you don't need a ride. But I've got him on speed dial."

"I understand."

"Okay." She knelt and gave her mother an awkward hug. "I've got one text I need to send, and then we'll have some iced tea and help the kids decorate eggs."

She went into the bathroom—the only place where she knew she could get a moment's privacy—and sat down on the edge of the tub. She contemplated calling Eduardo, but she figured the damage had already been done. She couldn't handle more confrontation, anyway. A woman only had so much strength.

She let her head fall into her hands. She didn't know if she'd been right to nearly kick her mom out, to lecture her, or to let her stay. She didn't know if there was any repair work that could be done with Eduardo. "Lord," she prayed, "help me. Show me the right thing to do."

A moment later, she heard loud voices in the kitchen—not angry, thankfully, just loud—and knew her alone time had come to an end.

She had to make a choice. Either she could cave in, be the weak woman she'd been in her marriage, or she could draw on the strength she'd gained from her community, her friends and her God.

She drew in a breath and typed a carefully worded text to Eduardo. Read it over and hit Send.

It probably wasn't going to fix anything. Eduardo was still a man, and though she was starting to realize how different he was from her husband, she knew he still had a lot of pride.

She liked that about him. He was proud of his heritage, proud of his work. Proud to be a strong man.

He was a strong father, too, and his decision to move out made sense. He had to protect his children and do what was best for them. They shouldn't have been subjected to the words they'd heard today.

What she'd texted him was unlikely to change that. But at least she'd tried.

Chapter 14

Eduardo was throwing toys and games into a big box when there was a knock at the door of the carriage house.

For a moment his heart leaped. Was it Fiona?

But no. He couldn't hope for that. Because whatever she said, he couldn't allow it to convince him to stay, to go back to her. Their differences were too great, the potential damage to his kids too real.

"Eduardo?" It was Dion's deep voice. "Need to talk to you, my man."

Eduardo shoved back the box, wiped his face on his sleeve and went to the door. "Come in. Kind of busy, though."

Dion walked into the center of the living room, looked around at the boxes and the chaos, and whistled. "You're serious about moving."

He nodded. "Mind if I keep packing while we talk? You can grab a soda from the fridge."

Dion slapped his back, hard. "I'll get both of us sodas. You can take a fifteen-minute break and listen to what I have to say, can't you?"

Eduardo didn't want to. He didn't want to lose momentum. He would rather not talk to anyone; just keep moving so he didn't have to think.

But he respected the older man, so he nodded. "Sure. I'll get the drinks."

"Sit on the porch?"

Eduardo shook his head. "Better to stay inside."

"Where are the kids?"

"They're with Lou Ann Miller. I... I didn't want them to see all this. They're upset enough. But they'll be back soon, so..."

"So hurry up and speak my piece? All right." Dion kept looking out the window, though. And a moment later, Eduardo saw why when Sam Hinton knocked on the door.

Eduardo narrowed his eyes at Dion. "Was this planned?" he asked as he went to let Sam in.

"Get the man a beverage."

Sighing, Eduardo did so. His friends were good men, no denying it, but they'd try to talk him out of what he was doing. And he couldn't let them succeed.

He walked back into the living room, shoved the soda can at Sam and sat down. "You guys have fifteen minutes. I'm watching the clock."

"What's prompting the move out?" Sam asked.

"I need a better environment for my kids."

"Seems like they've been happy here, from what Susan has told me."

"They were. Until Fiona's mother arrived to rub in all our differences. Economic and...background."

Dion frowned. "What did she say? Anything you haven't heard before?"

"It's not about me," Eduardo said. "I understand that some people didn't grow up knowing how to deal with differences. But she said stuff that Fiona's kids picked up and repeated to mine."

"Stuff about your being Latino?" Sam asked.

Eduardo nodded. "And poor."

Dion lifted an eyebrow. "Are you poor, or just a tight-wad? Nobody I know saves as much as you do."

Eduardo glared. "It's called *frugal*. I spend money on what's important."

"Nothing for anyone to criticize there," Sam said. "Besides, the way your business is taking off, you're headed toward being extremely comfortable, financially."

Eduardo waved a hand. "That's all beside the point. The big problem is that Fiona agrees with her mother."

"She *does*?" Sam frowned. "Where'd you get that idea?"

"I told her about what happened, and she didn't even get upset. She just walked away. She didn't care."

"Let me ask you something," Sam said. "Does the Fiona you know seem like a person who'd agree with that nonsense? Who wouldn't care that children had been hurt and stereotypes perpetuated?"

He looked at his hands and instantly knew the answer. Slowly, he shook his head. "That's not how she is."

"What I'm wondering," Dion said, "is whether you're going to let one ignorant woman push you out of your home."

"And away from the woman you love," Sam added.

"Hey, hey now!" Eduardo tried to wave away the words. "Nobody said anything about love."

"But it's the truth, isn't it?" Dion asked quietly.

The question hung in the air.

"I do love her," Eduardo said slowly. "But I have to protect my kids."

"From what, ignorance?" Dion shook his head. "They're going to face that in this world. It's not okay, and I hope one day it will change, but right now that's the society we live in. Their names and their coloring, everyone's going to know they're Mexican, even though they've grown up here in the Midwest. Better teach them how to deal with it rather than running away."

Eduardo had opened his mouth to speak, but now he closed it. Was that what he was doing? Running away?

Was that what he wanted to model to his kids?

He knew it wasn't. Sam and Dion were right.

Were they right about the rest of it, too? Could he stay and try to make a go of things with Fiona, as they seemed to be suggesting?

He rubbed the back of his neck and didn't look at them. "How am I supposed to manage the fact that Fiona has so much more money than I do? Her kids have stuff I wouldn't buy my kids in a million years."

Sam frowned. "I don't think of Fiona as being real materialistic, nor teaching her kids to be that way."

"I've seen her shopping at the discount store, like everyone else," Dion added. "What do her kids have that your kids want?"

"Cell phone, the latest Lego kit..." Eduardo trailed off. When he said it aloud, it didn't sound like a big deal.

"She got her kids cell phones?" Sam asked.

"I think her mom brought along a bunch of expensive gifts." Which wasn't Fiona's fault, of course, any more than the sacks of candy his own parents gave to his kids could be blamed on him.

Dion leaned back in his chair, cradling his head in his interlaced hands. "I get where you're coming from with the money thing, for sure. I mean..." He glanced at Sam. "I have feelings for a Hinton. Daisy could buy me and everything I own with her pocket change."

Sam narrowed his eyes at Dion. "Money doesn't matter, but you're an old man compared to her."

"She doesn't seem to mind," Eduardo said mildly. He understood that Sam was protective of his sister, but you couldn't miss the way Dion and Daisy looked at each other.

"We're not talking about me." Dion deliberately turned away from Sam to focus on Eduardo. "We're talking about you, and how you're making some stiff-necked move that has your kids *and* Fiona's kids *and* Fiona herself crying their eyes out."

"Fiona's been crying?"

"So I hear."

"She's a good woman," Sam said. "Pretty good friends with me and Susan these last few years, and I haven't seen a mean bone in her body. Good mother, good Christian, humble..."

"A looker," Dion contributed.

"Hey!" Eduardo glared at him.

"She *is* pretty," Sam said.

"And if you don't like us noticing," Dion said, "how're you gonna like it when some other guy steps in and claims her because you had too much pride to court a rich woman?"

"What do your kids think of her?" Sam asked.

"They love her. Sofia was hesitant, at first, because of loyalty to her mom. But she and Fiona seem to be getting close."

"And would they love a woman who looked down on them for their background?"

Eduardo didn't answer, but he knew they wouldn't. His kids had good instincts about people. They knew Fiona's heart was in the right place.

They all sat there a couple of minutes, watching the soundless baseball game on the television.

"You sure you're not feeling some survivor's guilt?" Sam asked abruptly. "When your wife dies, it can be hard to let her go and move on to being happy with another woman. Believe me, I struggled with that."

Eduardo shrugged a little. "Could be." Elizabeth would have encouraged him to move on and find love again; they'd even talked about it. But until now, his sense that he hadn't been enough of a protector had kept him from doing that.

"Have you taken it to the Lord?" Dion asked.

"I..." Eduardo stopped. He'd prayed some, sure. And he'd expressed his anger to the Lord when his kids had been hurt that morning. But had he really prayed before deciding to move out?

Voices and clomping footsteps broke into their meeting, which, Eduardo realized now, had gone on quite a bit longer than fifteen minutes. "Dad, we're home," Diego called.

Both kids stopped when they saw the other two men there, altered their usual manner into company politeness and shook hands.

"Hey, you two," Dion said. "How'd you like to do a little fishing with Mr. Hinton and me?"

"And then have some burgers at my house?" Sam added.

Eduardo looked at his kids and then at his friends. "Let me talk to them for a minute," he said.

"Take your time," Sam said. "I'm heading home to start those burgers. They'll be good, and Mindy will be glad to have somebody to play with."

"I've got fishing poles in the back of my car," Dion said. "Come on out when you decide."

"Thanks." Eduardo clapped them both on the backs as they walked to the door.

On the porch table, he noticed the phone he hadn't looked at in hours. Reflexively, he picked it up and checked.

One text.

From Fiona.

He clicked on it.

Whatever you may think of me, I don't want your kids to feel like they've been kicked out or that I feel the same way my mother does. I'm sorry for the things my kids said to yours. It won't happen again.

And then he turned back to find both of his kids looking at him with puppy-dog eyes.

"Do we *have* to move, Dad?" Sofia asked. "I'm sorry I talked about wanting a phone. I don't want one anymore and, anyway, I think Lauren's mom is taking hers away."

"And Diego said I could play with his Lego set. I don't need one of my own."

"And we don't care if we're poor," Sofia said.

"We're not…" Eduardo scrubbed a hand over his face. "We have plenty. More than a lot of people in the world. And material things aren't what's important, anyway."

"We know that!" Sofia said.

"So can we stay here, Dad, please?" Diego begged.

Eduardo looked over his shoulder through the screen door. There was Fiona's house. Probably, there was Fiona.

And her kids. And her mother.

He went to the door. "Hey, Dion," he called after his friend. "Instead of taking my kids fishing, how would you feel about babysitting six kids a little later? I've got something to set up."

"Six kids and two dogs," Diego added. "Don't forget Sparkles and Brownie."

Dion spun and strode back toward him, a wide grin on his face. "Sounds like I might need some help, but I'm completely game for it. I'll see if Daisy can come over."

"Do that," Eduardo said. "Because I've got some work to do."

"You want to *what*?" Fiona said to her mother after they'd eaten a late dinner.

"I want to take care of the children while you mend fences with Eduardo," she said. "He's actually quite charming."

Fiona blinked. "When did you talk to Eduardo?"

"When you were fixing dinner."

"Oka-a-a-ay," Fiona said. "But…are you sure Eduardo wants to talk to me? And are you sure you can manage the kids?"

"I have help," her mother said, pointing out the window.

Dion and Daisy stood halfway between the carriage house and the big house, talking heatedly. Then they smiled. Then laughed. And then Dion opened his arms to give Daisy a long hug.

Fiona looked over at her mother. "You're sure about this?"

Her mother squared her shoulders. "I'm sure. Go on now. He's waiting for you."

So, Fiona walked down her front walk and there was Eduardo. Not in his truck, but on foot. He was so handsome he took her breath away. "Take a walk?" he asked.

He must want to apologize, maybe explain his moving out. It wasn't much, but it was all she was going to get, and she wasn't going to waste it. She was going to treasure every remaining moment with this man.

"Okay, sure." They fell into step together, walking down to the back of her property, to a path that wound between the cornfields and the old barn.

Before she could lose her nerve, she spoke up. "I'm sorry about my mom," she said. "Between her gifts and the things she said…translated through the brains of little kids… I'm not surprised you'd be offended. That you'd want to move out."

"I'm sorry I blamed you for your mom."

"If it helps, she's going to try not to do it again. I gave her an ultimatum."

He lifted an eyebrow. "Ever done that before?"

"No. But I should have."

They walked along together, the creek beside them rippling.

"I… I think I was premature in saying I wanted to move out," he said finally.

"Really?" Hope sprung up inside her.

"The kids are really upset."

It was all about the kids, then. And that was fine. Good, even. "Mine were, too."

"And I was upset, too, Fiona, because the truth is…" He stopped and took her two hands in his so he was facing her. "The truth is I don't want to move out. I want to…" He looked up at the darkening sky.

All of a sudden, she felt like she was going to explode. "Look, Eduardo, I'm sorry about what happened, and I hope you'll stay for the kids' sakes. But I can't deal with this semi-romantic vibe we've got going here. It's making me crazy. Kissing me, letting me get close, then pulling back… I don't want to be treated that way."

Instead of answering, he tugged her to the edge of the cornfield. "Look at that."

"Aww, fireflies." Her heart softened.

"No, over here."

"Aaaah!" Fiona jumped closer to Eduardo when she saw what looked like two giant people.

He put an arm around her. "They're not going to hurt you. Come meet them."

A couple of steps later, Fiona realized how foolish she'd been for being afraid as she looked up at the cheerful straw pair dressed in colorful rags.

"They're *scarecrows*! But…they weren't here before, were they?"

"They're new." He paused, then added, "Take a look at her necklace."

Fiona moved forward and bent toward the female scarecrow. Something sparkled around her straw neck.

Her heart gave a great thump. She glanced back at Eduardo.

He was watching her, a nervous smile on his face. When she smiled back, he stepped behind the scarecrow, unfastened the beautiful necklace and came back to hold it out, showing her.

"Do you like it? It's been in my family for over a hundred years, but I know a lot of women like more modern styles. Elizabeth did. I just... Well, I treasure this necklace, and I'd like for you to wear it if you like it, too."

"I love it," she said honestly. "But I don't really *get* it."

He grasped her hand in both of his. "Can you forgive me for being so hot and cold? For having baggage and taking a while to figure things out?"

She hesitated.

"That's why I made the scarecrows. Because I've been scared. Scared of not being a good enough protector and provider. Of just not being, well, *enough*."

His heartfelt confession and the sincerity in his eyes tugged at her heart. "Of course you're good enough. You're wonderful." She stole a glance at the necklace, an intricately wrought silver pendant crowned by a large round diamond. A family heirloom. So much what she would have chosen herself.

"Fiona, I know we need to get to know each other better. I know it's too soon to make a commitment. But I'd like to work toward that with you. I want you to have this as a symbol of the future we might have together, with God's help."

She stared into those liquid brown eyes and tried to breathe.

"Because I love you, Fiona. I love your gentleness and your energy and the love you give your children. And maybe this is shallow, but I love how gorgeous you are."

The tone of his voice was sincere and so was his face. And in the warmth of that, the last hard, brittle fragments of her own not-good-enough worries melted away. She stepped closer to him. "I love you, too, Eduardo. And yes." She paused, her chest filled with amazement. "I would be incredibly honored to wear this and get to know you better and maybe…at least, think about building a life together. If our kids agree."

He clasped her to him then—a tight embrace that enveloped her, promising strength and safety and, most of all, love. Minutes later, he softened the embrace and pulled her to his side. "As for the kids," he said, "mine adore you. And I think—based on what she said this afternoon—that Poppy is going to be able to accept me. She was the toughest case."

"All of my kids will be thrilled." She leaned against him, still hardly able to believe it. Eduardo had said he loved her. He wanted to make a commitment to her.

He shifted so he could study her face. "How do you feel about our economic differences? I don't have as much money as you do."

She shrugged. "Doesn't matter to me. I didn't earn my money."

There was a great rustling and shushing in the bushes beside them. Brownie ran out into the clearing and started barking at the scarecrows. Sparkles limped

over and nudged him as if in reassurance, and he qui-
eted and went to sit at Fiona's side.

A moment passed and then all six kids burst out,
some from the bushes and some from the cornfield.
"Get married, get married, get married," they chanted.

Fiona pressed a hand to her mouth, whether to stop
laughter or tears, she couldn't say.

"Come here, all of you," Eduardo said. "Sit down."

So the kids sat in a circle around them, with Brownie
and Sparkles joining in, climbing from lap to lap.

"Were you kids listening to what we said?" Eduardo
asked them, his voice serious.

Lauren and Sofia glanced at each other. "We weren't
exactly *listening*," Lauren said.

"We just *overheard* a couple of things," Sofia added.

"Like that you might get committed," Diego nearly
shouted.

"That means married!" Lauren and Sofia said together.

"Get married, get married," Ryan started, and the
others took up the chorus again.

Fiona looked at her youngest, who was participating
in the chant but looking a bit confused. "How do you
feel, Poppy?" she asked. "What if we became a family,
after we've thought about it more?"

"Would I still be the baby?" she asked.

Fiona glanced at Eduardo to find him looking at her.
He leaned closer and whispered in her ear. "Do you
think we might have just one more baby, together?"

Fiona closed her eyes against the sudden tears of joy
that sprang up in them.

Eduardo got it. He loved babies and kids. He didn't
see seven kids as excessive. If all this worked out, they'd

have one more opportunity, if God blessed them with it, at having a baby again, at raising it together.

She reached out to tug Poppy onto her lap. "You'll always be my very special Poppy."

"And I think you're special, too," Eduardo added. "Every one of you kids. You're God's gift to us."

"And if we were blessed with one more gift, what could be more perfect?" Fiona murmured to him beneath the children's excited chatter. "I'd love to have one more. With you."

Epilogue

Fiona knelt to adjust the maroon-and-ivory ribbons on the sides of the seats and checked the aisle's white runner for folds and rough spots.

"Mom, what are you doing?" Lauren scolded. "It's almost time for the wedding to start!"

"I just want everything to be perfect," she said.

Eduardo appeared and held out his hands, tugging her to her feet. "Everything is perfect. Come relax for half an hour before the ceremony."

"I need to—"

"You need to relax," he said firmly and guided her toward a corner of the newly renovated Farmingham Wedding Barn. "Sit," he said, holding a chair for her and then pulling up another beside her. "Are you feeling okay?"

"I'm fine, Eduardo!" But she let her hands rest over the bump of her belly, propped her feet on a hay bale and admitted to herself that it felt good to sit down.

Eduardo was the most caring of husbands, especially now that she was in her seventh month of pregnancy. It had all happened fast, but it was what had worked, what they'd wanted. They were madly in love and couldn't wait to be husband and wife, and anyway, with six kids, there wasn't time or space for a long, drawn-out courtship. Although, she and Eduardo *had* taken a lovely honeymoon to a small island off the coast of Florida.

Fortunately, all the kids were thrilled about the new little brother to come.

"Go away! You're not supposed to see me!" Miss Minnie's shrill, nervous voice cut through the barn's peaceful quiet. Her niece and several other friends spoke to her in soothing tones, straightening her simple ivory gown.

And then Mr. Love, resplendent in a grey tuxedo and red vest, approached his bride on his granddaughter's arm. "I know the groom isn't supposed to see the bride before the ceremony," he said, "but that's not a problem for me." He touched the sunglasses that shaded his unseeing eyes. "Can't look at much of anything, but I can imagine plenty. I know you're a gorgeous sight to behold."

Fiona turned to Eduardo as the elders made their way to the back of the barn. "I'm just thrilled that they're the first couple to marry in this barn."

"They won't be the last." A deep voice behind her startled her, and she turned to see Daisy and Dion.

Daisy thrust her left hand in front of Fiona's face. "He just proposed!" she practically screamed.

"That's wonderful!" Fiona hugged her friend, who looked like she now had all the happiness in the world, while Eduardo pumped Dion's hand.

The children were leading guests to their seats and the minister gave them a wave, and she nodded. They were ready.

Mr. Love and Miss Minnie, ready to start anew in their eighties.

Daisy and Dion, finally overcoming their barriers and committing to a life of love together.

And she and Eduardo... She'd no sooner had the thought when he wrapped his arms around her from behind. "I love you so much."

"I love you, too."

As the guitar and piano music began and Poppy scattered rose petals along the short aisle between the rows of chairs, Fiona closed her eyes.

Her business. Her friends. Her children. All thriving.

And the love between herself and Eduardo...blossoming and growing. And coming to fruition in the child that grew inside her.

"Thank you, Father," she whispered as the congregation stood and the "Wedding March" began.

* * * * *

Get 4 FREE REWARDS!

We'll send you 2 FREE Books plus 2 FREE Mystery Gifts.

FREE
Value Over
$20

Both the **Love Inspired®** and **Love Inspired® Suspense** series feature compelling novels filled with inspirational romance, faith, forgiveness and hope.

YES! Please send me 2 FREE novels from the Love Inspired or Love Inspired Suspense series and my 2 FREE gifts (gifts are worth about $10 retail). After receiving them, if I don't wish to receive any more books, I can return the shipping statement marked "cancel." If I don't cancel, I will receive 6 brand-new Love Inspired Larger-Print books or Love Inspired Suspense Larger-Print books every month and be billed just $6.49 each in the U.S. or $6.74 each in Canada. That is a savings of at least 16% off the cover price. It's quite a bargain! Shipping and handling is just 50¢ per book in the U.S. and $1.25 per book in Canada.* I understand that accepting the 2 free books and gifts places me under no obligation to buy anything. I can always return a shipment and cancel at any time by calling the number below. The free books and gifts are mine to keep no matter what I decide.

Choose one: ☐ **Love Inspired**
Larger-Print
(122/322 IDN GRHK)

☐ **Love Inspired Suspense**
Larger-Print
(107/307 IDN GRHK)

Name (please print)

Address   Apt. #

City   State/Province   Zip/Postal Code

Email: Please check this box ☐ if you would like to receive newsletters and promotional emails from Harlequin Enterprises ULC and its affiliates. You can unsubscribe anytime.

Mail to the **Harlequin Reader Service:**
IN U.S.A.: P.O. Box 1341, Buffalo, NY 14240-8531
IN CANADA: P.O. Box 603, Fort Erie, Ontario L2A 5X3

Want to try 2 free books from another series? Call 1-800-873-8635 or visit www.ReaderService.com.

*Terms and prices subject to change without notice. Prices do not include sales taxes, which will be charged (if applicable) based on your state or country of residence. Canadian residents will be charged applicable taxes. Offer not valid in Quebec. This offer is limited to one order per household. Books received may not be as shown. Not valid for current subscribers to the Love Inspired or Love Inspired Suspense series. All orders subject to approval. Credit or debit balances in a customer's account(s) may be offset by any other outstanding balance owed by or to the customer. Please allow 4 to 6 weeks for delivery. Offer available while quantities last.

Your Privacy—Your information is being collected by Harlequin Enterprises ULC, operating as Harlequin Reader Service. For a complete summary of the information we collect, how we use this information and to whom it is disclosed, please visit our privacy notice located at corporate.harlequin.com/privacy-notice. From time to time we may also exchange your personal information with reputable third parties. If you wish to opt out of this sharing of your personal information, please visit readerservice.com/consumerchoice or call 1-800-873-8635. **Notice to California Residents**—Under California law, you have specific rights to control and access your data. For more information on these rights and how to exercise them, visit corporate.harlequin.com/california-privacy.

LIRLIS22R3

Get 4 FREE REWARDS!

We'll send you 2 FREE Books plus 2 FREE Mystery Gifts.

FREE
Value Over
$20

Both the **Romance** and **Suspense** collections feature compelling novels
written by many of today's bestselling authors.

YES! Please send me 2 FREE novels from the Essential Romance or
Essential Suspense Collection and my 2 FREE gifts (gifts are worth about
$10 retail). After receiving them, if I don't wish to receive any more books,
I can return the shipping statement marked "cancel." If I don't cancel, I will
receive 4 brand-new novels every month and be billed just $7.49 each in
the U.S. or $7.74 each in Canada. That's a savings of at least 17% off the
cover price. It's quite a bargain! Shipping and handling is just 50¢ per book
in the U.S. and $1.25 per book in Canada.* I understand that accepting
the 2 free books and gifts places me under no obligation to buy anything. I
can always return a shipment and cancel at any time by calling the number
below. The free books and gifts are mine to keep no matter what I decide.

Choose one: ☐ **Essential Romance**   ☐ **Essential Suspense**
                     (194/394 MDN GRHV)   (191/391 MDN GRHV)

Name (please print)

Address   Apt. #

City   State/Province   Zip/Postal Code

Email: Please check this box ☐ if you would like to receive newsletters and promotional emails from Harlequin Enterprises ULC and
its affiliates. You can unsubscribe anytime.

> **Mail to the Harlequin Reader Service:**
> **IN U.S.A.:** P.O. Box 1341, Buffalo, NY 14240-8531
> **IN CANADA:** P.O. Box 603, Fort Erie, Ontario L2A 5X3

Want to try 2 free books from another series! Call 1-800-873-8635 or visit www.ReaderService.com.

*Terms and prices subject to change without notice. Prices do not include sales taxes, which will be charged (if applicable) based
on your state or country of residence. Canadian residents will be charged applicable taxes. Offer not valid in Quebec. This offer is
limited to one order per household. Books received may not be as shown. Not valid for current subscribers to the Essential Romance
or Essential Suspense Collection. All orders subject to approval. Credit or debit balances in a customer's account(s) may be offset by
any other outstanding balance owed by or to the customer. Please allow 4 to 6 weeks for delivery. Offer available while quantities last.

Your Privacy—Your information is being collected by Harlequin Enterprises ULC, operating as Harlequin Reader Service. For a
complete summary of the information we collect, how we use this information and to whom it is disclosed, please visit our privacy notice
located at corporate.harlequin.com/privacy-notice. From time to time we may also exchange your personal information with reputable
third parties. If you wish to opt out of this sharing of your personal information, please visit readerservice.com/consumerschoice or
call 1-800-873-8635. Notice to California Residents—Under California law, you have specific rights to control and access your data.
For more information on these rights and how to exercise them, visit corporate.harlequin.com/california-privacy.

STRS22R3

HARLEQUIN
PLUS

Try the best multimedia subscription service for romance readers like you!

Read, Watch and Play.

Experience the easiest way to get the romance content you crave.

Start your **FREE TRIAL** at
<u>www.harlequinplus.com/freetrial</u>.